First Tuesday

First Tuesday

by

Oren Tasini

Chaucer Press Books
An Imprint of Richard Altschuler & Associates, Inc.

Los Angeles

Distributed by University Press of New England

First Tuesday. Copyright © 2013 by Oren Tasini. For information, write to the publisher, Richard Altschuler & Associates, Inc., at 10390 Wilshire Boulevard, Los Angeles, CA 90024, or visit www.richardaltschuler.com.

ISBN-13: 978-1-884092-92-3
ISBN-10: 1-884092-92-6

Library of Congress Control Number: 2013941323
CIP data for this book are available from the Library of Congress

This novel is a work of fiction. Names, characters, places and events are the product of the author's imagination, and any resemblance to actual persons, living or dead, businesses, organizations, characters, events or locations is purely coincidental.

Chaucer Press Books is an imprint of
Richard Altschuler & Associates, Inc.

All rights reserved. No part of this publication may be reproduced, stored in a retrieval system, or transmitted, in any form or by any means, electronic, mechanical, photocopying, recording, or otherwise, without the prior written permission of Richard Altschuler & Associates, Inc.

Printed in the United States of America

Distributed by University Press of New England
1 Court Street
Lebanon, New Hampshire 03766

To my girls (in the order in which I met them)
Tammy, Sara, Madeleine

CHAPTER 1

The jingle jangle noise was far away but getting closer, intruding into his dreams of passion and well-endowed women. The phone? The phone! He lunged for the phone, hoping to still its noise, and at the same time glanced at the clock on his nightstand. It was 3:46 a.m. The wonders of technology and digital clocks; they precisely recorded historic moments. Although he did not know it, this was an historic moment for John "Jack" Banner, Esq.

He missed the phone on his first try, knocking it off the hook and then grabbing it before it hit the floor.

"Hello," he mumbled, his mind half awake and his voice still sleeping.

"Is this John Banner?" At least the caller hadn't asked if he had woken him. What a stupid question that would be at 3:46 a.m., thought Jack. (Now it was 3:47 as the LCD crystal advanced and lit up.)

"Who wants to know?" A quick response, given the late hour and the rude awakening. Jack was particularly annoyed given the pleasant dream he was having, which was now interrupted, about that blonde receptionist at the law firm. She was definitely interested, but he was still considering the propriety of dating an "employee." Of course he was an "employee," but in the hierarchy of law firms there were classes of employees—with the associates being a low form of employee, beneath which lay the support staff and finally the receptionists, at the bottom of the food chain and pecking order. To hell with it he decided. She was single and attractive. He would ask her out on Monday.

The caller continued, "My name is Carlos Martinez, and I need your help."

"Call me in the office on Monday. I'm in the book under Kelly, O'Brien & Mason."

"You don't understand. That's how I got your name. I'm in jail and you're my one phone call."

"Well, buddy, you made two mistakes tonight. One was getting busted. The other was calling me. I don't do criminal work." Jack started to hang up the phone.

"Please, if you don't bail me out I'm a dead man! They'll be sure I don't survive the night in jail. They'll kill me for sure."

At this point, Jack wasn't sure if Martinez was a nut case, and he wasn't about to find out. "Look, buddy, I don't know who you are and I don't much care. It's three in the morning and I'm sorry you got busted for dope possession or whatever . . ."

"Hey, man, listen to me. This is serious stuff. Do you have a TV?"

"Yes," Jack replied, his curiosity piqued.

"Well, then you'd better turn it on before you hang up the phone and throw away a chance to be famous."

Jack paused and considered the options. If he turned on the TV and the guy was a nut case he could go back to sleep and be no worse for the interruption. If he turned on the TV and what he heard in any way was connected to one Carlos Martinez, his life might be in for some change. Whether for better or worse could not be known. To help in the decision, Jack ran a quick mental checklist: single, mid 30s, good looking, bright future in prestigious law firm. On the other side of the ledger was: predictable life with only mild excitement. Jack flipped on his TV.

". . . and over the nation's capitol hangs a pallor of sorrow over tonight's events. Police are releasing few details, but it appears that a large explosive device was detonated as the president-elect's limousine left the Kennedy Center for the Performing Arts at approximately 10:35 this evening."

"Jesus Christ!" Jack exclaimed as he sat upright in bed watching the video, his heart pumping with adrenaline, wide awake now.

The TV announcer continued, "President-elect Arthur Davis, who was elected in a narrow victory less than a month ago, and his wife, Amanda, were killed. The president, who was attending the performance with the president-elect, as a courtesy, was whisked away by a cavalcade of Secret Service agents. Sadly, several of the agents riding in the van following behind the president-elect's limousine were killed when the force of the explosion destroyed their vehicle. The president was rushed to Bethesda Naval Hospital, but the White House has refused to release details of his condition. The FBI and Secret Service have a suspect in custody but have not released his identity."

The announcer continued but Jack's mind was racing. He looked at the phone receiver in his hand and then at the TV. The probability that the two were connected caused his stomach to turn and his heart to pump even faster.

"Mr. Martinez, please tell me you have nothing to do with what I just saw on the TV."

"I wish I could, but . . ." A voice in the background at the other end interrupted, "Times up, Buddy. Let's wrap it up."

"Mr. Martinez, where are you?" Jack asked.

"I'm at FBI headquarters on Pennsylvania Avenue. You'd better hurry, man, because if you aren't here before they lock me down you're never going to meet one Carlos Martinez." Then the line went dead.

Jack was on his way out the door in five minutes, having thrown on sweat pants and a sweatshirt and a winter coat. It hadn't occurred to him to dress up for the occasion—a decision he would later regret when his picture was splashed on the front page of newspapers across the world, as the lawyer for the man who had killed the next President of the United States.

The cold winter air felt good against his face as he strode towards his car. It was a brand new BMW 7 series, one of his few impulse purchases and certainly not a sound investment. But it was fun to drive. In a few minutes he was out of Georgetown and cruising down Pennsylvania Avenue; and with the light traffic, he was soon approaching the FBI building at 10th and Pennsylvania. About three blocks away, Jack realized that reaching his destination would not be simple. There were flashing lights from police and emergency vehicles and TV crews and crowds of bystanders, causing traffic to back up for blocks. Jack made a quick decision. He pulled down a side street, parked and locked his car, and started in a slow jog toward FBI headquarters. The entire block surrounding the building was cordoned off. The news crews had bathed the area in spotlights, and a number of reporters were on the air transmitting their reports. Around the building were dozens of police officers and men in trench coats. Some had their weapons openly displayed. For the rest, the trench coats could not conceal the bulge of firearms. Jack felt a moment of doubt. The rush of the moment had overwhelmed his innate sense of caution. He steeled himself and moved forward.

He approached one of the barricades and called out to a man who looked like he possessed some authority. "Excuse me. I have to get inside."

The man he had called was wearing a trench coat and an earpiece. He slowly walked over to Jack, eyeing him with suspicion, his hands disappearing in the folds of his coat. Jack kept very still, not wanting his purpose to be misconstrued.

"That's real cute, mister, but this area is off limits to reporters."

"I'm not a reporter. I'm a lawyer and I'm here to represent the guy you arrested." Jack purposely kept his voice low, not wanting his words or identity to be overheard.

The man looked at Jack impassively. "You expect me to believe that? Most lawyers I know wear suits and ties. You look like a bum."

Jack had to admit the man had a point, but the hour was late and his temper was short. "Look, Mr. Nazi. I got a call from a Mr. Carlos Martinez to come bail him out down here. Now the TV said the police weren't releasing the name of the suspect, so how else would I know his name? So you'd better get on that walkie-talkie of yours or I'm going to walk over to those reporters over there and spill my guts!"

The agent paused for a moment and then reached inside his coat. Jack suddenly remembered Carlos Martinez's words of his feared demise and thought, for an instant, that this man was about to silence Jack forever. He sighed with relief when a walkie-talkie emerged from the folds of the trench coat.

"What's your name?"

"Jack Banner."

"Alpha One to base. Do you read me?"

"Alpha One this is base, over."

"I've got a guy down here who claims he's the mouthpiece for the perp we're holding. Name is Jack Banner. Please advise, over."

"Hold your position, Alpha One. We have to talk to the man, over." There were several minutes of awkward silence as the man in the trench coat stared at Jack and waited for instructions. Jack bounced from toe to toe in an effort to keep warm. The walkie-talkie crackled.

"Alpha One come in, over."

"This is Alpha One, over."

"We are sending personnel to your position to escort the man you are detaining. Hold your position until their arrival, over."

"That's a roger, over."

After another awkward wait, Jack could see three more men advancing to where he stood with the first agent. When they arrived, they pulled back the barricades.

"Sir, please come with us. We have been instructed to take you to see Director Stevenson." Over his shoulder, Jack could see that some of the reporters had sensed that something was happening. All those trench coats in one place had to mean action. "Please, sir, we need to move quickly."

As he said this, the man reached out and firmly grabbed Jack's arm, propelling him towards a ramp that led down under the building. The trench-coated men who stayed behind quickly closed the barrier and turned to stem the tide of reporters scurrying towards them. With the man at his arm pushing him in earnest, Jack soon arrived at the entrance to the building. It was a set of sliding glass doors, which parted as Jack and the FBI agent stepped through. Beyond the glass doors was an x-ray machine—and chaos. FBI agents were running back and forth through the halls shouting into walkie-talkies. Just beyond the x-ray machine stood men armed with machine guns and bulletproof vests.

Two of them walked toward Jack. "Sir, show us your I.D. and we will have to search you. Please turn around and place your hands in the air." Too shocked to reply, Jack did as commanded. One of the men checked his I.D. and quickly patted him down. "He's clean."

The FBI agent who had escorted Jack into the building turned to him and said, "Please follow me." The agent stepped through the metal-detector, forgetting that he was carrying an assortment of firearms. The x-ray machine made a loud buzzing noise, and all the armed men nearby who had not seen the cause of the noise, but only the result, turned with weapons at the ready.

"Jesus, Evans! You trying to get yourself killed?" yelled one man. The remaining agents relaxed and Jack followed Evans through the x-ray machine. They headed toward the bank of elevators just beyond the x-ray machine. Evans pushed the button and the elevator slid open. Jack and Evans entered and were followed by two more agents.

"Two's company, four's a crowd," joked Jack. No one laughed.

The elevator stopped at the third floor. When the doors opened, the two agents stepped out first. Jack followed with Evans behind him. They moved down the hallway. It was standard government issue: linoleum floors, fluorescent lighting, poor paint job. Things were not as chaotic here, although occasionally a door would open and slam shut, and someone would scurry down the hall. They stopped in front of a set of thick, oak doors that had a brass plate with the word DIRECTOR engraved on it. Evans opened the door and motioned Jack to enter. They were in a reception area. Unlike the hallway, the reception area was luxurious. The couches were plush and inviting. Artwork depicting the American West adorned the walls. Thick carpet covered the floor. Beyond the reception area was another set of double doors. To the left was a large secretarial desk occupied by a more than middle-aged woman.

"Gentlemen, the director is expecting you. Go right on in."

"Wait a minute," Jack said. "I'm here to see my client, not for a guided tour."

"My orders were to bring you here," Evans explained. "I do what I'm told and this is where you'll stay until I'm told otherwise. The other two agents stared gravely at Jack to enforce Evans's words. The discussion was cut short as the double doors opened and revealed Gary Stevenson, director of the FBI.

"Mr. Banner, there is no need to be concerned. You will be able to see your client shortly. I just wanted to talk with you for a moment or two." Stevenson was fiftyish, tall and handsome. He had known President Hampton for years and helped immensely in his tough first election campaign, convincing the right to support a Republican candidate about whom they had their doubts. The previous president had appointed him. His reward for his assistance to Hampton had been a continued tenure as Director of the FBI.

"Please, why don't you come in." The director turned and headed back through the double doors. Jack followed and one of the agents closed the doors behind them, leaving them alone. The office was as richly appointed as the reception area, but with a more personal touch. His family pictures lined the desk. Framed pictures with notable public figures and citations lined the wall behind his desk. The director stopped in front of his large, oak desk and turned to face Jack, as he sat on the edge of the desk.

"This is an enormous and tragic event in our history, Mr. Banner. May I call you Jack?"

"Sure, why not. Can I call you Gary?"

The director didn't respond. "As I was saying, Jack, this is a very serious matter. The national security of the nation is at stake, and I'm not sure you know what you're getting into here. The history books will devote many chapters to this event."

"Well, I know that you've arrested my client, and I presume due to the treatment I've been accorded that it has something to do with the murder of the president-elect. How am I doing so far?"

"Very quick with the jokes, Jack," replied the director. "But, alas, you have only touched the tip of the iceberg. The bomb explosion tonight was only one of several hundred across the nation. Ten state governors have been killed as well as fifteen United States senators and thirty members of the House of Representatives."

Jack was stunned by this revelation. He tried without success not to show it. What was he getting into?

"Your, um, client is a major suspect in a wide-ranging conspiracy to overthrow the Government of the United States. That is nothing to joke about. Are you familiar with a group known as the Liberation Front?"

"Only what I've read in the papers. Left wing, violent tendencies, but hardly powerful enough to overthrow the U.S. Government."

"Well, apparently they don't think so." The director walked around his desk and sat down. "We have received a communiqué from their revolutionary council claiming responsibility for the bombings and assassinations that took place tonight. The contents, which I can't divulge in detail, include particulars that only the perpetrators would know."

"That's all very interesting, but what does that have to do with Mr. Martinez?"

The director looked at Jack with some disgust. "Jack, you have a bad habit of interrupting. As I was about to say, Mr. Carlos Martinez has been under surveillance for some time regarding his connection to the Front. Shortly after the explosion at the Kennedy Center, he was spotted in the vicinity and arrested by an FBI agent who recognized him. He was carrying a 9mm machine pistol. Apparently, he wanted to see the results from his handiwork. So you see, Jack, yours will be a difficult task. Are you a solo practitioner?"

"No. I practice with Kelly, O'Brien & Mason."

"Oh, Jim Kelly and I play golf together. I wasn't aware they had a criminal department."

"They don't. I don't do criminal work. I'm a commercial litigator." Jack didn't like the direction this conversation was taking. "Look, this is all very interesting, but if you don't mind I'd like to see my client."

"Of course . . . of course. I'm sure that Jim will be fascinated, come Monday morning, when he finds you've taken on this case with such . . . gusto." The director reached for the intercom button on his desk. "Marge, would you tell the agents to come in and escort Mr. Banner to the holding area?"

"Right away, sir."

The director stood up and walked back around the desk with his hand outstretched. Jack realized that he had been standing the whole time and had never been offered a chair. He looked around the office. There were no chairs other than the director's chair. The man knew how to play the Washington power game. Keep them waiting and make them stand.

"It's been a pleasure meeting you. Good luck and give my best to Jim."

The director shook Jack's hand and then tried to release it. Jack held it firm and looked steadily in the director's eyes. "I don't know what game you're playing here. You're probably better at it than I am. But I don't know Jim Kelly and he wouldn't know who I was if I ran him over. I'm just a drone in his big firm. I do know this: I'm a lawyer and I'm sworn to uphold the law. You may have tried and convicted Mr. Martinez, but I intend to ensure that he gets his day in court with some other lawyer or me. You can threaten all you want, but it won't make a bit of difference. So I'd appreciate it if you would cut the crap and let me see my client."

Jack released the director's hand, wheeled around and headed towards the double doors. They opened by some magical force and the trench-coated men were waiting for him.

From behind him, Jack heard the director say "Take good care of him, gentlemen, he'll need all the help he can get."

CHAPTER 2

After Jack had left, the director activated his speakerphone. "Jenkins, I'm ready for you now."

"On my way, sir."

While the director waited for Jenkins, he considered the turn of events and the possible ramifications. The president's wounds were minor but would require some time to heal. He would be able to resume his duties in a week or two. More vexing was the question of who would now be president. Stevenson was a lawyer by training, but his knowledge of the legal ramifications was sketchy at best. President-elect Davis had defeated the incumbent president in a close and bitter election. He was to be sworn in on January 20th. What would happen now was unclear to Stevenson. Would the vice president-elect succeed the president-elect? Would a new election be required? He reached for a legal pad on his desk and wrote, "Call legal department. Find out procedure in event of death of president-elect. ASAP!"

More troubling was the impact on the social fabric of the country. Since the World Trade Center attack, the U. S. had been vigilant to avoid another domestic terrorist attack. The government had in fact foiled many plots over the years by a variety of foreign extremists. Now a large, widespread, homegrown terrorist organization had struck a devastating blow to the country. The Front had called for an uprising and there were reports of civil unrest in the major cities. The last few years had been difficult on the less fortunate, as a severe recession had gripped the country. The Front had a strong following in these groups. The National Guard had been called out and the military had been alerted.

The director's intelligence showed that the attacks had been coordinated with precision and professionalism—over 200 bombings occurring within seconds of each other. This had to mean sophisticated command and control and a widespread network of personnel. Previous reports had discounted the ability of the Front to mount such an attack. This was particularly troubling. Had a foreign power assisted the Front? It was unlikely the Russians would do so; relationships were acceptable, if not ideal, and democratic reforms were finally taking hold, moving the Russians more and more toward stable capitalism. The Russians had to know that helping the Front would be tantamount to an act of war. Instinct told the director it wasn't the Russians. Perhaps the Front was receiving assistance from a foreign group or a country controlled by Islamic radicals. The war on terror was never ending, and such a strike against America, in conjunction with the Front, could not be ruled out. It was just too early to tell. Who the hell could it have been?

The director swiveled his chair to look out his window. As he mulled through the other possibilities, his thoughts were interrupted by a knock on the door and the entrance of Steven Jenkins, the assistant director.

"You know, boss, you really need another chair in here. I'm getting awfully tired of standing during all these briefings." Jenkins had a sarcastic smile on his face. He and the director had been together long enough that humor was permitted even in the most serious of times. Jenkins was some ten years younger than the director. A career FBI agent, tall and handsome, and a graduate of West Point, he was a poster boy for the FBI.

"I'll take it under advisement. Let's start with what you have on the lawyer." The director picked up a pencil and his pad.

Jenkins began to read from a computer printout. "John Banner, Esq. Goes by Jack. Born August 8, 1959, Hartford Connecticut. Graduated Dartmouth, 1985. Law degree Georgetown University, 1988. Never married. No kids. Both parents deceased. Here's an interesting note. Brother Thomas Brian Banner killed in Vietnam, 1968, during the Tet Offensive. His brother was Special Forces, quite a distinguished war record." Jenkins flipped through the war record as he continued. "Nominated posthumously for Congressional Medal of Honor. Saved his battalion by holding off overwhelming enemy forces single handedly."

"Let me see that." The director reached for the file.

Jenkins handed over the sheet in the file regarding Thomas Banner and continued his description of Jack Banner. "Registered Democrat. Has no history of political activity. Belongs to a few environmental organizations, but not active. Belongs to the local bar association and the like. We haven't had time to make inquiries on the local level—friends, neighbors, the like—given the late hour. We'll have our people out first thing a.m."

"What's your analysis, Steve?"

"Well, his record looks clean. He appears to be an ordinary Joe. But it seems strange that the Front would go to all this expense and effort and then leave their guy Martinez hanging out to dry. Maybe Banner is not what he appears. My gut tells me he's clean, but it doesn't make sense."

The director doodled on his pad and then looked up at Jenkins. "Your conclusion is based on the assumption that we arrested the right guy. What if Martinez is innocent and this lawyer really is a random contact?"

"What are you talking about, boss? We caught the guy red-handed with a weapon, at the scene. He is a known Front member."

"What I'm talking about is that the likely suspects don't add up. We have to explore the unlikely and the outlandish. There are only a few countries in the world that could mount this kind of op, right?"

"Yup," answered Jenkins.

"Most are allies," continued the director. "The Brits, the Israelis. Russia and China would gain no benefit. The Arabs have the dough, but not the organization or the people with this kind of skill. Given all that, what is the likelihood that the Liberation Front, which has been less than a flyspeck on our windshield, could do this?"

"Not likely," answered Jenkins.

"Well, if we're right, then Mr. Banner may have bitten off more than he can chew. I want you to keep twenty-four-hour surveillance on him, but keep it loose. I don't want him or the press getting wind of this. Also call over to the CIA and ask them to put out an alert to their bureau chiefs regarding any tips on who ran the op. That should keep you busy for a while."

"Yes, sir," said Jenkins. He turned and started to leave, knowing through years of experience that the director was finished. As he reached the door the director called out.

"Jenkins, what was said in here was for your ears only. Let's not start the conspiracy buffs going until we have some hard facts."

"Yes, sir," he said. As he closed the door to leave, Jenkins had an uneasy feeling. In all their years together, he had never seen the director look so worried.

CHAPTER 3

The FBI agents escorted Jack to the elevator and from there down to the holding area. Prior to entering the holding area he was searched again. Jack wondered how they thought he could have obtained a weapon since being searched and passing through a metal-detector, but he relented without protest.

Once the search was completed, they led Jack through a locked steel door and into a hallway with a row of cells. Jack had never been in a jail before. It looked as he expected, claustrophobic and intimidating. Some of the cells were occupied. The sad and angry demeanor of the occupants reinforced his opinion. Caged animals just waiting to eat their masters. He had always thought that he would sooner die than be locked up in a cell, with all freedom of movement restricted. Some of that fear and anxiety began to come over him and he shivered involuntarily.

"Pretty cold in here," he said to no one in particular. The agents led him to the sixth cell on the left. Inside the cell, on the bunk was Carlos Martinez.

"Your lawyer's here to see you, you worthless piece of trash," said one of the agents; and then, turning to Jack, continued, "Take as much time as you need. It won't matter. He's going to fry in the end. Yell out when you're done and I'll send someone to get you." With that he nodded to one of the other agents, who produced a key and opened the door. Jack hesitated then stepped into the cell. The door was swung shut with a clang, then the bolt thrown. The FBI men turned and departed.

"Man, am I glad to see you!" Carlos Martinez rose from the bunk and reached out his hand. Jack shook it and sized up the man in front of him. He was dressed in blue jeans and a fatigue jacket over a gray sweatshirt. His olive skin bespoke of his heritage. He appeared to be around Jack's age. His black hair was cut short. Although Jack never professed to be an expert on the subject, he imagined that women would find Martinez quite attractive.

"I wish I could say the same about you," Jack answered. "It appears you may be the most infamous man in America right now. And apparently not too bright. Like I told you on the phone, I don't know anything about criminal law."

"That's OK, I don't need a lawyer. I just needed to contact someone, so that the feds would know, that someone knew, I existed and I was here. People like me have a funny way of ending up hanging themselves in jail, if you know what I mean." Martinez began to pace around the cell, what little room there was. He stopped and stared intently at Jack. "What I need you to do is leak my name to the press. Let people know I'm here. Otherwise, I am a dead man."

Jack was momentarily confused. He expected this man to need his great legal mind, to pronounce his innocence to the world. But Mr. Martinez did not act like an innocent man. "Before I do anything I need to get your story straight. The evidence they have is pretty damning. I mean . . ."

"Look, if you're asking whether I did it or not, I didn't." As he said this, Martinez motioned for Jack to come closer. Jack stepped toward Martinez. "Just between you and me I'm no virgin. But I can tell you this. I was there to off the guy, but someone beat me to it. I'm the fall guy. So what I need you to do is to go out to all those vultures out there and announce to the world who I am and what I'm accused of and how I'm innocent."

Jack was stunned. The conversation was not what he had expected. "If you're part of this thing I can't help you. I'll find you another lawyer, but I'm not going to help you with some publicity stunt."

Martinez smiled. "I guess you're not too bright either. You don't have no choice, because now your ass is on the line. Someone with a lot of clout put this plan together. They probably already know you've come to see me. They have to figure I know too much. That makes you dangerous. Who knows you came here tonight?"

Jack paused for a long time, another wave of fear gripping him. No one knew he was here, except the "feds," as Mr. Martinez called them. He had rushed out of his apartment at three a.m. on this great adventure whose potential ramifications were becoming more and more worrisome.

With his long pause conveying his answer, Martinez rambled on. "Just like I thought . . . no one. If I go, you go. The only way is to focus the spotlight on me and on you. Too much publicity will scare away anyone who is out to get me. I'm really sorry to get you involved in this, but I had no choice."

Suddenly Jack had an odd thought. "How did you pick me anyway?"

Martinez smiled a broad smile. "When I was a kid I had a cat named Banner. Your name just jumped out at me, like a cat."

Suddenly the cell felt smaller and smaller to Jack. He had an urge to run, to call the guards and get the hell out of there and be done with Mr. Martinez. But for some reason he didn't. Instead he walked over to the cot and sat down. His mind was racing. Could it be that he just walked into a major conspiracy to overthrow the United States Government? If it had just been Martinez, he would have figured him for a crackpot, but the director of the FBI had confirmed it all.

"Are you a member of the Front?" Jack asked. Martinez nodded.

"Tell me what happened."

"All I know is I was told to kill the president and that my acts would cause a spontaneous uprising of the masses. No one told me what was really going down. But you see, I had a feeling something funny was going on. Lots of meetings of the heads of the Front with unfamiliar faces. Guys in suits, with lots of money to throw around. I believe in the Front's philosophy—"power to the masses"—but I'm no fool. I realize I was set up. But I'm not going down silently. Someone has corrupted the movement, appropriated the message for the wrong purposes. I can't let that happen."

"Alright, alright," Jack said. "What we need to do is get you a real good criminal lawyer. I don't even know what to do now. I suppose you'll be arraigned shortly. That's where you plead and then a bail hearing is set."

Martinez grabbed Jack by the shoulders, his voice rising, the pretense of whispers suddenly gone. "I don't have time for that. I won't be alive tomorrow if you don't go out there and talk to the press. After that you can back out, but right now I need someone to know I'm here. It's not an unreasonable request, is it?"

Jack pondered for a moment and then decided he would have his fifteen minutes of fame.

"I'll do it." Jack turned to leave the cell, calling out to the guards, "We're done in here." Then, turning to Martinez he said, "I'll find you a criminal lawyer. Someone sharp. Do you have any money?" Martinez shook his head.

"Well, it doesn't matter. Every publicity-hungry lawyer in the country will want this case. I'd like to say it was a pleasure meeting you, but the jury is still out on that one. Don't talk to anyone but me. No matter what the FBI says or does, ask for your lawyer. You understand?"

Martinez nodded. The footsteps echoing down the hall signaled the arrival of the agents. They stood in front of the door. The FBI men unlocked the gate and motioned Jack out. As the door clanged shut, Martinez shouted to Jack, "Make sure they know who I am." Jack kept walking without looking back, the apprehension growing as his fate swirled in the uncertainty created by this stranger and his call for help in the middle of the night.

CHAPTER 4

The agents led Jack out the way he had come. Down the elevators, past the hordes of agents, and out into the cold night. He was surrounded by four agents—one in front, one on each side and one behind. They hustled him up the ramp and towards the barricades through which Jack had entered.

"Stick close, Mr. Banner. We need to move fast and not attract any attention," instructed the agent in front. He was the original agent Jack had met at the barricade. Agent Evans was behind him. Jack was only half listening, considering Martinez's warning and his promise to Martinez. Up ahead, he could see the glare of spotlights from the television cameras and reporters milling around hoping for a story. As they approached the barricades the agent in front reached to move the barricade, while the agents at Jack's side grabbed his arms and propelled him forward. The agents, to their misfortune, had not realized that the sight of four agents escorting someone, anyone, was for the reporters like blood in the water for a shark.

Off to Jack's left there was a shout. "Look! Over there! Something's going on." There was a rush of five, then ten, then twenty reporters as they spotted Jack and his escort. The ones furthest away broke into a run to be in on the kill. In less than ten seconds a female reporter was within a few feet of Jack with a microphone in hand, which she thrust forward towards Jack and the agents.

"Does this guy have anything to do with the assassination? Is there any information we can have on anything? Is it true there is a suspect in custody?" She hurled the questions one after another, not waiting for an answer.

The agents ignored her, strengthened their grip on Jack, and tried to push him forward more forcefully. An FBI car screeched up to the curb some twenty feet away, and the agents desperately tried to get Jack to the car before the mob of reporters closed off all escape. There was a small opening, rapidly closing. The doors to the car were thrown open, and the agents thought for a moment that they would make it. Jack did too and, with Martinez's warning now sounding an alarm in his head, he realized this would not be a good thing for him or his latest—and hopefully not last—client. Jack stopped abruptly, startling the agents at his side, who had, up until then, received no resistance. They stopped for a moment. The agent behind Jack collided with the threesome, further interrupting their momentum. The momentary pause was enough. The crowd of reporters now surrounded them, blocking their passage.

One of the agents tried to use his official powers. "We are agents of the Federal Bureau of Investigation. Please let us pass." His effort was futile.

A male reporter in the front of the crowd shouted out, "Is it true that the president narrowly missed assassination? Has the National Guard been called out?"

"We will not answer any questions. You must let us through."

"I have a statement to make," Jack said, not loud enough for the crowd of reporters to hear but loud enough for the agent in front of him to hear. He turned to Jack with a look of horror on his face. His life's work and proficiency rating was about to be screwed up by some loud-mouthed lawyer.

Jack started again but this time louder. "I have a statement to give . . ."

One of the reporters heard him and boomed out in a loud voice, "Quiet, he is going to make a statement." The message was passed in a chorus of "Quiet . . . a statement." The throng of reporters had grown to enormous proportions. The glare of the lights blinded Jack, but as far as he could see were the faces of eager reporters. Jack paused for a moment. The crowd was strangely silent. They had pressed in close, so that the agents could not have moved Jack if they wanted to.

The lead agent made one last, half-hearted attempt. "Please, Mr. Banner. I don't think this is a very good idea." Jack ignored him.

"My name is Jack Banner. I am the attorney for Carlos Martinez. Mr. Martinez has been arrested by the FBI for the murder of the president-elect. My client maintains his innocence. In the great tradition of our democratic system, which will be severely tested by the tragic events of this evening, he is innocent until proven guilty. I have nothing further to say."

There was a moment of silence, and then bedlam. Some reporters raced away to file their stories. Others turned, with cameras rolling, to give live feeds and reports. Others hurled questions at Jack in rapid succession.

"Is Mr. Martinez a member of the Front?"

"Are you a member of the Front?"

"Is it true that U.S. nuclear forces have been put on high alert?"

This last question stunned Jack. He started to respond and realized he had no answers. He turned to the agents. "Get me out of here." They started to push forward. The crowd of reporters had thinned somewhat, as they had acted upon the scoop of Jack's statement. At the same time, a group of agents had emerged from headquarters and began to engage in crowd control. With a great deal of effort, they reached the waiting sedan. The agents at Jack's side threw him inside the car.

The car made a screeching U-turn on the side street and then made a right turn onto Pennsylvania Avenue. The car continued straight on Pennsylvania Avenue, passing to the south side of the White House, its sirens blazing. As they passed the White House, Jack could see a helicopter circling overhead and Army troops deployed on the South Lawn. The assassins would not get a second chance to kill this president. Once past the White House, the car turned right on 17th Street and then picked up the continuation of Pennsylvania Avenue. With the late hour and the blaring sirens, they made good time into Georgetown. Within minutes they pulled up to Jack's house at 33rd and P Street. As the car pulled to the curb, Jack realized that he had never told the agents where he lived, yet they knew. He thought about asking, then just shrugged his shoulders to himself and stepped from the car. His house, actually a townhouse, was an old Georgetown brownstone, with a flight of brick stairs leading up to the front door. As he climbed the stairs, Agent Evans was close behind. "Mr. Banner, we'll have to search the house first."

Jack turned to face him. "To hell you will. Last time I checked, the Fourth Amendment was still a part of the Constitution. Do you have a warrant?"

"I'm sorry, sir. You misunderstood. We're not searching for anything. It's for your protection. Direct order from the director. From now on I'm your shadow. We would like to station a man in your house, too."

Jack pondered this for a moment. Martinez had mentioned his life being in peril enough to make Jack a believer. "OK. You can search the house, but no man inside. I'm not going to be living with some FBI agent in my kitchen."

"But sir . . ."

"No buts. Tell the director you did your best, but I'm a son of a bitch and completely unreasonable. We've met, so he'll believe you."

Evans started to protest, but he realized it was futile. He motioned towards the car and two agents hopped out and headed towards the stairs. Jack removed the keys from his pocket and opened the door. The two agents and Evans, with guns now drawn, entered the house. "Stay here," Evans shouted as he lunged through the door.

After a few minutes, Evans returned. "It's all clear. You can go on in."

As Jack headed in the house, he heard the sound of engines and screeching tires. Evans swung around, gun at the ready. The car was a news van, trailed by a carload of reporters. The hunt was on. Evans holstered his weapon. "Better run for cover, Mr. Banner. I'll keep them at bay."

Jack paused. This Evans seemed like a nice chap, but he was the FBI. Jack just shook his head and stepped into the house. "Sleep tight, Evans."

CHAPTER 5

Jack awoke the next morning with a start. A siren was blazing outside his window. He sat upright on the sofa, his heart beating quickly. A shot glass lay on the floor next to the couch. The throb in his head completed the picture. The siren faded away. Slowly he gathered his thoughts and his senses. As he did he began to hear a low buzz outside his window. He shook his head clear, got up from the couch and strode towards the window. He pulled the shade to the side and looked out onto the street. The street in front of his house was filled with reporters and camera crews. He recognized a few of the reporters on both the local and national level. By instinct, he looked to his front stoop to see if his newspaper was there. It was. Jack was tempted to retrieve the paper, but his good sense got the better of him. It surely would have started a stampede.

As this thought struck him, he saw Agent Evans emerge from a sedan parked in front of his house and walk towards his door. As he did so, a group of reporters tried to follow him, peppering him with questions, all of which Evans ignored. Several other agents herded the reporters away. Evans climbed the stairs, and when he reached the stoop he picked up Jack's paper and knocked on the door

Jack crossed the den toward the front door. When he opened it, Evans handed him the paper. "Thought you might want to catch up on world events. Not that much is happening."

Jack took the paper and returned the joke. "As long as the 'Skins' keep winning, nothing else matters."

"Time for a security check. Mind if we look around again?"

"Why not. In for a penny, in for a dollar."

Evans looked over his shoulder and waved to his fellow agents. Four agents emerged from two other cars parked in front of the house. Two climbed the stairs while two more proceeded to the back of Jack's townhouse. As the two agents passed by Jack, Evans asked, "Do you need anything? It is going to be mighty tough for you to just go to the grocery store from now on."

Jack paused for a moment. It was Sunday. He didn't need anything, but he did need to be somewhere. It was a trip he made every Sunday. "Actually, I have somewhere I have to be. Is there any way to get rid of all those damn reporters?"

Evans paused. "Can't get rid of them, but maybe we can play hide and seek. Do you have any coffee?" The question caught Jack off guard.

"Sure. Do you want some?"

"I'd love a cup. Then we can discuss our lives together from here on in. It seems the director has made you my personal project. Kinda like big brothers/big sisters."

Jack chuckled. He stepped back from the door and Evans entered the house. They proceeded into the kitchen. Evans shed his coat and Jack proceeded to make coffee. The kitchen was modern, but not spacious. The prior owner had updated it, and the modern appliances often went unused for long stretches of time. The coffee maker was not one such appliance. Jack sometimes lived on coffee alone. Soon the aroma was filling the room.

Evans made himself right at home. He plopped down onto one kitchen chair, stretched his feet onto another, and surveyed the room with a public servant's envy. Banner obviously had done well for himself. Of course now he was in deep shit and was probably just a candy ass who would end up dead or turn tail and run. But for now Evans liked him and the coffee smelled super. "Nice place you got here. What's a place like this cost?"

"Thanks." Jack ignored the question. "How do you like your coffee?"

"Black." Jack handed him a hot cup of coffee. They were interrupted by one of the agents as he poked his head into the kitchen.

"All clear, chief."

Evans nodded and the agent departed. He took a sip and then stared at Jack. "You haven't even looked at the paper. Aren't you curious?"

"Curious about what?"

"About what you look like in the paper?"

Strangely, the thought had never occurred to Jack . . . all the reporters and cameras. It would only be logical that his picture would be in the paper. He reached for the paper that he had placed on the kitchen table and unfolded it to the front page:

PRESIDENT-ELECT DEAD, PRESIDENT INJURED
PLOT TO OVERTHROW GOVERNMENT THWARTED
Suspect in Custody

Jack's eyes scanned down the page, and there, in the center, was his picture. He looked somewhat like a deer trapped in headlights. Even worse was the way he was dressed. He looked like someone should look at three in the morning, but it wasn't a pretty picture. The accompanying articles summarized what Jack had learned from the director in their meeting, about the explosions and assassinations that had taken place nationwide. Martinez was prominently featured, as well as a profile of the Front. Jack's statement was quoted in full. After a few minutes, he put the paper down.

"What kind of man is your director?" Jack asked Evans.

"Can't say I know him personally, but professionally he is first rate. Always backs up the agents one hundred percent and never passes the buck when the heat gets turned up, or if an operation goes bad."

Jack changed the subject, storing the information in the back of his mind for future reference. "You said you could get me somewhere?"

"That depends on where you need to go."

Jack became a little bit annoyed. "I thought I was still free to come and go as I please, as a private citizen, so what business is it of yours?"

Evans was unruffled. "That's true, but if you want my help, first I need to know why. I'm not gonna put my ass on the line for no good reason."

Jack calmed down. "Hey, I'm sorry. It's just a touchy issue with me. Every Sunday I go down to the Vietnam Memorial to pay my respects to my brother. Haven't missed a Sunday since I moved to D.C., and I'm not going to let the three-ring circus outside stop me."

Evans appeared moved. He paused for a moment, and let out a deep sigh filled with empathy. "I was in 'Nam. Lost some buddies there. I think we could make it happen. In order to do it, we will have to move fast. How long do you need to get ready?"

"Give me thirty minutes to shower, shave and dress."

"Good enough. That will leave me plenty of time to make the arrangements." Evans rose from the chair and headed for the front door. "Thanks for the coffee. Pretty damn good for a single guy. Could you give my wife some lessons?"

"You're welcome. It's all in the beans."

"See you in thirty minutes." And with that Evans turned and left the kitchen. Jack made his way upstairs to the bedroom. By force of habit he flipped on the TV as he undressed for the shower. CNN was on. Jack stopped undressing and sat transfixed as CNN replayed the assassination of the man who would have been the next President of the United States. This was no Zapruder 8mm film. This was high-resolution video from three different camera angles.

The video began with the president and the president-elect emerging from the Kennedy Center with their wives. They were talking casually, if somewhat awkwardly. A number of reporters shouted questions, which were ignored. The foursome walked toward the president-elect's limousine. A Secret Service agent stepped forward and opened the door. The president-elect's wife, after saying her good-byes, entered the limousine. The president-elect and the president continued talking. The president-elect gestured toward the limousine, inviting the president to join them. The president laughed and shook his head. A presidential aide approached the president from behind and whispered in his ear. The president nodded his head in acknowledgment and said his final good-byes to the president-elect.

The president-elect entered his limousine and then two Secret Service agents entered behind him. The video then cut to a new camera angle, showing the president walking toward his limousine parked up ahead of the president-elect's limousine. The president entered his limousine and it pulled away from the curb, followed by his escort vehicles. After it was clear, the president-elect's limousine began to pull away, followed by his escort vehicles. About 100 yards from the curb it happened. A tremendous fireball erupted, engulfing the limousine. The vehicle following the president-elect's limousine was also engulfed in flame.

Then there was pandemonium. Secret Service agents deployed from vans in front of and behind the now-destroyed limousine, weapons at the ready. Several tried to approach the limousine but were turned back by the intensity of the flames. There were cries and shouts from the spectators.

Then the CNN video replay ended. The anchor reappeared on the screen. "You have just seen a tragic and sad chapter in our nation's history. Throughout the nation, in every state, there is shock, anger, and fear. We go live to Judy Simons in the president-elect's hometown of . . ."

Jack reached for the remote and flipped off the TV. He sat heavily on the bed. As an ordinary person, he was shocked by the video. Taken together with his involvement with Martinez, the video was all the more disturbing. He was struck again by the improbability that he was at the center of this incredible event. Yesterday he had been an average citizen, in an ordinary job. Now he was . . . well, he wasn't sure what he was, but he sure was different from yesterday. He rose from the bed and continued to undress mechanically, his mind occupied with what to do next. He would, as he had told Martinez, have to find a criminal lawyer. His firm had a criminal department, but it specialized in white-collar crime. A nice name for bloodless crimes that robbed either the American taxpayer or widows and orphans, as opposed to a shakedown in the street. He doubted there was anyone tough enough, or savvy enough, in his firm to handle this case. There would be dozens of the top criminal lawyers calling him, looking for a piece of the action, but how would he decide whom to recommend to Martinez? The only solution would be to screen the lawyers and then allow Martinez to decide, with Jack's input and advice.

Jack then pondered his own future. The presence of Evans and his people made it clear that Jack's life was going to be drastically different for the time being. He was not a man who was good with change. Not inflexible by any means, just set in his ways. Could he handle the demands that would be placed on him in the next several days and weeks? He had held up extremely well so far. The FBI director had tried to bully him and Jack had faced him down. His statement to the reporters had been coherent and forceful. Most important, he had kept his word to Martinez. Jack was old-fashioned in that sense, a man's word was his bond. Through his actions, he sensed that he had Evans's grudging respect. Why that was important, Jack wasn't sure, but it was. Perhaps it gave him confidence that if his life was on the line—a thought that had occurred to him, but which he pushed to the background—he could handle it.

Some of this bravado was rooted in Jack's belief in the system and the rule of law. People always said that the system was lousy and that the wheels of justice not only ground slowly, but also ground people up in the process. Jack, to the contrary, believed that the legal system, although imperfect, was the glue that held society together. People settled their disputes in court, instead of in the streets. The latest turn of events caused great conflict in his mind. Martinez had said that if Jack didn't make an announcement about Martinez and his existence he would be dead; and he implied, not too subtly, that Jack would meet a similar fate. Yet Martinez had been in FBI custody. Jack was not naive, by any means, but he didn't believe that the FBI would murder a prisoner. That wasn't how the system worked. Martinez was innocent until proven guilty. He would get a fair trial and be judged by his peers.

Jack also believed that the institutions of government would protect him as well. Now the whole country was up in flames. The news reports claimed that all was calm and that the military and local police were in control of the situation, but did this massive terrorist act signal the beginning of civil unrest and conflict? Could a constitutional democracy survive such a blow? Jack had always played by the rules, and believed that if you played by the rules, eventually you came out ahead. His belief was shaken but not shattered. He rose from the bed and headed to the shower. He was an officer of the court, part of the system and, as such, as long as he played by the rules he could not be harmed or touched. The thoughts helped Jack, and by the time he stepped into the shower he had stilled his self-doubt. He could handle this. He lived in an ordered and civilized society with rules and laws; they would protect him as they always had.

CHAPTER 6

After he finished his shower, Jack dressed and made his way down the stairs. Evans was waiting in the foyer. Standing next to him was an agent of about Jack's height and weight. Evans looked at Jack, sizing him up. "Looks like I guessed about right. McMillan, give him your coat."

The agent shed his trench coat and handed it to Evans. "You have a coat, counselor?"

"Yeah, it's in the hall closet." Jack crossed the foyer and opened the closet door. He removed his gray wool overcoat. He turned and handed it to Evans. Evans admired the coat and handed it to the agent. He gave Jack the agent's trench coat.

"Here's the plan. I'm going to call in two more agents. After about two minutes, they will escort 'you', in the form of Agent McMillan, to one of the cars in front. They will be moving fast and will be sure to attract some attention. Once it gets hectic out there, I want you to casually step outside and make your way down to the corner, east of the townhouse. That's a left when you exit the building. A car will be waiting. Get in the car, and then duck down in the seat. Got it?"

"Yes."

"OK, let's get ready to move." Evan reached in his pocket and pulled out a walkie-talkie. "This is team leader. Prepare to initiate."

Evans turned to Jack. "Step back into the den. When you hear the sirens go off, make your move. Remember, head down, left out the door, keep walking, and act natural. Whatever you do, don't look back."

Jack stepped back into the den, and Evans crossed to the front door and opened it. Two agents mounted the stairs and entered Jack's townhouse. Agent McMillan turned up the collar of his coat. One of the agents handed him a cap, which he pulled tightly on his head. Evans led the way out the door. The sight of the cavalcade of agents with a person in tow set off the reporters. The FBI had cordoned off the entrance and sidewalk in front of Jack's townhouse. The reporters were close enough to see that something was happening, but not close enough to spot the ruse. The agents moved quickly, but not too quickly. The reporters were drawn to the agents like bees to honey. About ten feet from the car the agent driving put on the siren.

In the house, Jack took his cue. He took a deep breath, crossed to the door and opened it. He descended down the steps to the sidewalk and took a left, thinking it was a good thing Evans had told him east was left; Jack had a terrible sense of direction. He kept walking, his peripheral vision looking for any signs that he had been spotted. It was about fifty feet to the corner. About twenty feet away Jack glanced back. That was a mistake. A reporter who had tired of the chase had turned around and was headed back toward his car. His eyes locked with Jack's for just a moment, but that was enough.

"Hey, that's him. That's Banner!"

His shouts attracted the attention of some other reporters and the chase was on. Jack swore under his breath at his own stupidity and started to run towards the corner. A nondescript sedan pulled up to the curb, and the door was flung open. Jack scrambled into the sedan and the car quickly pulled away. He had just enough of a lead. By the time the reporters had started their cars for the chase, the FBI sedan was hurtling down 34th Street, its siren clearing traffic. Once it passed, the traffic resumed its flow, preventing the pursuers from taking up the chase. Jack breathed a sigh of relief.

CHAPTER 7

Within twenty minutes they had reached the west end of the mall—the site of the Lincoln Memorial and, in its shadow, the Vietnam Memorial. They had parked the car south of the Lincoln Memorial. Reaching the Vietnam Memorial required a walk in front of the Lincoln Memorial. Jack was escorted by two agents and, as they walked past the Lincoln Memorial, they passed the reflecting pool at its foot. To the east was the Washington Monument, which was reflected in the pool, and beyond that was the Capital Dome. It was a sight that never ceased to impress Jack. History and power, past and present, all brought together in the buildings and monuments stretched along the mall. As they approached the Vietnam Memorial, Jack was surprised to see Evans standing at the pathway entrance to the Memorial. He must have laid down some rubber to beat them there.

"That was a big screw-up, counselor. I hope you're a better lawyer than a listener, or your client Martinez is in big trouble. Next time follow my instructions."

"Hey, I'm really sorry. I just looked for a second. It won't happen again."

"It better not, or the director will have my ass." Evans changed the subject. "We've posted some agents down there. Obviously, we can't close down the Memorial. It's reasonably quiet, but if you get in any trouble just let out a yell and we'll come running." Evans then stepped back, clearing the path to the Vietnam Memorial.

Jack started down the tree-lined path. It was not particularly long and, after a short distance, Jack could see the bronze sculpture that marked the entrance to the Memorial. The sculpture had not been part of the original Memorial but was added later. The sculpture was, however, a perfect addition to the Memorial. It was not the typical war sculpture depicting brave warriors. Rather, it was a sculpture of three soldiers: Hispanic, African-American and white. Their fatigues were open at the collar. They carried their weapons casually. One soldier had his weapon tucked behind his neck, his arms cradled over either end. They appeared tired, forlorn, fatigued. Uncertain men, not boys, fighting an uncertain war.

Just beyond the sculpture was the Memorial itself. When the design was first announced it had generated enormous controversy. Many thought it was not appropriate and disrespectful. Jack could not have disagreed more. It was composed of black granite and set into the side of a hill—actually, it was a part of the hill—and shaped in a "V." At each end the Memorial was at a low point, not more than a foot high, from which it gradually rose to its peak, some ten to twelve feet, at the center of the V. Etched into the face of the granite were the names of all those who had been killed in Vietnam, beginning in chronological order from each end and meeting at the apex, at the center. It was incredibly powerful to behold. People approached the Memorial in hushed tones, walking slowly in front of the marble walls along the path that ran the length of the Memorial. As they looked at the names engraved on the walls, their own images were reflected in the smooth, polished, black marble. They reached up and touched the names; some leaned their heads against the wall, some wept. People left poems and gifts and mementos for the dead. They gathered together here to mourn and remember their loved ones. This was a living Memorial.

Jack continued down the path and began to walk along in front of the marble panels. About two thirds of the way to the center, he stopped and scanned the panel. About half way up his eyes focused on a name: Thomas Brian Banner. Each panel had a year engraved at the top. This panel said 1968. His brother had been killed during the Tet Offensive, in the city of Hue, South Vietnam. His death had also meant the end of Jack's family—and his life as he knew it. His brother, Tommy as he was known, was nine years his senior. He was all the things Jack would never be: high school quarterback, valedictorian, a lady's man, even at eighteen, and, beyond that, a genuinely nice kid. His parents and Tommy had argued for months about the war. Tommy felt it was his duty to go. Mom and Dad tried to convince him that he could get a student deferment and, like most middle class kids, avoid the war. It had all come down to one final argument in the family kitchen. Jack was supposed to have been in bed, but he was sitting at the top of the stairs listening.

"Why do you want to go? I mean, it's not really our war. What do you care about some godforsaken country in the middle of nowhere?"

"Look, Dad, we've been over this a hundred times. I want to serve my country. I've been given so much. I think I owe something back."

"Fine, join the Peace Corp!"

Jack's mother chimed in. "Honey, it's not that we don't respect your opinion. We just don't want to see you get hurt, or . . ." She began to cry.

"Mom, I'm really sorry. It's just something I have to do and it's my decision to make."

The argument must have gone late into the night. The next thing Jack remembered was his brother rousing him from his sleep. "Hey, squirt, you'd better not let Mom and Dad catch you up here or there will be hell to pay. Let's get you into bed." Jack rose to a sitting position.

"Are you really going to Vietnam?"

"Yes."

"Are you going to get killed?" The question was asked with the matter-of-factness of a ten-year-old, with no appreciation of its implication or meaning.

"Of course not. I'll be back before you know it."

"Can you call me from there?"

"Probably not. But I'll write every week. I promise."

Tommy kept one of his promises. Jack got a letter every week, until the day in December of 1968 when the chaplain knocked on their door and changed his life forever. Adolescence had been surprisingly uneventful. His parents were too involved in their grief to notice his rebellion. With no resistance, rebellion became boring and Jack soon quit trying. His mother was an empty shell, and her death at an early age was a blessing. The last word on her lips was Tommy's name. His father tried to give Jack a normal childhood. He was a decent man, but the death and loss of his wife—his first and only love—to grief overwhelmed him as well. Jack learned to conceal his pain, learned that to live was to feel, and to feel was to feel pain, so he stopped living.

He fled home as soon as he turned eighteen. College was a blur of drugs and alcohol, with an occasional class thrown in to break the monotony, delaying his graduation. He prayed for God to take his life, and did all he could to make the wish come true, trying ever more potent blends of the best drugs his campus had to offer. Then one day Tommy came calling. Jack had abandoned all belief in anything spiritual, and he would have passed this vision off to the drugs, were it not for the electricity in the air. His previous trips had been warm and fuzzy; on this night there was a crispness and clarity he had never experienced before. He tried to shake it off but there—clear as day—was Tommy sitting on the end of his bed.

"Hey, squirt, I gotta tell ya, you look like hell."

"Tommy, is that really you?"

"Yes, it's me, Jack."

"I've really missed you, Tommy."

"I know, squirt. I've missed you too. Listen, I don't have much time. I needed to get special permission to make this trip. I just came to tell you one thing. It wasn't your fault. Get your act together before it's too late." Then he was gone.

"Tommy, Tommy!"

"Man, Banner is hallucinating again. Hey, Banner. Wake up, man. We have to ramble. Banner?"

"Forget it. He's wasted."

"Wasted. Wasted." Jack mumbled to himself as he stood before the wall.

"It really was a waste, wasn't it?" The voice came from Jack's left. He turned and saw a strikingly beautiful woman facing him. She was of medium height with beautiful auburn hair flowing down to her shoulders, eyes the color of emeralds and decidedly delicious curves, apparent even under her winter coat.

"Oh, I'm really sorry. That was so rude of me to interrupt your thoughts like that. It's just that I was thinking what a waste it was. All those young men dying, for what? And then you said what a waste and I just . . ." Jack's expression must have been totally unsympathetic, because she stopped speaking and stared blankly at him.

Jack rescued the moment. "No need to apologize. It's nice to know someone shares my feelings." He reached out his hand. "I'm Jack Banner, pleased to meet you."

She paused, then stretched out her hand. "I'm Alison Stevens."

They shook hands. She paused and gave Jack a quizzical look. "Wait, not *the* Jack Banner, the man whose picture was splashed all over the front page this morning?"

"One in the same," Jack intoned proudly.

"Wow! I mean that's incredible. You're not going to believe this, but I sat up all night thinking about you. I mean, not you exactly, but . . ." She was beginning to ramble on again, but Jack found it so endearing that he let her continue, curious to see how she would get out of the hole she was digging. He was struck by the fact that, even at such a serious moment and time in his life, the sight of a beautiful woman, of the possibilities that might follow, fully captivated him. She continued, "You see, I'm a lawyer too, and I was thinking what a case that would be to have. I'm with the ACLU and this is a case that we would all kill for; and then to meet you here."

Jack wasn't sure he had heard correctly, so now he did interrupt. "Did you say you were a lawyer?"

"Yes."

"And you just happened to be here and ran into me just by luck?"

"Well, yes I did." From the tone in his voice she realized what Jack was thinking. She started to laugh. "You thought I planned all this? Well that's just ridiculous. When I said thinking of you, I didn't mean *you*, you. I meant the case. Your picture wasn't in the paper until this morning. Second, how could I know you would be here? Do you think I'm a spy or something?"

"No, just a lawyer out to land a big case."

She lit into him with fury. "That is so stupid and egotistical! If I had wanted the case I would have called you on Monday and asked you for it. You probably think that I was going to use my feminine guile to come down here and seduce you into giving me the case. That's just what a woman would do, wouldn't she? Well screw you, buddy!" Alison turned briskly and headed up the pathway running along the monument. The exchange caught Jack by surprise. He started to go after her, but suddenly Evans appeared at his side and grabbed his arm.

"What the hell was that all about, counselor? I was about to bring the troops down on her."

"It was nothing. Just a lady friend I hadn't seen in awhile. We ended on bad terms. She wanted to have the last word." Jack felt bad lying to Evans, but one thing he had learned in the last twenty-four hours was that life was strange and unpredictable. If he told Evans the truth he would have eight agents following her around for weeks. She didn't need that; no one did. Besides, Jack was intrigued and wanted to find out more about Ms. Stevens. The FBI snooping around would screw that up too. He knew her name and where she worked. That would be enough.

"We'll, it's time to get going."

"Sure, sure, let's go," Jack said, only half listening while straining to get one last look at Alison Stevens, as she strode off defiantly, never looking back once. She didn't give a damn about him; he loved that in a woman. Evans tugged at his arm again and they headed back to the car.

CHAPTER 8

Across town a phone rang in a dingy hotel room filled with smoke and empty takeout food cartons. The phone made the man jump. He had been waiting for the call but still jumped.

He picked up the phone and said nothing. It could only be one person.

"Contact. We have to meet. You know where. Tomorrow. Two."

The man hung up and went back to his takeout food. He could do nothing now but wait.

CHAPTER 9

The President of the United States, Peter Hampton, was not a happy man. He hated hospitals and, on top of that, he hated being sick. It was a typical male thing, but for him it was almost an obsession. The president always needed to be on the go and active. Being stuck in a hospital bed was entirely foreign to him. Even worse, he was surrounded by people trying to make him feel better, which only made him feel less well. There were nurses and doctors and Secret Service agents and aides and family and well-wishers coming and going all the time. In the room at the present moment were two nurses, three Secret Service agents and the senate majority leader's wife. After a full day, he had had enough.

"Berlin," he called to his chief of staff, Howard Berlin. Berlin was his most trusted aide and resident hatchet man. Every president needed someone to do the dirty work. Not only did Berlin do it exceptionally well, he relished it. Berlin moved over next to the president. "Get these people out of here. I need some peace and quiet and I need it now. You stay."

Berlin nodded. He turned to face the people in the room, which was actually a suite with a sitting area and a living room adjacent to the area where the president lay in his bed. The nurses and the majority leader's wife were in the sitting area. The Secret Service agents stood vigilantly near the door. Berlin cleared his throat. "Excuse me, the president would like to be alone now." The majority leader's wife looked somewhat insulted, having interrupted her day's activities to come see the president. As she rose to leave, she shrugged her shoulders with great effect. One of the nurses started to protest, but Berlin silenced her with a wave of the hand.

"I promise, if he so much as sneezes, I'll ring the panic button." This seemed to satisfy the nurse. She and her colleagues departed as well. The Secret Services agents were used to the need for privacy in matters of state, and all but one of them followed the nurses without protest. The president could never be truly alone with anyone, including his chief of staff. But in this situation one agent was sufficient precaution. Berlin closed the door leading to the living room.

"Thank God," exclaimed the president. "I thought they would never leave." He quickly got down to business. "Where do things stand, Howard?"

"Well, we've released a statement expressing your deep remorse at the death of the president-elect and the senseless acts of terrorism. We've also made clear that you are in good health and that the powers of the presidency have remained in your hands at all times. The VP dialed up the Soviets . . . sorry, the Russians . . . and assured them that things are in complete control. The Ambassador to the United Nations will make a statement to the Security Council tomorrow a.m., reiterating the same principles. CIA reports that everything is calm. Pentagon has reduced force readiness to DEFCON 2—ready but not looking for trouble."

"When can I go on TV to assure the public that all is well and that I'm fit as a fiddle?"

"They have you on at eight p.m. tomorrow night, assuming clearance from the doctors."

"Fuck the doctors. I'm fit as a fiddle and I am out of here tomorrow morning."

The phone rang at the president's bedside table. It was a secure phone. Only the powerful in Washington had the number. Berlin hated that phone, just like he hated that damn black bag with the nuclear codes. The "football," they called it. When the president had been knocked unconscious, the Secret Service agent who carried the football had immediately left the scene to find the vice president. The football had to always be with the next person in the line of succession who could unlock the codes and unleash the dogs of war. Like the football, the phone symbolized power, and to Berlin, power he could not control was a frightening thing.

"Yes," the president said. "Good, good." He was nodding his head. "Keep me informed." He hung up and looked at Berlin. "Head of the joint chiefs. The requests for National Guard troops have stopped. Apparently things are quieting down. Only New York and L.A. are reporting any significant problems. By tomorrow morning everything should be under control."

Under control? thought Berlin. Sometimes the president amazed him. The whole country was up in flames and he was talking about control. Berlin had to hand it to the president. Sometimes he was a real pain in the ass, but in a crisis he had no rivals. Berlin had first seen that feature back in his days as a staff member for the then representative to the House of Representatives. Berlin was fresh out of college, but he had an innate sense and ability to put his hand on the pulse of the American public. In doing so, he had put the president out in front on numerous issues that, at the time, seemed controversial. When Hampton gained a reputation as a forward-looking and dynamic thinker, his rise to the presidency began. Berlin's reward had been rapid promotion and the undying loyalty and faith of the president. However, being out front was risky and, more often than not, Berlin and the president had worked long into the night trying to put out the flames of controversy. In those late-night hours, as Berlin fretted and worried, the president was steady as a rock. He always rose to the occasion and the crisis would pass.

Now, as the president's chief of staff, he had control over access to the president, and that was power he could control; that kind of power he loved. He had been crushed when the president had lost the election. He still didn't know why. The American public was so fickle. They complained and moaned about the state of this and the problem with that, and then they had elected a totally inexperienced person to be president, instead of the steady hand of President Hampton.

The president interrupted his thoughts. "Howard, I want you to send a personal note, to be signed by me, to the wives and husbands of each and every senator, congressman and governor who was killed last night. I want a meeting with the heads of the CIA, FBI and NSC tomorrow, followed by a briefing by the Joint Chiefs of Staff. After that I want a meeting with the White House Legal Counsel. The succession process is now thrown into the area of the unknown. I am familiar with the essence of it, but I need an expert opinion."

"What do you mean?"

"What do I mean? I mean who the hell is going to be the next President of the United States come January 20! It is not as cut and dry as you may think, Howard."

Berlin was taken aback. In all the excitement and confusion, he had assumed that the president would continue to be president just as he had been. The constitutional implications had never been a consideration. The future was not a concern. Berlin had been a history major in college; he was not a lawyer. Somewhere in the back of his mind he thought that the Twelfth Amendment to the Constitution addressed the issue in one way or another. He was worried again. There was a sense of power and a course of events that he could not control. Damn that made him edgy.

He brought his nerves under control and refocused on the president. "That's an excellent point. I'll have the White House counsel prepared to brief you on that tomorrow. Well, Mr. President, I best be going. No matter what you say, a little rest will do you good."

"To hell it will. But you're right, you better be going. There's a long road ahead of us and we best be prepared for any and all eventualities."

Berlin turned to leave. The unease had not completely left him. The president called after him as he exited the room. "Remember, I want to be on TV tomorrow at eight, come hell or high water." Berlin nodded his head without turning. It was like the old man was running for reelection again. He pulled his cellular phone from his coat pocket and dialed the White House Press Office. Prime time it would be.

CHAPTER 10

This Monday morning would certainly be different than most for Jack Banner. Evans and his friends had made sure Jack avoided the hysteria outside his office building and in the lobby. A phalanx of the FBI's finest had been able to hustle him in through a service entrance unseen. He was beginning to admire those guys. Unfortunately, they could not eliminate the hysteria that greeted him when he disembarked from the elevator on the 11th Floor at the offices of Kelly, O'Brien & Mason.

As he exited the elevator, he was confronted by the receptionist, who looked completely and totally frazzled. The phones were ringing constantly and she repeatedly and rapidly attempted to answer the calls. Jack was a bit puzzled by her state. This was the same receptionist he had been dreaming of when Mr. Martinez interrupted his slumber. Generally she looked quite calm and always greeted him with a warm, cheerful and, in Jack's mind, provocative "hello." As Jack approached the reception area, the source of her irritation became clear. Usually Jack had no messages when he arrived in the morning. Today there was a stack at least four inches thick for him. He reached carefully for them, afraid of what they might hold. He began to flip through them: NBC, *Newsweek*, *The Wall Street Journal*, WTOP, a local news station, John Ladimeer, world famous criminal defense lawyer. The vultures had descended even more quickly than he had expected.

Without exchanging a word with the receptionist, he started to walk toward his office, still flipping through the messages. As he turned the corner he was almost run down by the office manager, Ms. Wendy Roberts.

"Oh, Mr. Banner, thank goodness you're here! It has been a total disaster. We're getting so many calls for you that our regular calls can't get through. You must do something."

Banner kept walking, ignoring her pleas. "What do I look like, AT&T?"

Ms. Roberts was momentarily taken aback. She gathered herself and stated emphatically, "Well, there is no reason to be rude about it."

As she spoke they rounded another corner and Jack's secretary, Elaine, came into sight. She was a pleasant lady, in her forties, and had been Jack's secretary for three years. A record of sorts. Jack had a reputation of being hard to work for. He never understood why. He turned his attention back to Ms. Roberts.

She appeared undaunted. As they passed Elaine's desk, Jack handed her the messages from the front desk. "Call all these people back. Tell them I have no comment. No interviews. No background stuff. Nothing. Call the ACLU, get a Ms. Alison Stevens on the line for me."

"Yes, Mr. Banner." He gave her a disapproving look. Jack had very few rules and almost no structure to his routine. That was probably what made him so hard to work for. His two rules were always be on time and call him Jack. Elaine always followed the first, but in times of stress she often violated the second. She caught Jack's look and quickly corrected herself.

"Yes, Jack." The "Jack" was long and drawn out to show her distaste for this particular rule. They passed her desk and headed toward Jack's office, with Ms. Robert's still in hot pursuit. At the doorway to his office Ms. Roberts paused. "Oh, by the way, Mr. Kelly wants to see you as soon as possible." She said it with intentional nonchalance, believing that the name of the firm's managing senior partner would strike fear in Jack's heart. It did give him momentary pause, but the recent events had made his patience for such things rather short.

"Fine. Tell him I'll be there as soon as I can."

Ms. Roberts seemed dumbfounded by his response. Having imparted her news, Ms. Roberts's mission was done. She stopped as if to say more, thought better of it, then wheeled around and was gone.

Jack crossed from the doorway to the chair behind his desk. It was not a large office. One wall was all windows, but the view was merely of the building across the way. The office was smartly decorated, mostly at his expense. The firm was rather stingy in that regard and in most others. But Jack had decided that if he was going to spend so much time in the office it should be comfortable, even if he had to foot the bill. A sofa lined one of the walls and all of them were adorned by a variety of artwork and photographs. He had also mounted the customary diplomas on the wall behind his desk, in frames of fine mahogany wood. A number of plants brought the room to life and increased the feeling of hominess. An Oriental rug was laid on top of the standard-issue wall-to-wall. All in all, not a bad place to spend ten to twelve hours a day, six days a week. Standard hours for a senior associate bucking for partnership.

Jack eased into his chair. It was a large, leather chair with armrests and a reclining footrest built in. Comfort was key. The phone rang. Jack pushed the speakerphone button. It was an annoying habit he had learned his first year with the firm. A partner, whose office was just down the hall, would call Jack and put him on the speakerphone. As they had worked closely on one particular project, the partner would call Jack all day long, always on the speakerphone. Not only was the guy too lazy to walk down the hall, he was also so arrogant that he used the speakerphone, even when not necessary. Jack found this so annoying he began answering the phone by pushing the speaker button, assuming it was the partner calling to harass him. The absurdity of it amused Jack. Two people not more than thirty feet apart communicating by speakerphone. The wonders of the technological revolution.

Elaine came on the speakerphone. "Mr. . . ." She started, stopped, and began again. "Jack, I have Ms. Stevens on the line."

"Thank you, Elaine." Jack reached for the phone. "Hello."

"Mr. Banner, I wish I could say it's nice to hear from you, but that would be a lie."

Obviously Elaine had failed to tell her about his rules. "Please call me Jack. I can understand why you feel that way. I'm calling to apologize. I was way out of line yesterday."

There was a pause on the other line. Jack could see her face in his mind. Its beauty was imprinted in his memory. He also felt a connection. Somehow, from the brief meeting, he had connected to her spirit. She was pondering whether to accept the apology graciously or make him grovel some more. He expected the grovel approach. She didn't disappoint.

"You certainly were. And now you think you can call up with a simple sorry and all is forgotten?" Jack's heart leapt. His reading of her had been right on the money. Beautiful, smart and stubborn. The perfect combination. His return approach had to be perfect. If he went for the personal "let's have dinner" approach, she would reject him out of hand. He had to appeal to her professional pride, play his best card now and hope for the best. Most of all he had to see her again. It was all he had thought of as he tossed and turned last night. The world was in chaos and she was all he could think about. A chance meeting, a brief encounter and he was hooked.

"No, no, of course not. I really wasn't calling for me."

"You weren't?" She sounded disappointed. Had he misread the situation?

He quickly continued, "No, actually I'm calling on behalf of my client. I've given this a lot of thought and I'd like you to meet him. I've spoken with quite a few lawyers in town and, to be blunt, they say you're one tough lawyer and that's what Mr. Martinez needs. Someone tough and not out for the book and movie rights. I think that's you. Am I right?"

"It certainly is." It was said without arrogance. It was a statement of fact.

"Good. Now, I can't make any promises. I'm going to have him meet several lawyers. The choice is ultimately his, of course, and you understand he has no money to pay?"

"That's no problem. I understand completely. But you can bet that once he meets me, he'll pick me. I'm the best there is."

"That's what they tell me. I'm planning to see him at four today, the FBI willing, of course. I'd like for us to meet at three, in my office. You'll need to explain the ins and outs of the criminal procedure for the next few weeks. Right now he only trusts me, so I have to be able to explain the situation to him and then ease you in. Sound like a good approach?"

"Fine. So long as you understand that when the case is mine, I run the show."

"Sorry, no can do. If he chooses you, I'm in all the way. I'm looking to expand my practice into the criminal area. I figure this would be good exposure. Learning at the knee of the master, so to speak. You'll be lead counsel of course, but my name comes right after yours. Deal?" Jack felt a little guilty. Here he was bargaining over a man's future so he could find out more about this woman. It was true that he wanted to expand his practice, but that too was a little cynical. His conscience was interrupted by her response.

"Deal. See you at three." Then she was gone.

Jack could barely contain his excitement. In just a few hours he would get a chance to see her again. And even better, assuming Martinez hired her, they would be spending hours and hours together. It would also be a very emotional and pressure-filled time; the perfect setting for falling in love. Jack was at heart a romantic. Not a lady's man, really, but he loved the romance in a relationship, the getting-to-know-you phase. And, of course, women loved that.

His thoughts were cut short by the buzz of the speakerphone. "Jack." It was Elaine. "Mr. Kelly just called. He wants to see you right away."

"Thank you, Elaine. While I'm meeting with him, would you please arrange a phone call from Mr. Ladimeer. He's the hotshot criminal defense lawyer. Make it about 3:15."

"Isn't that when you told me you're expecting Ms. Stevens?"

"Yes, it is. Please arrange the call."

"As you wish."

Jack hung up the phone and walked out of his office. He headed down the hallway back toward the reception area. Immediately behind the reception area was a staircase that connected the 11th and 12th floors. Mr. Kelly's office was on the 12th Floor. The receptionist was still busily answering calls. Jack was sure she gave him an over-the-shoulder glance as he passed by. He climbed the stairs two at a time and made a right at the top. After several more turns, he arrived at the threshold of the seat of power at Kelly, O'Brien & Mason.

Jim Kelly was a good old boy in the Washington tradition, which was perhaps different from a good old boy in the southern tradition. After all, Washington, D.C. was south of the Mason-Dixon line. In the South, a good old boy knew everyone in town and always had a beer handy and the pickup truck ready. In Washington, a good old boy knew all the right people and knew how to fix a problem for those in power. He could throw a fundraiser on two days notice, put people and the deals together in order to keep the money flowing for everyone.

Despite having been with the firm for six years, Jack seldom came in contact with the man. He had a reputation in the firm as a stickler for detail and a rigid adherence to the bottom line. He personally conducted inventory with the office manager on a yearly basis. Jack was sure that this would not be a pleasant experience.

Guarding the gate to the kingdom was Ms. Hathaway. She was the loyal and trusted administrative assistant to Mr. Kelly for over twenty-five years. Jack wasn't sure what the difference between a secretary and an administrative assistant was, except that an administrative assistant did personal errands for the boss, whereas a secretary felt such tasks beneath her. Ms. Hathaway was always sure to point out, however, that she was an "administrative assistant." She even had business cards to prove it. She was, in fact, a kind lady, which was surprising, given that she ran interference for

Mr. Kelly on a daily basis, and often put up with some very unhappy and upset people, including her boss. Her kind manner was the way she defused situations.

As Jack reached her desk, she gave him a warm smile. "Jack, how are you?" Elaine must have told her about his rule. Without waiting for an answer she continued. "Mr. Kelly is waiting for you. Go right on in."

Jack took a deep breath and entered Mr. Kelly's office. The view from this office was nothing short of spectacular. It faced south and looked down upon Pennsylvania Avenue and the north entrance of the White House. Beyond that were Constitution Avenue and the Washington Monument. The office was richly appointed, at firm expense. On the walls were photographs taken with past presidents and other Washington dignitaries. Mr. Kelly was behind his desk talking on the phone. He motioned to Jack to be seated, and held up his index finger to indicate that he would just be a minute. Jack took a seat on one of the chairs in the front of the desk. Mr. Kelly was true to his word, and in a moment had wrapped up his conversation.

He hung up the phone and looked at Jack. "Well, it appears you've had quite a weekend." Jack had no response. Kelly got up from his chair and crossed the room toward the entrance. He closed the door as he continued to speak.

"I've had a long talk with my old friend Gary Stevenson. He's quite concerned about your safety. Those FBI agents must make you feel pretty secure."

"We'll, sir, I'm certainly grateful, but I must say a little suspicious. Unsolicited kindness always makes me a little nervous."

"Gary mentioned that, too."

"What's that, sir?"

"That you're something of a wise ass. The partners I've spoken to say the same thing. Bright, hardworking, but a wise ass." Jack was about to say something to confirm his reputation, but Kelly continued.

"How long have you been with us Jack, five years?"

"Six, actually."

"Hmm. Another year and you'll be eligible for partner. How do you like your chances?" Jack didn't like where this conversation was going, but at the same time he felt a connection to Kelly. He was a straight shooter, in the sense that he didn't pussy foot around. After the last several days, a few direct questions were refreshing.

"Well, it all depends. If it's based on merit, I'm a shoo-in. I work as hard as anybody here and my work product is better; and, of course, my billable hours are near the top as well. On the other hand, if it's a question of politics, I'm history. I don't follow firm policies, I don't conform to unwritten firm etiquette and I don't kiss anyone's ass."

Kelly paused as he considered Jack's answer. "Directness, I like that. The way I see it, this most recent turn of events could make you or break you. If the case goes well, and by that I mean Martinez takes a plea and we look to be the champions of the poor and downtrodden, you're a hero. On the other hand, if the situation gets ugly, drawn out, and it looks like we support people who murder our presidents, you're finished. Given all that, I think I'd like to assign Richard Steele to help you out; he's our top white-collar crime guy."

Jack was sure this conversation was going to get even worse, so he decided to get it over fast and take his poison. "I'm sorry sir, but that just won't be possible."

"Not possible? What do you mean not possible? Last time I looked you worked for me. And, also, the last time I looked you signed an agreement that said all cases or legal matters in which you became engaged would become the property of the firm, whether located by you individually or on firm time. So, you see, the case now belongs to this firm, which means it gets staffed as the senior partner, which happens to be me, decides."

Now Jack paused. He had to admit that he was out of his league butting heads with Kelly, but he had the trump card, the winning hand. He had Martinez, and he knew that Kelly wanted this case in the worst way. However it came out, it meant exposure for the firm, and exposure meant revenue. A lawyer probably invented the Golden Rule.

"Everything you say is true, but if we do it your way we lose the case. I can promise you that. I've met Martinez and he doesn't trust guys like Steele; and, with all due respect, guys like you. Three-piece suits and attaché cases make him nervous. If you descend on him he'll can us. However, he trusts me. Second, I've already arranged competent co-counsel in the form of a gifted criminal lawyer with a history of defending these kinds of cases. Third, and this may be hard to swallow, I think he just might be innocent. I'm sure you'd agree that he deserves his day in court. We have the resources to give him that and make a good name for ourselves if he is innocent. If he's not, well, we did our duty as lawyers and officers of the court. It's the only ethical thing to do."

Jack thought for a moment that Kelly was going to strike him. He became visibly upset and rose from his chair. He leaned across the desk and shook his fist at Jack. "Don't come into my office, in my firm, and talk to me about ethics and what's right and wrong! You think you're pretty tough, don't you. Well, let me tell you about tough. I came from a little coalmine town in Pennsylvania. My father died from black lung at forty-five. My mother raised five boys on her own. Nothing was ever handed to me. Everything I have in my life is mine because I made it that way. Now when I make a call to the White House, the president interrupts whatever he's doing, including taking a crap, to take my call. So if you want to play tough, if you want to play with the big boys, you better be sure you've got what it takes. Do you have what it takes, Banner?"

Jack found himself staring out the window, down at the White House. He was collecting his thoughts, pondering his response. Once again the enormity of the situation started to creep up on him. He was debating the fate of a man accused of killing the next President of the United States, the man who would have occupied the White House at which Jack now stared. Did he have what it takes? He wasn't sure, but he knew he needed to find out.

"Well, sir, I'm not sure. But I can tell you this. We, and I mean you and me, really have no choice. For some bizarre, unknown reason Martinez called me in the middle of the night. And by chance I work for you. The real question is not whether I have what it takes. The question is whether or not you trust my judgment. The question is whether you believe I'm right. That's what you have to decide. If I'm right and we do it your way, we lose. If I'm wrong and we do it my way we lose. I think I'm right. What do you think?"

There was an awkward silence when Jack finished. He wanted to rush in and fill the void with some more comments, but he held back. Now Kelly was staring down at the White House, embroiled in his own thoughts. He had his hands together beneath his chin, fingertips to fingertips. He rocked slightly back and forth in his chair. Then he swiveled his chair to face Jack.

"Who's the lawyer you've retained?" Jack could barely contain his excitement.

"Her name is Alison Stevens. She's with the ACLU."

"The ACLU. Nice touch! Gives an oppressed, working-class feel to the whole thing. I think I've heard of her." Kelly began taking notes on a yellow legal pad. "Here's the deal. We run with it your way for now. If it gets too hot to handle, or the thing starts to go down in flames, we pull the plug. I'm going to call Kelleher and McCain, a public relations firm. We'll need to have a press conference and state our position. I want you to report to me on a daily basis as the case progresses. Whatever staff you need, you let me know. Just remember, Banner, it's both our necks on the line, but I have a lot more to fall back on. So don't blow it."

"You can count on me, sir."

Kelly stood up, which was a signal that the meeting was over. Jack stood up and turned to leave. His body language must have said victory because Kelly called after him.

"Don't get too cocky, kid. Doing it your way was really doing it my way. Know what I mean?"

Jack didn't look back. He headed out into the hallway, whistling.

CHAPTER 11

The president was a much happier man. Against the advice of his doctors, he had checked out of the hospital. The doctors had strenuously objected, but that was just to cover their butts; and having signed all the necessary legal release documents, they discharged him like any other patient.

He was now comfortably ensconced in a large, overstuffed sofa in the Oval Office, receiving the briefing he had requested the prior day. Berlin was seated next to the president, as always. It was another way for him to control access and, thus, control the power. Also present in the room was the Chairman of the Joint Chief of Staff, General Perkins. He was in the middle of his briefing on the military situation, including the state of domestic unrest in the United States. The president, always attuned to political necessities, had decided to include the ranking members of both parties in Congress: the Senate Majority Leader, Luther Ahmason, from California, and Representative Stan White, from New York, on the Democratic side, and Senator Scott Stilin and Representative Dan Crowell on the Republican side. Also present was the White House Legal Counsel, David Rothstein, and the head of the National Security Council, Andrew Weaver. The CIA and FBI had not been invited to this briefing. They would brief the president in a separate meeting scheduled later in the day.

General Perkins's report was encouraging in some respects, but not completely reassuring. There was no unusual military activity, and the readiness level of U.S. force had been reduced accordingly. The domestic situation was still not under control. Although many National Guard units had been withdrawn from most major cities, unrest was still being reported in many outlying areas. There seemed to be no organized resistance, but some grass roots support was being noted in various locations. The military had acted swiftly against the Front, but the Front's plea for public unrest was being followed by many people, and riots continued in many cities. The general wrapped up his briefing.

"Thank you, general. Any suggestions on how to handle the domestic unrest?"

Senator Stilin responded first. "Mr. President, we need to make it clear to the people that their needs and concerns will be addressed. It is time for strong but compassionate leadership."

"I agree, Scott. I intend to emphasize that in my speech tonight," replied the president.

The president turned to the head of the National Security Council, Andrew Weaver. "What do we have in the way of INTEL, Andrew? We need to find out who committed these barbarous acts and take decisive action."

Andrew Weaver was a tall and elegant man in his late fifties. He was a product of the finest East Coast prep schools and colleges. He had served his country for over thirty years since graduating from Princeton University, first as an agent for the CIA and then, ultimately, as head of the president's National Security Council.

"Mr. President, first let me assure you that justice will be served." Weaver had a flair for the dramatic. He paused after his opening sentence to allow the gravity of his words to be felt. He adjusted his glasses and continued. "We have activated our most skilled intelligence teams to get to the bottom of this. We feel, based upon the sophisticated nature of the attack and the coordination, that a foreign government must have had some involvement. The Front was not capable of acting alone in such a manner. Unfortunately, as of today there are more questions than answers. We have established that the explosives used were C-4 plastique from a large shipment that was stolen from an army base. Other than that, the rest is sketchy at best. It's just too soon to give a complete and adequate answer."

"Thank you, Andrew."

The president then turned to the White House Legal Counsel. "Well, David, where do we stand from a legal point of view?"

David Rothstein stuck out like a sore thumb in this group of blue blood Americans. He was from the Bronx, a graduate of the City College of New York and Harvard law school, by way of brilliance and scholarship. His politics were decidedly democratic and far to the left of that spectrum. His position as White House Legal Counsel was a result of political patronage from the ranking senior senator from New York. The senator had split from his party, endorsed Hampton for president, and had delivered New York in the president's first election. His reward had been plenty of jobs programs for his state. In addition, when appointments were made, the senator's own chief counsel, Rothstein, became White House Legal Counsel; better to keep an eye on the sheep with a wolf in sheep's clothing.

Rothstein was in his late forties, with a full beard dotted with specks of gray. In contrast to the Brooks Brothers suits and military uniforms of the other participants, he wore khakis, a sports coat and no tie. He only owned one tie. Some considered him irreverent, others eccentric. None doubted his brilliance. He stood with a yellow legal pad in one hand.

"Well, it appears we are in uncharted constitutional waters." He addressed those gathered as he would a law school class. Setting the stage, then defining the issues, and as all good lawyers, never giving a simple yes or no answer. "There has never been a situation where a president-elect has been murdered or died prior to taking office. As you know, there have been instances of a sitting president dying in office, and the procedure is quite straightforward for that. Article II, section 1, of the Constitution provides that the vice president succeeds to office and serves the balance of the term."

"Of course," chimed in one of those in attendance.

Rothstein seemed not to notice and continued. "However, the Constitution is less clear on the situation we have here."

"How so?" asked the president.

Rothstein turned to face and address the president. "Well, sir," he continued, "The Twentieth Amendment provides that if the president-elect dies prior to inauguration day, the vice president-elect assumes office. It further provides that if there is no vice president-elect chosen or he or she is not qualified, then Congress may by law determine who shall qualify."

"Still not following you, David," the president said. "We had an election, the vice president-elect is alive, he becomes president. What am I missing?"

Rothstein tried to hide his sense of triumph, having led the little class into his trap. He replied without any sense of the excitement in his brain.

"Well, sir, the Twelfth Amendment to the Constitution, which governs the procedure for the election of the president and vice president, in conjunction with the Twentieth Amendment, seems to have a . . . well . . . a loophole, for lack of a better term." He paused for effect, saw that now his audience was fully engaged and rapt with attention and continued.

"As you know, contrary to popular belief, when voters step into the ballot box and pull the lever, they don't actually vote for the president whose name appears on the ballot. They vote for electors, who collectively compose the Electoral College. Each state has a number of electors equal to its representation in Congress, plus you throw in the District of Columbia with three electoral votes, for a total of 538. The people chosen as electors, in turn, choose our president and vice president. The Twelfth Amendment states, and I quote: 'The electors shall meet in their respective states and vote by ballot for President and Vice-President.' Whoever gets a majority of the votes of the electors is president, and the person who gets the majority of votes of the electors is vice president. If no majority is obtained, the election is decided by the House of Representatives as to the president, and by the Senate, as to the vice president.

"Although the Constitution provides that the method of choosing who the electors are for each state is determined by each state, the Constitution also provides that Congress determines the date when the electors are chosen, which date 'shall be the same throughout the United States.' Congress has done just that, and by legislation has designated the first Tuesday in November, what we know as Election Day—as the day the electors are chosen. Most states, in turn, have passed laws that say, in effect, the electors placed on the ballot are deemed elected on Election Day based on the votes cast for the candidate to whom they are pledged. Again, by law, the electors are then required to meet on the first Monday after the second Wednesday in December following the election. They meet in each of the states, cast their votes and then send their votes to the Senate, as required by the Twelfth Amendment. The Senate is required to meet on January 6 to count the votes as delivered to them by each of the states. The applicable statute contains a very detailed procedure about certification of lists and delivery to the Senate, etc. I won't bore you with the details."

Representative Ahmanson interrupted this time. "So, if I'm following you, you are telling us that this group of electors need not choose the person for whom the people voted? That seems incredible to me."

"Sir, you are right on target," Rothstein replied. "And your question brings up one of the great debates in constitutional law: Must the electors vote for the person to whom they have pledged their vote when placed on the ballot, or may they vote for whomever they please? We have no clear answer, as the Supreme Court has never ruled on the issue. The closest the court has come to answering the question was back in 1952, in the case of *Ray v. Blair*. In that case, the court held that in connection with a primary the Democratic Party could force a delegate to pledge his vote to the candidate chosen in the primary as condition to serving as a delegate at the convention. However, the court's holding was quite limited on the Twelfth Amendment issue. The court stated, in essence, that even if such a pledge was unconstitutional in the general election regarding the Electoral College, it was not so in a primary, where the delegate voluntarily participated and agreed to be bound by party rules. Moreover, the decision was 5-2, with neither Justice Black nor Frankfurter participating. Justices Douglas and Jackson filed a vigorous dissent, essentially saying that the Electoral College was an awful system. In their words, the Electoral College is, and I quote, 'a mystifying and distorting factor in presidential elections which may resolve popular defeat into an electoral victory.' Nonetheless, they concluded that the Constitution is the Constitution, and nowhere is an elector required to vote for any particular candidate. They are in essence free agents."

Representative White interrupted. "How did we come up with such an awful system?"

"Good question. There are two plausible explanations. In his Federalist Paper Number 68, Alexander Hamilton explained that the system would place such an important decision in the hands of an esteemed group of people, selected by the population, to in turn select the president. His trust in the common man was not all that great. The second answer, one that I prefer, is slavery. The Constitutional Convention was a struggle between the slave states of the south and the free states of the north—a precursor to the Civil War. On the issue of presidential elections, the northern states appeased the south by giving them the system they wanted. Because slaves were not counted as citizens, but rather as property, the southern states did not want direct presidential elections for fear of being outvoted by the more populous northern states. Even more significant was the ability of the southern states to include provisions that each slave would count as three-fifths of a person for apportionment purposes in determining representation in the House of Representatives, but not be given the right to vote. Because the electoral system is based on apportionment, that is, the number of electors is equal to the representation in Congress, the southern states had control of selection of the electors based upon a census counting slaves. At the same time, slaves were not permitted to vote in the election of a state's representatives who decided who the electors would be. The South had its cake and could eat it too. The slaves being counted for apportionment gave the South increased representation based on counting those who could not vote."

General Perkins tried to interrupt with a question, but Rothstein talked right over him. "Now, if we had already had the meetings of all the electors and the results certified in the Senate, I believe the issue would be less murky. The new president would probably be deemed elected on January 6, the votes of the electors having already been cast, and the new vice president would have succeeded him and be sworn into office on January 20. I don't believe an elector's vote can be changed once cast. Once the vote is made, the results are certified, sealed and sent on to Congress. However, the day set for the electors to meet is the third Monday in December. That's over three weeks away. Given the circumstances, some or all of the electors could conceivably change their votes. It's anybody's guess what happens then. Given the closeness of the election, if enough electors change their votes, it would change the outcome of the popular election."

The general could no longer contain himself. "Do you mean to tell me that you can't tell us who will be president come January 20!"

"That is correct. Since the adoption of the Constitution, a handful of electors have, in fact, cast their votes for someone other than the person to whom they were pledged. Usually it was done to protest against some policy or another. Many states do not even require a pledge from the electors as to their vote, and most that do have no penalty, or minimal penalty, for failing to do so. Indeed, I suspect prosecution for such a crime would not be high on the list of any prosecutor I know."

Rothstein paused for a moment and the room was silent.

Senator Stilin spoke first. "Mr. Rothstein, you say the Supreme Court has never spoken on this issue?"

"No, sir. Other than the case I mentioned, they have not."

"Could we request a ruling from them on the issue? I mean it appears we may have a constitutional crisis on our hands."

Rothstein rubbed his beard thoughtfully. The professor in him was now in full glory. "Well, that would be convenient, but not possible. The Supreme Court does not grant advisory opinions. There must be what is known as a 'case or controversy,' that is, an actual dispute, not some hypothetical scenario. For all we know, the electors might elect the president-elect, although, with all due respect to the dead, I'm not sure they can vote for someone who is not alive. Then upon his election and then death, the vice-president might succeed to office or, perhaps, the electors would elect the vice president-elect in his place; a perfectly plausible outcome. For just that reason, the court will not consider a case unless some party with standing objects to how the electors actually vote."

"So all we can do is wait and see what happens?" the president said, his utterance sounding like both a question and a statement.

"I'd like to give you a more definitive answer, Mr. President, but the law is not always so clear."

"Thank you, David. That was an excellent presentation. I'd like for you to consider what possible steps could be taken from a legal point of view once the electors have met and the votes cast and counted. We should be prepared for any eventuality. We have a few weeks, so let's get all our ducks in a row."

This was Rothstein's cue to leave, but he did not take it; instead he responded, "I'm not sure that would be appropriate, Mr. President." Most of those assembled looked at him quizzically, the president included.

"Excuse me?"

"Well, sir, I perceive an inherent conflict of interest. I believe I am merely an employee of the United States Government while you, on the other hand, are a candidate for president and conceivably could use the information to benefit you and your party. It is within the great range of possibilities that you could still be elected president, notwithstanding the results of the election. Or you might decide to challenge the results of the Electoral College vote by the electors. Given all that, it seems to me that it would be improper to utilize the services of an employee of the United States Government, such as myself, to your personal benefit."

The puzzlement in the room turned to shock and anger. Berlin practically leapt out of his chair, ready to go on the attack. The president placed a hand on him, restraining him. "I appreciate your candor, David, and your point is well taken. The thought had never really occurred to me. I assumed I had lost the election and was operating under that premise. I'll look to the Republican National Committee for my answers. I will, of course, continue to look to you for assistance on any legal questions regarding matters of state."

"You have my fullest loyalty, Mr. President, as always."

"Well, gentlemen, this has been most enlightening. I appreciate your coming." The group rose as one except for the president, who remained seated. Berlin crossed to the door and ushered the participants out. The mood was somber, serious as they left. The president and Berlin were left alone. Berlin crossed back to where the president sat and seated himself on a chair across from the president. Neither one said a word. Berlin's mind was racing with excitement. They were back in the race. By some twist of fate and the ruminations of a lawyer refugee from the 1960s, they had hope. In his head he was calculating the electoral votes. You needed 270 to win. The president-elect had gotten 271. A slim margin, by Electoral College standards. Rothstein hadn't addressed a thought that now occurred to Berlin. When a presidential candidate wins a state he gets all the electoral votes. Rothstein didn't explain how that worked. His conclusion was that all the votes were now up for grabs and that the "winner-take-all" system was no longer in effect.

The situation was perfect. The vice president-elect was a zero. He had no popular support and limited political support, mostly in the Midwest. He had been selected to balance the ticket and help win the Midwest, which he had done. With the election just over, the president's political machine was still in place. First . . . leaks to the press about this Electoral College question, if they hadn't investigated it already. They probably had, but a leak would accelerate the process. Within twenty-four hours, every elector would know that they could vote however he or she wanted.

Second, they had to make a list of all the electors and compile a list of those most likely to change their votes: conservative democrats, southern democrats, and independents. Then a full court press. Personal calls from the president and then follow-ups from prominent party members. Berlin could hear the pitch in his head: "This is a critical moment in history. The country needs a seasoned leader like President Hampton."

The president interrupted his thoughts. "Well, Howard, I guess there's nothing we can do now except wait."

"Wait? I don't agree, Mr. President. We need to do everything in our power to see that you are the one elected on January 6 when those votes are counted in the Senate. Your country needs you now more than ever."

"I appreciate the compliment, Howard, but the people have spoken and they didn't choose me. It would be unseemly for me to take advantage of such a tragedy to my own personal benefit."

"Mr. President, it wouldn't be for your benefit. It's for the benefit of the country."

"I'm sorry, Howard. I know how hard you worked during the campaign and I appreciate all your years of service, but I'm afraid it's over now. Time to move on. I will not authorize any effort on my behalf to change the votes of the electors."

"But sir . . ."

"No, Howard. It's not subject to discussion, is that understood?"

"Yes, sir."

The president rose. "Well, time to meet with the Belgian Ambassador. We must continue with business as usual." He crossed to the doorway and once there stopped and turned to Berlin, who sat forlornly on the couch.

"Don't look so sad; think of all the money you'll make with your book on the White House years." Berlin managed a small chuckle and the president was gone. After he left, the chuckle turned to a laugh, and then continued until it became a cackle. It was not a form of joy, but of triumph. Don't make an effort on his behalf? Who the hell did he think he was? He was not about to throw it all away because the old man had lost his spine. When it was over, and they were again inaugurated, he would tell the president what he had done, and when he had, he would thank him. But for now, it would have to be kept secret. He picked up the phone.

"*Washington Post*, may I help you?"

"Glen Spivey, please."

"One moment."

"White House desk, this is Spivey."

"Glenn, my friend, it's Berlin. I am about to give you the scoop of the century."

CHAPTER 12

The man from the hotel was glad to be out of his room. Takeout was getting old and daytime television was driving him toward insanity. The regular meeting place was Houston's in Georgetown. It was a restaurant bar on Wisconsin Avenue, south of M Street. In the 1960s, the Kennedys had made Georgetown trendy again. It was ironic that the last time he had been in D.C. was because of the death of a president. From Dallas to D.C. to nonexistence. That's how it always was in his line of work. His meetings were often in public places. It attracted less attention than a meeting in some remote and desolate location.

They had taken a booth alongside the bar. The caller was dressed in a dark-blue suit, a crisp, white dress shirt, and conservative, patterned tie. His hair was cropped short. He could have passed for any of the thirty-something yuppies that filled the office buildings on K Street. More careful analysis by a trained eye would lead to a different conclusion. He carried himself in a decidedly military way: ramrod straight, each move deliberate and purposeful. His eyes were constantly scanning the terrain, looking for suspicious movements and, ultimately, danger. On this particular occasion, he went by the name of Mr. Smith. Corny, but simple.

The man across from him was dressed in a decidedly nonmilitary manner: casual clothes, hair down below his collar. He was, however, no less serious in his purpose and equally as deadly.

"The operation was sloppy. You left too many loose ends."

The caller was unfazed by the criticism. "That's why we called you in to pick up the pieces."

"Well, I'm getting damn tired of being the maid. I tried to tell you guys that framing up Martinez was a bad idea unless you could be sure he was dead before he got nabbed. Now you've got the feds and who knows who else poking around."

"Hey, it was unavoidable. We needed to throw them off the track. Buy some time. Make sure all the 'evidence' is in place, so that Martinez takes the rap." The caller suddenly turned serious. "The future of our nation was at stake. Risks had to be taken. We took them. Now we have to be sure the risks pay off. If you take care of business, it will."

"Save your sanctimonious crap for your brethren. I pray to the almighty dollar and you can be sure this is going to cost you. I trust the down payment has already been deposited?"

"It has. One million as you directed, the balance upon completion."

"Did you bring the information I needed?"

Mr. Smith reached down under the table and brought up a briefcase. He placed it on the table and laid his hands on top of it. "'Everything you need is inside. He is being arraigned on Tuesday. The route to and from the courthouse is inside. The best place is probably in the courthouse or on the way in or out. The place will be a mob scene with the press and all that. Security will be loosest there. The hallways are narrow. Also, there is a drop ceiling throughout. I provided you with the duct layout if you decide that's the way to go."

"What about the lawyer? Do I whack him too?"

"I'm afraid so. We have to assume he told the lawyer enough to make trouble. That's why it's so important to do it soon. The longer we wait the more loose ends we have to tie up."

"Don't worry. I'll get the job done. Make sure your people are in position to create the diversion."

"We'll be there. We started this and we'll finish it. Our country is depending on us."

"Yeah, right." He rose from the table, taking the briefcase. He started to reach for his wallet and then thought better of it. "Tonight the drinks are on you."

CHAPTER 13

Jack hadn't been able to work all day since his meeting with Kelly. Even more difficult was concentrating on work, with the anticipated arrival of Alison Stevens. A number of his colleagues had stopped by to hear, firsthand, the tale of his exploits. Jack had been intentionally circumspect, even with those lawyers he considered his friends. Martinez's cautionary words were his overriding concern. The fewer people who knew anything, the better.

Most amusing were the senior partners, who previously never gave him the time of day, inquiring about how they could help or if he needed "anything." In his mind Jack could see them calculating the increased revenue per partner that the case might bring. It also saddened him greatly. The law was no longer a profession. It was a business, and like any other business, the focus was on the bottom line. Lawyers were commodities, not people. Occasionally, he would run into an old timer who would reminisce longingly about the "good old days," when all the lawyers in town knew one another. Courtesy was common and required for survival. If one lawyer acted uncivilly or improperly he was blackballed and the other lawyers in town referred no further business to him. It had been a calling, much like the priesthood, and few answered the calling. Those who did operated by a strict code of ethics. Those days were long gone.

His musings were interrupted by Elaine. "Jack?" She was standing in the doorway.

"Yes?"

"Ms. Stevens is here to see you."

His heart leapt. He had glanced at his watch fifty times that day, hoping that this hour would arrive, and it finally had. Jack tried to maintain his composure.

"Why don't you show her in and ask her if she'd like some coffee?" Elaine departed without a word and a moment later returned with Alison Stevens. She took Jack's breath away. She was dressed in a black silk dress that had the perfect blend of professionalism and femininity. It suggested both power and sexuality. Her hair was pulled back in a bob, still radiant while restrained. Back in the late '70s and '80s, as women entered the legal field they thought that to compete they had to dress like men. They wore awful women's suits, with ridiculous scarves and bows meant to mimic ties.

Although incredibly ugly, the women were caught in a bind. If they dressed with too much style they were not taken seriously. If they dressed like the men, they were derided as too masculine looking. The glass ceiling was very thick. Fortunately, as more women entered the law, they could begin to dictate the dress to their liking. Alison Stevens was obviously a lady with a lot of style as well as brains.

Jack rose from his desk and met her at the doorway, his hand outstretched. He hoped his hands weren't sweaty. "It's good to see you again, Ms. Stevens. May I call you Alison? I insist everyone calls me Jack."

She paused. "Of course, Jack." Her grip was firm but feminine. Her touch sent a shiver down his spine.

Jack gestured towards the sitting area in front of his desk, where there were two chairs and a coffee table. "Please have a seat. Did Elaine offer you some coffee?"

"Yes, she did. I imagine it's on the way." She laid a leather valise on the coffee table and pulled out a legal pad and a number 2 pencil. As she sat down, Jack crossed to his desk, where he picked up a yellow legal pad and a pen. He then joined her in the sitting area. The pad was balanced on her knee. Her legs were neatly crossed. He felt like he was on a first date, and wanted to make sure he said and did the right thing. "Well, we have a lot of ground to cover and I'm afraid not much time to do it in, so we better get started."

"I couldn't agree more." Elaine returned with the coffee and departed. "The way I see it, the government's case is weak. They arrested our client at the scene, but they have to link him to the crime. His being there with a weapon doesn't help, but that's merely circumstantial. They need witnesses who will testify that he was involved in the conspiracy. I'm sure they don't have that now. Of course we won't know until we see the indictment. We have an advantage in that the government will have to reveal all its information and evidence to us."

"Well, there is one slight problem."

"What's that?" Alison asked.

Jack paused for a moment. The next statement would indelibly cast her fate. Jack felt he could not force her to throw in her lot with him. It wasn't fair to her. She had the right to have a say in her future.

"I don't mean this as an insult, Alison, but I have to ask it and I hope you take it in the spirit that I say it."

She looked extremely annoyed. She uncrossed her legs and leaned forward. Jack didn't want to say it, but he did.

"Are you sure you want this case? Based on what I know, it could be very dangerous."

Her response took him by surprise. She started to laugh and the laughter caused her to relax. She leaned back, continuing to chuckle.

"I'm glad you find this so amusing." Now there was an edge in his voice. It cut her laughter short. She smoothed out her skirt to aid in regaining her composure.

"I'm sorry. I didn't mean to laugh. You see, I was a prosecutor before I went to the ACLU. I prosecuted drug dealers, mobsters, and killers of the worst kind. I've got more bounty on my head then the FBI's most wanted. Don't get me wrong. I worry sometimes at night when I'm alone in my apartment, but life's too short to always be looking over my shoulder. So spit it out, Banner."

Jack got up to close the door. He returned and sat down. It was his turn to smooth his slacks. "Martinez told me he was part of a conspiracy to kill the president-elect. He was there to kill him, but someone beat him to the punch."

Alison was about to respond but was interrupted by Elaine's voice on the intercom. "Jack, Mr. Ladimeer is on the line."

Jack looked at Alison. "Do you mind? This will only take a second and we've been playing telephone tag for a day."

"No problem," Alison said, but inside she was seething. The little s.o.b. was trying to embarrass her. She sipped on her coffee, so as not to explode . . . as if he thought she didn't know what he was up to: Everyone in the criminal defense bar knew George Ladimeer. Jack was obviously shopping the case around and he wanted to rub her nose in it.

Jack walked over to his desk and picked up the phone. "Mr. Ladimeer. May I call you George?" Jack turned to look at Alison. She met his gaze while continuing to sip her coffee. He smiled as he listened. She did not smile back. "George . . . George . . . I appreciate your enthusiasm for the case, but the purpose of my call was to let you know that I've already found a lawyer for my client. I wanted to let you know personally, as a courtesy."

Alison put down her coffee, a look of surprise on her face. He wasn't trying to show her up. He was trying to impress her. That made her even madder. Jack was listening again. "Who? Alison Stevens, she's with the ACLU . . . You've heard of her? Yes, a very fine lawyer. I will keep you in mind if anything comes up. Thank you, George."

Jack hung up the phone and crossed back to the sitting area. He took his seat under Alison's withering stare. "What the hell was that all about?" she demanded.

"What was what all about?"

"The call from Ladimeer just happened to come while I was here?"

"Yes."

"That's bull and you know it. I don't know what game you're playing but I'm not impressed. Is this part of some extravagant seduction for you? Throw me the case and hope I'll go to bed with you? We're talking about a man's life here. I take that very seriously. Obviously you don't. I don't think we can work together." She stood up from the chair, grabbing her valise.

Jack stood up as well. "Hold on a minute. I think there's been a misunderstanding. I've gotten literally hundreds of calls about this case. I need to take those calls when they come in. It's important not to insult people, especially important ones in the legal field like Ladimeer. I'm sorry if your ego can't handle that." Jack was again skating on thin ice with her. She was so volatile. It seemed that the littlest things set her off. At the same time she was tough as nails. She wasn't going to take any crap from him or anyone. She didn't care about the danger the case might put her in. But why the chip on her shoulder? OK, so he had set up the call to come while she was there, but that was only to impress her, not upset her.

Alison stopped gathering up her stuff. She looked at Jack. Was he lying or not? She couldn't tell. Was she doing what she accused him of, letting her emotions cloud her judgment? She couldn't allow that to happen. She took a deep breath to compose herself and then sat back down. Jack followed suit.

"Look," she said, "we need to set a few ground rules. First, we can't let our emotions get in the way of our work. I apologize. I broke that rule just a moment ago. It won't happen again. Second, we need to be straight with one another. You're probably right about the danger. Even without that, this case is going to be very rough. The full weight of the United States Government will be against us, not to mention the media circus. I've got to know that I can trust you and count on you. You have to feel the same way. Third, we're equal partners, but I make all the calls on trial strategy. The rest we decide together. Sound fair?"

"Completely. I should apologize also. I should have let you know that call was going to be coming."

"Apology accepted. Now, you were saying . . . ?"

He related his meeting with Martinez. When he was finished the intercom rang again. Jack looked at the phone apprehensively, then at Alison. They both smiled. She nodded her head and Jack walked over to the phone. "Yes, Elaine? Good. Great."

He hung up. "The FBI has said we can see Martinez in half an hour. After what I've told you I would understand if you wanted to decline the case. But I'd love to have you on board."

Alison again stood up and placed her pad and pencil in her valise. Jack again admired her. Her manner was unhurried and without tension. She had a confidence and purpose about her that was calming and reassuring. He felt drawn to her, wanted to reach out and touch her, to share in that confidence and steadfastness. She finished putting away her belongings and looked up at him, their eyes catching for a moment. He looked down, feeling guilty that she had caught him gazing at her.

"I'm ready."

"After you." She moved toward the door and Jack grabbed his coat from the back of the door.

CHAPTER 14

The putts were going left and that was a bad sign. The chief justice of the United States Supreme court, Donald Kincaid, was an avid golfer and, even at age 75, an excellent putter. However, when distracted his putts tended to pull left. Something about not staying with the line of the swing long enough. The putting machine in his office received a daily workout. Today was no exception. He stroked another putt along the green pile carpet. It also was left, and he banged the head of the putter against the ground. Frustrated, he placed the putter against his desk and began to pace the office floor.

The chief justice had been on the Supreme Court for thirty years. That made him an expert in both constitutional law and politics. Although his primary dedication was to the law, his true loyalty and love was for the court itself: the institution and its history that placed the court at the center of American history and made it the linchpin of a democratic society. It was the existence of the court system, and the Supreme Court, as the highest court in the land, that allowed democracy to survive. The citizens had recourse for their disputes to a forum that was not beholden to the government, and as to each citizen it was wholly impartial. Yet for all its power, it was an extremely weak institution. Because it remained independent from the government, it had no army, means to raise funds or even to enforce its decisions. It relied solely on the people's belief in democracy and the rule of law for its power. As such, its decisions had to be reasoned and founded on both moral and legal grounds. The impact of its decisions had to be considered, for if the people lost faith in the courts, its edicts would not be enforced and lawlessness and anarchy would follow.

The assassination of the president-elect caused him great consternation. As a student of the law, he knew the constitutional dilemma the country now faced. He had his law clerk fully researching the issue. His concern was that the issue would be brought to the court for resolution. The court might have to choose who was president. That was unsettling for him. The decision could have enormous repercussions and could place the court in the center of a political controversy. What if the losing party chose to ignore the court's decision? There had been rumors that when the court had ordered Nixon to turn over tape recordings of conversations in the Oval Office, discussion in the White House turned to martial law and suspension of the Constitution to prevent such disclosure. Surely the people would not have allowed that and civil unrest would have ensued. What if the man the Supreme Court chose turned out to be a poor president or a tyrant? The people's faith in the court would be lost forever.

At the same time, the court could not avoid the issue if a case or controversy were presented to it. This also would diminish its authority. So troubled was he that he had called a special meeting of all the justices for later in the week. They would have to consider all the possibilities so they would be prepared to act when the time came; the future of the court and the nation depended on it.

He walked back to his desk and picked up the putter. He lined up another putt. He smoothly stroked the round white ball. It appeared to be straight when it left the putter head but slowly, imperceptibly at first, and then more and more, it headed left of the target, rolling past the putting machine along the rug, and finally on to the granite floor near the entrance to the office. The chief justice watched with disgust as the ball clattered along the granite, hopped over the threshold of the door and rolled noisily down the hallway.

CHAPTER 15

Across town, the director of the FBI was struggling with a dilemma of his own. He had called a meeting of his top personnel to analyze the assassination and to identify possible suspects. Jenkins was there as always. Also present was the head of the FBI's Counterterrorism Unit, Skip Hodgkins. For years the bureau had dreaded the possibility of a profound foreign-hatched or domestic terrorist attack, and now it had finally happened—and on his watch! Several of his top field agents were there. They had been flown in overnight from around the country.

Since his meeting with Jack, Stevenson was more convinced than ever that the Front, as they knew it, could not have been responsible for the attack. Preliminary reports from field offices didn't fit the profile of known Front activities and capabilities. The operation had just been too sophisticated. Some of the timing devices on the explosives were state-of-the-art. His munitions experts were in awe and envy of the handiwork. Dozens of Front members had been arrested all over the country. The field agents had been called in to report on the interrogations. The reports had been disquieting. They were seated around a large conference table in the FBI's Situation Room. Stevenson turned to Skip Hodgkins.

"Skip, fill us in on what we know so far." Hodgkins was a tall, muscular man. He had served in the Green Berets and only a foolish man would challenge him in a test of wills or strength.

"From what we have gathered in the last forty-eight hours, the Front has apparently undergone something of a transformation. One that I am sad to report we did not detect. Approximately six months ago the Front was co-opted, infiltrated, taken over—whatever you want to call it—by a number of highly-skilled and well-trained professionals. They had plenty of money and access to weaponry and explosives. They also talked the talk, in that they convinced the existing leadership that an armed insurrection was the only means to achieve the Front's goals. Our reports are sketchy, but they are described as white males, thirty to forty years old."

Stevenson interrupted, not as much to ask a question as to confirm his suspicion. "Is it our conclusion that these infiltrators merely used the Front for their own agenda?"

"It appears that way. Our intelligence shows that the infiltrators numbered maybe ten or twelve at the most. They needed a number of people, in many different locations, to pull this off. The Front was ripe for the picking. Our efforts at counterintelligence had restricted their activities; their popularity had diminished, their funding was drying up. These guys promised them the moon, when all they saw was the bottom of the barrel."

Stevenson paused, contemplating the next question with great care. "I want you to think about this question before anyone answers. Were these men sponsored by any foreign government?"

The room was quiet for a moment. If the answer was yes, then the result would be an international crisis with a high likelihood of armed conflict. The United States could not countenance the assassination of its future president. On the other hand, if the answer was no, then some insidious, indigenous force was at work. A sophisticated, homegrown terror network, its objectives unknown, had unleashed its full fury. Brent D'Angelo offered the first response. He was the head of the Midwest Field Office. His agents had pulled in the suspects who had first revealed the existence of the "infiltrators."

"Based on the descriptions, they are clearly part of a homegrown American group. All the statements we have describe them as standing out like sore thumbs. The Front is very ethnically and racially diverse as an organization; these guys were just the opposite. They could be recruits, deep plants, but I doubt it. I think we are dealing with local boys." Those seated in the room each nodded their heads in turn as the director scanned the room.

Stevenson again took control of the discussion, turning to Skip Hodgkins, posing the question delicately. "If they were sore thumbs, Skip, why did we miss them?" Hodgkins was quiet. He looked at Stevenson and then surveyed the room. Everyone had the same thought but no one wanted to say it. Jenkins broke the silence.

"Everyone in this room has the highest security clearance, so let's cut to the chase. The only way that we could have missed this was either the Front was practicing extremely effective disinformation or we have a leak in the bureau."

It had been said. The unthinkable. A spy, a plant, a mole. Every intelligence agency's nightmare. Unfortunately, in this case, it made sense and they all knew it. The Front had been at the top of the FBI's agenda. Millions of dollars had been spent and hundreds of agents had been assigned to stamp out the Front. Somehow, the Front had not only defeated that effort, but had also become an entirely new and dangerous organization, run by trained professionals. An informant within the bureau would have enabled the Front to anticipate the bureau's actions and react accordingly, in order to prevent discovery of its metamorphosis.

Stevenson scanned the room. He knew it could not be any of these men. They had all been together too long and subject to the highest scrutiny over the years: lie detector tests, random searches of home and offices, and financial disclosures to prevent payoffs or bribes. No, most likely the leak was at a lower level, by someone with access to information, but not subject to intense scrutiny. Intelligence was a funny business. It was all about information and getting as much of its as possible. At the same time, the key to its success was limiting access to that same information once gathered—contradictory impulses and desires leading to a schizophrenia of purpose.

"Skip, I want you to implement at once the Prompt Disclosure Protocol. If we have a leak we need to plug it fast." The Prompt Disclosure Protocol was the bureau's response to possible leaks. It required a complete review of the flow of information to determine all persons who had access to any information that was related to the Front, so as to identify the potential source of the leak, from the lowest file clerk to the highest officer, including the director. A special squad of agents was then assigned to investigate each person who had such access, until either the leak was discovered or it was determined beyond certainty that no leak existed. Notwithstanding the director's admonishment, this leak would not soon be plugged without some luck. The volume of information and the number of people were just too great.

The director continued, "Second, nothing said today leaves this room." They all nodded in agreement.

"Good." The director glanced at his watch. "We will reconvene at five p.m. tomorrow. That is a little more than twenty-four-hours from now. I'm meeting with the president at 6:30. I'd like to be able to tell him something concrete, if possible."

They dispersed with a sense of purpose and vigor. They all wanted to be the one who found the person who had betrayed them.

CHAPTER 16

Frank Ruffulo had been the mayor of Winnetka, Illinois, for a number of years. This, of course, meant that he had been active in Democratic politics. Few people in Illinois got elected without the aid of the Democratic machine. Ruffulo had dined with Mayor Daley in his heyday. As a result, he had been asked to be an elector every four years and faithfully attended the electoral vote in the state capitol. He didn't really understand what it all meant. The party bosses told him where to go and how to cast his vote, and he had done as they asked.

Over the last three years, he had grown disillusioned with the Democratic Party and politics in general. The country had taken a turn for the worse. Too much crime, too many taxes, too few good jobs. The assassination of the president-elect and the other government officials had confirmed his worst fears; the country was going to hell in a hand basket. He had even considered not running for reelection, but he had been in politics so long that he didn't know what else he would do. That's what made the phone call he received that afternoon so intriguing. Some fellow from Washington, D.C. had called and asked him how he was going to cast his vote at the meeting of the electors in Springfield in three weeks. Ruffulo told the fellow he had hadn't given it much thought, which was true. Did he have a choice, he asked? Of course, said the caller. They had then discussed the repercussions of the assassination. The discussion of Article II of the Constitution went over his head, but the gist of it was that Ruffulo could vote for whomever he pleased.

The caller had then made a case that the reelection of President Hampton would be good for the country. In this time of crisis, the country needed experienced leadership. Ruffulo had to admit that that made sense, but what the hell had the president been doing for the last four years? He didn't want to be rude, so he remained silent on that point. Ruffulo told the caller he would certainly give it some thought. The caller said he would check back in the next several days.

Since the phone call, Ruffulo had been doing some serious thinking. Being Mayor of Winnetka was important, and he had impact on people's lives. The opportunity presented to him now dwarfed that by comparison. He could decide who would be the next president of the most powerful nation on earth. More important, that power was a valuable thing. People might pay a lot of money for that kind of power. Being Mayor of Winnetka didn't pay a whole lot, and social security didn't amount to much. The caller had asked if there was anything—with emphasis on the word "anything"—he could do to help Mr. Ruffulo with such a difficult decision. Did that mean the mother lode or public works projects for Winnetka? He had to be careful. The whole thing could be a hoax or, worse yet, a setup by the police or FBI. How could he find out what "anything" meant without catching his own ass in a trap? He would have to give that some thought. He had only a few days to decide some very serious stuff. It was almost too much too bear. He should probably head home and talk it over with his wife, Mable, but all the thinking had given him a headache. A trip to Jimmy's Bar and Grill was what he needed. Have a few, clear his head, talk it over with the boys . . . of course in a way they wouldn't know what he was really talking about: *If you had a chance to make some money, but the way was a little bit questionable, what would you do?*

A moral dilemma for the ages, but one never before faced by Ruffulo. If only this opportunity had come at a younger age. All those years that he had gone to Springfield with no idea of the power he held in his hands. As he donned his hat and gloves, he considered the years of lost opportunity. It only seemed right that he make up for lost time. Well the boys at Jimmy's would help him figure it out. That was one thing of which he was sure.

CHAPTER 17

The trip to see Martinez had not gotten off to a good start. Evans had been waiting for them in the reception area and this had immediately upset Alison. She wanted nothing to do with the FBI. It took fifteen minutes to convince her that it was for her own protection, and the only way to get through the media circus in the lobby. Jack wasn't so sure, himself, about the FBI, although he had come to trust Evans. Actions spoke louder than words, and so far Evans had lived up to his promises. Finally, they had convinced her to accept the ride, by promising her that after the meeting she could go as she pleased. Evans had helped in this regard, by telling her that his orders were to stay with Jack at all times, and that was exactly what he intended to do. This had mollified her, and they made their way through the crush of reporters to the FBI sedans. Alison had fumed the entire way over and Jack's efforts to get her to discuss the case had been unsuccessful. Her answers were terse and not illuminating.

Once at FBI headquarters, her mood did not improve when she was subjected to a brief search of her belongings and asked to pass through the same metal-detectors Jack had passed through two days earlier. In the elevator, on the way up to the holding area, she continued to give Jack angry looks. Finally, they arrived at an interview room, where they waited for Martinez to be brought in. She said nothing as they sat in the stiff plastic chairs. Jack stared out through the windows covered with wired mesh, and began to feel the same anxiety he had felt during his first meeting. Impressively, Alison's demeanor quickly changed when Mr. Martinez was led into the interview room. She sat upright and alert. Martinez looked warily at her as he entered.

"Who's that, man?"

Before Jack could respond, Alison stood up and reached across the table that separated them, her hand outstretched. "I'm Alison Stevens. Mr. Banner has asked me to assist him in your defense."

Martinez did not seem impressed, and he did not reach for her hand. Alison pulled her hand back awkwardly. He turned to Jack.

"I told you I didn't need a lawyer. I just needed you to get the word out about me. From the newspapers, I see you did a good job of that. So if you don't mind, I'll do the time. I'll have three squares a day and a roof over my head. That's better than what I've had before."

Jack wasn't sure what to say. Martinez's attitude didn't surprise him, given their first encounter, but his current attitude was a bit cavalier. It also didn't jibe with his mood on their first meeting. Then he had talked about not taking the fall for someone else's actions. Had someone gotten to him? He had told Martinez not to talk to anyone. Had he not heeded his advice? He was about to inquire into the possibility when Alison leaned her body across the table and looked Martinez right in the face.

"The way I see it, Mr. Martinez, you have a really dumb attitude for a couple of reasons. One, in case no one told you, killing a President of the United States is a capital offense. That means the death penalty. Now maybe someone can say the guy wasn't the president yet, but do you want to take that chance? Second, if you're innocent, as Mr. Banner says you say you are, how long do you think the guys who set you up will let you last in prison? You know, I once prosecuted a guy who took the rap for an organized crime boss. He was really cocky and tough, like you are. He lasted two weeks in the joint.

"Now, if all that doesn't impress you, here's something that might. Ever heard of the First Amendment? Well, your exercise of those First Amendment rights is sure to be worth a lot of money—TV, movies, video. My colleague, Mr. Banner, is with a really fancy law firm, and they've assembled the best public relations team money can buy. Now, Mr. Martinez, that can all be yours, or you can keep your mouth shut and roll the dice. Frankly, I don't give a damn. What I care about is that the system works; that those who want a chance to prove their innocence get it. The rest can rot in jail or underground for all I care."

There was complete silence in the room. Martinez was leaning back slightly, the full force of Alison's diatribe thrusting him back. Jack suppressed a smile. She was so transparent, but so convincing. Had she read Martinez right? The next few moments would tell.

The silence was broken by Martinez's laughter. It was a deep and booming laugh. "You're alright, lady," he managed through the laughter. "A little on the dramatic side, but still alright. I think we can do business together." He grabbed a chair and seated himself at the table.

"Good," Alison said, pulling out a legal pad and her number 2 pencils. "Now, let's hear the story from the beginning. I just want the facts, no conclusions. Just what you saw and what you know as a fact."

An hour later they had the complete story, or as complete as Martinez could remember. Martinez's family had been immigrants from Honduras. They had settled in Los Angeles. His father had worked hard to support his family, but with no education and few skills it had been hard to make ends meet. Martinez had dropped out of school at sixteen to help support the family and, consequently, fallen into the same trap as his father. His inability to get ahead and to find financial security led to disillusionment. He could never understand how a country so rich could have so many poor residents.

The Front had been a rumor in his neighborhood for six months. The people talked about a group that was dedicated to changing things for the poor and working class. That sounded right to Martinez. When he had been approached he was immediately receptive. He went to several meetings and, although he did not pretend to understand all the theoretical underpinnings, the basic concept was clear to him. Those in power would not relinquish their power willingly. Only force could wrest control from the elite and place it in the hands of the people.

Martinez had plunged in with enthusiasm. The leader of his local cell of the Front, Hector Rodriguez, was from Honduras, like Martinez, and equally disenchanted with the "System." However, unlike Martinez, Rodriguez had a university education. Rodriguez spent many hours educating Martinez about political philosophy and history. A whole new world was opened to him. He began to read anything he could get his hands on: philosophy, religion, politics. Martinez discovered that he was not stupid but, rather, uneducated. The Front also trained him in the ways of the revolution, sending him off to a paramilitary camp in the wilderness of the mountains of California.

Despite the best efforts and intentions of the members of the Front, its effectiveness was limited at best. The United States Government had been relentless in its pursuit of Front members. Funding had also been a problem. The Front relied on bank robbery to fund many of its activities. The FBI's close surveillance had culminated in the arrest of many of the most skilled bank robbers, resulting in a severe cash shortage. It was at this point when what seemed, at the time, to be salvation arrived. Martinez was still not at the highest decision-making level, but word had filtered down of some new members who had joined, and who had an immediate and positive impact on the Front. They brought plenty of cash and seemed to have an endless supply of it. They were also highly skilled in paramilitary operations, and were well armed with the most sophisticated and powerful weaponry.

Martinez had asked Rodriguez about the rumors one day. Rodriguez had pulled him aside. "Don't ask too many questions. These guys are very serious and very paranoid. Questions make them nervous. When the time is right, you will know everything."

Martinez had done as suggested, then several weeks later there were more rumors; this time of a purge at the top of the leadership carried out by the new members. Certain members of the Revolutionary Council were demoted and the new members took charge. When the word "demoted" was used, it was said quietly, like the word "cancer." Again, when Martinez asked, Rodriguez told him not to and to be patient. "Historic change requires absolute faith in the chosen leaders." Martinez wasn't sure what that meant, but he trusted Rodriguez and again kept his mouth shut.

Martinez paused in his story to get up from the table and stretch. Jack and Alison exchanged serious glances. Although unspoken, they had both wondered whether Martinez was a nut case. Now they knew he wasn't. His story so far was clearly not fiction. It was told in a straightforward manner and was internally consistent as to times and dates. Lies always ended up revealing inconsistencies, as the teller tried to separate fact from fiction. Martinez took his seat again and continued.

"About six months ago, Rodriguez told me that a special mission had been planned for me and that I was to appear before the high council for a briefing. I asked him what it was all about, but he told me he didn't know. Well, I was sweating bullets the whole day before the meeting. That night they put me in a car blindfolded and we drove around for what seemed like an hour, making all kinds of turns and stops and starts. Finally, we stopped and they led me into a building. A warehouse, I think, by the sound of things. I could hear foghorns and the building sounded big and empty. They led me into a room and, when they took off the blindfold, I was standing in front of a long table. Seated at the table were three guys, and I looked at them and it just blew my mind."

"Why was that?" Alison asked.

"Because these guys looked like they had just stepped out of the suburbs, man. All the other guys in the Front were brothers, man. These guys were as lily white as they come. They must have realized what I was thinking, because this one dude says, 'Don't let our race and appearance fool you, Martinez. We are committed to the cause. We want to end the injustice and inequity of the capitalist system. We think we can do that. Will you help us?'

"It really wasn't a question. It was a demand. Sure, I said, what do you want me to do?"

"Would you recognize him if you saw him again? Jack asked.

"I think so. It was kind of dark. But I spent a long time looking at him because, like I said, I was so blown away."

"I didn't mean to interrupt. Go on."

"Well, then the first guy sits down and this other dude, who looks just like the first guy, stands up and says, 'We knew we could count on you.' He says his name is Mr. Smith. Yeah, I believe that. But this guy, I was afraid of him right from the start. You know how some guys give you the creeps just looking at you. Well, he was one of those guys. He would as soon kill you as give you the time of day. Then he says, 'Mr. Martinez, we are about to give you the chance of a lifetime; a chance to change history and to help your people at the same time. But first we have to know, are you prepared to die for the cause?' I tell him yes, and this is where it gets really hairy. He pulls out a pistol and points it at my head. 'You are surrounded by the FBI,' he says. 'You know complete details of the operations and organization of the Front. Your capture will mean the complete destruction of the Front. What are your orders?' I look around and I see the first guy standing in the corner with his automatic in his hands. I realize for the first time that there is a bunch of other people in the room. They all have automatic rifles. Mr. Smith is staring at me and I realize I'm dead either way. If I don't tell him to shoot me, they kill me because I can't be trusted. If I tell him to shoot and it's loaded, I'm dead. I have no choice. I have to call the bluff. So I say, 'My orders are to kill me. I cannot be captured and jeopardize the Front.' The dude pulls the trigger, and seeing as how I'm sitting here, you know what happened. I guessed right. Well, that seemed to break the ice. They had me sit down and brought me a whiskey to calm my nerves. The third guy at the table, Mr. Jones, starts to tell me how the time is right for revolution. Then they hit me with the 'Plan,' as we called it. It was pretty heavy stuff. They started talking about how cutting off the head of the dragon would kill the dragon. How we needed to kill all those at the top of the power structure: congressmen, senators, governors and, of course, the president. So, after about an hour, I ask them what they want me to do. There is a big pause and then Mr. Smith comes over to me and puts his arm around me and says, 'We want you to kill whoever is elected as president.'"

Jack and Alison exchanged another serious glance. Martinez continued, "At the time, I thought it was a great idea. You have to remember, I was a true believer. In many ways I still am. The system stinks, man. Not for folks like you, who have money and degrees hangin' on the walls. But guys like me, we don't get no justice. Never have. Never will.

"So I tell them I'm in. And to make a long story short, that's how I end up outside the theater the other night with a gun under my coat. They tell me that my killing the new president is the signal to start the revolution. They briefed me on the new president's schedule and set up an elaborate timetable. We practiced it over and over again. How to get as close as possible, where the Secret Service agents would be standing, how many would be there.

"Well, that night I'm nervous as hell. I follow the Plan to a tee, but then I hit a snag. The Secret Service, or someone, sets up the crowd-control barriers farther away than expected. There's no way I could hit him from there. I start searching around for another way to get closer and then . . . kaboom! All hell breaks loose. The explosion knocked me flat and everyone around me too. I'm stunned, because I have no idea what's going on. It's not part of the Plan, so I figure someone else beat us to the punch. As soon as I catch my breath, I start to take off, but some cop sees me hustling off and he stops me. I tried to stay cool, but he called in back-up and when they pat me down they find the gun. The rest I think you know."

Everyone in the room was silent for a moment. Alison scribbled some notes on her pad as she digested the information. Jack was not a note taker. He felt it better to digest the information as it was relayed. If you took notes, often you missed what the person was saying. He broke the silence.

"But it was the Front that carried out the assassinations, or at least that's what the FBI has concluded. The director of the FBI told me himself."

Alison looked at Jack with great disgust and despair. "Of course they did. Unfortunately for Mr. Martinez, he was the fall guy."

"Like I said, lady, you're alright. The Front did the killing, no question about it. Why do you think I would rat out on them? If they had been stand-up with me and told me I was just a decoy, no problem. I could have dealt with that. But man, they double-crossed me and that makes them no better than the people the Front is dedicated to fight. I was just a pawn in the bigger game."

Alison tapped her pencil on the legal pad. Then she began to make some doodles on the pad as she spoke. "The way I see it, Mr. Martinez, you have two options. First, we try to plead you to a lesser charge in return for your cooperation. The information you have is valuable. We will, however, have to act fast if we choose that option. The government is bringing all its resources to bear on this case; and if they obtain the information on their own or from someone else before you give it to them, then it is of little use to them, or to you. The second option is to plead not guilty and build our case on the fact that, though you conspired to kill the president-elect, you did not actually commit the killing. The difficulty in that strategy is that as a conspirator you are liable for all the acts of your co-conspirators. If a jury doesn't believe your story, they could come to the conclusion that you participated in the conspiracy leading to the assassination by the detonation of the bomb."

Martinez absorbed the information and began to pace the room again. Alison glanced at Jack, tilting her head slightly and opening her hands as if to ask, "What do you think?" Jack shrugged his shoulders.

Martinez turned to face them. "If I do plead, what kind of sentence will I get and how can I be sure the Front or someone else won't try to get rid of me?"

Alison paused for a moment and again began to doodle as she spoke. Jack noticed this and filed it away for future reference. Obviously it was a sign of her anxiety.

"That depends on the prosecution and on their case. If they need you they'll deal. If it is an open-and-shut-case, they won't. We'll know more after we've been given access to the state's evidence. On the second point, I can't guarantee anything. We can ask for witness protection, but that's no guarantee. My recommendation is that I at least talk to them about a plea. If they tell us no dice, at least we know where we stand."

So far, Jack had listened attentively without interjecting himself too forcefully in the dialogue. Alison had plunged in aggressively, taking charge and probing for information. Jack, in contrast, had watched and listened. One of his most valuable qualities as a lawyer was his ability to listen to people and divine what they were not telling him, or what they really meant between the lines. To him, Martinez's body language and tone of voice indicated that he was not telling the whole story. His last comment to Alison had been the final piece of the puzzle.

"I have just one question." Alison and Martinez looked at him. "Who the hell are you really afraid of?"

Martinez protested, "What the hell are you talking about?"

Jack then resorted to one of his favorite negotiating tactics. He began to gather up his things as if to go, accompanied by great protestation and indignation. It was akin to "It's my ball and if I can't play I'm taking it and leaving." He grabbed his coat and began to put it on. He looked at Alison.

"Listen, I don't know about you, but I don't like being jerked around. This guy is taking us for a ride and I don't want any part of it. You can have the case if you want."

He grabbed his briefcase and headed towards the door. Now was the crucial moment. He needed Alison to play along to make Martinez come clean. If she contradicted Jack, it would give Martinez a way out. On a personal level, it was also a crucial moment. How she reacted would reveal the extent to which they were in tune and in harmony with one and other. It would also reveal whether she trusted his instincts, trusted him, and believed in him. As he grasped the door handle, his heart was lifted by her voice.

"Wait, Jack, I'm with you." She rose from the table and headed towards the door. Jack turned toward her and their eyes locked for just a minute. Alison smiled slightly. As she reached the door, Jack opened it and stepped aside to let her pass through. She paused and they both turned to look at Martinez, their poses conveying to him that this was his last chance. He sized them up for a moment and appeared ready to protest. Then he slumped down in the chair, looking defeated.

"Alright, Alright. I'll tell you the whole story." Alison and Jack closed the door to the interview room and crossed over to the table where Martinez was seated. He looked up at them with a frightened and desperate look.

"What I'm about to tell you will put all our lives in danger. Are you ready for that?"

Jack and Alison looked at each other. Alison answered for both of them. "The way I see it, Mr. Martinez, we don't have much choice. By coming here we have jumped in feet first. If what you know is so dangerous, exposing the truth is the only way to save any of us now."

He sighed and nodded. He began to tell the full story. Alison took furious notes. Jack could only listen with rapt attention. It did not take him very long. What he knew was very little, but the implications were extraordinary. The impact of its disclosure would shake the foundations of the country. What he had learned was that the activities of the Front had been directed by some outside force. Martinez did not know who exactly, but he knew that it was "an inside job." His details were sketchy, but the conclusion was inevitable: Someone within the United States Government had helped plan the assassinations.

It was purely by accident that he had discovered this. Being curious, Martinez had not listened to his friend Hector. Through his curiosity, he had heard conversations he should not have. After that night in the warehouse, he had been kept close to the high council. They frequently moved their headquarters to avoid detection. Martinez had moved with them. One of his jobs had been cleanup crew in the kitchen. The Front was very big on communal work. One day he was working in the kitchen. Smith and the fellow council members had asked him to bring them coffee. After leaving the coffee, he sneaked back to the doorway and listened.

"Did you call Washington for the new requisitions?"

"I did."

"What did they say?"

"The money will be wired within twenty-four hours. But the job has to be done soon."

"I can't wait to get out of this hellhole and back to living off the federal dole."

"I know what you mean. Does our government pension keep building while we're stuck out here?"

The room filled with laughter. Then Martinez heard a sound behind him. Someone else was coming. He quickly continued down the hall to the kitchen from where he had come. After that night, he had tried to find out more, but he could not. Martinez contemplated escape, but it was not possible. He was watched closely and, because of the frequent moves, he often had no idea where he was. With each move he was blindfolded.

Eventually he would deduce the location, only to be moved again. Then before he knew it, it was the day of the Plan.

Martinez sat slumped in the chair, fear mixing with fatigue. Jack and Alison exchanged worried looks. Jack began to regret that he had ever answered the call from Mr. Martinez. But as Alison had said, the dye had been cast. They were up to their eyeballs in a whole lot of trouble. Jack only hoped that he and Alison had as many lives as Mr. Martinez's cat, which was the reason for them being there in the first place.

CHAPTER 18

The president stared into the camera, waiting for the red light on the top to come on, signaling that his picture and voice were being broadcast into living rooms throughout the United States and, in the age of global communication, the world. The president had chosen the Oval Office as the setting for his speech. It was the site from which all presidents made their most important speeches. He was seated at his desk. Arrayed on a credenza behind him was an assortment of family pictures. This also was a typical tableau for presidential addresses from the Oval Office. He had a copy of the speech in front of him, but this was just for show, because on either side of the camera were two Teleprompters that would scroll the speech for him. These were also mostly for comfort. The president had a photographic memory and he had committed the speech to memory after just two readings. The red light came on.

"My fellow Americans. By now, I am sure that you know the details of what can only be described as an attack on all those who love this country. A dissident element, with no regard for the sanctity of the democratic system and our republic, has sought to destroy it through the murder and assassination of your duly elected president, governors, congressmen and senators. Let me assure you that this plot has not, will not, and cannot succeed. There is no widespread revolt or revolution. Calm reigns in all our major cities. This was a small group of fanatics and our local police force and the FBI, in a joint effort, have crushed the group, known as the Front.

"I have met with the key leaders in the House of Representatives and the Senate, and they have already set into effect the procedures for succession in order to place new congressmen and senators in office pending the holding of new elections. I have also talked with the key leaders of the legislatures in those states whose governors have been assassinated, and have also been assured that the succession process is running smoothly.

"In telling you this, I do not mean to be insensitive to the families of the fallen. Our hearts and our prayers go out to them. I have declared a thirty-day period of national mourning in their memory. But the work and life of this country must go on. Only a powerful and assertive response to this cowardly act can assure the sanctity of democracy.

"I have also met with my key advisers and with constitutional scholars to determine the fate of the office of the president. Just a scant two weeks ago, I conceded defeat to my noble opponent, who now has been cut down in the prime of his life. In the spirit of democracy, I would have been present on January 20 to witness his inauguration and the passing of power in an orderly and peaceful fashion, which is the hallmark of this great nation. As president, I have always been honest with you and so I will be honest with you tonight. Who will be the next president is in doubt. Under our sacred Constitution, which has served us so well these 200-plus years, the people have chosen electors who, as set forth in the Constitution, will soon meet in the state capitols to cast their ballots to elect the next president. Our Constitution allows them to vote for whomever they desire to be president, and I urge them to follow the will of the people in this unprecedented situation, for it is they who choose our leaders. We must remember that this nation was founded on the principle that it was formed and governed of the people, by the people, for the people. This is not a time for doubt or division. This is a time for unity. I am, as I have been throughout my life of public service, prepared to act in the best interests of the country.

"Let me also take this moment to assure all our allies throughout the world, and to warn our enemies, that this nation is prepared to meet its commitments and to defend its borders. Peace has been restored throughout the land and the acts of cowards and terrorists will not bring down this great nation that has survived a civil war, depression, two world wars, and terrorist acts around the world against our country. I urge you to go out from your homes tonight and to be with your family, friends and neighbors and to celebrate with them the great gift of democracy. We are, and shall remain, the greatest nation on earth.

"God bless you and God bless the United States of America."

CHAPTER 19

Jack and Alison were silent as they rode in the FBI sedan. Jack considered their next move. Their lives were in danger. What Martinez had told them meant they could trust no one until they knew the whole story. Was it the CIA, the military, the FBI who was involved? He felt he could trust Evans and his men. If they were part of the plot they would have killed Jack and Alison already. It would have been too dangerous to allow them to meet Martinez. Any information conveyed to them could then be related to other people. Once the dissemination of information began, the number of people who knew them would quickly grow. It also occurred to him that the FBI might be the only thing keeping them alive. Their round-the-clock surveillance made it difficult for anyone else to reach them. He was also greatly concerned about Alison. He had to convince her that she also needed FBI protection. That would be a difficult task.

Evans turned to face them from the front seat. "Where should we drop you, Ms. Stevens?"

"Actually, Mr. Banner and I would like to have dinner. Can you take us to Adams-Morgan? There is a nice Ethiopian place I'd like to try." She gave Evans the name of the restaurant. Adams-Morgan was the trendy area of Washington, replete with ethnic food and music. It was rundown and chic at the same time.

Evans looked at her quizzically and then at Jack, who merely nodded. He wasn't sure what she was up to, but she had played along with him and he could only do the same.

"I'll have to get clearance from HQ on this one. Besides, my shift is almost up. I have to coordinate a shift changeover. I guess dinner would be a perfect time to do it."

Evans coordinated the shift change over the radio. They soon arrived in Adams-Morgan. In this situation, Jack was glad to have the FBI escort. Parking in Adams-Morgan was a nightmare. It was an older residential area with a strip of restaurants. There were no public parking lots or garages, and the streets were not equipped to handle the volume of traffic. That didn't matter to the FBI. They pulled right up to the restaurant. The FBI entourage got there first and cleared the way for Alison and Jack. The maitre d' approached them.

"How many?" she seemed oblivious to the situation, and assumed the FBI agents were part of the party. Alison handled the situation with aplomb.

"Just two. No smoking please." Evans stepped forward to intercede. He drew the maitre d' aside and pulled out his identification. As he explained the situation, her eyes grew larger and she nodded with serious understanding. When she returned she said in hushed and respectful tones, "Please, right this way."

She seated them at a booth. Evans and his men fanned out in the restaurant. One remained by the front door while one headed to watch the back entrance. Several others canvassed the restaurant and the bathrooms. The maitre d' handed them a menu and a wine list. "It is a pleasure to have such honored guests. I hope you enjoy your dinner."

After she left, Evans came to the table. "What did you tell her?" Jack asked, motioning to the departing maitre d'.

"I told her you were members of the British Royal Family."

Jack and Alison chuckled. Evans continued, "My shift is over. Agent Duncan is taking over the detail. He's a good man. So listen to what he tells you. I'll see you in the a.m. Ms. Stevens, it was a pleasure to meet you." He turned and walked toward the exit.

Jack turned to Alison. "So now can you tell me what the hell is going on? I like Ethiopian food, but this is a little much."

"It's simple, really. You and I need to talk. Based on what Martinez told us we have to assume your place is bugged. Mine probably is too. So are our offices. They can't bug a restaurant if they don't know we're going to be there."

Jack could only nod his head in agreement and amazement. The two of them made a good team. She had the smarts. He had the instinct. He could only compliment her. "Good thinking. But how do you know about bugging and that sort of thing?"

"In case you forgot, I used to be a prosecutor. I know all about bugs and illegal searches." A waiter came to the table and told them about the specials. They each ordered a mixed drink and asked for some more time to decide. The waiter left.

"Well, Ms. Stevens, I guess I have to defer to your depth of experience. What do you suggest we do now?"

She took a deep breath and slowly traced some patterns on the tablecloth with her fingers. It was akin to doodling without pencil and paper. Jack admired her hands. The fingers were long and graceful, her nails manicured but with no nail polish. Her skin was smooth and, he suspected, soft to the touch. He again found himself admiring her beauty. She must have sensed him looking at her, because she raised her eyes to meet his and blushed slightly.

"One, I agree with you that our lives are in danger," she said. "Having the FBI around may be a pain in the ass, but it makes sense. Assuming we trust them."

Jack sighed with relief. At least she agreed with him on that point.

"Two, I think we can trust Evans and the others we know. Any new agents should be viewed with suspicion."

"Agreed," Jack replied.

She continued, "I think our first step is to go to the press, but I think we need something more. No one is going to print a story of this magnitude without corroboration. The question is how do we get it? Martinez's information is so sketchy, assuming it's true in the first place. Do you think it's true?

"Yes, I do," he answered. "And I'll tell you why. First, he has no reason to lie. It doesn't exonerate him of involvement, so why would he make it up? We both agree he's not crazy, right?"

Alison nodded.

"Second, when I had my meeting with the director of the FBI, I got this sense that he thought there was more to the story. Call it instinct, but the guy didn't believe for a minute that the Front pulled this thing off."

"So far your instincts have been on target."

"Thank you, Alison. I believe that is the first compliment you've given me in our short relationship."

"You're welcome. OK, were both lawyers. We have a client. We need to prove his case. What do we do?"

"Easy. Take discovery," answered Jack. Discovery was the grist that fed the litigation mill: depositions, interrogatories, requests for production. These were the mounds of paper filed by lawyers in an attempt to seek the truth. Prior to the formalization of discovery procedures, known as Rules of Civil Procedure, lawyers tried their case by ambush. On the day of trial there was no knowing what your opponent knew. That was deemed not to be in the interests of justice. Rules had been passed to allow each side to "discover" everything the other side knew and what the evidence would be at trial. Now extensive discovery was the norm. In some ways it had served its purpose. Discovery went on for so long and cost so much that most cases were settled. Mostly it was subject to abuse, with no purpose other than to harass the opponent and beat him into submission with an avalanche of paper.

"Very good, Mr. Banner. You go to the head of the class. We serve subpoenas on the head of the CIA, FBI, the branches of the armed forces, the NSC, the NSA. Everyone we can think of. We set their depositions and ask for all documents regarding the Front, covert operations, the works." Their drinks arrived and the conversation paused. They again asked for more time to decide on their order, as neither of them had even looked at the menu.

Jack interjected, "That sounds good in theory, but let's get real. If someone knows something, it's not going to be written down, and he or she isn't going to tell us about it. Second, the government is going to fight us tooth and nail all the way: motions for protective order, motions to quash, national security. Even if they're not part of the conspiracy, they will still resist our efforts. It could, no—it will—take years."

The real fun in the discovery was the efforts by the opposition to resist discovery. Such efforts took the form of motions for protective order or motions to quash where the party asked the court to "protect" them from the overzealous and overreaching efforts at discovery. These efforts to prevent discovery often took more time than the actual discovery itself. Jack had once heard a lawyer say that there are two types of lawyers, trial lawyers and litigators. The latter pushed paper in an attempt to avoid trial; the former wanted to get in front of a judge or jury as fast as possible.

"Right again," Alison said. "But look at it this way. Think of an ant pile. If you stick a stick in it and stir it around, all the ants come rushing out in a mad frenzy. It looks all disorganized. But if you are an expert in ant behavior, you know that it all is completely organized and systematic, with a specific purpose. The ants react to defend the nest. That's what our ants will do. They will react to protect the nest. Those who react the most are the ones we know are involved. Plus, we have an ace up our sleeves."

"And what is that?" asked Jack.

Like any good lawyer trained in the Socratic Method, Alison answered with a question. "What was one of the last things Martinez told us?"

"Watch our butts?"

"No, before that. He said they were going to be wired money."

The light went on in Jack's head. She really was good. Alison continued, not wanting to let Jack steal her thunder, "If we can find the money, we find them. There has to be a paper trail. Wire transfer orders, receipts, deposits, something. With the amount of activity they undertook and the geographic area they operated in, there is no way they kept that kind of cash on hand or transported it around the country. Money is bulky and heavy. There had to be accounts at several different banks. If Martinez can identify locations and cities where he was located, we can subpoena bank records."

"But under what names and at which banks? Are we going to subpoena every bank in the country? Like I said, that could take years. I'm not sure we have that kind of time." The statement had double meaning with regard to their predicament and the pace of litigation generally. Jack had once spent three years exclusively on one case. Alison's experience was similar.

"I know what you're saying, on both counts. At the same time, we can go to the press, get the story at least rolling. That way our necks may be safe. Besides, we have to start somewhere. Martinez can help us narrow it down, but if we have to, yes, we'll subpoena every bank in the country. That's where your firm comes in. You have paralegals and attorneys to spare. Besides, hopefully the ants will tip their hand first, but litigation is hard work you know."

"Yeah, I know. I should have been a doctor like my mother wanted."

"Well, it's not too late to go to medical school."

"And miss all this fun? No way. Enough business for one night. Let's plan to meet at my office tomorrow morning. Right now I'm hungry, so let's order and you can tell me your life story."

"Only if you tell me yours first."

"A deal, but leave out your old boyfriends. I'm the jealous type."

"You don't give up, do you?"

Jack just smiled. The waiter saved him as he came to take their order. Jack watched Alison as she ordered. Her actions were so measured and precise, even in the most mundane of activities. She surveyed the menu with a seriousness of purpose, making her selections carefully and deliberately. There was also complete self-confidence. She quickly captivated the waiter with her questions about the menu and the specials. She was showing him that she cared about what he did. She had a magnetism that attracted people to her. It made Jack wonder whether his attraction was no different than the waiter's, but even more, he wondered if the signals she was sending him were no different than those the waiter perceived. Was her warmth and magnetism calculated or natural? His thoughts were interrupted as the waiter asked Jack for his order.

His style was the exact opposite of Alison's. He merely glanced at the menu and haphazardly ordered a number of dishes, more with an eye to variety than what the dishes contained. Alison was equally impressed and puzzled by his mannerisms. Superficially, Jack seemed cavalier and impetuous. But as she had witnessed today, he was bright and his instincts for people uncanny. He was also tough and fair. A lot of men would have run from the "feminist speech" she had laid on him in his office. He genuinely seemed to respect her skill as a lawyer, his flirtations notwithstanding. She suspected there was more to him than met the eye. He was also extremely handsome, she had to admit.

The waiter finished taking Jack's order and departed. "So where should I start?" he asked Alison.

"Wherever you want."

"Well, I hope you have all night. My life story is a pretty long one."

"All night, no. But if we don't finish tonight, you can finish another night."

"Are you asking me for a date, Ms. Stevens?"

"Consider it a business meeting, Mr. Banner."

"I'll take what I can get."

The rest of the evening went quickly. Jack told Alison his life story. She, in turn, told him hers. She had been raised in an upper-middle class family in Greenwich, Connecticut. Her father had been a successful lawyer on Wall Street and had provided comfortably for his family. Alison was the oldest of three daughters. She had been destined to follow in her father's footsteps. Her only hope of rebellion had been in her career path. She would be a lawyer, but she had vowed to dedicate her skills to serving the public interest. She admitted to Jack that it wasn't much of a rebellion.

The ACLU was low paying, but her father had established a trust account that allowed her to live well.

They talked politics and religion. She was, of course, liberal and a Democrat. He was conservative and a Republican. She was Catholic. Jack wasn't sure what he was. They swapped a few war stories. Alison's were much more interesting, because her clients were people. Jack's were, more often than not, faceless corporations. It was a ballet of words and gestures, and slowly a bond of friendship was formed and, perhaps, much more. Only time and events beyond their control would decide how much more. Soon the food was finished and the restaurant began to empty. Agent Duncan approached the table.

"I don't mean to rush you folks but it's getting late and we really should be getting you home. The less crowded the streets, the easier we are to spot."

Jack motioned for the bill. The waiter came hurrying over. "How was your meal?"

"Excellent." He laid the check on the table. Alison and Jack rose from the table and Jack took out his wallet. Duncan interceded.

"This one is on the United States of America. Compliments of the director himself."

Jack and Alison looked at each other with raised eyebrows. "Tell the director thank you and that we should do lunch sometime," Jack said.

Duncan didn't respond. He motioned them to the door, where the other agents were waiting. Alison led the way. They exited the restaurant and got into the ubiquitous FBI sedan. Duncan got in front.

"Ms. Stevens, we'll drop you first. We've established a security perimeter at your townhouse. Please stay away from the windows."

They drove in silence, until they reached Alison's townhouse in the Northwest section of D.C. Outside of Georgetown, this was the nicest part of Washington. Alison's townhouse was far more impressive than Jack's. It was the size of a house, but was called a townhouse because of its configuration and attachment to adjoining townhouses. Jack exited the car with Duncan and Alison and they walked together toward the door. Unlike Jack's arrival the other day, things were quiet here. The press had not yet gotten wind of his co-counsel. After the arraignment, that would all change.

Jack gave Duncan a look and he took the hint to make himself scarce. "Goodnight, Ms. Stevens. We'll be here all night. If there is any problem, just holler."

Alison fished for the keys in her purse. She was a little nervous, but finally found them. She placed the key in the lock and engaged the bolt. As she pushed the door open, she turned to face Jack.

"Well, goodnight. I'll see you in the morning."

"Does this mean a goodnight kiss is out of the question?" Jack leaned his body in to hers, but she gently placed her hand on his chest.

"Under the circumstances, I think so. It's just too complicated. One of us has to think straight, and if it has to be me, so be it." She said it without much conviction. Once again, Alison felt the tug of many different emotions. She could not allow herself to become involved with this man, for many different reasons. Her life had always been in control, but Jack lived with no regard for control or discipline. He said and did what he felt, when he felt it. He was her complete opposite; the cliché was too much to bear. If she relented and let him kiss her, she imagined so many things that could happen, some good, some bad. He did not know her, did not know about her life and how she had come to this point. What would he say if he knew the truth about her? She wanted to unburden herself to him, but if she did, the danger would only increase. She was relieved when Jack pulled back.

"You're right. It is too complicated, but I'll consider it a rain check." Their eyes met briefly, both stating the obvious. In a different time and a different place she would have invited him in, and from there, no one could say what would happen or where their relationship would lead. In normal times, they would at least have a chance, a moment. But in the situation and place that they were in, they were frozen in time. Their lives were on hold until this giant thing that had descended upon them was resolved. And, then, maybe the moment would be there again, and maybe it would not. In all things in life, a moment longer in the shower or eating breakfast or talking on the phone can forever alter fate, leaving one at a spot too soon or too late to connect with the events that alter the path of life.

"Then I'll see you in the morning. I'd better go while my resolve is firm. I'll see you in the morning." Jack turned and went back down the steps into the waiting FBI sedan. Alison watched him leave. Then she entered her house, locking the door once inside.

She had hardly removed her coat when the phone rang in the room to her left. It was her cell phone, in her purse by the door. Knowing she had to take this call, she raced to get it before the fourth ring, when it would roll over to voice mail. Fumbling through her purse, she snatched it on the third ring.

"Hello?"

"Alison, it's Debbie."

"Hi, Debbie. How are you?"

"Great. Listen, I heard your name on the news tonight. Is it true? Are you really representing that Martinez guy?"

"It's true."

"Well, does that mean we're still on for dinner on the tenth?"

"We'll have to see. Debbie, can I call you back? I just walked in and I'm really tired."

"Sure. Sure. Call me at work this week. You remember the number, 657-1384."

"I remember, Debbie. Thanks for calling."

Alison hung up. She walked briskly across the foyer to the study opposite the den. As she walked she repeated the series of numbers aloud, "657-1384." She crossed to the bookshelf and reached up to remove a book from the third shelf. It was a book of names. She flipped to the page with Deborah. She counted ten lines down the page. Then she counted over six words. Reaching for a pad and pen, she wrote down the first letter of the sixth word. She did the same for the fifth, seventh, first, third, eighth and fourth word. When she was done she had a series of letters, all within the first seven letters of the alphabet. ECEFCBD: 535-6324. Alison replaced the book. She reached for another set of books on the first shelf of her bookshelf. When she removed the books, it revealed a panel. She pressed firmly on the panel and a latch released, allowing the panel door to swing open. Inside was a cellular phone. It was not an ordinary phone, because it had the capability to scramble the conversation to prevent interception. She entered the phone number.

It took only one ring before the phone was answered.

"What have you found out?"

"He's on to something, but I'm not sure what, and neither is he."

"Will he find out?"

"With time, I think he will. Martinez knows enough to get him started. Banner is smart and his law firm is behind him one hundred percent. I think it's more a question of when, rather than if."

"It's the when that worries me. Does he trust you?"

"Yes."

"Stick close to him. Whatever he finds out, you are the first to know. Understood?"

"Yes, sir."

"Next contact in 48 hours." The line went dead. Alison replaced the phone in the hiding place and replaced the books. She tore off the sheet of paper and ten sheets behind it, in case she had made an impression of the numbers. She crossed back into the foyer. A staircase led downstairs to the kitchen. Once in the kitchen, she crossed to the stove and ignited the gas burner. In her younger days she wouldn't have even written down the numbers. She was slipping in her old age. She placed one end of the pages in the burner. As the pages burned, she felt overwhelmed with guilt. Jack really did trust her. More than trusted her. That much was obvious. And she had to admit she had feelings for him as well. Part of her training was to be honest with your feelings. Hidden feelings might betray the mission. The heat began to singe her fingers. She dropped the pages into the burner and, as she watched them become ash, she hoped that she would not have to choose between him and her duty.

CHAPTER 20

Howard Berlin was in seventh heaven. He was seated in his office in the West Wing, surrounded by total chaos. Papers containing the names and biographies of all the electors were strewn across his large desk. His annotations and notes regarding his conversations with the electors were scribbled in the margins and on numerous legal pads scattered on the desk. He had been on the go for forty-eight hours, with no time for sleep and little time to eat. He had had to keep up his regular duties as chief of staff. His current task had been squeezed in frantically in the remaining time available. He looked out the window and noticed for the first time that it was morning. He looked at his watch. Close to six a.m. Time to take a break. He rose from his desk and stretched.

After his discussion with the president, he had assembled his two closest staff members, Nancy Pasqua and Ed Broberg. These two owed their professional careers to Berlin, and were young enough and naive enough to trust him completely. He had called them to his office and explained that the president had requested Berlin to mount a quiet and subtle canvas of the electors to gauge the possibility of reelecting Hampton as president. Pasqua and Broberg were, of course, ecstatic. Their loyalty to the president was genuine. Berlin had explained that secrecy was of the utmost importance. They could mention this to no one, including their families or other staff members. The president had insisted on this. If there was a leak, it was traceable to only four people. They should not even discuss it with the president himself.

Pasqua and Broberg dove in with enthusiasm. Each state had a number of electors equal to the number of representatives and senators. In total there were 538 electoral votes representing the 435 members of the House of Representatives and 100 members of the Senate, and a single representative each from the District of Columbia, Puerto Rico and Guam. The race had been extremely close. In the election, the president had won states totaling 267 electoral votes while his challenger had won 271; 270 electoral votes were needed to become president. Berlin needed to swing a mere three votes to his side to reelect him as the president. Their first step had been to confirm the support of the electoral votes pledged to the president. This had been relatively easy. The president's support was solid in the south and the west, where he had won a majority of his electoral votes. These electors had expressed a clear disdain for the vice president-elect and had pledged their firm support for the president. Berlin was somewhat concerned about the possibility of slippage. At some point, the Democrats would come to the same conclusion he had, and they would look to pick off some of his votes in favor of the vice president-elect. They might even offer up some third party candidate, sensing the weakness of the vice president-elect. With that in mind, Berlin had mapped out a series of follow-up calls by Pasqua and Broberg, reminding the electors of their commitment and throwing in a threat of presidential reprisal for disobedience and a reward for obedience.

Next they had gone to work on conservative Democrats and some moderate Republicans in key states won by the president-elect. Here the going had been slow. Some had maintained their allegiance to the Democratic ticket. Others had been non-committal. None had yet offered to switch their votes. It was a weighty decision, rife with serious implications. With this information, Berlin realized he needed a more forceful strategy that would require the president's unknowing participation. He was doubly glad he had leaked the contents of the president's briefing, where Rothstein had advised them of the legal implications of the succession dilemma. He had done so in order to create a sense of crisis and urgency. This fit in perfectly with the plan he was now hatching. The leak would generate press coverage and public opinion polls. Berlin had also planned a series of announcements and activities for the president over the next several weeks, designed to show a vigorous and active president, not a lame duck. The country would rally to the president in this time of crisis as they always did. The timing of the meetings of the electors would be perfect. Three weeks was plenty of time to build support and not too much time in which to lose it.

This also solved his second problem. Secrecy. Eventually someone would find out about his activities and then the president would find out. At that moment, Berlin had to be able to show the president that the people wanted him, and that Berlin had acted not in self interest but in the interests of the country. Berlin could point to the polls, the pledged electors, hopefully 270 by then, and convince the president that he owed it to his country to serve a second term. It was a risky gamble, but Berlin didn't have much to lose. He had reached the top and he had nowhere to go but down. His memoirs would fetch a handsome price whether he left in a blaze of glory or an inferno of scandal. It was worth the risk to be so near the candle for just a few more years. He smiled as he pondered a second inaugural address with him seated at the elbow of the president.

CHAPTER 21

Larry Lefteski was less sanguine than Howard Berlin. He was downright frightened. He was standing in the center of Rock Creek Park, in the middle of the night, waiting for a rendezvous with what he expected would be death. It should not have been that way. Lefteski had only himself to blame. He was a nighttime computer operator for the FBI. He also happened to be a grade "A" computer hacker. He could gain access to almost any computer system in the world with a laptop computer, access to Internet broadband, and some special software he had designed while killing time during graduate school. These two facts, together with his employment by the FBI and his expertise in going where no man had gone before, combined with a third fact of his life: Too much free time had led him to unauthorized entry to the FBI's computer system.

The FBI had spent millions of dollars to create a secure computer network. The system had the latest security features to avoid penetration. This was a necessity. The system was constantly being tested. Much of this was in the form of protection from foreign governments. On top of that was the irresistible urge of computer hackers throughout the world. These denizens of the dark recesses of the computer information superhighway saw every computer system as a challenge, because, like the mountain, it was there. With their high speed Internet access and ever more powerful home computers and networks, they had assaulted the citadel for years with no success. Many, who had tried and failed, had the even more unfortunate experience of a visit from the FBI and an arrest for unlawful attempts to gain entry to the FBI computer network.

But every system has a flaw, inherent in the combination of computers and humans. Since passwords are needed to access computer systems and computers are rigorously precise, humans do whatever they can to remember them. While they are not supposed to write passwords down where others will find them, they sometimes do because they are fallible. Hackers thus often search for passwords on scraps of paper in dumpsters and other places where people thoughtlessly discard vital information.

And so Larry had found the password. While in between jobs, he had been working for the FBI as a glorified file clerk. He culled information for the various research departments of the bureau and then categorized and indexed that information on the computer system. It was work far below his talent level, but Lefteski was, at his core, a flake and a misfit. He had held a series of jobs but his brilliance always clashed with his superior's sense of job decorum and hierarchy. Calling your boss an "ass" when he wouldn't accept your brilliant, but wholly impractical, solution to a problem did not lend itself to job security. He wasn't sure how he got a job with the FBI given his past job history, but hired he was.

Initially he had enjoyed the job and minded his own business. Then he had been relegated to the graveyard shift. The boredom and lack of human contact throughout the late night hours led him to thinking, and that led him to trouble. His first foray had resulted from an innocent discovery one late night as he wandered the halls of the FBI during his break. He had strolled into the office of a field agent and sat down at his desk to drink his coffee. While sitting, he had casually sifted through the agent's drawer. The agent had written down his user name and password. Lefteski had himself written down the information. Several nights later, he again entered the agent's office and accessed the system from the agent's terminal. Lefteski assumed that the system would not trigger a warning if the access were from the expected terminal even though the late hour of the access might raise some questions. He was able to read several quite interesting reports on counter-terrorist activities in the United States. For several days thereafter, he imagined teams of agents swooping down on his desk and arresting him. When nothing happened, Lefteski grew bolder and tested the levels to which he could gain access from the agent's terminal without detection.

After several weeks on the job, Lefteski had been about ready to quit the FBI and move on. The work was boring, and true to form, he and his superior had clashed. The source of their conflict was trivial. The FBI had a required indexing system, using specific subject codes and topics, into which all material was to be categorized. Lefteski had resisted this rigid system and categorized research in a more "logical" fashion, leading to a run-in with his supervisor. One night while riding the Metro after work, he was mulling over his decision to quit, when another passenger who approached him interrupted his thoughts.

"Are you Larry Lefteski?"

As Lefteski turned to face him, a sickening feeling began in the pit of his stomach. The man was in his late thirties, crisp white shirt and dark suit underneath his tan trench coat, short-cropped hair and muscular build. He had FBI written all over him. Lefteski quickly looked at the doorway, hoping to escape. But the doors had closed and the car was moving away from the platform. It probably wouldn't have mattered because standing by the door was a clone of the man—strong, determined, and deadly serious. Lefteski was speechless, and so the man continued.

"I'm with the United States Government. We know you work at the FBI and we need your help with a matter of utmost urgency."

Lefteski didn't know what to say. Shouldn't the man say you're under arrest, or you're in big trouble? Instead, he was saying they needed his help. Maybe this was a trap. The FBI wanted him to confess to something because they had no proof of his meandering through the computer system. It was probably that damned supervisor. One night as Larry was coming back from his break—and a short trip through classified files—the supervisor had confronted him and grilled him as to where he had been and what he had been doing. At the time he thought he had provided a sufficient explanation. The fat pig! Lefteski wondered what the guy would think if he mentioned some of the supervisor's extracurricular activities with the young receptionist in the supervisor's office. The man brought him back to reality, gently but firmly grabbing his arm.

"Why don't we get off at the next station."

It was a demand, not a question. Lefteski looked around the car. The other passengers were oblivious to his predicament. The subway car began to slow as it approached the next station and, as it did, Lefteski's body remained in motion, shoving him gently against his new acquaintance. The bulge from a gun beneath his coat was unmistakable. The train stopped at Metro Center and the passengers streamed towards the door. The man kept a firm grip on Lefteski and led him toward the door, his accomplice just a few paces ahead. After they had exited, the man steered him towards the escalators leading to the street high above. They rode one escalator to the turnstiles. Lefteski fumbled in his pocket for his Metro ticket, which contained a magnetic strip encoded with his fare information necessary to enter and exit the Metro System. The accomplice ahead passed through the turnstile. Then Lefteski fed his card into the turnstile and the gate opened with a slight whoosh. He scooped up his card, which still had some fare remaining on it. The man behind him followed closely. They rode a second escalator up to the street level, standing to the right, as other passengers walked past them. As they rode up, Lefteski turned his body slightly to get a better look at the man behind him. He was the obvious leader of this operation, lean, taut and determined with piercing blue eyes. After another thirty seconds they reached the street level. The man steered him toward the curb. The accomplice was a few steps ahead of them, opening the door of a sedan parked at the curb, its motor running. Lefeteski wanted to scream, to run, but he did nothing. The man forced him into the back of the sedan and then climbed in behind him. The car sped from the curb and, as it gathered speed, the man turned to him.

"Please be assured that no harm will come to you if you cooperate. You can call me Mr. Smith. I can't tell you very much, I'm afraid, but what I can tell you is that we know of your activities. If you do as we say, the documentation of your activities will be destroyed and your life will continue as you know it. If you tell anyone of our meeting, call a lawyer, the police, the repercussions will be most serious."

"I don't know what you're talking about!" Lefteski protested. They were passing out of downtown Washington, headed west on Pennsylvania Avenue, then down 17th Street toward Constitution Avenue. Lefteski's mind was spinning.

Mr. Smith continued, taking no notice of Lefteski's protests. "Quite frankly, Mr. Lefteski, you are in deep trouble. Fortunately, the right people discovered what you were doing. We know that you have been accessing information from the FBI computer regarding the activities of the FBI in combating the Front. We have reason to believe that there is a Front operative within the FBI. It is our suspicion that the information being generated by the FBI is being influenced and distorted by that person in an effort to subvert the efforts of the FBI. We need your help to uncover the traitor."

Lefteski began to protest again, but Mr. Smith held up his hand. Lefteski fell silent and Mr. Smith continued. "We can use the information you give us to set a trap. Once a week someone will call you. Take this book." He handed Lefteski a copy of *The Exorcist*. Lefteski took the book without thinking. "The caller will identify himself with a series of numbers. Write the numbers down. Turn to the pages in the book corresponding to the numbers. Then follow the instructions written on those pages. Do you understand?"

"No, I don't. I mean, I do about the book, but not about all this, about you. Who are you?"

"Trust me. You don't want to know. If you try to find out, I will kill you. If you tell anyone about this, I will kill you. As of this moment you are a dead man. Only I can save you. And you can save yourself by doing as I say. Now, once again, do you understand?"

"Yes, I do."

"Good. The first call will be in one week. Gather all the information you can about the Front. The caller will instruct you what to do with it."

The car pulled up to the curb. Lefteski looked out. They were at the Rosslyn Metro Station. Mr. Smith opened the door and motioned for Lefteski to get out. He numbly complied. "Until we meet again." The door slammed shut and the car drove off.

Since that night, Lefteski had complied with all the requests and instructions. At first he had been petrified of being killed and then of getting caught, but after a few months it settled into a routine. Not as simple as brushing your teeth, but definitely part of life. Then the bottom had dropped out. The bombings by the Front had created a frenzy within the FBI. They had egg all over their face. How could the FBI have let such a powerful group emerge when all along the FBI had been touting its anti-terrorist efforts? An analysis of the intelligence gathering process had begun at every level. Word of spies and traitors had spread throughout the bureau. Lefteski knew it was just a matter of time until he got caught.

The last call had come as a relief. The caller had given him the page numbers and, when he looked up the pages, the instructions called for a meeting in Rock Creek Park. And so that was how Larry Lefteski had ended up in this spot, at this time. It was a desolate picnic area, made more desolate by the late hour and the freezing cold. They had used this drop-off before. Lefteski was not optimistic about his fate. He had no alternative. Mr. Smith and his friends had shown him their true power and reach on a number of occasions. At several meetings they had told him about intimate details of his life, where he banked, where he had dinner, to let him know that they could find him at anytime and do whatever they wanted. It would have been fruitless to run. Lefteski was not stupid. But he didn't intend to go quietly. His ace in the hole, his hand from the grave was still in play, even as he stood waiting for his fate to be revealed. He had programmed his home computer so that if he did not input a given password every twenty-four hours a file would be communicated from the computer via e-mail to the FBI's Counter-Terrorist Division. The file contained everything he knew, which he realized, as he had prepared it, was not much. It described Mr. Smith and his men and the activities in which Lefteski had participated. It listed the drop-off dates, times and places. It summarized the information he had passed along.

Lefteski had entered the password before he had left for the meeting. The clock was ticking. An approaching car interrupted his thoughts. The car stopped and Mr. Smith emerged from the back seat. One of his accomplices, whom Lefteski had taken to calling Mr. Jones, emerged from the front seat. They crossed the fifty feet to where Lefteski stood.

"Good evening, Larry. How are you tonight?"

"That remains to be seen." Lefteski had gone beyond being scared. He was resigned to his fate. "This is the end, I suppose?"

"Events do seem to have overtaken us, Larry. I was hoping it wouldn't come to this, but it has." He reached into his coat. Lefteski took a deep breath and a step back. "You have been good to your word, Larry, a true loyal soldier, and for that you should be rewarded."

"Rewarded?"

"Yes, of course." From his coat Smith pulled a thick envelope. He handed it to Lefteski.

"What's this?"

"A new passport, the account code for a Swiss bank account, and an airline ticket as well. The account has a million dollars in it. That will be enough, won't it?"

Lefteski was speechless. This just didn't make sense. He was sure they were going to kill him, but instead they wanted to give him a million dollars?

"This is a joke, right?"

"No joke, Larry. Just one catch. From this moment on you no longer exist. From here you go to Dulles and then you disappear. Use the tickets, the passport, the money and the instructions inside. Follow the instructions precisely. If you don't, remember the promise I made when we first met? It will come true. As you can see I'm a man of my word." Smith gestured toward the sedan. "My colleague will drive you to Dulles. You can be proud of what you've done, Larry. Your country is forever in your debt."

Lefteski walked in the direction of the car. His mind was pulling in many different directions. What a strange twist of fate. From the jaws of death to a millionaire. Mr. Smith walked alongside him and opened the door to the car. As Larry entered, Mr. Smith said, "Remember, Larry, your life is in your hands and mine. Don't disappoint me."

Just as Mr. Smith was about to close the door, Lefteski saw the jaws of death opening again. The ticking time bomb he had left. Shit. Sometimes he was just too smart for his own good. If he told Smith about it, he was, once again, a dead man. He could only hope against hope that whoever found the computer message could not figure out what he was talking about. A good hope because he knew very little about Mr. Smith. In this case, a little ignorance would go far. Once he got to Switzerland, the million dollars could take him a long way. Mr. Smith shut the door and the car pulled away into the darkness of Rock Creek Park. Lefteski felt relief and exhilaration. A million bucks. That would sure buy a lot of computer software.

CHAPTER 22

Glenn Spivey had been on the go since the call from Howard Berlin. He was the White House reporter for the *The Washington Post,* a position that he filled rather admirably. He had won two Pulitzer Prizes for his investigative journalism. Not bad for a boy from City College of Brooklyn. It was three a.m. but he wasn't sleepy. He did his best work late at night. The tip from Berlin about the succession question had been a bit of a washout after the president's speech. The whole newsroom and the town were abuzz about who would be the next president. Spivey was disappointed that Berlin's tip "of a lifetime" had been a dud, but he quickly put aside his disappointments. His instinct told him that there was more to this story than met the eye. He hadn't won two Pulitzers for nothing.

His calls to his "sources"—a journalist's term for what others called snitches, rats or stoolies—confirmed his instincts. The power of journalism was a thing to behold. People wanted to tell him things. All he had to do was ask. He seldom paid his sources and when he did it was very little. Yet still they came. The motivations differed. Some loved the power and danger. Some had an ax to grind or a score to settle. Others looked to soothe their feelings of guilt. His first Pulitzer had been the result of an exposé on a connection between organized crime and local politicians in the District of Columbia. It had all started so simply. One of the local politicians had been visited by God and told to confess his sins. He had chosen Spivey as his confessor.

In this case, his sources had very little concrete information, but something was clearly happening. They were burning the midnight oil at all the major intelligence agencies. Lots of activity, lots of high-level meetings. His CIA source said that things were relatively quiet overseas. The CIA was prohibited from engaging in intelligence activities within the United States. That meant that the focus was domestic. His White House source, Berlin, had given him enough details on the briefing of the president to make it worthwhile to dig some more. He had spent several hours online in the newspaper's computer system, reading old articles about the Front and its activities. Either the reporters had missed the boat or their sources weren't as good as Spivey's. The articles began with the first story about the Front, following the first bombing, almost five years ago. Subsequent articles traced the increased Front activity. Then about eighteen months ago, the tide had seemingly turned. The articles described a massive and effective anti-terrorist effort by the FBI that had destroyed the Front as a terrorist organization.

At the very least, he had a story about FBI incompetence, but that was small potatoes. Spivey had tried to reach the lawyer defending Martinez, but the guy refused to return his calls. His law firm had released a colorless press release about the ongoing investigation and how every person is presumed innocent until proven guilty. Spivey leaned back in his chair and clasped his hands behind his neck. There was definitely an angle here, he just hadn't found it. The phone on his desk rang.

"Spivey."

"Is this Glenn Spivey?" The caller was a female.

"That's what I said."

"Do you want the real story about the Front?"

Spivey grabbed for a pen and paper, cradling the phone on his shoulder. "Yeah, you and a thousand other crackpots are going to give me the true story."

"I'm no crackpot. I have proof of who really killed the president-elect."

Spivey was silent. He felt a sudden chill traveling up his back, raising the hair on his neck. It was true that he had received lots of crackpot calls, but this one was different. The tone was simple and straightforward. Crackpots told convoluted stories in a rushed manner, because they feared they would be cut off at anytime. This caller was silent as Spivey contemplated his response. Silent and confident.

"Mr. Spivey, are you still there?"

"I'm here. When can we meet?"

"Tomorrow night. Same time. Jefferson Memorial. Come alone. Don't be late." The line went dead. Spivey hung up the phone and then began to smile. He leaned back again in his chair, contemplating his third Pulitzer Prize.

CHAPTER 23

Jack's trip to the office was similar to the previous day, but now it was a routine, making it less trying. His mind was preoccupied with the events of last evening, so the trip was even more of a blur. It felt like when he would drive somewhere and, when he arrived, could not remember any details of the trip. Jack had barely slept, what with the tension and excitement over the path his life had taken. On top of that, things with Alison seemed to be progressing quite nicely. She seemed to genuinely like him, perhaps even more than like. His previous relationships with women could best be described as numerous. She was someone who might change all that. Jack smiled involuntarily. He was on a runaway train and having the time of his life. At his side, Evans noticed the smile.

"A productive evening?"

"Huh? Oh, yes. Very productive." Jack was glad to see Evans again. Duncan had been competent but colorless. By now Evans had been briefed on the events of the previous night, so he knew Jack and Alison had gone their separate ways. The comment was intended to convey to Jack that Evans understood his attraction to Alison. What wasn't to understand? Once the car pulled up to the curb, the pack of reporters descended again. Evans and the other agents cleared a path for Jack. The reporters shouted questions at him.

"Mr. Banner, how is your client going to plead at the arraignment tomorrow?"

"Is it true that Martinez is a Russian spy?"

Jack ignored all the questions and followed closely behind Evans. Soon they were in the elevator.

"Having fun yet, Banner?"

"Sure. I could get used to a pack of reporters following me around and probing every detail of my life. It's like running for office." They reached Jack's floor. As they exited the elevator, the receptionist gave him a seductive look. He ignored her. Evans and his entourage peeled off. They would leave one man at the elevator and one at each of the fire stairwells. Yesterday they had intercepted a few reporters, but so far no assassins. He walked up to Elaine's desk.

"Good morning, Elaine."

"Good morning, Jack."

"Could you please arrange a meeting with Mr. Kelly for this morning? Also, have Ms. Flanagan and Ms. Jacobs, our star litigation paralegals, come down to my office as soon as possible."

"Yes, sir."

Jack went into his office and sat behind his desk, collecting his thoughts. He and Alison had arranged to meet this morning in his office. Kelly had promised him full use of the necessary staff and he intended to take him up on the offer. The first step was to serve all the subpoenas that he and Alison had discussed. In civil litigation, that was easy. He didn't have the vaguest idea how to do that in a criminal proceeding. The second step was to prepare for tomorrow's arraignment. Alison would have to brief him on that as well. It would be a simple affair. Martinez would plead not guilty. Bail would likely be denied, given the severity and nature of the alleged crime. Alison had mentioned that they might file some motions to be heard at the hearing. His thoughts were interrupted by the arrival of Ms. Flanagan and Ms. Jacobs. Jack beckoned them to enter and motioned for them to be seated in his sitting area, where he and Alison had had coffee the day before. He joined them.

"Good morning, ladies."

"Good morning," they answered almost in unison.

"Whatever you're working on, get rid of it. Until further notice you work for me." They started to protest but Jack held up his hand. "Don't worry about the other partners. Just give me a list of the projects you're working on and I'll get it taken care of through Mr. Kelly."

The incantation of Kelly's name seemed to satisfy their concerns. There was nothing worse for a paralegal than to be caught in a squeeze between partners. Someone's work wouldn't get done and the paralegal would take the blame.

"As I'm sure you know, this firm will be defending Mr. Martinez. Our experience in criminal law is limited at best. That's why I've asked for you two. I think you are our best and brightest paralegals, and I'll be looking to you to bone up on the criminal procedure as fast as possible. That is your first assignment. I'm meeting Ms. Stevens, who will be my co-counsel, at ten. I'd like you to sit in on that meeting. We'll outline a plan of attack at that time." They were both scribbling furiously on their legal pads. Neither was more than twenty-five years old. They were young and eager, not yet beaten down by the long hours and stress that came with the practice of law. He knew they were both single. Given last night's revelation from Mr. Martinez, he wasn't sure it was fair to involve them in what might turn out to be a deadly affair. He would have to give them a choice at some point based upon full disclosure. For now a veiled warning was sufficient.

"One more thing." They stopped scribbling and looked up at him intently. "This is obviously a case with enormous implications for our country and for all those involved. Our client is accused of killing the next President of the United States. You can tell no one, and I mean no one, of what you learn. Not your boyfriends, your parents, your best friends. If you do, not only is it a breach of your ethical duty, it could possibly endanger people's lives, including your own and your loved ones. Do you understand what I'm saying?"

Their eyes were wide. They both nodded their heads.

"If either of you are uncomfortable with this, I perfectly understand, and I can find someone else. It will be just between us."

Ms. Flanagan spoke up. "Mr. Banner . . . uh . . . I mean, Jack." His rule was well known throughout the firm. "I can't speak for Stephanie, but I'm thrilled to be given the opportunity." Jack turned to Ms. Jacobs. She nodded in agreement.

"Good. Excellent. Then we'll meet back here at ten." He stood up and they followed suit, gathered their legal pads and left. The intercom buzzed. It was Elaine. "Mr. Kelly says he can see you now."

"Thank you, Elaine." He checked his watch: 9:45. "If Alison arrives while I'm gone, please bring her up to Mr. Kelly's office."

"Very well. Do you want the ten in your office or in a conference room?"

"In the conference room. We'll need the room. And Elaine . . . ?"

"Yes?"

"Why do we use this stupid intercom when your office is not more than fifteen feet from mine?"

She didn't answer the question. "Would you like me not to use the intercom?"

"Please." She hung up in exasperation.

Jack left his office and, as he passed Elaine's desk, she gave him the "evil eye." He smiled back. Their banter was part of the daily routine, a sign that their working relationship was a good one. His thoughts turned to his meeting with Mr. Kelly. Jack had promised to keep him apprised of the situation. He intended to do that. Jack needed Kelly's support in order to get the cooperation he required to try the Martinez case. Jack also had not lost sight of the fact that his future with the firm would be decided by this case, assuming he wanted a future with the firm. The last few days had caused a lot of soul searching on his part. Before Martinez's call, his life had been on a predictable path. Too predictable. That had changed with one phone call. Right now, he was too close to the events to make a clear decision about whether that was a good thing or a bad thing. If he and Alison got Martinez off, he could write his own ticket as a lawyer, not to mention for TV and book rights. Then again, being with Alison had allowed him to see the other side of the street, where the practice of law had a noble purpose instead of a profit motive.

He forced his mind to focus on the meeting. What would he—and could he—tell Kelly? He and Alison had concluded that they could trust no one, but he had to give Kelly some idea of what was going on. At some point, he and Alison would have to tell someone. If Kelly had the connections and clout he was rumored to have, his friends might come in handy in a pinch. Then again, with an alleged conspiracy within the government, those friends could very well be the enemy. Jack just didn't have enough information to make an informed decision. He would just have to play it by ear. He was doing a lot of that lately.

Ms. Hathaway was at her usual post and she exchanged pleasantries with him, as she ushered him in to see Mr. Kelly. As with the first meeting, he was on the phone and motioned for Jack to take a seat. Jack wondered if he intentionally made calls before meetings so his guests would have to wait. If so, it was a habit that Jack would have to adopt. It made the guest extremely uncomfortable.

Kelly wrapped up the phone call. "Good morning, Jack."

"Good morning, sir."

"Well, what do you have to report?"

Jack paused, again, wondering how much to share with Kelly. Was he an enemy or an ally? If he was an enemy, he already knew what Jack was about to tell him. His knowing what Jack knew wouldn't change much, because, in fact, Jack knew very little. If he was an ally, he might be able to help, given his power and friends in high places.

"This is going to sound a little paranoid, but according to our client, Mr. Martinez, the assassination was a conspiracy involving some person or persons within the United States Government."

Kelly said nothing. He rose from his chair, crossed to the door and closed it. He returned to his chair.

"Does he have proof?"

"Not solid proof. Just his observations. Things he overheard and saw." Jack gave Kelly a quick summary of the conversation with Martinez. Kelly listened attentively, not interrupting. When Jack was done, Kelly leaned back in his chair.

"Is this Martinez a nut case?"

"I've asked myself the same thing. I think not. He tells his story in a coherent and logical fashion. Times and dates correspond and flow. What he knows he didn't make up. The question is his interpretation of what he saw. It certainly sounds suspicious. These yuppie, paramilitary guys taking over a left wing, ethnically diverse revolutionary group. But maybe their parents didn't give them enough love and it's a form of rebellion. We need to shed some more light on the facts we know and see what shakes loose."

The intercom buzzed on Kelly's desk. He picked up the phone. "Yes. Send her in." He replaced the phone. "Ms. Stevens is here."

Ms. Hathaway appeared in the opened door, ushering Alison in. Both Jack and Kelly stood up. "Come in. Come in." Kelly crossed to the door, his hand outstretched. They shook hands warmly. Alison's face showed slight surprise at the warm greeting. "Did Ms. Hathaway offer you something to drink?"

"Yes, she did, thank you."

"Please have a seat. Jack was just giving me an update on where we stood." Alison shot Jack a glance, uncertain how much he had told Kelly. They had never decided how much to tell and to whom. Had he spilled the whole story already? Kelly's next comment made it clear that Jack had.

"Jack and I were just deciding whether Martinez's conspiracy story holds water. What do you think?"

Alison hesitated. Not knowing what Jack had said she did not want to reveal too much. She looked at Jack. He gave her a slight nod. "I think his story is plausible. The question is, can he prove it or, better yet, can we as his lawyers prove it."

"Jack's sentiments exactly. You two appear to make a good team. How do you suggest we go about that?" Kelly was in the role he played so well. The mentor, the leader. Coaxing others to find the answers. Bringing out the skills of others to achieve a defined goal. Alison and Jack outlined the strategy they had outlined at dinner—what now came to be known as the "ant strategy."

"Good. I like it. As I've said before, the resources of the firm are at your disposal. I also have some other sources that I'm going to consult. I'd prefer that they remain nameless for now. But if I find out anything I'll let you know."

Jack interrupted, "I need you to clear the decks for Ms. Flanagan and Ms. Jacobs. I've enlisted their help."

"Consider it done."

Kelly rose from his desk to signal that the meeting was over. Alison and Jack did the same. They all walked toward the door. "I don't have to tell you two to be careful. If you need my help, my door is open."

"We will," Jack replied. As they walked away from the office, Jack could sense Alison's anger. "Is there a problem?"

"Yes, there is. How could you tell him everything without consulting with me first? I thought we were together on this thing."

"We are. The way I see it, he can either help us or maybe he's one of the ants. What I told him should stir up the nest pretty good."

CHAPTER 24

Jenkins rushed into the director's office with a broad smile on his face. Sometimes it was better to be lucky than good. "We might have just gotten our first break. A supervisor over in records has a hard-on for one of his employees. A guy named Lefteski. When he didn't show up for work, his boss called the Prompt Disclosure Squad."

"Maybe he was sick today."

"That's what I thought. But we had the computer jockeys run a search. Turns out, there were a high number of entries into the database on the Front during the shifts that Lefteski worked. The access was from a number of computers located in his section, but using an agent's password—an Agent Reynolds."

"How did he get the password?"

"We questioned Reynolds this morning. Turns out he violated the number one rule and wrote his password down and left it in his desk. When he was being reassigned, his temporary desk was in Lefteski's section. Reynolds is clean. He passed a lie detector test with flying colors. It looks like Lefteski used Reynolds's password to access the information on the Front."

The director interrupted, "Then he passed it to the Front, which explains why our counter-terrorist activities appeared to be working. In fact, they were one step ahead of us the whole time. They knew our every move as they planned the assassination. Where is Lefteski now and what do we know about him?"

"We don't know where he is. Checked his apartment. No one home. We're in the process of getting a warrant to search his apartment. His personnel file shows that he was somewhat of a malcontent. His boss wasted no time in pointing the finger at him. His coworkers say he was a computer hacker. That explains the fact that the systems operator never picked up any unusual activity. He accessed the database from different terminals at different times and intermittently, so as not to raise any red flags."

The director leaned back in his chair. "Do we know what he knows?"

"Pretty much everything we knew about the Front."

"Well, we really have egg on our face now. I'll have to brief the president and the attorney general. Steve, let's make sure there are no leaks from our end. Once I tell the president and the AG, all bets are off. The press will have a field day with this one. Keep me posted."

"Yes, sir." Jenkins turned to leave.

"One more thing. How is our tail on Banner going?"

"Fine. Evans says he's an alright guy. Nothing suspicious, no strange phone calls or meetings.

"Good. That's all for now, Steve."

Jenkins left and the director reached for the secure phone. "This is Director Stevenson for the president." There was a pause as the call was routed. "Mr. President, I have some troubling news for you. Yes, I can be there at five."

CHAPTER 25

Frank Ruffulo was still struggling with his problem and his conscience. He had spent a long night with the boys at Jimmy's, to no avail. They just didn't understand the dimension of his problem and he couldn't share enough of the details with them to make it clear what a difficult decision he faced. His wife knew something was on his mind. She kept asking him if everything was alright. He said it was, but that was a lie.

Ruffulo was pleased in one way. His first instinct had been to accept the offer to make it "worth his while," but the more he thought about it the less he liked it. True, he was disillusioned with the government and the direction in which the country was headed. But that didn't mean he should sell out his principles for a little payoff. In an attempt to clear his head, he went for a walk. It was pretty cold. Hell, it was always cold in Illinois in the winter. Eventually Ruffulo found himself in front of a church. Not just a church, but *his* church. The church in which he had been christened and married. He hadn't been to confession in a long time. Was it two, no, three, years? Purgatory looked like a sure thing. He decided to go in.

The church was a simple structure. It had stained-glass windows and Gothic architecture typical of the Catholic churches he had known and seen. The pews ran down either side of a central aisle. To the right were the confessional booths. Ruffulo paused for a moment, gazing at the altar and the statue of Christ on the cross that dominated the church and the pews. He remembered how frightened he had been as a small boy, imaging the pain and suffering of Christ on the cross, and more frightened when the priest intoned that Christ had died for the sins of others. That was, indeed, a large burden for an eight-year-old. Involuntarily he found himself walking toward the confessional booth, peering back at the crucifixion scene, feeling the eyes of Christ gazing upon him. He parted the curtain and entered the confessional. As he knelt, the priest slid open the partition that allowed conversation between the sinner and the confessor.

"Father, it has been three years since my last confession."

"And what sins have you come to confess?" It was Father O'Leary. He was a young priest, relatively new to the parish, the fresh breed that accepted the tenets of the church but bristled at its rigid hierarchy. His ideas of more openness and democracy within the church made him a rebel. His posting to the parish in Winnetka was an attempt to bring him to heel. He resented that, but he was dedicated to his work and tended to his parish with enthusiasm and compassion.

"I have committed many sins, father, but it is a sin that I might commit that troubles me most."

"There is no sin that cannot be forgiven. Still, it is better to nip a sin in the bud if possible. How can you prevent this sin from occurring?"

"I'm not sure I can, and I don't know if I want to."

"Then why did you come here today? Obviously you are troubled."

Ruffulo could feel himself perspiring. He began to feel claustrophobic in the small confessional booth, his heavy winter coat adding to his discomfort. Why had he come? He wasn't sure. The church had just been there and it seemed the right thing to do. But was it mere coincidence? He had set out to get some fresh air, but the route he had taken was not the usual one he took when trying to clear his mind. Was he looking for a solution or someone to soothe his guilty conscience? In his heart he knew he was a weak man and that, in the end, he would take the money and sell his vote to the highest bidder. A big payoff was what he needed. For that he could sell his soul. Yes, absolution was what he needed, but this priest was trying to redeem his soul. He didn't want that or need it. He rose to leave.

"Wait, my son. It is never too late to change the path your life is on. The fruits of temptation have a bitter aftertaste. Your conscience brought you here; let it be your guide." The words echoed in Ruffulo's ears, as he hurried toward the church door and out into the cold winter air. He made it home in record time, breathing heavily as he climbed the steps to his apartment. His wife was watching TV when he arrived.

"Hey, honey, how was your walk?"

"Fine. Fine. We got anything to eat?"

"There's some leftover meatloaf in the fridge. Oh, I almost forgot. Some guy called for you. Said it was real important. He wouldn't leave his name, just his number. I left it by the phone."

Ruffulo's stomach dropped. He walked over to the phone on the hall table. The number began with area code 202, a Washington, D.C. phone number. As he picked up the phone to dial, he could feel the eyes of Christ boring into his back.

CHAPTER 26

Justice Kincaid was seated behind his desk. His young law clerk was seated opposite him. The clerk was a bright lad. All the clerks were. They came from the top 1 percent of the top 1 percent of the nation's law schools. They were also naive and clueless as to how the real world worked. As a justice and their mentor, he tried to impart to them how what they did in this ivory tower had an impact on the world outside the tower. When a new clerk brought him his first well-crafted opinion, complete with footnotes and a thorough legal analysis, his first question was always, "How would the decision affect the man on the street?" Invariably this would draw a puzzled look from the clerk. "Isn't justice blind?" they would ask. The chief justice would then explain that the rule of law depended on the confidence of the people. If the laws made no sense to the average man, he would not follow them and lawlessness would rule the land. The next opinion was always so much different than the first. It gave him great pleasure to see these bright minds understand the import of their work.

His meeting with the other justices was scheduled for the day after tomorrow, and he wanted to be fully prepared to address all the issues and answer as many questions as possible. His clerk had briefed him on the constitutional issues. The conclusions agreed with those of David Rothstein. The clerk did not know this, because the clerk did not know that Rothstein was a former clerk of the chief justice. The chief justice remained close to many of his clerks, and he and Rothstein were especially close, sharing their love of the game of golf and the law. It may have been considered improper by some that the chief justice would converse with Rothstein on the subject, but where the future of the court was concerned, the chief justice was known to cut a few ethical corners.

This was a disquieting conclusion, because it brought to the fore his concern that the court might be the arbiter of such an explosive political controversy. Unfortunately, the political controversy now had a constitutional dimension. If the question were presented to the court regarding the constitutional procedure as regards the president-elect's assassination, the court would have to decide the question. For all the reasons he had contemplated the previous day, he did not want that to happen. The only hope was if the question never reached the court. The president had increased that likelihood by promoting the election of the vice president-elect. That removed at least one person with standing to object to any result. But what if an elector or an ordinary citizen appealed to the court for its interpretation? The court had to be prepared for any scenario and then do its best to avoid issuing any decision. He had not expressed this conclusion to the clerk or his fellow justices. It seemed to an outsider that this was an abdication of the court's responsibility, when in fact it was essential to the operation of a democracy with checks and balances. The courts merely interpreted the laws that were enacted by the popularly elected representatives. All they could do was wait and be prepared. That was satisfactory to the chief justice. He hoped he would never see the day that his beloved court would be forced to decide a question that might plunge the country into chaos.

CHAPTER 27

The vice president-elect was far more interested in deciding who would be the next president. Ed Simmons had come a long way and he wasn't going back anytime soon. He was a senator from the state of Missouri, who had started out selling insurance on the dusty prairie and then found his true calling in politics. His position on the ticket was a combination of hard work and geography—Missouri being neither south nor west but close enough to draw support from both regions of the country, and yet decidedly not northeast, so as to cost him support in that region either. He had been a party loyalist for many years and contributed to the campaigns of fellow Democrats. He had been good at selling insurance and was equally good at selling himself and other politicians. He was well known nationally and had converted that notoriety into fund raising. When the time came for selecting the vice president he had called in his chips. He was young and a position on the national ticket, win or lose, would prove helpful down the line. Serving eight years as vice president was a cakewalk. State dinners, a few funerals and then, in eight years, his own run for the presidency. The death of the president-elect had accelerated the timetable—or so he had thought, especially given the president's concession speech the prior evening.

But suddenly the situation was changing. His campaign manager, Amy Hall, had received a strange call from one of the political bosses out in the field in Illinois. Someone was rallying support for the president among the electors. The effort had been subtle and almost imperceptible to the average observer, but Simmons had built his career on attention to the little things and the little people. He remembered names the way most people remembered where they were when the first man landed on the moon. He always returned a favor with a favor. People were his thing, and the connections he made in his district and around the country always paid dividends. Several of the electors had called and reported strange inquiries about how they intended to vote.

This came as a shock to Simmons and his staff: How they intended to vote? They assumed it was a done deal, tempered, of course, with the sadness at the death of the president-elect. They had consulted with the Democratic National Committee. The legal staff was at first dumbfounded by the question. Later they had called back and said, yes, there was some question about the election process and what would happen next. They would get back to him.

Next they had called the president's campaign staff and denied any knowledge of the effort. *And Nixon didn't know about Watergate.* Well he was damn sure not going to stand around and let them snatch the presidency from his hands. He had worked too hard and too long for that. He and Hall were contemplating what moves to make and how to respond. They were seated in a suite of hotel rooms that was to have served as their transition headquarters before the move to the vice-president's quarters in the Old Executive Office Building. Now it was their war room.

She paced the floor as he laid out a strategy. "We need to contact all our electors and make sure they're solid. If there's a chance they can change their minds, let's not give them a chance—or a reason—to change it. I want you and Delancy to split the list and make the calls. Any fence-sitters give to me and I'll get involved." Delancy was his director of communications and a veteran of politics and dirty tricks.

"Next, we need exposure in the press. We need to get my face on television and in the papers. Set up as many network and print interviews as you can. I think we should schedule a press conference as soon as possible."

Hall interjected, "We have to be careful not to appear insensitive and opportunistic. You have to appear presidential. I'll get the speechwriters started on something to open the press conference. Dillard," she yelled over her shoulder.

Matt Dillard, the head speechwriter, appeared at their side. He was young, as most of the staff was, but tested in the fire of a campaign. They had been working nonstop and thinking on their feet for over a year. Now they were in the homestretch and full of adrenaline.

"We're going to schedule a press conference. We need a speech. It should start off somber, condolences for the families, concern for the nation. Then gradually turn to take charge, full of action and decisiveness."

"But it can't overreach," Simmons added.

"We need it as soon as you can have it." Dillard nodded his head and departed.

The phone next to Simmons's chair rang. Hall reached over and answered it. "Yes. Right. OK. Can you fax it? Great." She hung up. "That was Anderson over at the DNC. They've been doing some overnight polling. Seems that 62 percent of the American public, if given a choice, is prepared to give the president another four years. Looks like we have our work cut out for us."

Simmons got up from his chair and began to pace the room. "This is incredible. We campaigned for one solid year, we crisscrossed the country, spent millions of dollars and won this election. Now it might have been all for nothing. In one night, some terrorists have wiped out an election and sent us back to square one. I just can't believe this can happen." The room was silent. Simmons continued, "Well, if we're going to go down, we're going to go down fighting. We know what we have to do, let's do it!" Hall and the others dutifully obeyed, going off to their appointed tasks. Simmons returned to his chair and picked up the phone and dialed. "Honey. I'm going to be home late. All hell is breaking loose here . . . and maybe everywhere."

CHAPTER 28

The FBI Director was seated in the Oval Office with the president and Howard Berlin, along with Attorney General Malcolm Williams. Stevenson didn't care much for Berlin. He was a weasel and everyone knew it, including Berlin. In fact, he reveled in the reputation, which made him all the more distasteful. Stevenson had briefed them on the new information they discovered about Lefteski and his presumed connection to the Front.

"So what you're saying is that the FBI blew it?" Berlin was on the attack. Stevenson had been expecting it, but he had no adequate response. Berlin was right. They had blown it. The president rose to his defense.

"This is no time for placing blame, Howard. What we need to do is find those who are responsible and bring them to justice. How does our case stand against this Martinez fellow?"

"Well, I'll defer to the attorney general on the legal aspects. From the investigation side, we know he was a member of the Front and he was at the scene of the crime. Other than that, it's hard to say at this time. We think he's our man, but we have some more leads to track down and interviews to make." Stevenson was about to continue and disclose the information that they had discovered about the infiltrators, but he didn't trust Berlin. In fact, after recent events, he didn't trust anyone other than his top people. A soldier knows that he can trust his own men and no one else. He had wanted this briefing to be just with the president. He was disappointed to find Berlin and the attorney general present. The rest of his information would have to wait until he could be alone with the president.

Attorney General Williams interrupted his thoughts. He was a lawyer of little skill, but with significant political assets. "What the director says is correct. We only have circumstantial evidence right now. But you can rest assured that we will bring the full force of the government to bear on this case. By the time trial comes, our case will be ready."

"Good. Good. But let's remember, everything is by the book. No shortcuts. No gray areas. I want to nail these bastards!" The president slammed his fist down on the desk. This surprised Berlin, as well as the president's choice of words. The president seldom showed anger and almost never used profanity. For some reason this was disquieting to Berlin, but he was not sure why. The others present in the room had no reaction, and Berlin attributed it to the stress of recent events.

"We will give it our best effort, Mr. President. You can count on us," said the attorney general sternly and confidently.

"Very well. If that's all gentlemen . . ." This was the president's way of signaling the end of the meeting. The attorney general rose to leave.

Stevenson interjected, "I have one more matter, Mr. President, but it is for your ears only." This was an extraordinary statement and an affront to the attorney general, who was the top law enforcement agent of the United States Government. The attorney general leapt to defend his turf.

"Excuse me, Mr. Director, but I can't imagine what information you could have that I would not be privy to."

The president turned to Stevenson. "Gary, I would have to agree with Malcolm on this." The first name basis was another trait of the president. He used it to defuse conflict by making the parties comfortable with one another. Berlin started to speak, but the president held up his hand. "Gary?"

Stevenson leaned forward in his seat to increase the import of his words. "Mr. President, these are difficult times. Protocol, hierarchy and hurt feelings will have to be put aside. The future of the nation is at stake and I cannot risk sharing the information I have with anyone, other than those I think have a need to know. If you trust my judgment on that point, you will honor my request. If you do not, and you ask me to do so, I will share that information with the attorney general and Mr. Berlin."

The president pondered for a moment. "Gentlemen, if you will excuse us, I would like to meet with the director alone."

The attorney general turned red with anger. "Mr. President, I must protest. This is highly irregular."

Berlin wanted to protest, but did not. He was after all merely a political appointee. He had no title, no power, other than his access and closeness to the president. He knew the president well enough to know that he made up his mind. Arguing would anger the president and diminish his power. He rose to leave. This had the effect of undercutting the attorney general's protest as well. Another effective paean to the president.

"Malcolm, I understand your concern. You will have to trust my judgment, as I have the director's."

"Of course, Mr. President, I understand." The attorney general gave Stevenson a harsh look as he rose from his chair and exited the room with Berlin.

The president also rose from his chair to stretch and pace. The director remained seated. "Well, Stevenson, what was so important that I had to offend my chief of staff and attorney general?" The president was behind his desk now, his back to the director, gazing out of the window behind his desk. The window was constructed of bulletproof glass. The grass that he gazed out upon was crisscrossed with sensors and other security devices, as was the fence that surrounded the White House. Concrete barriers stood between the street and the outer fence to prevent a bomb-laden car from being driven too close. The head of the most powerful nation in the world was in fact a prisoner. He could never travel alone or spontaneously decide to catch a movie or a ballgame. Everywhere he went, a cocoon of security surrounded him. All presidents chafed at the restrictions, but few questioned them. Recent events had made it clear how perilous the job was.

"Mr. President, our preliminary investigation indicates that a wide-ranging conspiracy was involved in the recent wave of bombings."

The president turned to face the director. "Not a surprising conclusion. You've briefed me previously on the Front and their activities."

"Yes, sir, I have. But our analysis of what we have learned since the bombings leads us to believe that the Front was co-opted by another group and is being set up to take the blame."

The president had moved from behind the desk and was now seated across from Stevenson. "Another group? What kind of group? Who are they?"

"That we don't know, sir." The director briefed the president on what they had learned about the "infiltrators" and their discovery of the leak through Lefteski. The president appeared deeply troubled. He stood again and began to pace.

"We've known each other a long time, Gary. What are we looking at here? Russians? Chinese? Those damn Iranians?"

Stevenson paused. This was the critical moment. Once the words passed from his lips, the wheels would be set in motion. Orders would be given, actions taken. People would die. Would some disappear without a trace? It all depended on the president's reaction. Would fear and uncertainty lead him to act irrationally and trust no one? Or would he rally those close to him and move in a purposeful and thoughtful manner to solve the problem? He did not know and could not know. All he could do was to do his duty and provide the information as he knew it.

"I wish it were that simple, Mr. President. But the truth is, in our opinion, this was a domestic operation. A domestic operation that was planned with the help of some person or persons within the United States Government." There, he had said it. Every president's nightmare. An overthrow. A *coup d'etat.* The president appeared stunned. The blood drained from his face and he let out a gasp.

"A military overthrow? Not possible . . . I mean . . ."

"I never said military, sir. I only said that some person or persons within the government were, are, involved in this. The intelligence they had was too good. The munitions and explosives too sophisticated. The command and control too precise. These were professionals and they were insiders. They were Americans running the operation. Whether they were military or CIA or some other covert group that neither you nor I know about, it's too soon to tell."

The president had moved over to the bar and poured himself a drink from a glass decanter of brandy. He gestured to Stevenson with his glass, but Stevenson declined with a wave of his hands. The president replaced the decanter. He walked over and sat in his desk chair, rocking slowly back and forth. "Who else knows about this besides you?"

"My top people. A half dozen at most. They will all keep it quiet, but the information will leak out somehow. Someone will find out about Lefteski, about the infiltrators. The question is how closed was the cell at the top? How many people knew the true nature of the conspiracy and how tight is the cell? My guess is it's pretty tight. We're going to need all our resources to crack it. You see the problem, of course?"

The president apparently did not, as he gave the director a quizzical look.

"Who can we trust? How can we be sure that those we turn to help us—the CIA, armed forces, NSA, even my own people—are not part of the conspiracy? They could impede our progress rather than support it. Even worse, they could destroy evidence, eliminate links in the chain, thwart our every move." He regretted turning down the drink. His head was spinning.

"What do you suggest we do then? We obviously can't do nothing." The president's resolve appeared to return. "I'll be damned if I'm going to let those people get away with this."

"First thing, sir, is to increase the security detail around the White House. We can't be sure their work is done. Next, I'd ask that you allow me to investigate this matter as I see fit for a period of one week. The people I trust, I trust with my life and the life of this country. Give us a week. After that, I should have a better focus, know who I, we, can trust. Until then, I would also ask that you discuss this with no one."

The president nodded his head, digesting the information. "I can give you a week, but no more. After that, good conscience and constitutional mandates require me to act."

"I understand, Mr. President. The week is more than reasonable under the circumstances. I value the trust you've placed in me. It would be best if I go about my business and make full use of the time." The director stood.

"Of course. Of course. I expect a briefing every twenty-four hours. Sooner with any new development, day or night."

"Yes, Mr. President."

The president got up from his chair and escorted the director towards the door, out of the Oval Office. He placed his hand on his shoulder as they walked. The gesture of a true politician. As they reached the exit, they turned to face each other. The president spoke first.

"Why would anyone do this heinous thing, Gary?"

"Sir, I don't know, but I intend to find out."

"I have complete confidence in you Gary, and your agency."

"Thank you, sir."

The president stretched out his hand and Stevenson shook it. "Good night, Gary."

"Good night, Mr. President."

As he turned to go, the president said, "You don't really think about that phrase often."

"What phrase, Mr. President?"

"Good night," he replied. "We say it all the time without thinking about its meaning. Tonight is not a good night. Not for us, or for our country. Let's make sure we can mean that we when we say it."

"I'll do my best, sir."

"I know you will, Gary. I know you will. Hopefully all our bests will be good enough."

CHAPTER 29

Jack and Alison and the firm paralegals, Jacobs and Flanagan, had been meeting the whole afternoon. They had taken over one of the firm's large conference rooms. It was typical of a conference room in any large law firm. A large conference table surrounded by ornate chairs. They were seated around the table, which was piled high with paper and law books. With the paralegals, they had outlined a detailed list of subpoenas and depositions they intended to take in the case. It was an ambitious list. More ambitious than was realistic. They intended to subpoena the CIA, the FBI, the State Department. Many, if not all of their requests, would be resisted on grounds of national security. They had one advantage in that the prosecution would be required to turn over all its evidence to the defense, including any evidence that was exculpatory. The only problem was with the assumption that the government would play fair. They did not know how wide or deep the conspiracy was. It was possible that evidence had been, or would be, destroyed. Jack and Alison had agreed that Flanagan and Jacobs would not be told about the information given to them by Martinez. It was safer that way. As far as they were concerned, it was a question of giving Martinez the best possible defense and the discovery was a way to do that.

They were all exhausted by the effort. It was close to eight o'clock and Jack suggested that they break for the evening. The case promised to be a long one. There was no sense in burning out early. After Flanagan and Jacobs had left, Jack and Alison discussed the arraignment scheduled for the afternoon. Alison outlined the procedure briefly. She would handle the arraignment, but Jack wanted to be familiar with the procedure. He interrupted her discourse.

"Do you think we need to be concerned with security?" I assume the FBI will handle it, but who knows. I'd better ask Evans to get his boss on the line."

"Good idea. I was pretty much done anyway." She rose to leave.

"Wait, where are you going? I thought maybe we could have dinner."

Alison shook her head. "Thanks, but I'm beat. Got a big day ahead of us."

"You sure?" Jack rose from where he was sitting to escort her out the door. He was confused and perplexed. There had been a marked change in her attitude toward him since dinner the previous night. She was acting aloof and distant. He thought he had broken through the barrier she had placed between them when they had first met. Now the wall was up again and he didn't know why. Had he pushed her too hard? Was the pressure of the case getting to her? Jack had decided, long ago, that with women directness was the best solution. Even this was a risky proposition. In his experience, women often told you one thing when they meant another. Intuitively, men were supposed to read between the lines and figure out when "I'm not upset" meant "I am," and learn how to deal with the statement "If you have to ask and can't figure out how to make it better, what good are you?" when you asked what was wrong. Even more confusing to him was the fact that women who complained that men were insensitive expected they would intuitively know women's emotions and how to solve their problems. It defied logic and common sense, but that, Jack supposed, was the fun in it. So he leapt.

"Is something wrong?" He was standing close to her. She turned and faced him.

"No, nothing. Like I said, I'm just tired."

"You sure? Because if I've done something to offend you or upset you I'd like to know." He reached out and placed his hand on her arm in a comforting gesture. At first she seemed receptive to the gesture. She took a deep breath.

"Its just that . . ." and then she pulled her arm away. "No, really, everything's fine." She pushed her way past him and headed toward the exit to the conference room. She stopped in the doorway and turned to look at him.

"Let's plan to meet at the courthouse at nine."

Jack was too confused to protest. "Sure. Sure. Nine it is."

"Good night, Jack."

"Good night, Alison." She strode briskly toward the elevator. As she exited, her FBI detail fell into step behind her. She was afraid to look over her shoulder. If Jack followed her and confronted her again she wasn't sure she could keep the truth from him. When he had asked her, she wanted to tell him the truth. But why did she want to pore her heart out to this man of all men? Because of her beauty and intelligence there were always men "after her." They had only two things in mind: sex and making her a good wife. She had time for the former on her own terms, but none for the latter. Somehow Jack had the ability to throw her off kilter, to get underneath her radar and penetrate her defenses. It was so obvious he was in love with her. And what was he to her? She didn't want to think about it. Couldn't think about. For both their sakes. Another time and another place, perhaps, but not in this lifetime. Thankfully the elevator came. Alison and the FBI agents entered the elevator. She pushed the "L" button. As the elevator descended, she felt a feeling she had not felt in a long time. A sadness that comes with losing someone you love. She tried to push back the memories and the feelings she had sworn she would never feel again, but she could not. She could almost feel him next to her, his voice, his smell. How many years had it been? Five? Six? Ten! She had been so young. He had been her instructor at the "college." It wasn't a college known to many, and the curriculum and staff were rather unusual. His name was Ben. With the rigorous training and close quarters, it was inevitable that they had fallen in love. He was dashing, handsome and brilliant. He was an intellectual with a purpose. They spoke long into the night, about a world where justice prevailed and the need for people who would dedicate their lives to achieving that end. Then they made love, a wild passionate love, baring their inner souls and desires as only true lovers could.

And then, after only a few months, it had all come to an end one dark, rainy night. He had gone off for a few days. He, of course, could not tell her where he was going, and she knew better than to ask. She had been in her room at the academy. The driving rain beat against her windows, and the wind blew the trees with a viciousness she could not ever recall seeing. All day she had been filled with unease, sensing something was out of place, amiss. There was a knock on her door. The director of the academy was standing there when she opened it. His face was all she needed to see. He was gone. The director went on to explain how he had fallen in the name of a good cause and would be sorely missed. She remembered little else. Alison had been brave and continued on with her life. But she had never felt the same joy in life since that night. A feeling had been missing. A feeling of a reason to live, a spark, a passion. Until just a moment ago, when Jack had touched her arm. She had felt his energy course through her and she wanted to reach out to him, to engulf him in her life and her in his, like so many years ago. And when she had pulled back, the feeling had gone. Now she wondered if it would ever come back. Or, even worse, would there be another chance? In her life, she had seen many people die; she had killed more than a few. Each death sucked out a part of her life. Maybe this man could put some of that life back. Her thoughts were interrupted by one of the agents. They had reached the lobby.

"Ms. Stevens, wait here with Agent Davis while we pull the car around."

"Of course." The first agent left her with Agent Davis. In a way it was humorous. The FBI thinking she needed protection. She would play along for now. The FBI sedan pulled up in front of the office building. Agent Davis exited the elevator and beckoned her to follow. Her heels made a loud echo in the now empty lobby. As they exited the building, the chill of the winter night hit them and they clutched their coats closer. The agent looked carefully to his right and left as they exited. He did not notice Alison's more discreet, but equally professional, inspection of the street. Davis held the door open as she entered the car.

If she had looked up, she would have seen Jack staring down at her from the conference room, his face a mixture of confusion and sadness that matched hers. He watched the car drive away. Then he turned from the window and went back to the conference table. He slumped in a chair and rested his chin in his hands. What was it with her? Whenever they got close, she pulled away. He sensed it wasn't him, but some external force holding her back. It was so maddening. Over the years he had met many women and thought he had loved a few, but with Alison there was an almost psychic connection. He could sense the rhythms of her mind and feel the hum of her soul. In her eyes, he saw a reflection of his life. A seemingly satisfying life, lacking inner peace and harmony. He was determined to break through the barrier and unlock the secret that closed off her heart to him. He wearily rose from the conference room and gathered his coat. Tomorrow would be a long day. He hoped that Evans would be on duty tonight. He needed a little cheering up. He turned off the light and headed home. He wished that she would be there to meet him, but for now that was just a dream.

CHAPTER 30

Spivey was on time, as usual. He always felt it best to be at a meeting first, especially a clandestine one. He liked to survey the lay of the land to make sure it felt right. He had never been in physical danger at any similar meeting, but caution was his watchword. He was standing in the rotunda of the Jefferson Memorial, staring out across the tidal basin at the Washington Monument. A statue of Thomas Jefferson dominated the rotunda of the memorial. It was amazing that at three in the morning this structure was open to the public. As far as he knew, there were rarely, if ever, problems with graffiti or vandalism at the nation's monuments. In fact, one of his favorite seduction routines was a late night tour of the memorials. On several occasions, the inspiration of the monuments had had intriguing effects on his dates.

His thoughts were interrupted by the sound of quiet footsteps. He turned to see a woman approaching across the rotunda. She was about five-feet-six-inches tall, with short blonde hair trimmed close to her head. She was dressed in dark slacks, a dark sweater and a dark blue parka. If Spivey had not spoken with her prior to the meeting, he would have guessed she was a man. She walked and carried herself in a decidedly masculine manner. She was carrying a manila envelope in her hand. She stopped about five feet away from him. She scanned to the left and to the right, not with nervousness but methodically surveying the land.

"Are you alone?" she asked.

"Yes."

"Were you followed?"

Spivey wasn't sure. He had made no attempt to conceal his tracks. Why would anyone be following him? "No."

"The information in the envelope is deadly. If anyone knows you have it, you're dead. If anyone knows we met, you're dead. Your only hope to survive is to publish it before they know you have it. Trust only those who need to know with it. Don't try to verify it or confirm it. If you do, you're dead, as is anyone you told about it. In my estimation, you have approximately four hours before they know it's gone. Another two before they figure out it was me who took it. After that, all hell will break loose as they try to find it. They know all my movements up until 0100 hours.

They only need to track down my last two hours. They can do it. Do you understand what I'm telling you?"

Spivey wasn't sure he understood anything. "No, I don't and who the hell are you?"

"We have no time to discuss this. Every minute we waste is a minute less you have to save your life and the life of this country. I was a part of the conspiracy to kill the president-elect. I am disgusted to admit I was brainwashed, led to believe that the actions were necessary to save our country. Then I found the Lord again. He showed me the errors of my ways. My mission is to reveal this deception. All the information is in the envelope."

"What if I don't want the envelope?" Spivey was very scared now. The same truthfulness he perceived on the phone was even more powerful in person. She was supposed to be his ticket to another Pulitzer, instead she sounded like an Angel of Death.

"You have no choice. These people are ruthless. They will stop at nothing to achieve their purpose. I left out one small detail. I mailed a letter to my ex-compatriots. It describes how we met and the information I gave you. I figure it gets delivered in three days, tops. If you get lucky and they can't figure out it's you I met, they'll know for sure when they get the letter."

"But why did you do that?"

"I had no choice. Too much was at stake. I couldn't take the chance that you wouldn't help me. I only have one shot and you're it." She stretched out her arm, holding the envelope out to Spivey. He didn't want to take it. He tried to keep his arms at his side, but his right hand slowly rose and took hold of the envelope. She released her grip on the envelope. "Remember, time is of the essence." She turned and started to walk away. Then, before she exited the memorial, she called back, "And God bless you." Then she was gone.

Spivey looked around frantically. Now he was worried that he had been followed. Or maybe she had been. This secret agent stuff was for the birds. He did the only thing he could think of. He ran. He sprinted across the memorial rotunda, down the memorial steps and along the pathway leading to his car. He fumbled in his pocket for his keys, almost dropping them as he tried to open the car door. He jumped in his car, his heart pounding in the last second before he slammed the locks shut, expecting to be accosted at any moment. His hands were trembling. He held the package on his lap. He reached for his cell phone but then remembered her warning. He flipped the envelope over and ran his finger under the flap to open it. He reached inside and grabbed hold of its contents and pulled them out. He had a little reading lamp attached to his dash. He flipped it on and directed it toward the papers he had pulled from the envelope. The stack was maybe an inch thick and appeared to be a memo of some sort. It was held together by a binder clip in the upper left hand corner. The top page was a single 8-1/2 x 11-inch piece of paper. Centered in the middle, in bold capitals, were the words "OPERATION RESTORE DEMOCRACY." Spivey folded over the first page, keeping the clip intact, and began to read, flipping the pages quickly as he read. It was so stunning that it took his fear away. His instincts as a reporter took over. Could this be true? If it was, he was going to get a Pulitzer and perhaps a medal too, not to mention book and movie rights. He had to get started right away on this story. He reached for his laptop sitting on the passenger seat. He flipped open the cover and pressed the power button. The little machine began to hum as it booted up, the hard drive grinding as the operating system kicked in. Spivey continued to read while the machine booted into Windows.

His concentration was so deep that he failed to notice the figure approaching from the rear of the car. He was dressed in similar garb to the informant Spivey had just met. Unfortunately for Spivey, this new stranger had been the last person his new acquaintance had the pleasure of knowing. She had been wrong. They had not had four hours. As part of a tightly woven organization, her presence had been missed far earlier than she expected. Even worse, those in charge had suspected that she might be a weak link in the chain. Unbeknownst to her, she had been under twenty-four-hour surveillance. They had to find out whom she had contacted and then eliminate the links. A call had gone out and the hunters were now on the loose. The man approached the window and raised his silenced revolver, pointing it at Spivey's head. At just the instant that he was to pull the trigger, the laptop beeped, having finished its booting process. Spivey reached for the laptop and momentarily saved his life. The man could not recall the motion he had set in course to pull the trigger. The gun fired, the window shattered, Spivey screamed. The bullet tore into the top of his skull, taking part of his brain with it. As he fell forward and towards the passenger seat, the assassin fired three more bullets into the car. One entered Spivey's back, narrowly missing his spine, passed through his lung, and tore an enormous hole in his chest as it passed back out. The other two bullets miraculously missed. The assassin reached in to unlock the car and make sure of his aim. Then, suddenly, from the corner of his eye, he saw a pair of headlights. Fortunately, for Spivey, someone else believed in late night seductions at the nation's monuments.

Across the parking lot, the man from the hotel and Mr. Smith were watching in a parked car. They also saw the car. "Shit!" said the man from the hotel.

Mr. Smith spoke into a walkie-talkie. His voice echoed in the assassin's earpiece, "Hold your position, Alpha."

The assailant closed the car door and ducked down next to Spivey's car. The young couple in the car drove into the parking lot and parked about fifty yards away. Spivey's car was between their car and the monument. They would have to pass by it to reach the monument. They did not exit the car. Five minutes passed and then ten. It was obvious they had no intention of visiting the monument just yet. The only question was how long they would stay in the car. Smith and the man from the hotel glanced at their watches. The plan had been to dispose of Spivey's body and any trace of him. Every minute they waited, they risked discovery. Killing the couple would create more loose ends. That was the last thing they needed.

"Alpha, can you reach the package?" The assailant rose up slowly from his crouching position and peered into the vehicle through the shattered window. The light on the dashboard was still on and it illuminated the interior of the car. Spivey was motionless. The envelope was visible down by the accelerator. The sheaf of papers was also visible, still bound together by the clip. "Affirmative," whispered the assailant into his cell phone. He slowly leaned his body through the shattered window, extended his torso and grabbed the envelope and the memo.

"Got it," he said. "What now?"

"Continue to hold your position." Smith looked at his watch. It had been fifteen minutes. Far too long. He couldn't wait much longer. The couple solved his problem for him. The dome light in their car went on as the doors opened. "Alpha, abandon your position." The assailant quietly crept away from the car. The couple was still enamored of each other and the man went around the car to embrace his companion. They kissed, giggled and kissed some more.

In the car, Spivey was bleeding to death. At most he had ten minutes without immediate medical assistance. Somewhere in the back of his brain he knew he was dying. He was slumped over in the passenger seat and could feel something hard underneath him. The computer. He rolled his body off of it, lying on his left shoulder with his back pressed against the dash. The LCD screen was bright enough so that he could see it. The computer was configured to automatically boot up and run Word on startup, and the empty page, waiting for words to be written, stared back at him. With the last of his strength he began to type, but could only muster three words.

The young lovers finished their embrace and began to walk toward the monument. Their path took them right past Spivey's car. The broken glass under their feet caused them to pause.

"Hey, honey, what's all this?" said the woman. The young man came up alongside her. They noticed the broken window and the light inside and moved closer to investigate. Suddenly a piercing scream filled the air. It was the last sound that Glen Spivey heard.

The assailant had joined Smith and the man from the hotel. Using an infrared camera, they snapped photos of the young lovers and then, with their lights off, exited the monument parking lot and drove onto I 395. As they drove off, the man from the hotel turned to Smith.

"How come everything in your operation gets screwed up?"

Smith was unruffled by the criticism. "Nothing is screwed up. We eliminated the leak. We retrieved the document. The only people who shouldn't have seen it are dead. Now all you have to do is take care of Martinez."

"Don't worry. I always take care of my end of the deal."

"For what we're paying you, you better deliver."

The man from the hotel flushed with anger. He turned towards Smith. "You don't scare me and I don't like to be threatened. I'll get the job done. You just make sure your men don't screw up tomorrow. Because if they do, we are all in deep shit. Now take me back to the hotel. I'm tired and hungry."

Smith said nothing. The driver looked at him for instructions. Spivey's assassin was seated in the front passenger seat. He stiffened, prepared to carry out any order that Smith might deliver. Smith smiled.

"Our friend is right. It is late and we are all a bit tired. We should call it a night. Tomorrow is an important day for us and our country."

They traveled in silence the rest of the way, each wondering when they would have a chance to kill the other.

CHAPTER 31

FBI Special Agent Perkins was tired, hungry and pissed off. He had been sitting in Lefteski's apartment for five hours. It was four a.m. and he was no further along than when he started. His task had been to remove the data on Lefteski's computer. It should have been a relatively simple matter. He was an expert in the area of computers. When he arrived he found the computer running. He had tried to gain access, but had been confronted with a series of passwords. With his decryption software he had managed to determine the passwords for several levels, but this had taken some time. With each level he penetrated, the password had become more random. Passwords that consisted of real words or a series of numbers were relatively easy to crack, especially since he had linked up to the FBI's central computer. It was just a matter of some serious random number crunching until the word or combination was revealed. Passwords consisting of a random series of letters, characters and numbers were more difficult to crack.

What was upsetting him now was the realization that a time bomb was ticking on the computer. Not a bomb in the explosive sense, but a computer time bomb that, if triggered, would destroy all the information in the computer's memory. If he accidentally triggered the bomb, he might be able to reconstruct the fragments of data, but with so much at stake, the slightest loss of data could have enormous repercussions. So he had to proceed slowly. That was fine with him, but the bosses at headquarters wanted results and wanted them yesterday. They wouldn't understand any computer mumbo jumbo about time bombs and destroyed data. He reached for his thermos and some more hot coffee. It promised to be a long night.

CHAPTER 32

Homicide Detective Rudy Hernandez had been on the District of Columbia police force for twenty years, and with D.C. ranking at the top of the list every year for murders per capita, his career had been a busy one. What he had on his hands now was a multi-jurisdictional nightmare, commonly known as a clusterfuck. The murder had occurred in the District of Columbia, thus involving his department. It had also occurred at a federal monument, thus involving the park police. Finally, due to the recent bombings by the Front, the FBI had asked to be informed of any unusual murders or incidents occurring in proximity to the assassination. This murder qualified. The worst thing for any crime scene was too many live bodies trying to examine and look at the dead ones. It caused nothing but problems. On top of that was the posturing by each agency and department to lead the investigation. The FBI always thought it was the top dog and tried to order Hernandez's people and the park police around. This upset the local police force and made them less likely to cooperate with the feds. All in all, not the way to run a murder investigation.

Hernandez had arrived on the scene and spoken with the first uniformed officer to arrive, a park policeman named Davis. The young couple had had enough sense to use their cell phone to call 911 and even more sense not to touch anything. Davis had described to Hernandez how he had found the body as it now lay in the car. The girl and the guy were all nerved out and could provide little information. Davis had called for backup and forensics, and the crime scene had been cordoned off. Once the forensic team arrived, they began combing the area. They found four shell casings, 9mm, and two entry wounds and two exit wounds on the deceased, now identified as Glen Spivey, a reporter for *The Washington Post*. They had also managed to recover the bullets embedded in the car. Lots of prints were on the car, but they could be those of any number of people, and probably not the murderer. The forensic team had also pinpointed the time of death within minutes of the discovery of the body. That was unusual for a crime scene. The young couple had probably just missed witnessing the murder.

Hernandez walked over to the car, ducking under the yellow police crime scene tape. One of the members of the forensic team, Hugh

Dunston, was examining the driver's side window into which the shots had been fired. He turned as Hernandez approached.

"Detective, I think I've got something." The key to forensic science was the principle that at each crime scene the perpetrator either left something at the scene or took something with him that could link him to the scene. Hernandez leaned in towards the window. Dunston pointed to the sill.

"There is a trace of some fibers that got snagged on the broken glass at the base of the window." As he said this, Dunston rose from his crouching position. "The way I figure it, he leaned into the window to finish off the victim." Dunston demonstrated by holding his hand out to simulate a weapon and leaned, but without touching the window, to avoid contaminating the scene.

Hernandez peered into the window. Police floodlights illuminated the scene. The victim's body was still slumped where it had been found. They had done some preliminary forensic work, but wouldn't move the body until the crime scene had been completely investigated. Something about Dunston's theory didn't make sense to Hernandez. It was the position of the body and Dunston's demonstration that made it click. "It doesn't add up. How tall are you?"

"About five ten."

"About average height, right?"

"Yes."

"So let's assume the perp is average height, fair enough?"

"Sure, odds are he is within plus or minus two inches."

"OK, look how you're standing and look in the window."

Dunston turned toward the window and peered in. Hernandez continued. "It's a clear shot from there, right?"

"I guess."

"So why does the guy lean in to finish him off? He unloaded three rounds. He's a pro. If more was needed, he could do it from where you're standing."

Dunston considered the theory. "But remember, it was dark; we have all these lights on now."

"Fair enough. But if it was too dark to see in the window, how could the killer be sure about taking the first three shots? He must have been able to see; the shots are too on-target and we know they were up close."

"OK, then what's your theory."

"I think the guy leaned in to get something out of the car. Something he couldn't reach." Hernandez walked closer to the car, bending toward the window, extending his torso as if to reach in, again without touching the vehicle. He peered into the car, talking as he did. "It must have been somewhere in the car, cause he could have reached the driver's seat without putting his body inside. Did you search the whole vehicle yet?"

"Yep. Didn't find much. We have it all inventoried. I'll get you a list. But one silly question." It was said with slight sarcasm. The forensic guys hated it when the cops played Sherlock Holmes. "Why didn't he just open the door and get what he wanted?"

"Nice try, kid." To Hernandez, anyone with less than his twenty years of experience was a kid, especially when they tried to one-up him. "You forgot about Romeo and Juliet over there. If the perp opens the door, it attracts attention. Especially if the dome light goes on."

Hernandez turned to his left. "Hey, Pettit. Get your sorry ass over here!" Joe Pettit slowly sauntered over, paying no attention to Hernandez's exhortation.

"Yes, sir," he said, not with any respect for authority but, rather, out of habit. He and Hernandez were partners and friends. They had worked many a case together and shared many a beer the last fifteen years. Good-natured ribbing was part of the job. A way to keep some sanity in the otherwise insane world they witnessed every night. Hernandez and Pettit had had some close calls together, and had saved each other's necks and lives to the point where neither was sure who was more indebted to the other. It was that way with partners. They shared all the hell and the pain together, and knew each other probably better than their wives—or, in most cases, ex-wives. Yet their lives were strangely split. When the shield came off, they rarely socialized together, or even spent much time together. But each knew that the other would lay down his life for him.

"We need to find out what this reporter was working on. Find out if someone was mad enough about his work to kill him. Call his editor, his colleagues, his family, if he has one." Pettit nodded.

"How are our friends from the FBI making out with the finest from the park police?"

"The usual. They're waiting to see if this is a case worth fighting about. Given the hour and all, I think they'd rather be in bed."

"Good. Let's keep it that way. Go over and tell them that we respect the multi-jurisdictional aspect of the case and that we intend to keep them fully apprised of the situation as it develops. Then tell them a task force sounds like the way to go, with them in the lead of course. Then get them the hell out of here."

"I hear ya." Pettit was a man of few words. It was one of his best attributes. His silent manner encouraged people to talk to him and unburden their souls. He left, making notes as he went. Hernandez called after him.

"Remember to use the word multi-jurisdictional." Without turning back or around, Pettit waved to acknowledge, but not necessarily accept the suggestion.

Hernandez was about to finish his conversation when a high-pitched beeping began to emanate from the car. It sounded like an alarm on a digital clock. He looked at Dunston. "What's that?"

"Sounds like an alarm."

"Gee thanks. I never would have guessed." They moved closer to the car and peered in the window. With their sight connected to the sound, they could identify the noise as coming from the laptop computer perched on the passenger seat signaling that the battery was about to be drained of power.

"Shit." Hernandez looked at Dunston. "You're the technician here, do something." Dunston opened the driver-side door, relaxed in knowing that in all likelihood the computer would save any file Spivey had been working on. He was not a hundred percent sure, however, so speed was necessary. A violation of forensic protocol, but this was a necessary evil. Suspecting the computer was in power-save mode, he hit the space bar and the screen came to life. The computer continued to beep. On the screen were the final words Spivey had written: "the secret is."

Hernandez could just make out the words over Dunston's shoulder. "'The secret is' . . . what? Is that all?"

Dunston used the cursor to scroll down the screen. It stopped at the bottom. There was nothing more in the file. "Yup. That's it."

"What other files are on that thing?"

"There could be hundreds or thousands. Depends on how big his hard drive is."

"Don't start talking dirty on me. "Dunston started to explain, but when he turned to face Hernandez he realized from his expression that his remark was in jest. "We can look at the five most recent files he was working on, but first I think we should save this file."

"Good idea."

"What should we call it?"

"How about 'secret'?"

Dunston typed the command to save the file to the hard drive. It was just in time. The computer shut down. "That's all the juice it has."

Hernandez straightened up. "I've seen some weird ones in my day, but this is really strange. A dying man scrawls his last message on a computer and we have no clue what it means. Alright, enough fun for one night. I think we need to get the FBI boys in on this one. I bet they have some hotshot computer jocks who can shake down that thing and see if any more tidbits surface. Log it, book it, and make your report."

"You got it." Dunston began to fold up the computer. Hernandez walked away from the passenger side and circled back around to the driver's side. He walked to the shattered window, wondering what the killer had been reaching for. Whatever it was, it was gone. The secret had died with Spivey. If only he had lived long enough to finish the message.

He left the car and walked toward the FBI agent in charge. It was time to be true to his words. A multi-jurisdictional case it would be. The wind kicked up for a minute and he pulled his jacket closer to him, thinking there must be a better way to make a living. Then again, it could be much worse. It could have been him lying dead in the car. Life was wonderful after all.

CHAPTER 33

It was a crisp autumn morning. Or was it winter? Jack could never remember when the seasons ended and began. All he knew was that, as he sipped his morning coffee and gazed out the window, the sky was a clear blue that only came with fall and winter. In summer and spring there was too much haze and humidity in the air. He had risen early that morning. An unusual thing for him. He didn't have to meet Alison at the courthouse until nine, and normally he would have slept until the last possible moment. This morning he had been wide-awake at six. He had showered and then watched the morning news on CNN. The headline was, of course, the upcoming arraignment of Martinez. The legal commentators were out in force, predicting strategies and outcomes.

After watching the news, he had read the morning paper. The headlines were the same as those on the television. There was a nice biography of him and Alison. They placed prominence on his brother's war record and Alison's ACLU connection. The reference to his brother awakened the old demons and memories. He wished he could be here now, so that Jack could ask for his advice and guidance. When he thought rationally, he remembered that his brother had only been eighteen when he left home. It seemed to Jack that Tommy had all the answers. In reality, he was a teenager looking for his own answers. That was why he had ended up in Vietnam.

The doorbell interrupted his thoughts. Evans was here to pick him up. He exited the kitchen and crossed the foyer to the front door. He opened it to let Evans in. The usual horde of reporters was camped out in front. He couldn't understand why lawyers had such a bad reputation. Lawyers didn't camp outside your house and pursue you at all hours of the night. These guys really needed to get a life.

"Good morning, counselor."

"Good morning. Have time for a cup of coffee?" This had become a morning ritual for the two of them. The circumstances that had thrust the two of them together had been totally random, but they had formed a bond of friendship. It most likely would not last beyond the time they were forced together, but it was a friendship Jack valued. Evans was a steadying force in an otherwise chaotic situation.

"Love some. But only if it's Vanilla Bean. That's my favorite."

Jack smiled. "You're in luck. That's what I brewed this morning." They headed toward the kitchen. Evans removed his coat and took his now usual seat at the table, as Jack prepared his cup of coffee. Cream, no sugar.

"Big day for you, huh, counselor?"

"I guess."

Evans's voice turned serious. "I want you to be alert today. If I tell you to duck, or run, or hide you do it fast. No questions asked."

Jack was taken aback for a moment. "Sure . . . sure. Whatever you say. But there's nothing to worry about."

"I hope you're right, but you've stirred up a lot of dust on this one. I hear the word that's filtering down in the agency, the rumors. Government plot, overthrow. My guess is a lot of people would like to see your client Martinez dead, and you're going to be standing next to him today. So like I said, keep your head up and your ears open."

"I hear you. Thanks for the concern. Now finish your coffee before it gets cold."

They sipped their coffee in silence for a few minutes. Evans perused the sports section, Jack the front page. The doorbell rang again.

"Time to go, counselor." Evans rose from the table and crossed to the sink to empty his cup. He felt at home in the kitchen. He rinsed the cup and placed it in the dishwasher. Jack did the same. Evans gathered his coat and they made their way to the front door. Jack got his coat from the hall closet and picked up his briefcase from its customary place by the front door. A blast of cold air hit them when they opened the door. The car was out front with the engine running, the exhaust fumes revealed in the cold winter air. The reporters shouted out questions but Jack ignored them. It was getting to the point that he didn't even hear them.

He entered the car and Evans closed the door behind him. As they pulled away from the curb his thoughts turned to Alison. He was looking forward to seeing her but was apprehensive as well. He had tossed and turned all night long trying to figure out what it all meant. He suspected that she had been hurt before. Or maybe that was just his ego looking for some reason why she was resistant to his advances. A sleepless night had revealed no answers, and in his current state he suspected that since a woman was involved it would be a long time before he had an answer.

Their trip to the courthouse was a quick one. The cavalcade of FBI sedans with lights flashing parted the busy downtown traffic. The federal courthouse was located on Constitution Avenue in the shadow of the Capitol Building and across from the West Wing of the National Museum of Art. The museum was another of Jack's favorite spots on the mall. The mini motorcade pulled into the circular drive in front of the courthouse. The by now ubiquitous gathering of reporters had been cordoned off with sawhorses and police. Jack exited the car and entered the lobby, where he found Alison waiting. The sight of her made his heart skip a beat and his breath shorten. She was truly beautiful. His doubts in the car dissolved. She looked at her watch instinctively and then at Jack. He walked towards her.

"Good morning, Alison."

"You're late."

Jack pointed behind him to Evans. "You'll have to blame him. He insisted on Vanilla Bean." Alison looked puzzled. "We can discuss it later. Unfortunately the judge isn't going to care whose fault it is. We only have a few minutes before court is in session. We'll have to talk while we walk." She turned and walked down the hallway toward the courtroom. Jack and the FBI agents fell in behind.

Jack caught up to her. "Hey, I'm really sorry I was late, but why the attitude?"

"It's not attitude. It's professionalism. We're in court now representing our client. Whatever there is between us personally I don't have time for that now. Understood?"

"Understood." Actually Jack was ecstatic. This was the first time she had even hinted at there being anything between them. He quickly suppressed his elation. She was right. All their attention had to be on the matter at hand. The arraignment was in many ways a formality. The defendant entered a plea and bail was set. It was, however, an important feature of the American criminal justice system. Under the Sixth Amendment of the Bill of Rights, all defendants were entitled to a speedy trial. In the days of the monarchy, the king could keep prisoners and opponents of the state locked up indefinitely without charge. The Constitution had changed all that. Now an arraignment was required within a relatively short period of time, so that the defendant could be charged and the process started whereby the state would have to prove, in open court before a jury of the accused's peers, guilt beyond a reasonable doubt. It was quite astonishing how the process had survived for over 200 years; how with all its imperfections it worked, because it assumed innocence and made the state prove guilt. Oppression and tyranny were impossible in a system where the light of day shone on the process.

They planned to ask for bail, expecting that the judge would turn them down. The high publicity and the seriousness of the alleged crime would leave the judge little choice. They would plead not guilty and the judge would set future dates in the proceeding. They walked in silence, Alison's heels resounding on the linoleum floor. As they approached the courtroom, an area to the right had been cordoned off. The shark pack of reporters was there too. When they saw Jack and Alison coming, they readied their microphones and cameras. The lights almost blinded them. Fortunately, the FBI had cordoned them off a sufficient distance that Alison and Jack could avoid their questions.

Jack let Alison pass in front of him, as he reached out to push open the swinging door that led into the courtroom. As they entered, there was a hum and buzz of voices. The courtroom was packed with spectators and more reporters. Heads turned toward them and the buzz, too, as they were clearly a topic of discussion. There was a center aisle leading up to the courtroom with seating on either side. Straight ahead, at the front of the courtroom, was the bench where the judge would sit. It was elevated above the rest of the courtroom. Jack and Alison walked down the aisle and took seats at the table to the left as they faced the bench.

The prosecution team was already there, and there were quite a few of them. Alison and Jack took out their legal pads. Jack leaned over to Alison and whispered, "Who are those guys?"

"The gray-haired guy is the assistant attorney general, Joseph Hayes. The guy next to him is the United States Attorney for the District of Columbia. The rest are just flunkies."

Jack counted ten flunkies, in addition to the two non-flunkies. They were waiting for Martinez to be brought in by the U.S. Marshals. Jack scanned the courtroom. It was not special in any sense, in terms of its architecture or decoration. It was typical of courtrooms, in that it had an air of importance about it. It didn't matter what the architecture or the style was. All courtrooms had a certain feeling: a feeling of respect, of tradition, of power. It was the courtroom of United States District Judge Thelma

Gold. Federal judges were appointed for life and Judge Gold had been one of the first African-American women appointed to the federal bench. She had a reputation as being fair, but tough. She expected respect and professionalism from those who appeared before her, and gave the same in return to those who complied. For those lawyers who did not follow her rules or guidelines, humiliation was swift and certain; but she was always sure not to place the sins of the lawyers on the clients.

Jack turned around to look at the spectators. As he scanned the crowd, he noticed a man toward the back who looked familiar. He had short blond hair, cut in almost a military style, a dark blue suit and striking blue eyes. He was firmly built. Jack was terrible with names, but had an uncanny recollection of faces. Once he had been at a party and recognized a guy he had taken a summer-school class with ten years earlier. Their eyes locked and Jack racked his brain trying to place this face with an experience or a name. The man stared straight at Jack, his eyes never wavering, but not showing recognition. Jack felt a chill up and down his spine and averted his gaze, still struggling to place the face. His efforts were interrupted by a commotion from the front of the courtroom. The U.S. Marshals were bringing in Martinez.

They had arranged to have a suit and tie delivered to him and to have his hair trimmed. He looked downright presentable. Certainly not the kind of guy who could kill anyone. All criminal defendants with good lawyers looked that way. The marshals led him over to the defense table. Martinez took the seat in-between Jack and Alison. Jack leaned over and whispered in his ear, "What took you so long? We thought you were standing us up."

Martinez smiled and chuckled. This brought a serious glance from Alison. She turned to Martinez. "It's not a good idea for you to appear callous. Laughing is not appropriate. When the judge comes in, you rise. Look serious and remorseful." She gave Jack a second and more serious look of reproach. Jack gave her his best "What, me?" face.

Their battle was interrupted by the bailiff's voice. "All rise for the Honorable Judge Gold. The United States District Court for the District of Columbia is now in session." In unison, those assembled in the courtroom rose. The judge entered the room and strode to the bench. As she took her seat there was a loud rustle as the others in the courtroom also took their seats. She shuffled her papers and then leaned over to her bailiff to say something. The bailiff nodded and departed through the door where the judge had entered. She adjusted some papers and then looked up.

"We are here on the matter of the *United States v. Carlos Martinez*. The charge is murder in the first degree, conspiracy to commit murder, assault and battery, illegal possession of explosives and firearms, and attempted assassination of the President of the United States. Before you enter a plea Mr. Martinez, I would like to put one thing on the record. I am aware of the significance and notoriety of this case. This will most likely be a long and difficult matter. Under no circumstances will I allow my courtroom to be turned into a circus. All parties, their counsel and the spectators who are present will abide by the rules of my court. There will be no exceptions and no second chances. I intend to see that the defendant gets a fair and speedy trial, as is his right. I also intend to see that the people get a fair chance to present their case. Now counsel, if you would enter your appearances."

Hayes stood. "Joseph Hayes, on behalf of the United States of America." He said it with great authority. That is all he should have said. Obviously he had not been in Judge Gold's courtroom before, because instead of sitting down he continued, "Your Honor, I would just like to say that this horrible crime against the government and its people will not go unpunished."

Judge Gold's booming voice filled the courtroom. "Mr. Hayes. Sit down!" Hayes was so stunned he immediately dropped in his chair. "Mr. Hayes, you obviously have not been in my courtroom before, correct?"

"Correct, Your Honor," he said, in a much less booming voice.

"I see Ms. Powers at the end of your rather long table. She appears frequently here. Did you bother to consult with her regarding my procedures?" All eyes in the courtroom turned to Ms. Powers. She was an Assistant United States Attorney for the District of Columbia. One of many. She tried mightily, without success, to disappear, by slumping down in her chair. She was only three years out of law school. Embarrassing the assistant attorney general did not bode well for her career.

"No, Your Honor," Hayes replied.

"Well, if you had, she would have told you about Gold's Rules. Ms. Powers would you please enlighten your colleague?"

Powers reluctantly rose from her chair. She looked straight ahead at the judge, not daring to glance at Hayes to her left. Her voice quavered. "Keep it short and sweet. No speeches. Address the court, the jury or the witness, never your opponent. Be on time. Be prepared, especially for the unexpected." She was amazed she remembered them, but she had seen all new lawyers receive the speech from the judge upon their first appearance and inevitable transgression.

"Excellent. Thank you, Ms. Powers. You may be seated."

She turned her attention to Mr. Hayes. "I'll chalk it up to the passion of the moment Mr. Hayes and let you slide on this one. You may represent the United States Government but remember that I represent the people who elected the president who appointed you. I'm here for life; you're just here until the next election. We're going to do things by the book. Got it?"

"Yes, Your Honor. My sincere apologies to the court."

"Duly noted. Ms. Stevens."

Alison and Jack rose. "Alison Stevens and Jack Banner for the defense." Jack was glad that Alison was there. He would probably have made the same mistake as Hayes. Alison remained standing, so Jack followed suit. Suddenly there was a low rumbling, and then the room began to shake, slowly at first and then more vigorously. Alison and Jack gripped the table for support, but then the ground beneath them began to shift.

The bomb had been planted in the basement just beneath the courtroom. It had been designed to focus the force of the blast straight up into the courtroom, in an attempt to limit collateral damage. The man from the hotel was good at his craft and the bomb was behaving as expected. The force of the blast hit the courtroom between the judge's bench and counsels' tables. The explosion sent the floor and other debris straight up until the blast met the ceiling and spread out, throwing debris, flame and smoke in all directions. Jack, Alison and Martinez were lucky on two counts. First, the construction of the building made it impossible to plant the bomb directly beneath them. It had been planted as close as possible to the defense table. Second, the initial force of the blast threw them to the floor and knocked over the table, so it shielded them from the secondary effects of the blast. They were also lucky in that Judge Gold insisted on old antique oak tables in her courtroom. No government issue for her. The sturdy table absorbed the brunt of the blast. They felt the heat of the flames and the force of the blast as the debris hurtled over their heads. The spectators in the gallery were less fortunate. The flames incinerated the ones in the front row. The others behind them were either impaled or crushed by flying debris. Within moments of the initial blast the fire sprinklers went on, briefly dousing the courtroom with water until the explosion ripped open the pipes, causing a deluge of water at the crater in the ceiling formed by the blast. There were screams and shouts of panic and the sound of running feet. And then, within a matter of a minute or two, it was over. It was quiet, except for the moans from the wounded, the falling water from the broken sprinkler pipes and the sound of crackling flames.

Jack and Alison lay dazed next to one and other. They were covered with bits of acoustic tile, plaster, wood and dust. The room was filled with smoke, and Jack could smell a fire burning. He sat up, brushing the debris off his body. He reached over and shook Alison gently. "Are you OK?"

"I think so." She sat up also. "How about you?"

"Fine. Fine. How about Martinez?"

Alison looked over at Martinez. His face and head were badly bloodied. Alison reached over and touched Martinez's chest. She could feel him breathing and his heart was beating. "He's alive."

"We need to get out of here."

"What about Martinez?"

"We can't carry him. Help will be here soon. Whoever started this may be back to finish it, and I don't want to be here when they do."

Jack looked around the courtroom to orient himself. He felt sick to his stomach. Bodies were strewn in the gallery and in the aisle, some dead, some moving. Piles of debris lay throughout the courtroom. To his right, he could see some of the prosecution team gathering themselves. Some had been fortunate because a similar table had protected them. Ms. Powers had not been one of them. She had been seated at the end of the table and the blast had hit her full force. She lay limp on the floor, bloodied, her eyes open and staring vacantly at the ceiling. In front of him was a gaping hole in the floor and in the ceiling above. The judge's bench was no longer there. The fate of Judge Gold was uncertain.

"It looks like we can get out through the main entrance." He stood up and steadied himself. He reached down, grabbed Alison's hand and pulled her up. She reached down and grabbed her purse. They walked gingerly and slowly toward the exit. The visibility was poor due to the smoke and dust, and in spots the falling water from the sprinklers cascaded down on them. As they made their way down the aisle, several court personnel came running toward them. "Are you two OK?" They nodded.

"The people in there need help. We're OK," Jack said. A security officer led them toward the door, as his colleagues raced into the courtroom. As they exited the courtroom they looked back and saw two men tending to Martinez.

Jack and Alison continued to walk out the way they came in. Their pace became steady and firmer and soon they were exiting out the front of the building. Emergency vehicles were quickly arriving on the scene and sirens could be heard in the distance. As they exited the building, Evans came running up to them. "Jesus, what the hell happened in there! Are you OK?"

"Yeah. It was either a gas explosion or a bomb. Which do you think it was?"

"Well, at least you've still got your sense of humor."

"Look, were fine. Martinez is in there. Can you make sure he's OK and stay with him?"

"Sure. Sure. I'll send some of my people back for you. Wait right here."

Evans ran toward the courthouse. Alison and Jack sat down on a ledge of a concrete planter. Alison started to shiver. Jack realized that he was cold too. It couldn't be more than thirty-five degrees outside. They were soaked from the sprinklers and their overcoats were inside. "I'll get us some blankets." He walked toward an ambulance that had pulled up into the circular driveway in front of the courthouse that fronted on Constitution Avenue. A paramedic was in the back pulling out supplies and equipment. He saw Jack. "Are you OK?"

"Yeah, fine. My friend and I just need some blankets."

"Sure. No problem." He handed Jack two heavy blankets. "Are you sure you're OK?"

"Yeah, I'm sure. Thanks for asking and thanks for the blankets." The paramedic smiled and quickly went back about his business, preparing for the casualties to be brought from the ruins. Jack turned and walked toward Alison. As he headed back he looked to his right and did a double-take. Standing off to the side was the man he had seen in the courtroom. The one he could not place. To the casual observer, he appeared to be a rubbernecker slowing down on the highway to see the crash. Jack was more than just a casual observer. He could tell that the man was not just an observer. He was surveying the scene. More significantly, he was looking at Jack, then at the spot where Alison sat, and then back at Jack, calculating the distance between them. Jack started to quicken his pace and then saw a sight that caused him to break into a dead run. He tried to get her attention by waving, but she wasn't looking at him. He wasn't more than a hundred feet from her. He called her name, but the noise of the sirens, the traffic on Constitution Avenue and the general commotion drowned out his voice.

What caused his fear was a small, red dot of light he could see on her chest. He only understood its significance because of a letter his brother had sent him from Vietnam. Tommy didn't often let the war intrude in his letters. He tried to remain upbeat at all times. But the grind of the war must have been too much for him that day, for he had detailed in his letter a night spent talking to a sniper on leave. The sniper had explained, in detail, how he would infiltrate behind enemy lines and wait quietly for hours, hidden in the brush. When the target would appear, he would train a laser on the victim, targeting his rifle with deadly accuracy. He never missed, he said, from over a thousand yards.

Somewhere a sniper had his sights trained on Alison. Jack continued his sprint towards her, wondering whether a similar rifle was trained on his back. He threw the blankets aside. When he was about thirty feet from her, she looked up and saw him. The fear on his face was clear and she looked at him with puzzlement. She stood up and Jack could see the dot adjust with her movements. He waved his hands and screamed at her. "Alison, look out!" is all he could manage. She started to move towards him, looking around and then suddenly down. She saw the dot of light and realized its significance. Her shoulders slumped in resignation. Ten feet away Jack leapt at her, his body hitting her squarely in the chest. He had come at her from her left and the force flung them to the right. He heard a soft, whizzing noise and then the crack of the bullet hitting the bushes and thudding into the ground. And then, quickly thereafter, another bullet hitting the cement sidewalk, sending up a spray of cement shards. He clutched her and rolled over and over, trying to find cover. She was still clutching her purse, which was wedged between them. They were now behind the planter. Jack was gasping for air. He let go of her and they scrambled to their knees behind the planter. The direction of the shots suggested that they were coming from in front of them. To their left and behind them, was the courthouse. There was an open expanse between the planter and the building. Behind them to their right, between the courthouse and the Canadian Embassy, were a courtyard with benches and a set of long, low steps leading to the North. It was one of the many open areas found in Washington, D.C. It had the advantage of having a number of trees and, also, an escape route back up towards Judiciary Square. Jack mentally calculated that if they stayed close to the western edge of the courthouse, it would shield them from the marksmen. This assumed that there was no second gunman. He stole a quick glance over the planter, hoping someone had seen their plight and was racing to their rescue. The commotion of the explosion eliminated all hope of that. The rescue was going on full force with no attention paid to the two uninjured survivors. He ducked down again.

"We can't stay here. We're sitting ducks," Jack said.

"Agreed."

"I think we need to head that way," Jack said, pointing towards the steps behind them. Alison turned to look where Jack was pointing and nodded her head. She was taking deep, slow breaths of air, trying to slow down her adrenaline rush, as she had been trained.

"It looks like it's about fifty feet to the corner of the building. That should be the first spot we run to. Keep low to the ground and run straight. The less time you're exposed the better."

Jack looked at her quizzically. She sounded like it was an everyday experience for her. "Well, in the movie I watched, they kept yelling 'serpentine.' What movies have you been watching?"

"This is no movie. Those guys are serious. We need to be the same." Again Jack was struck by the strange duality of her personality. On the one hand, she had been clearly frightened when she realized, as Jack did, her impending fate. Now she was tough and combat ready. She really was an enigma.

"Alright, whatever you say." He reached out for her hand.

"No. You go first, then I'll follow."

"Are you crazy! Once the guy sees where we're headed, he'll focus on that point. You'll never get across fast enough."

"There's no time to argue. Only you and I and Martinez know the truth. For all we know, he could be dead by now. At least one of us has to stay alive." Jack couldn't argue with her logic.

"You're right. You go first."

"We don't have time for this male chivalry, bullshit." It was the first time he had heard her swear, but he was not going to back down.

"Either you go first or we go together . . . or we sit here. It's up to you." She surveyed his expression for a moment, and realized he would not be deterred.

"Damn it. Alright. I'll go first, but you follow when I'm halfway across. That way there will be two targets and the shooter will have to choose one." Again, Jack couldn't argue with her logic, but the thought of being target practice was unsettling. They turned and faced the corner of the building, staying in a crouch. Alison reached down and removed her heels, tossing them aside, but holding on to her purse. She got into a sprinter's stance and Jack did the same. She rocked back and forth three times and then launched herself towards the building, running in a crouch towards the corner of the courthouse. The trees lacked foliage but the branches were enough to throw off the gunman's sights. Halfway across, a bullet cracked along the pavement, sending up splinters of concrete. Jack momentarily froze, his body ready, but his mind not willing. Then he thought of Alison. Above all he wanted to be with her, to see her again at the corner of that building and thereafter. He leapt from behind the planter, his legs and arms churning, lungs filling with the cold winter air. He imagined he was with Tommy, racing home for dinner. The first one home was the winner. There was no prize but the sheer joy of beating your brother and sharing that moment in time together. He could hear Tommy's voice, "You can do it squirt." A bullet whizzed by his shoulder, thudding into the cold, hard ground. He could see Alison ahead of him. She had almost reached the corner when the uneven payment caught her in an awkward stride. She tumbled forward onto the concrete walkway, rolling head over heels to keep her momentum going forward. Then she righted herself and scrambled forward on all fours, like a crab. Jack's heart rose when she reached safety. Then he was standing beside her. They were both breathing heavily again. They leaned against the wall of the building to catch their breath.

"I guess that was the easy part," Jack gasped. Alison smiled. At least their guess had been right. Based on the bullet marks on the concrete and the one that had passed Jack, the building they were leaning against blocked the shooter's angle.

"You ready?" she asked. Jack nodded. Alison pointed in the direction of the steps. "We need to stay as close to the building as possible, until we reach the top of the stairs, and then we run like hell."

"Sounds like a plan." They had made their way along the building for about fifty feet when they spotted a figure approaching them from the opposite direction. He was dressed in the traditional FBI garb of a trench coat and suit. He was waving at Jack and Alison. When he got within fifteen feet, he shouted, "Mr. Banner. Ms. Stevens. Evans sent me looking for you. He's worried sick about you." As he got within a few feet of them, he displayed an identification card.

"I knew that Evans would come through." Jack stretched out his hand.

"Glad to meet you. I'm agent Johnson. Like the hotel," said the man from the hotel, reaching to shake Jack's hand. In his business, it helped to be able to play many different roles. His shooter had botched the job and now he was going to be the cleaner. It really was hard to find good help.

"What are you all doing back here?" he said to Jack and Alison.

"Someone was trying to kill us. They were shooting at us with a sniper scope!" Jack exclaimed.

"Jesus!" said the man from the hotel, quickly pulling his gun from its holster and ducking low. Jack followed suit, but Alison remained standing. The man from the hotel turned towards Jack and pointed the gun directly at his midsection. It took Jack a moment before he realized what was happening. He looked at the man from the hotel blankly.

"I think you can put your gun away. The building blocks his view."

The man from the hotel did not lower his gun. He walked toward Jack, casting a quick glance towards Alison, who stood motionless. "I'm really sorry about this. You seem like a nice guy. You were just in the wrong place at the wrong time. It's nothing personal. Just business."

Jack started to back up toward the building. He didn't think to run. It would have been futile anyway. The man from the hotel was a dead shot. As Jack backed up, a root from one of the hedges caused him to trip and fall to the ground. The man from the hotel continued moving forward.

Jack looked quickly at Alison for one last time. Then he closed his eyes. He heard a loud retort of the gun. He smelled the gun powder and then waited for the pain. It never came. After a moment, he opened his eyes. The man from the hotel lay at his feet. A pool of blood was growing near his head, as it poured out of his head in spasms with each beat of his heart. Alison stood ten feet away in the traditional firing position, a gun clenched in both hands, feet spread apart. The man from the hotel had made a fatal mistake. He had been angry that the job had been botched and, in his anger, he failed to pay enough attention to the situation. Ordinarily, he never would have let Alison get behind him. He really should have killed her first. But anger had clouded his judgment and cost him his life. Alison lowered the gun and reached down to place it in the purse that now lay at her feet. She closed the distance between them, stepped over the body and reached out her hand to Jack.

"Come with me if you want to live."

Jack was speechless. He was too stunned to do anything. He reached out his hand and she helped him to his feet. They walked briskly but carefully along the edge of the courthouse. At the top of the crest of the hill they were on D Street. The Judiciary Square metro station was two blocks away. They walked past the District of Columbia municipal courthouse and the D.C. police station. They drew strange stares from passers-by—a woman and a man with no overcoats and she with no shoes. Most had seen stranger sites in the nation's capitol, so all they drew were brief glances. They crossed D Street to the metro station entrance. As they rode the escalator down into the underground station, Jack turned to Alison.

"My God! You just killed a man."

Alison said nothing. They reached the bottom of the escalator. The warm air in the heated station felt good. With all the excitement, Jack had forgotten how cold he was. Alison was too preoccupied to notice. They bought their fare cards and went through the turnstile.

"Where are we going?" Jack asked.

"The airport."

"And then?"

"Nowhere."

"What do you mean nowhere?"

"I'll explain later." It was too much for Jack to take. She had just killed a man. She refused to tell him anything, including where they were going. He was about to challenge her when she looked at him with great sincerity. She grasped his hands and looked at him intently.

"I know this is a lot to take, but you've got to trust me."

It was enough for Jack. He remained silent. He did trust her. He didn't know why, but his instincts never failed him. It wasn't blind love. If she wanted to, she could have let him die. She had killed to save him. They rode in silence on the metro. When they reached Metro Center, they got off to switch to the Blue Line, which would take them to National Airport. At each end of the station were large department stores. Given the continued strange glances, Alison suggested a quick stop. They picked out jeans, a long-sleeve shirt, sneakers and a winter coat for Jack, as well as some comfortable hiking boots; and a casual outfit, comfortable shoes and an overcoat for Alison.

They changed into their new clothes. Alison reminded Jack to keep the old ones in the bag. They would dispose of them later. After they changed, they left the metro station and entered a local drug store. Alison bought some black hair-dye and blonde hair-dye for her, two pairs of scissors, and two compact mirrors, as well as sunglasses, a Redskins cap and a scarf. Again she paid cash. Within half an hour, they were back on the metro headed to National Airport. Alison wasn't sure what the plan was going to be. She was improvising. The most important thing was to stay alive until she could make contact with her superiors. The one good thing had been that the assassin she had killed had not recognized her or known of her significance. That meant her cover was still good. It had taken her years to develop her cover. Law school, all those years at the ACLU. Her ability to blend in and appear to be an ordinary lawyer of the left wing was critical to her mission.

The Blue Line dropped them at National Airport. After a short walk from the metro station, they entered the main terminal. Jack followed Alison to the United counter. She bought two tickets to Dallas with a credit card. They went to the Delta, US Air and American counters. Alison bought two tickets to Los Angeles, Pittsburgh and Denver, respectively. She had Jack buy two tickets to London on British Airways. Just in case, Jack used his law firm credit card. No sense getting stuck with the tab.

When they were done, Alison said, "Follow me."

"So which tickets are we going to use? I vote for London. Shoot, I forgot my passport." Alison was relieved to hear his sense of humor again.

It meant he was returning to his normal personality. The first killing you witnessed was the worst. It never got easy, just merely bearable.

"None. Like I said, we're not going anywhere."

She led them to the restrooms. She reached inside her bag and handed Jack the black hair-dye, the scissors and the Redskins cap. "Go in there and get your hair real wet. Give yourself a little trim. Nothing too obvious. Then put the dye in and work it in. Dry your hair as best you can, then put the cap on. I'll meet you out here in ten minutes."

Jack went into the bathroom and looked around. He walked over to the sink and tried to appear nonchalant. A man was washing his hands in the sink next to him. Jack washed his hands slowly, waiting for the man next to him to finish. When he did, Jack quickly ran his wet hands through his hair, rewet them several times, and then ran them through again. He heard the door swing open. He quickly entered one of the stalls and locked it. He took the dye from the package and applied it to his hair. He worked it into the hair, rubbing vigorously, as the directions provided. He removed the mirror and placed it on top of the flat metal surface of the toilet-paper dispenser. He carefully clipped his hair. It evoked memories of the haircuts his mother would give him and Tommy. Never stylish, but never the subject of ridicule. Something must have rubbed off, because he found himself quite adept and quickly trimmed an even inch off his hair. He tried to grab the clippings and place them in the toilet, without complete success. He was also careful to keep all the packaging and to place it back in the bag. He was sure Alison would be proud of his newly found instincts. He placed the cap on his head and exited the stall. He walked over to the sink and, with no one around, quickly lifted his cap to see the results. Not too bad.

Alison was waiting for him in the hallway. The scarf covered her hair, but he could see the fringes of her blonde and much shorter hair. He smiled at her. She smiled back.

"I guess it's a good thing we're not hairdressers," she said.

"Speak for yourself. I think I look downright dashing."

"No time for that now. We need to get moving."

They walked through the airport to the Hertz rental counter. Alison walked up to the counter "Hi. I'd like to rent a car for a week. Do you have any midsize?"

The counter attendant accessed her computer. "Sure do. Is a Ford Taurus OK?"

Alison pulled out a VISA card. As she laid it on the counter for the clerk, Jack noticed the name embossed on the card, Susan Blauser.

"Ms. Blauser, I'll need to see your driver's license, too." Jack froze. Alison didn't miss a beat.

"Sure, no problem." She rummaged through her wallet, pulling out a driver's license with her picture in the name of Susan Blauser. Jack tried to act casual. The clerk quickly processed the charge. She swiped the credit card through the magnetic reader. The machine produced a receipt that the clerk presented to Alison. Alison signed "Susan Blauser." Within forty-five minutes "Ms. Susan Blauser" and her rented Ford Taurus were on the road. They headed up the GW Parkway until they reached Route 66 and headed west, out to Virginia. They stopped for lunch and then a mall to buy more clothes, suitcases and toiletries. This time Alison paid cash. In the mall was a drugstore, where Alison bought more hair dye. They dumped their old clothes in a dumpster behind the mall. They drove for about an hour until they reached a Best Western. They registered as Mr. and Mrs. Blauser. "I always knew I was going to marry you," Jack said.

When they got to the room, Alison suggested they try and rest. It was close to three p.m. and they had been on the go since early in the morning. Jack didn't think he could sleep, but he had to admit that he was tired. He lay down on the bed. When he awoke, it was dark outside. He glanced at his wristwatch: 6:15. Alison had left one lamp on. He rolled off the bed. He could hear the shower running. There was a sink outside adjacent to the bathroom. He washed his face and brushed his teeth. Then he went back to sit on the bed, rubbing his head to clear the cobwebs.

He heard the water go off and, in a minute, Alison came out of the bathroom, a towel wrapped around her torso. She had used more of the hair dye. He was taken aback that her long, brunette hair was now short and blonde. It didn't change how beautiful she was. Jack was sitting on the bed and admired her sensuous figure beneath the towel.

"I preferred you as a brunette, but blonde will do." He rose from the bed and crossed towards her. "By the way, I never thanked you for saving my life." He reached out and placed his arms around her. She didn't resist or protest. "You can tell me what this dark secret is that you're hiding. You said I should trust you. Well you should trust me too."

Alison was torn with emotion. He was a good and decent man and she wanted to be honest with him. She didn't truly know what feelings she had towards him, but when the gun was pointed at him she had feared losing him. She had acted not only out of her duty, but also out of desperation to save him. But what she told him would forever change his feeling towards her. Her life was not just one dark secret, but many. Could he handle the truth? She wasn't sure. But she felt right in his arms and she pulled herself close to him, pressing her head against his chest. Her wet hair dampened his shirt. She looked up at him. "I wish I could Jack. I really do. But I can't. Not right now."

"Alison . . ." He started to protest, but she silenced him, placing her index finger on his mouth.

"Shhh. How about no more talking for now." She stretched her neck up toward his face and he leaned down to meet her. Their lips met and Jack pulled her close to him, his hand moving up to cradle her face as they kissed. He moved one hand back down to caress her back and then gently pulled the towel away, tossing it to the side. He broke the embrace of her lips and moved down to nuzzle her neck. She stepped back from Jack, took him by the hand and led him to the bed. Her naked body was as beautiful as he had imagined. When they reached the bed she slowly unbuttoned his shirt and then kissed his bare chest as she undid his jeans. He stepped out of his jeans and then pulled her to him again. They kissed with a sense of desperation. Two people adrift in a stormy sea, clinging to each other like lifeboats. They fell on the bed, their passion building.

"Alison, I think I love you."

"Shhh. I said no more talking." And talk no more they did.

CHAPTER 34

Agent Evans could feel the perspiration dripping from his underarms. He had been with the FBI for twenty years. In that time, he had faced down criminals and thugs and other assorted malcontents, but he had never been this nervous before. He was standing in front of the director's desk. Jenkins was seated to his left, in a chair brought in especially for the occasion. To his right stood his immediate supervisor, Moss Duncan. This was his first time meeting the director. It was sure to leave a lasting impression in both their minds.

"Agent Evans, was it not my direct order that you guard and protect Mr. Banner and that you know of his whereabouts at all times?"

"Yes, sir."

"And can you tell me where he is now, or the whereabouts of Ms. Stevens?"

"No, sir."

"And why is that, Agent Evans?"

"Well, sir . . ." Evans started to explain, but then he looked at Moss Duncan, whose face had a clear expression of warning. There was no way to explain it. He had messed up and now he had to face the consequences. At least he was a twenty-year man. He had his pension. Maybe he could hook up with some private outfit or a state police force. He wasn't that old. Maybe it was time to move on.

"Well, sir. There really is no explanation other than I failed in my assignment. I could blame the heat of the moment or the confusion. But the bottom line is, I blew it."

The director clearly was not prepared for this, because he stopped his assault and leaned back in his chair. After a few moments, he leaned forward again, looked at Jenkins and then back at Evans.

"I appreciate your candor. I've discussed your prior service record with Jenkins and Duncan. They both speak highly of you. In my mind, that says a lot. I've always believed in giving everyone a second chance. We need someone to help us find Banner. I've read your surveillance reports. You seem to have a good grasp on him as a person, developed a rapport with him. That could be useful. On the other hand, I understand you have twenty years under your belt. If you saw fit, I would approve a voluntary resignation, which would assure full benefits."

The director was throwing him a rope. It was unclear whether it was a lifeline or a noose. If he accepted the offer of resignation he would be comfortable financially, but with his self-esteem and reputation destroyed. If he stayed on, the director was implying that future failure could result in discharge for cause and the potential loss of his financial benefits. He weighed his options. It was his fondness for Jack that tipped the scales. Evans was not an idealist by any means. His tour in Vietnam had convinced him of the folly of acting in response to principles and morals. One man's principles were another man's evil. In his life, he had molded his philosophy around people and relationships, not ideology. He had developed this approach while in Vietnam. At first he had stuck with all the black soldiers in the unit. But then, as time went on and battles were fought, he discovered that all the black soldiers were not his friends, nor did he like all of them. By the same token, not all the white soldiers from Georgia were KKK rednecks. He learned that a person was not a Democrat or a Republican, or white or black, or left wing or right wing. Each person had his own set of beliefs and experiences that shaped who he was. If you labeled people, you often got the wrong label; and prejudging them never got you to find out what was in the package. Jack was one of those people with whom he had developed a bond. He could sense that Jack was a good person. Evans knew he had to do whatever he could to help him.

"Sir, I'd appreciate a second chance."

"Good. From here on in you work with Jenkins directly on this one. All your other assignments are off your desk. I've cleared it with Duncan. It is critical that we find Mr. Banner and Ms. Stevens. Tell me what you know so far."

"Well, we know that Ms. Stevens and Mr. Banner were last seen entering the Judiciary Square metro station about ten to ten-thirty this morning. They purchased some clothes and other items at a department store in Metro Center. We know that both Ms. Stevens and Mr. Banner purchased airline tickets at National Airport. We had agents check all the flights, and Interpol checked the flight into London. They were not on any of the flights for which they bought tickets. After that, the trail runs cold. Other than the ticket agents at National, no one else at National recalls seeing them. We're still canvassing the airport and the area around Metro Center with their pictures, and we're hoping to get lucky."

"What about the dead guy outside the courtroom?"

Jenkins interceded, "Forensics says one single shot to the head, 9mm. Assuming it was Banner or the lady lawyer, they were a crack shot. Time of death within an hour of the bombing. The gun he was carrying is untraceable. We ran his fingerprints through the computer and got nothing. Then we send it up to the boys at Langley. They tell us they can't tell us who he is. Not that they don't know. The information requires the highest security clearance. It requires an executive order or court order to release the information. That means only one thing."

"Rogue agent," said the director.

"Exactly," said Jenkins. Duncan and Evans nodded in agreement. Like any organization, the CIA had its share of bad apples. With the CIA, a disgruntled employee was more dangerous than an ex-postal worker. CIA rogue agents didn't act out of anger or revenge but out of pure greed. Expertly trained in espionage, their services fetched a high price. The CIA kept tabs on all agents whom they suspected had left the agency to branch out on their own. To avoid embarrassment to the agency and to the current administration in power, the list was a closely held secret.

"I'll be meeting with the president. I'll ask him for the executive order. In the meantime, let's circulate his picture to all field offices on the chance that someone has run across our Mr. X. Anything else?"

"Yes," responded Jenkins. "We found a number of slugs from a high-powered rifle near the spot where Mr. X—I guess we are calling him—was found. From what we can tell from the trajectory and the location of the surrounding buildings, it had to come from the roof of the National Gallery. We've canvassed the roof, but have found no shell casings or other evidence of a shooter."

"What's your conclusion?"

"It's a little early to say, but my guess is someone took a few shots at Banner and Stevens and missed. They made a run for it and ran up against Mr. X and somehow laid him to rest. Frankly, I find that hard to believe. I mean, an ex-agent being taken out by a couple of lawyers. They may talk you to death and bury you in paper, but marksmanship tends not to be their specialty."

They all smiled. The director interrupted, "That's a good point, Ed. We don't really know if Banner or Ms. Stevens killed him. In fact, we don't know if some other party or person was there when the shooting occurred. Let's keep all our options open."

He turned to Duncan. Evans was sweating a little less profusely, grateful that the conversation had turned to other topics. "How's Martinez?"

"They think he will be OK. He has some pretty nasty head wounds and he's still unconscious. The doctors think he'll be fine after a few days of recovery."

The director stood up from his chair and started to pace behind his desk. "This is absolutely insane. First, an assassination of our future president, and then a bombing of a courthouse in an attempt to kill the assassin before he can implicate others. I'm not going to stand for this, gentlemen. We have our work cut out for us. Let's get cracking."

"Yes, sir," they said in unison. Jenkins rose from his chair to escort Evans and Duncan out. He turned to the director. "You need me, boss? I've got to go check on Martinez's security arrangements."

"No, Ed. I'm OK. Inspector Duncan, Agent Moss, thanks for your time."

They nodded and departed with Jenkins, closing the double doors behind them. After they left, the director sat down behind his desk. He picked up the phone and dialed a number. After a few rings the call was answered.

"It's I," said the director and then listened.

"No, we don't know where they are. They're on the run."

He paused again to field a question.

"I understand your concern. I agree. If we don't find them first, the whole lid is going to blow off the can. We need to call a meeting. I'll arrange it with the others. Be ready."

The director hung up the phone and then began to dial the "others." It would take a day or two for them to assemble from around the country. He hoped they had that much time.

CHAPTER 35

Alison and Jack lay entwined in the bed. He was asleep again. She was awake. Listening to his breathing. They had made love once more. He had said he was hungry before he had fallen asleep. Alison had promised to get some food. She gently disentangled herself from him and slipped out of the bed. She dressed quietly, grabbed the room key, the car key and her purse. As she opened the door, Jack stirred slightly. "Where you going?" he mumbled.

"To get some food. Remember you were hungry?"

He mumbled something and went back to sleep. She pulled the door shut and headed out to the rental car. She recalled they had passed a Chinese restaurant a few miles before the hotel. She turned over the ignition and pulled the car out of the motel parking lot and into the traffic. About a mile away, she saw a gas station and pulled in. She drove in past the pumps and around to the pay phone in the back. Before she turned off the ignition she checked the gas gauge. Half full. She would have to remember to fill up later.

She pulled out her Susan Blauser credit card and placed a call. A familiar voice picked up the phone. "I've been waiting for your call."

"I know. Things got a little out of control. I think we should abort the mission. The plan is no longer viable."

"Is he with you?"

"Yes."

"Where are you?"

"I'd rather not say."

There was silence on the other end. Her answer was clear insubordination. "We can easily find you by tracing the calling card call."

"True. I thought of that. But it's a pay phone. We'll be miles away by the time you get here."

Again there was silence. "What do you propose?"

"I have a plan. Let me handle it my way."

"You were always good at improvisation. Fine. But no loose ends. That includes Mr. Banner. Understood?"

"Completely. By the way, did I get confirmation of the renewal of my insurance policy?"

This time Alison could sense a stony silence. The voice on the other end understood her message. "No. But I'm sure in the event of your untimely demise, the appropriate beneficiaries would be notified?"

"That's what the policy provides. In fact I recently updated it and put it in a safe place. I'm pretty sure they got my last payment, but just checking."

"Not to worry. I'll keep an eye out for it, but I'm sure nothing is going to happen to you in the near future."

"One can only hope. I'll check in soon." She hung up the receiver, her hands shaking. She got back into the car and started to drive back to the hotel. Her calm quickly returned. In all her years, she had never questioned those above her. She had blindly followed their commands and orders. She had also taken a lesson from Ben. Obey, but trust no one. Always be prepared for the day when you needed to protect yourself. Over the years, she had collected information about her activities and those who directed them. The philosophy they followed was based on good intention, but she had also been taught that all men could be corrupted. Now she faced a situation where, for the first time, she would not do as she was told. What would the result be? It should be that her judgment would be trusted. Her long service entitled her to no less. But in this battle, all were expendable and should those above her decide it was so, she needed the ultimate protection. The knowledge she had was power. It was stored in a safe place. In fact several. With letters to different people she could trust, to be opened only in the event of her death and instructing them where the information was hidden. It wasn't foolproof. The recipients of the letters might not follow her instructions out of fear, or simple laziness. Once they had the information, the stakes became even greater. The danger increased and many she had chosen would balk, and the letters would be destroyed once they were received. But she hoped that at least one would do as she asked. All she really needed was the threat. Even the slightest possibility of exposure was taken seriously. She had bought some time. Not much. As event unfolded, others would have to act. It was what was required and she understood that.

She pulled into the strip mall where she had seen the Chinese takeout place. She parked the car and walked into the restaurant. It had a pleasant smell. It was reasonably crowded given the hour. A good sign. Alison scanned the menu. She realized that she hadn't asked Jack what he liked. She would have to guess. It was like the dating game. "Your mate's favorite Chinese dish is?" She smiled to herself. She placed her order and took a seat in one of the red plastic chairs lining the wall. The restaurant was overheated. She shed her coat, draping it over her lap.

Her mind turned back to the hotel. From the moment she had met Jack she had tried to keep her distance. He was relentless in his pursuit of her. Her initial reaction of annoyance was genuine. She had worked too hard over the years to establish herself in her profession. Both of them actually. To be patronized by some male chauvinist pig was galling. As she spent more time with him, she realized he was not at all like that. He was flippant, but not callous. He was intelligent, hardworking by all measurement and truly caring about his work. She also had to admit that he was extremely handsome, and the physical attraction was intense. Her need for him in the hotel was not just because of the situation. The circumstances allowed her to surrender to her true emotions. The risks she was taking were immense. She had done it for only one reason. Jack. If others had had their way, he would be dead and the operation terminated. She had put herself in the firing line for him. Alison had never done that before for anyone, let alone a man.

The hostess called her name, interrupting her thoughts. She paid for the food and walked back out to the car. By instinct she scanned the immediate vicinity for anything that looked out of place. She had developed a sixth sense over the years. Her antenna did not reveal any cause for concern. She got in the car and started the ignition. The rumble of the engine had a strange effect on her. It triggered in her a memory of another time and another place, and then all the memories of her secret life flooded back to her. Strange places, dark places, death and destruction, ostensibly in the name of good. In the past, her passion for her cause had overcome all doubts and filled her with energy and fire. Now the memories made her feel tired, alone, and sad. It was time for it to end. She had had enough. She placed the car in gear, resolute in her conviction. She would find a way out of this mess and then she would build a new life. She hoped it would be with Jack. But no matter what, there was no going back. Of that she was sure.

CHAPTER 36

Derek Holden was an expert in forensics. He had a Ph.D. in physics and chemistry. He could have been a professor at any college or university in the world. Ever since he had been a little boy, explosions had fascinated him. It had started with caps, continued with fireworks and finally, when he was old enough to buy them, explosives. Fortunately for civilized society, he was a well-grounded and completely sane person, and had decided to make good use of his skills. This was especially so given that his senior thesis had been the construction of a nuclear device, albeit absent uranium. Not that he could not have obtained some. He enjoyed his profession and valued his freedom too much to take that kind of risk.

His life's work had led him to the FBI. He was now the chief forensic scientist for the FBI, specializing in the area of explosives and munitions. Through a combination of science, art and instinct, he could reconstruct almost any explosion. Determining where the bomb was placed, what it was made of, how big it was, and, most important, who made it. The latter was the result of years of building a database of all known explosions of suspicious origin investigated by police and intelligence agencies around the world. Holden, with the help of his assistants, had catalogued them on a computer. Each bomb had its own signature. Bombers liked certain packaging or materials or placed the bombs in certain ways. Sometimes it was pure laziness or obsessive habit rather than ingenious bomb making. By entering information about the bomb into the computer, a map could be generated with the location and description of all similar bombings.

It was a foregone conclusion that Holden would be the one to investigate the bombing at the Kennedy Center. Other agents under his supervision had been sent to the other sites that had been bombed by the Front. Unfortunately, he had fewer assistants then there were bomb sites, and so the progress would be ongoing for many weeks. Preliminary reports had revealed that all the bombs were made from C-4, a plastic explosive, popular due to the bang for the buck. Each batch of C-4 had its own chemical signature. The signature of this C-4 showed that it was from a batch that had been stolen from an army base over three years ago. That didn't help much. Stolen was how the army described any missing weapons or munitions. Often that meant that some soldier had found a way to supplement his meager pay. It was a serious problem, one that Holden never understood. Didn't the idiots consider that some day they might be the targets of the same explosives they were hustling out the back door? Maybe that's why they were taking orders instead of giving them.

One of the unusual aspects had been the timing devices. Actually, pieces of them. They were quite sophisticated. C-4 was rather simple to blow up. That was its beauty. It was highly stable and could be shaped and packaged. It was also reasonably easy to ignite. A simple timer would do, attached to a small charge. The timer completed the circuit, igniting the charge and then the C-4. In this case, the bomber or bombers had gone for what seemed like overkill. Holden could only surmise that it was the need for precise timing. The bombs had all exploded within seconds of each other across the country. This was a clue in and of itself, but one for which Holden could not yet assign significance.

The job now before him lay sprawled at his feet. The wreckage of the limousines from the Kennedy Center explosion had been brought to a warehouse just outside of Washington. The wreckage had been arrayed as it had lain in the wake of the explosion. First there was the president's limousine. It had been relatively unscathed. The back window had been blown out. The force of the explosion had hurled debris into the passenger compartment and tossed the occupants of the limousine violently about. That was what had caused the president's injuries. The next vehicle was the president-elect's limousine. Not much of it was left. The various parts that had been scattered by the explosion were also spread about the warehouse. They were being identified and catalogued by other staff members. Finally, there was the Secret Service van that had followed behind the second limousine. It had also suffered major damage. This fact alone led to the immediate conclusion that the force of the blast had been toward the back of the president-elect's limousine. Perhaps right under the back seat.

Holden walked toward the second limousine. It was a twisted hulk. The explosion had originated under the street, beneath a manhole cover. Pictures of the gaping hole were arrayed on a bulletin board to his left. All the windows had been blown out. The roof had been torn off. The doors had been ripped off and the frame was mangled and charred by the flames from the explosives. The upholstery had been vaporized by the blast. *To think this was an armored limousine.* The panel between the front and back seats of the limousine no longer existed. It was now just a shell of the vehicle. Still, the shell and the parts scattered about the warehouse told a story. The chapters about the story of the bomb were unclear as of yet, but Holden would write them, of that he was sure. Despite the macabre scene, he felt the thrill he always felt from the power of destruction.

Something had bothered him right from the start. He had examined the pictures of the bodies of the president-elect and his wife. It was unpleasant, but necessary to his job. There wasn't much left of them, but he did notice that the front part of their bodies had suffered significant trauma but the backside had not. This was inconsistent with an explosion ripping up from the pavement and through the bottom of the limousine.

The crime scene investigation revealed traces of gravel and other debris in the limousine and imbedded in the bodies. It also didn't make sense to him that the van behind the president-elect's had been so seriously damaged whereas the president's limousine in front had suffered significantly less damage. His assistant, Susan Powers, had attributed this to the fact that the van was behind and moving toward the limousine, and the president's limousine was moving away; and also that the explosion had occurred toward the back of the limousine. However, analysis of the video showed that all the cars were moving at the same speed and each was equidistant from the other. Any moment he was expecting additional video to see exactly where the explosion was in relation to the limousine's body.

He walked closer to the limousine. He looked through the frame of what had been the back window and down toward the floor. There was a clear outline of a hole where the bomb had exploded through the underside of the car. The jagged edges of the metal were thrust upward and there were scorch marks on the underside of the metal. The hole was, in fact, located toward the back of the vehicle. Maybe Powers was right. He turned to walk away. And then he saw something out of the corner of his eye. He might have missed it had it not been for the bright spotlights bathing the scene. It was a glint toward the back of the vehicle. It was similar to sun reflecting off a metal watchband. He carefully stepped into the interior of the vehicle's shell. The object was imbedded in the frame between the interior of the car and the trunk. Only the fact that the limousine was armored had allowed that part of the steel frame to be intact. He leaned over and stretched toward the trunk, pulling a flashlight from his pocket and shining it on the object. He knew right away what it was; and then it clicked and all the pieces fell together. He knew he would figure it out. It was just a matter of time.

"Powers!" he yelled. "Call the director. Tell him I've got something he's going to want to see."

CHAPTER 37

The director had gotten there as fast as he could. If it had been anyone else but Holden, he would have minimized the urgency of the call. Holden was the best and the director knew it. They had reached him at home after eleven. He had immediately called Jenkins. By the time they had linked up and made it out to the warehouse, it was close to midnight. They were seated in two folding chairs inside the warehouse. Holden had placed a projection screen and bulletin boards in front of them. His assistant Powers was there. Other than the four of them, the warehouse was empty. This gave it an eerie feeling, with the destroyed vehicles arrayed just to the right of where they sat.

Holden was standing just in front of the bulletin board, a white projection screen, a large flatscreen TV and DVD player. "It's really rather obvious and I feel pretty dumb not having seen it right away. Unfortunately, the conclusion was too difficult for me to absorb, so I think, subconsciously, I ignored it."

"Enough with the psychobabble; let's get to the reason you called us out here in the middle of the night," Jenkins said. He and Holden had always had an antagonistic relationship. The late hour only made it worse.

"The reason I called you out here is this." He reached in his pocket and took out a plastic evidence bag. Inside was a misshapen piece of gold-colored metal. He handed it to the director.

"What's this?"

"What does it look like?"

The director turned over the bag in his hands, examining it more carefully. It had the heft and look of real gold. On one side he thought he could make out the shape of an eagle and some olive branches. He looked up at Holden knowingly and Holden nodded slightly. He turned to Jenkins. "This is a presidential tie clip. It has the presidential seal on it." He passed it to Jenkins.

"Correct," said Holden. He was enjoying himself immensely, letting the pieces of the puzzle out one at a time. How long would it take them to put the pieces together?

"Where did this come from?" Jenkins asked."

"I found it in the wreckage of the president-elect's limousine. Lodged in the rear frame, near the trunk."

"Is it genuine?" asked the director.

"Yes, it is. Only 100 of those are in existence. Each bears a special imprint to note its authenticity that can only be seen with powerful magnification. I put that under the electron microscope and found the imprint. The president only gives them out to VIPs and especially close friends," explained Holden.

"Who was wearing this one?" Jenkins asked.

Holden didn't answer. Instead, he pointed to Powers at the back of the room. She dimmed the lights. Holden stepped toward the DVD and pushed the play button. On the projection screen appeared the images of the president and the president-elect standing in front of the Kennedy Center, chatting amiably. The president-elect was facing toward the camera as it did a slow zoom. When his upper torso was centered in the frame, Holden froze the picture. "Now the next image you're going to see is the frame magnified with fractal software to reduce pixilation. That means graininess, to those of you at home." He smiled at his joke. No one else did. He pointed to Powers, who turned on a second projector. The image appeared on the screen.

"What do you see?" asked Holden.

"A striped tie, no tie clip," said the director.

"Correct. Next image." The picture flashed on the screen. It showed the two Secret Service agents entering the limousine. "The next image is this one enlarged." He motioned to Powers and she projected the next picture. Before Holden could ask the question, Jenkins interjected.

"I think we get your point, no tie clip on either one."

"Correct again."

The director and Jenkins were beginning to see where this demonstration was going. Holden hit the play button. It showed the president-elect and his wife bidding the president goodbye. The president-elect's wife entered the car. The two men and the president's wife continued to chat, until an aide whispered in the president's ear. The two men shook hands. The president proceeded towards his limousine. The president-elect entered the car, followed by the two Secret Service agents. Holden stopped the video.

"We get the point," Jenkins said. "But what does it prove? That tie clip could have been in there for weeks or months or even years."

"I thought the same thing. Only one problem. Actually, three problems. I removed some tissue and blood from the tie clip. Blood type O positive. Same as the president-elect's. My guess is the genetic testing will show a match. Second, notice the shape of the tie clip. It's smashed at one end. The way I found it suggests that it was a projectile passing back to front, through the president-elect's body and then lodging in the rear frame. Mere luck that anything stopped it and it wasn't hurled out the back. Third problem, and biggest from a statistical point of view. I checked the history on the limousine. It was just put into service two weeks ago."

Jenkins and the director were silent, as the conclusion became apparent.

"An inside job," said the director mournfully.

"It certainly would seem so. If you need further proof, come look at this." Holden gestured toward a bulletin board to his left. The director and Jenkins got up from their seats and walked up to the bulletin board. A series of photos was displayed. The first was a shot of the hole in the pavement, from the explosion. The rest were various photos of the wrecked limousine. Holden picked up a large pointer and directed it at the first photo.

"The first photo shows the explosion that originated under the pavement. Note the diameter of the hole. Not as large as one would expect from an explosion of this magnitude. Now look at this second photo. It's a close-up of the floor of the limo. What do you see?"

"A hole, showing the force of the explosion. Shards of metal twisted upward, away from the origin of the explosion," Jenkins said, clearly losing his patience.

"Look closer. Don't see what you expect to see; see what is there."

Jenkins looked carefully, as did the director. They both shook their heads, not able to decipher Holden's clues. "What if I told you this photo was taken from the underside of the limo."

"That's impossible. The force of the explosion would have been up, not down."

"The first explosion *was* from the bottom."

"The *first* explosion?"

"Yes, the first explosion. Watch this." He motioned to Powers. She dimmed the lights again and started the DVD. "This is a super-slow-motion video of the explosion. The car pulls away from the curb. Then, boom! The first explosion from underneath the car and then—almost at the same time—a second explosion, from inside the vehicle. Watch the back of the vehicle."

Jenkins and the director sat transfixed. The car almost didn't move, the video was so slow, but it was clear to the naked eye. First, a plume of smoke and fire and debris spewing upward. Then, almost simultaneously, a larger explosion moving laterally. They could see glass and metal, fire and smoke being hurtled out of the back of the limousine.

Holden continued, "My guess is that they hoped to make them go off at the same time. Then it would have been less obvious. Remember a few years back, Hurricane Andrew? They suspected that the most severe damage was caused by tornadoes but they could never prove it. The destructive pattern distinctive of a tornado was obliterated when the hurricane blew through, right after. That's what they hoped would happen here. The two explosions would mix together and the evidence of the second explosion would not be apparent."

"Who else knows about this?" asked the director.

"Just me, Powers, you and Jenkins," answered Holden.

"Good, let's keep it that way." He looked first at Holden and then at Powers, the intensity of his stare showing his resolve. They each nodded their assent. He didn't need to look at Jenkins. He turned back to Holden.

"I want the full report ASAP, but for my eyes only."

"Yes, sir."

The director and Jenkins headed towards the door. Holden fell in step next to them. Powers remained behind. "Sir, there's one thing more." The three men stopped and formed an impromptu circle. Holden glanced over his shoulder. Powers was busily engaged in taking down the displays and rewinding the video. Holden dropped his voice to a whisper. "I thought the fewer people who know this the better."

The director instinctively lowered his voice as well. "Yes, what is it?"

"There was an inscription on the tie clasp. Unfortunately, a good part of it was obliterated. I haven't had a chance to get it under our most powerful electron scope. So far all I can make out is "Thanks," and then later on a letter "P."

"Let us know as soon as you know more." The director said.

"I will."

He turned to Jenkins as they walked out. "I suspected this was an inside job, but not that much inside. I had better go see the president again."

Jenkins nodded, a look of concern on his face. "This could get really out of control."

"Well, it's our job to see it doesn't."

CHAPTER 38

The Chinese food was surprisingly good. Alison had guessed right about what Jack would like: vegetable moo shoo, steamed dumplings and white, not fried, rice. They were both hungry after the day's events and most of the food was quickly eaten.

"Now what?" asked Alison.

"Dessert," Jack said. "I have something tasty in mind." He reached out for her, but she pulled away playfully.

"You have a one-track mind. Besides, that's not what I meant. We need a plan. An objective and a method to reach it."

"Agreed. The goal is simple. Figure out who is behind this whole mess. How we do that is a little more complicated."

Alison stood up and started to pace the room. "Well, we can make an assumption that whoever did it figures we know something. They weren't content to just kill Martinez. They were after us too."

"But we don't really know anything, except for what Martinez told us."

"True, but let's consider what he told us. " Alison walked over to the nightstand and picked up a pad of paper. "You have a pen?"

"Afraid not."

Alison grabbed her purse and rummaged through it, finally coming up with a pen.

"What exactly do you women carry in your purse? I mean us men manage to get through life with just a wallet."

"Yeah, but you're always asking us for things you don't have, like pens."

"Point well taken."

Alison sat on the edge of the bed. Jack was sprawled out, resting his head on the pillows at the head of the bed. Alison continued.

"First, we list what we know for sure. Then we list what we can assume. From that, we figure out what we need to find out and how."

"OK, I'm game. First, we know someone killed the president-elect and that someone was the Front."

"Yes and no," interjected Alison. "According to Martinez, the Front was co-opted by some outside force, most likely some element within the United States Government."

"Exactly."

"So now all we know is that someone killed the president-elect." Jack swung his legs off the bed and sat up next to Alison. "Not to be a pessimist, but I don't see how this is going to get us very far. We don't know shit. And even if we did, what can we do about it? Whoever did kill the president-elect is now after us. If what we think is true, then the full weight of some element or elements of the United States Government is against us. I don't particularly like those odds."

Alison turned to face Jack. She looked deep into his eyes. There was no fear in them. That was good. He looked confident but perplexed. He was not experienced in these kinds of things, and unfamiliarity bred confusion.

"Well," she said, "we need to improve the odds in our favor. Any ideas?"

Now it was Jack's turn to pace. He got off the bed. She in turn slung her feet up on the bed and reclined. There was silence as he paced the room. In his mind, he began to recount the events of the past few days. It was close to a week now. The call had been on Saturday morning. Tomorrow was Thursday. His once sedate life had been turned upside down. He had met the director of the FBI, been in a jail cell for the first time in his life, held a press conference, survived an explosion, been shot at and fallen in love. The last one made him smile, and he turned to look at Alison. She smiled back, still waiting for his response to her question. He stopped and looked at her.

"OK, I think I have an idea, but to get it done you're going to have to level with me."

"What do you mean, level with you?"

Jack came back and sat down next to her. "Look, Alison. I'm no idiot, OK? The things you did back at the courthouse and at the train station are not the kinds of things that you learn in law school. You have a past that we both know you are hiding from me. I need to know the truth."

"Jack, I . . . I . . . I just can't." She looked down and started doodling on her pad. "I wish I could, but the less you know the better." Jack reached over to her and put his hand on her chin. He lifted her face towards him and looked into her eyes.

"It won't matter to me Alison. No matter what you say, I'll still love you."

She pulled away from him and stood up quickly, throwing the pad and the pencil on the bed violently. "Love!" she shouted so loudly that Jack flinched. "What do you know about love? Love isn't some quick roll in the hay and a moonlit carriage ride. Love is giving part of yourself to someone unconditionally, not knowing if you'll ever get anything back. Love is sacrifice and pain and, in the end, love is never happiness. So if it's love you want, get it from someone else." Then she began to cry. The tears ran down her cheeks. She tried to wipe them with her hands but the tears soon became sobs, wracking her body. Alison wrapped her arms around her midsection and then collapsed to the floor.

Jack was too stunned to move. He was overwhelmed by her emotion. He was also deeply affected. The words she had spoken echoed his own feelings. Since that day when the chaplain had arrived at the door, Jack had never allowed himself to love anyone, to give himself to anyone. The risk of the pain and the loss was too great. That had changed the first day he saw Alison. The way the sun shone off her hair, the life in her eyes, the spirit in her voice. All the walls around his soul had tumbled and he had felt free for the first time in a long time. The feeling intensified whenever he was with her.

He lowered himself to the floor, sitting next to her, and pulled her towards him. She was still sobbing and resisted his embrace for a moment, but then relented. Jack held her tightly, trying to vanquish her pain. "Shhh. Shhh. It's alright." He brushed the hair from her eyes. Then he wiped the tears from her cheek.

"It's . . . not . . . alright," she gasped in-between sobs.

"Alison, I have something to say, and I want you to listen, OK?"

She nodded.

"I know that there must have been something in your life, in your past, that caused you great pain. I know there was in mine. I lost someone I loved very much. He meant the world to me. And when he died, part of me died. I spent a long time trying to get back that part of me, or maybe I was trying to kill off the rest of me, so it wouldn't hurt so badly. Did you lose someone you loved?"

"Yes, very much." She was becoming more composed now.

"I suppose you never really get over it, but you do learn to live with it. Life is a strange journey. Do you believe in God?"

She looked up at him. "I'm not sure. I've seen so many evil things, it's . . . it's . . ." She started to cry again. Jack pulled her close.

"I got a visit from my brother once. I think God sent him. I was really wasted in college one night, actually every night. My brother came down from Heaven, sat next to me, and told me that it wasn't my fault that he had died. He told me it was time to get my life in shape. I did, at least on the outside. But inside I've always felt incomplete, until now. So I don't care what you've done, or who you loved, or even why you were sent to meet me that day. It doesn't matter. I love you and I will always love you no matter what. And if I die tonight, or tomorrow, or next week, my life will have been complete."

Alison had stopped crying. There was silence as Jack's words hung in the air.

"Jack, I've killed people," she said softly.

"I know, but you did it to save me. I understand."

"No, you don't understand." She straightened herself and moved away from him. They were sitting about a foot apart on the floor. "Before today, I've killed people. It was part of my job."

Jack looked at her blankly, absorbing the impact of her words.

"They were all evil people. At least that's what I was told. And I truly believed that was the case. I always thought that made it acceptable. But I bet someone loved them. Didn't they? Everybody is loved by someone. So the way I felt when I lost the one I loved and the way you felt when your brother was killed, did someone feel that way about the people I killed? Did they have kids, husbands, wives?"

She paused. "Actually, that's a lie, they weren't all evil. Some just were in the wrong place at the wrong time. So now I question everything I have done and everything I have lived for. My whole life has been a lie."

Now Jack was looking down. His mind was swirling in confusion. Alison reached out with both hands and placed one on each side of his face. He turned towards her.

"My orders were to kill you if that was necessary. Now, do you still love me?" She said it in a low voice, but filled with venom. Alison rose from the floor and crossed over to the window. There was a small crack between the curtains and she stared out into the dark. Silence hung in the air. Alison felt almost relieved that she had finally been able to unburden part of her soul. Now she was afraid of the consequences. She had not wanted to tell Jack, but something inside her had forced it out, willed her to reveal herself to him. In the parking lot she could see a family unloading their car. The father was carrying a little girl, who was fast asleep. The mother guided a boy, maybe nine, towards the room. He was bleary eyed. It was dark and late, but the children were at peace in the security of their parents' watchful eyes. Would she ever hold a child like that? Would she ever feel security like that?

Alison felt Jack coming up behind her. In these few minutes, Jack had processed his life and what Alison had told him. For too long he had been cautious and alone. He knew he could not go on without her. He placed his arms around her and pulled her toward him. He too focused on the family making their way across the parking lot.

"That could be us some day," he whispered. "But if we want to get there, we have to trust each other."

Alison turned to face him. Her eyes were still wet from the tears. "I do trust you, Jack. It's me I don't trust."

"I trust you Alison, with my life. Now I want you to tell me the whole story, from start to finish."

"I can't do that Jack, I really can't, but I know some people who can—and will." She crossed over to the phone and picked it up. "Start packing. After this call they will know where we are. It's time to move." Jack started quickly throwing what limited belongings they had together as Alison dialed. He listened intently as he packed.

"It's me again. I'm sure you're having a meeting soon. I need to be there with my friend."

She listened for a moment. "He has a right to know. He's willing to put his life on the line. You at least owe him an explanation."

Again, she listened. "Fine, we'll be there."

She hung up the phone. She looked at Jack. "Tomorrow at midnight you'll find out everything you need to know. I hope you're right about this, Jack, because after tomorrow night there is no turning back, no way out, except to finish it. Do you understand what I'm saying?"

"Yes, I do."

She walked over to him and grasped his hands in hers. "Don't do this for me, Jack, or for love. Do it because it's the right thing and because you want to."

Jack squeezed her hands and pulled her toward him, kissing her gently on the forehead. "Doing it for you, and for love, is the right thing. Now let's get out of here."

Within ten minutes they were on the road in search of a room for the night.

CHAPTER 39

Detectives Hernandez and Pettit were earning their living this week. Two nights, two murders. Not necessarily unusual in their line of work. Tonight it was a young, white female. Jane Doe. No ID. Nude, found floating in the C & O Canal in Georgetown. It would have passed for another routine homicide, were it not for an alert patrolman looking to earn his gold detective's shield. Having been a former military man himself, he immediately noticed the victim's strong build and military-style haircut. Even after having floated in the water for many hours, she looked the military part. The patrolman had also read the morning bulletins to report any suspicious murders or other criminal activity. He had called the watch sergeant, who had called the captain, who had called Hernandez and Pettit, rousing them from their warm beds and into the cold night.

By the time the detectives arrived, the coroner and the cops on the beat had fished the body out from the canal and placed it in a body bag. The area was cordoned off. A search for evidence was underway.

Hernandez walked up to the rear of the coroner's van. The body bag was on a gurney, waiting to be loaded in the van. "Any guess on time of death?" he asked the coroner's assistant.

"Hard to say. Cold water makes it difficult. My guess is twenty-four hours, give or take."

Hernandez motioned to the body bag. "Mind if I take a look?"

"Be my guest." He stepped aside and Hernandez walked over to the body bag and zipped it open. No matter how many times he did it, the sound of the zipper always gave him a chill. The woman's face stared up at him, the illumination of his flashlight adding an even more ghostly quality. She was young, no more than thirty, with short, blonde hair and lifeless, vacant eyes. The spark of life extinguished. That was another thing that always got him, how lifeless the eyes were. The eyes truly were the windows to the soul. The coroner's assistant had moved along beside him.

"Single shot to the left temple. Looks like a 9mm. As you can see, not much bruising around the entry wound. They probably put her in the water right away. Kept down the swelling and the bruising."

"Any sign of sexual assault or a struggle?" asked Hernandez.

"No on the first. Yes on the second. She put up quite a fight, from what I could tell from the other bruises on her hands and arms. Again, not much swelling due to the ice water but still noticeable."

"How would you describe her physical condition?"

"Excellent. She worked out regularly. Weights, aerobic conditioning. Almost no body fat to speak of."

"Consistent with military training?"

"Most definitely."

Hernandez zipped up the bag. "Thanks for the info. Let me know as soon as you have the full autopsy report."

"No problem, detective. "

Hernandez turned and walked toward the canal. Pettit was talking to the eager patrolman who had roused them from sound sleep. He joined them and Pettit introduced him.

"Nolan. This is my partner, Hernandez."

"Good to meet you, sir. Patrolman Nolan extended his hand and Hernandez gave it a perfunctory shake.

"Tell us how you found the body."

"Well, sir, I usually make my rounds down here between midnight and two a.m. A lot of homeless hang out down here, especially under that bridge over there." He pointed over his shoulder to a bridge spanning the canal and supporting the road running perpendicular to the canal. There's been quite a bit of drug activity down here lately. A few of the homeless got roughed up. So I've made it a point to make sure there's no trouble down here."

He paused, expecting Hernandez and Pettit to commend him on his altruistic behavior. He received none and continued on. "When I got down here, first I checked under the bridge and it was all quiet. Just Ozzie hanging out by the fire and one other guy sleeping under there. Then I walked down along the canal. That's when I saw the body."

"Did Ozzie or the other guy see anything?" Pettit asked, his voice adding sarcasm to the name "Ozzie."

"Haven't asked him," answered Nolan, being sure to refer to Ozzie as him. Detectives could sure be a pain in the ass. "I figured that was your job."

Pettit ignored the barb. "Thank you, patrolman. Be sure to file your report."

Nolan took this as his cue to leave. He was glad to be out of there, anyway. His shift was over and finding the body had given him the creeps. Pettit and Hernandez watched him climb the bank of the canal.

"Well, Pettit, did you enjoy abusing that young patrolman?"

"Most definitely. Should we go find Ozzie?"

They walked along the canal toward the bridge overpass. A couple of patrolmen were keeping an eye on Ozzie and his companion. As Pettit and Hernandez got closer, an unpleasant odor wafted out from under the bridge. It was a mixture of human sweat, urine and feces. The homeless men had erected a small cardboard and wooden shelter under the bridge to ward off what cold they could. The city had shelters, but many felt safer on the street. There were cans and bottles and other litter strewn about. Ozzie was standing under the bridge in a too-small overcoat and too-long pants. He was clapping his hands and bouncing from foot to foot to stay warm. The elements and the abuse of his body had taken their toll. He was probably thirty-five but looked fifty. Pettit and Hernandez walked up to him.

"Are you Ozzie?"

"Maybe." The smell of alcohol was strong on his breath.

"Well, assuming you are, did you see anything unusual here last night or tonight?" asked Hernandez.

"I didn't see nothing. I mind my own business."

Pettit stepped a little closer. "Maybe a night in jail will refresh your memory."

"Jail would be good. Warm, free food." Ozzie took a step back and looked down, avoiding Pettit's stare. His bravado was a thin veneer.

Hernandez stepped between them and placed his hands on Pettit's arm, tugging gently. "Come on. We're wasting our time with him. I guess someone else will get the reward."

Pettit followed Hernandez's cue. "Whatever. It's fucking cold out here. I'm ready to call it a night." They turned away from Ozzie. He never even let them take a step.

"Reward? Like for what?"

The detectives turned back towards him. "Yeah, the city gives out a reward to anyone who helps solve a murder. What is it Pettit? Five hundred bucks?"

"I think it's a thousand. But old Ozzie here says he didn't see anything, so no way he's getting the reward. Have to be some other lucky stiff."

Ozzie's eyes practically sparkled. A thousand bucks could go a long way. New coat, maybe some long underwear. A month maybe in one of the flop houses over in Southwest. "Well, I might've seen something. Dependen' of course on how soon I might get my reward."

"Listen, Ozzie," Hernandez said, as he walked up close to him. "Like my partner says, it's fucking cold out here and we really don't feel like wasting our time and freezing our asses off. So cut out the bullshit. You give us something, we'll make sure you get the reward. The fine officer over there will take you down to the station and get the particulars on where we can reach you, and if what you tell us pans out, the money is yours. But you only have thirty seconds and then we're out of here. So if you have something to say, say it."

Ozzie could practically taste the money. But he remembered that cops were sneaky. Last time he had talked to the cops it had cost him fifteen months upstate. *Cooperate and we'll go easy on you. Yeah, right.* Then again he hadn't done anything wrong this time, so what harm could be in it?

"I saw the whole thing."

"What whole thing, Ozzie?"

"The lady down there. I saw them whack her." The story came tumbling out. "You see Rex and me. That's the other guy over there." He pointed to Rex standing with another patrolman some forty feet away. "We were just hangin' out and drinkin' a little. Well, Rex he passed out, and I was just finishin' off the rest of the bottle when I hear this lady screaming. I looked down the hill and I saw this lady being tugged and pulled at by three guys. She was all tied up and she didn't have no clothes on, and at first I thought they were going to have their way with her, if you know what I mean."

"Yeah, Ozzie, we get your drift," said Hernandez. He looked at Pettit, who nodded. It was a look they had shared many times. Over the years they had learned to tell who was lying and who was telling the truth. Between the two of them they had never been wrong, so they had developed a signal, a special look and a nod. Ozzie's voice and his mannerisms all said that he had seen an awful thing. Now he was glad to tell about it, to share it with others. It was funny that way. Killers and witnesses were the same. They had to tell the story in order to unburden their souls. Ozzie continued his narration.

"Then they cut off the ropes. She tried to make a run for it, but they tackled her. She put up quite a fight—and then boom! And that was it. Then they dumped her in the water and scrammed out of here."

"What did the men look like?" asked Hernandez.

"It's awful hard to say. I mean it was pretty light with the moon and all." They looked up at the three-quarter moon. "But still it's pretty far away. I could see that they were pretty sturdy looking guys, nice coats on. Looked warm anyways. I can tell a good warm coat when I see one." He looked wistfully at his own threadbare coat. That one thousand dollars was looking better and better.

"Ozzie, that's a very compelling story. And we would like to believe you, really we would. But you expect us to believe a broken-down old drunk like you saw all that and then you just hung out here, didn't call the cops or anything?" Pettit said, his voice rising.

"Why should I call the cops? Cops are nothing but trouble. Besides, this is my home. I ain't got nowhere else to go."

"Very sad, Ozzie. Very sad." Although they believed him, the detectives had to press him, see if he would stick by his story. "I don't know Ozzie; that reward may be slipping away." The response was even better than they could have dreamed.

"Maybe this would change your mind." Ozzie reached into his coat pocket and pulled out something. "I found this down by the river. I went down to see if the lady was alive. She wasn't. This was lying by the bank. Now do I get my reward?"

Hernandez pulled out his flashlight and shined it on the object. It was a piece of gold jewelry. A pin of some type. It looked vaguely familiar to him. He looked at Pettit, who shrugged. Pettit pulled an evidence bag from his inside coat pocket and held it out. Ozzie extended his hand out, holding the pin above the evidence bag, but not letting go.

"When do I get my five thousand dollars?" he asked.

"Nice try, Ozzie," replied Hernandez. "It's a thousand. Like we said, you go with the officer over here and he'll get you taken care of." Ozzie smiled and dropped the evidence in the bag. Pettit sealed up the evidence bag. "By the way Ozzie, don't be leaving town anytime soon."

"Whadda you mean?"

"Oh, didn't we tell you? You have to appear at trial to collect the thousand," Pettit said matter-of-factly, as if the proposition was an obvious one from the beginning.

"Appear at trial?" Ozzie exclaimed. "I knew you cops were no good sons of bitches." Ozzie was getting excited and started waving his arms. "I never should of trusted you. Trial! I want my thousand dollars and I want it now!"

Hernandez interceded, "Well, if the case is resolved before trial you'll get your money sooner." Hernandez reached into his coat and pulled out his wallet. "Here's a little pocket money." Hernandez peeled off a pair of twenties and presented them to Ozzie. Ozzie examined them with some disdain, refusing to believe that his thousand dollars was now forty.

"Hey, if you don't want to take it Ozzie, it's no skin off my teeth." Hernandez began to put the money back in his wallet. Before he could, Ozzie snatched it from his hands and then turned and stalked off, muttering under his breath. "Wait 'til my lawyer hears about this. ACLU gonna help me."

Hernandez motioned to the uniformed officer. "Go after him. Make sure he fills out the paperwork to get his dough." The uniformed officer went off in search of Ozzie.

Hernandez turned to Pettit. "Well, we best get this over to our FBI friends. They should be able to help us figure out what it is."

Pettit nodded. "You sensing a pattern here? Two nights, two murders, both 9mm, and what looks to be a professional job."

"As I'm sure you know, I hate to admit when you're right; but yeah, I get that distinct feeling our reporter friend and this lady knew each other. Let's run a missing persons report. Nice young lady like that doesn't disappear without someone noticing. Let's roust one of our nice junior detectives out of bed and get them on it. Start with the military bases. See if anyone has gone AWOL. I'll book the evidence and get it over to the FBI."

A cold wind kicked up and Hernandez pulled his coat closer. "Pettit, let's make a vow. Next year at this time, we're in Miami drinking daiquiris. Deal?"

"Deal."

It was the same vow they had made every year, for the last fifteen. Both knew it wouldn't happen, but the dream kept them warm and that was enough.

CHAPTER 40

Berlin and the president were seated in the Oval Office, going over the day's schedule. The president was seated behind his desk. Berlin was seated opposite him. They had started every day the same way for the past three-and-a-half years: coffee and breakfast and a planning of the day's events. The schedule was tightly orchestrated. Everyone wanted access to the president, and Berlin was careful to dole it out in small measures. The president liked it that way too. He was the CEO of the world's largest company and, as much as possible, he delegated decision making and authority to the heads of each of the agencies. Only the most serious policy decisions, especially those involving foreign affairs, merited his consideration. Pick good people and then rely on them. That was his philosophy.

Berlin's mind was only half on the schedule. He ticked off the day's events: cabinet meeting in the morning; consultation with Congress on the elections to be held to replace the assassinated members; meetings with some lobbyists on the proposed budget. It was amazing how the process barely skipped a beat even in the most tragic of times. The government really was a world unto itself.

The other half of Berlin's mind was on counting delegates. His numbers showed he was close. He needed 270 of the votes. He was very close to flipping the three votes he needed, but there was slippage in those who had originally committed to the president and now were having second thoughts. The swing votes would be the most difficult. The electors were confused about their role and their obligation. They were talking to party officials, friends, lawyers, and priests, and getting all kinds of different answers. Berlin knew he couldn't do it on his own. He needed the president's help. He had tossed and turned all night trying to decide the best way to get the president on board. The president had been resolute in his opposition. When he made up his mind, there was no changing it. That part of his personality had been pivotal in the first election. The people wanted someone who was decisive and would not falter. Berlin had come to the conclusion that he could not bring up the subject directly. If he challenged the president, he would stand fast in his position. He would have to use a more subtle approach. The president intruded on his thoughts.

"You with me here, Howard, because you look like you're a thousand miles away?"

"What? Huh? Yes, sir, I'm with you. It's just that I was thinking about a phone call I received this morning and debating whether to tell you about it." *Right, Berlin thought, and if I ask you not to think of pink elephants what will you think of?* The president snatched the bait.

"Well, Howard, I've always told you I depend on you to be candid with me. That's why you are where you are. You tell it like it is and I need someone like that around. That's the problem with Washington; too many yes-men. I can take it Howard, so spit it out."

Berlin paused and took a deep breath, heightening the president's curiosity. "One of your key supporters called and asked if you had considered the ramifications of the recent events and the possibility of you serving a second term." Before the president could jump on, Berlin quickly continued, "I told him in no uncertain terms that you had ruled it out and that was that. Frankly, it's not the first call like that I've received, and I just thought you should know about it."

The president's response almost caused Berlin to jump and scream for joy. "I've been giving some thought to it myself. Not reconsidering, mind you, but wondering whether I was too hasty in dismissing the possibility. It should really depend on what the people want. The recent events call for strong leadership. First, the assassinations and then that episode at the courthouse yesterday. What has this country come to? By the way, any word on what became of Martinez's lawyers?"

"No, sir, the FBI is still looking for them. They seem to have disappeared."

The president continued, "People voted for the president, not the vice president. Then again, I have to consider my historical legacy. We had a very successful first term. I don't want to taint that record by being perceived as trying to take advantage of such a tragedy. I couldn't even begin to consider it, unless I was sure that it was in the best interest of the country and that the people would support me. It's obviously a very delicate matter, Howard."

"Obviously, Mr. President." Berlin could barely suppress his smile. He had been around the president long enough that they had developed their own language. The president was asking him to test the waters without formally asking him. That way the president could deny any involvement or knowledge if the effort proved unsuccessful, unpopular or politically damaging. Plausible deniability. If it was unsuccessful, Berlin would be the scapegoat and that was OK with him. The risks were high, but the reward even higher. "I have no doubt that the people would support you, Mr. President. Why don't I make a note to remind you in a week or so about our conversation? Will that be enough time for you to mull it over?"

The president leaned back in his chair. "Yes, I think so."

"We should be getting to the cabinet meeting, sir."

"Yes, of course." They rose from their chairs. As always, Berlin waited for the president to go first. The Secret Service was waiting outside the Oval Office. They fell into stride behind Berlin and the president. On their way to the cabinet meeting room, they passed by Berlin's office.

"Mr. President, can I catch up with you? I have to make a quick call to check on a scheduling item."

"Of course, Howard." Berlin peeled off into his office. He passed his secretary's desk and gave her a brief nod and greeting and then walked into his office. He picked up the phone from his desk and dialed an inside extension number.

"Broberg, it's me. I just met with the president. He wants a firm count by five. Get Pasqua on this too. We'll meet at four."

Berlin hung up the phone and rushed out to the cabinet meeting. He was feeling sky high. Maybe he could pull it off after all. The thought of four more years at the center of all that power was almost more than he could handle.

CHAPTER 41

Vice president-elect Simmons was also counting votes, and the outcome was encouraging but not 100 percent satisfying. If the electoral vote were held today, he would win. But there were still two weeks until the meeting of the electors. A lot could change in that time. The president's speech the other night had been both a positive and a negative. He had seemed to withdraw his name from consideration, but the speech was a powerful and evocative one. His approval ratings in overnight polls had gone through the roof. Simmons, on the other hand, was a relative unknown. His staff had outlined a number of appearances and speeches in order to keep his name in the headlines, but since the assassination he had been relegated to the inside of the paper, while the president was on the front page. He deserved to be talked about at the same time, or before the president. He had been elected by the people, not the president.

Simmons had met with party leaders and they were prepared for all eventualities. They were engaged in a fullcourt press on all the electors to firm up their votes. Fortunately, a lot of favors were due and the party was calling in all its chips. If all else failed, a legal challenge was being prepared. Simmons liked the odds, but something was still not right in his mind. While in the Senate, he had been on the Intelligence Committee. The committee had conducted an investigation and hearings on the Front. The main philosophy of the Front was the lack of economic equality in the United States. The president-elect had been sympathetic to their views. He had run on a platform of equal economic opportunity for all Americans and a leveling of the playing field—and he meant it. Some had labeled him a socialist, but his theory was that more equality created more stability, which led to more economic growth. Given that, why would the Front have killed him?

Perhaps they had decided that decisive action was necessary. Still, all the pieces did not fit together. He did not get where he was by not having all the facts. He had some friends in the intelligence community. He picked up the phone. It was time to call in some more favors.

CHAPTER 42

Jack and Alison quietly ate their breakfast. Jack was hungry, but Alison just pushed her food around the plate. It was a greasy spoon on the outskirts of Maryland. They had decided that Virginia would be too hot for them, so they had hopped on the Beltway and made their way into Maryland to a hotel that was as seedy as the one the night before. A quick stop at a local mall had outfitted them with some new clothes. Alison felt it was important to continually change their appearance. They had a whole day and night to kill before their meeting. Jack had suggested a little sightseeing at a few Civil War battlefields. Alison had nixed the idea. She was particularly downcast and Jack wasn't sure why. He suspected the confessions of the previous night had unsettled her, but he had decided long ago to never try to guess what went on in the mind of any member of the opposite sex.

"Cat got your tongue?" he joked.

Alison looked up with a half smile. "No. Just thinking."

"That could be dangerous."

"Not any more dangerous than things are now."

"True, but at least we're famous." He motioned to a woman in a booth across the aisle. She was holding up a copy of *The Washington Post*. The front page was facing them. It was adorned with a picture of the courthouse and one picture each of Jack and Alison. A bold headline proclaimed "CHAOS CONTINUES IN NATION'S CAPITOL." Alison cringed and looked quickly down at her plate.

"Great, it's just a matter of time before someone recognizes us."

"Doubtful. The way we look no one will recognize us." Jack stroked his newly forming beard for effect.

"I hope you're right."

"So, what can you tell me about this meeting tonight?"

"Nothing."

"What do you mean 'nothing'?"

"Just that. I swore an oath of secrecy. I take it seriously. You'll know everything tonight, from people who can tell you. I can't."

Jack appeared disappointed and they sat in silence for a few minutes. Alison reached across the table and placed her hands over his. "Jack, I'm sorry. Please don't take it personally. It has nothing to do with us."

Her touch and her voice melted his resistance. He smiled at her. "I understand."

"Let me ask you something."

"Uh-huh."

"Did you notice that guy at the courthouse? He was watching us so intently. I was sure I knew him from somewhere."

"There were a lot of people there, Jack. Can you be more specific?"

Jack closed his eyes and tried to picture the man. "Medium build, dark suit, dark overcoat. Short-cropped hair. Intense blue eyes."

"That describes half the men in America."

"No, not with eyes like that and a look like that. It was the look of a killer. I saw him outside the courthouse too, just before the shooting. He was looking at you and it gave me the creeps. I know I've seen that guy before, and it's driving me crazy. I never forget a face. Anyway, you done?" he asked.

"Yeah, I wasn't really hungry."

"I noticed." He motioned to the waitress for the bill. She brought it to the table and laid it down.

"Everything OK, folks?'

"Yeah, super." Jack laid down the money and the tip and they headed towards the door. They passed by the booth where the lady had been reading *The Washington Post*. She had left the paper behind. There was a separate insert on the assassination and Jack scooped it up. He leafed through it on the way to the door. The center pages showed, frame-by-frame, the sequence leading up to the explosion at the Kennedy Center. Halfway through, Jack stopped dead in his tracks.

"Oh my God, I remember!"

"Remember what?" Alison asked.

"Where I know that guy."

"What do you mean? How?"

"Quick, we have to get out of here so I can make a call on my cell."

"Why?"

"No time for questions."

He walked back to the cashier as fast as he could without arousing suspicion. Alison was just a step behind him. *Great, she thought, nothing like drawing attention to us.* The cashier was finishing with another customer and Jack waited impatiently. When the customer left, he stepped up to the cash register and practically threw his money at the cashier. She looked at him askance but had seen stranger customers and just gave him his change. Alison and Jack quickly exited the restaurant and walked toward the car as Jack pulled out his cell phone. First he searched the number, with a momentary thought that always came to him: Why hadn't I thought of Internet search? Then he pushed it from his mind. When the number came up, he tapped his phone again to start the dialing. After four rings, the call was answered.

"Newsroom," Jack said. The call was routed.

"NBC4. This is Carla."

"Hi. I need to speak to the general manager."

"That would be Mr. Abrams and I'm afraid he is in a meeting right now. Would you like to leave a message?"

"No. I really need to speak with him right away. Could you please interrupt him and tell him Jack Banner wants to give him an exclusive interview."

"I'm sorry, Mr. Banner, I'm under strict instructions not to disturb him."

Normally Jack would not have been quite so rude, but the circumstances left him no alternative.

"Carla, do you like your job?"

"Yes, I suppose."

"Good. Because if you don't tell Mr. Abrams I'm on the phone and he finds out you let the story of the century get away, you'll be looking for a new one."

There was a pause. "Can you hold?"

"Sure, Carla, but not for very long."

Within thirty seconds a breathless Stan Abrams picked up the line.

"Is this really Jack Banner?"

"One and the same."

"How do I know it's you?"

"Actually, you don't, until you meet me. Would forty-five minutes be OK?"

"I'll be here."

"Good. Here's what I need when I get there." He told Abrams, then quickly searched for directions on his phone and started up the GPS.

"Follow these directions," he said to Alison.

"Now are you going to tell me what that was about?" she asked.

"I'll tell you while we drive, but if I'm right, by tonight we'll be able to tell your friends who killed the president-elect."

CHAPTER 43

Agent Evans was hot on the trail. His reputation was hanging in the balance and that meant a lot to him. The director was counting on him to find Jack and Alison. He had retraced their path after the assassination, and, as before, the trail went cold at National Airport. He had checked Dulles Airport, the bus stations and train stations. No luck. Evans was getting an uneasy feeling. The way they had disappeared showed all the marks of a professional. Banner was smart but had no experience in espionage or intelligence. Other than the airline tickets, there was no evidence that he or Ms. Stevens had used credit cards or banks card or even cashed a check. The airline tickets were clearly an attempt to throw them off track. Somehow they had access to money and somehow they had disappeared, despite the fact that their faces were splashed all over the newspapers. That could only mean one thing: Alison was not what she seemed.

Evans had done some digging and, on the surface, everything about her appeared ordinary. Work at the ACLU. Law school. College. What was strange was what wasn't there. Alison had never had a parking or speeding ticket. She had never owned any property or purchased any stocks or investments. Evans had called her colleagues at the ACLU. They all agreed that she was a great lawyer and a fine coworker, but not one could provide any details about her personal life or her family. None could remember ever having dinner with her or going to a movie. Names of boyfriends were vague or perhaps nonexistent. Evans had tried to contact her parents without success. A maid had answered the phone and informed him that they were out of the country and not reachable. The pieces of the puzzle did not fit and that made him nervous. His concern was heightened by his fondness for Jack. He was out there somewhere and, most likely, oblivious to the mysteries surrounding Alison Stevens. Evans had seen how Jack acted around Alison. You would have to be blind not to see Jack was obviously not thinking with his head, and that was dangerous for any man, let alone one in Jack's position.

Evans hoped to find the answers and a degree of comfort in the FBI reports spread in front of him. The first one related to the murder of a reporter at *The Washington Post*, Glen Spivey. He had come across the item on the murder of Spivey yesterday and had given it little thought. As requested, the local cops were reporting all suspicious and unsolved murders to the FBI. Fortunately it was stored in his mind when the report came in of a Jane Doe found floating in the C & O Canal. The M. O. appeared to be the same: 9-mm, no sign of robbery, a professional hit. He had contacted the officers in charge: two D.C. cops who seemed to be good eggs. They had filled him in on the details. He had no doubt that the murder was connected. The Jane Doe was not yet identified.

He also had in front of him the reports from the computer specialist on what was found on Lefteski's computer. It described the events from his first being approached by Mr. Smith up until his planned meeting for the evening that he disappeared. Evans drew four circles on a pad and wrote the names of Spivey, Jane Doe, Lefteski and Mr. Smith in each circle. Lefteski and Smith were connected. Lefteski had been co-opted to work for Smith and to provide him with information on the FBI's investigation of the Front. This was consistent with the FBI information that the Front had been infiltrated and taken over by some outside force. He assumed Lefteski had met the same fate as Spivey and the Jane Doe, but an APB had been issued on him as well. He drew a line between the two circles.

The connection among Jane Doe, Spivey and the other two was not clear. Evans had checked with *The Washington Post*, and Spivey had not been working on any articles regarding the Front. It was not even within his area of expertise. Organized crime had been his forte. With no information about Jane Doe, he could only surmise that somehow all four individuals knew each other or were in some way connected. His secretary interrupted his thoughts, as she leaned into his office.

"Sir, your package is here."

"Great. Have them bring it in." He had asked for the evidence collected on the two murders. The D.C. cops had been most cooperative and he had arranged for a runner to bring them to his office. The runner came in carrying two cardboard boxes. He placed them on the floor.

"You'll have to sign for these."

He produced a clipboard and indicated the line where Evans was to sign. When Evans was done, the runner departed. Evans hefted the first box onto his desk. It was related to Spivey's murder. Spivey's personal belongings were inside plastic evidence bags. His clothing was stained brown from blood. Evans pulled out the evidence bag and examined the clothes through the plastic, only briefly. The forensic report would give him the information he wanted. Underneath the clothing was Spivey's computer, also wrapped in a plastic bag. Evans picked up the bag containing the computer but, again, did not remove it from the plastic. The computer jogged his memory about the police report. He pulled out the report and reread the portion on what had been discovered on the computer. According to the officers, Spivey had written "the secret is" on his computer just before his death. Evans found this hard to believe, but both the detective and a forensic guy on the scene had sworn to it. Evans scratched his head. This case was getting stranger and stranger. What was the secret? And did it have anything to do with Spivey's murder? The rest of the box contained some items from Spivey's trunk and some pictures of the crime scene. Nothing much of interest. Evans replaced the items and placed the box on the floor.

He put the second box, regarding the murder of Jane Doe, on the table. It was practically empty. She had been found nude so there were no clothes and no personal belongings. The box had some soil samples collected at the scene and some debris found there that was collected. The last item was a piece of jewelry. It seemed strange that it was in the box, because it was a lapel pin. He was sure she had been found nude. He pulled out the report and read it again. A local homeless man, who had allegedly witnessed the incident, had found the lapel pin. He claimed that Jane Doe had ripped it off one of her attackers. Evans was ready to dismiss the report until he got to the description of the assailants. Although it had been dark, the moon had been out and it was a clear night. The description matched, almost exactly, the description given by Lefteski of the infiltrators. Evans read the report again, pulled out the Lefteski report and compared the two. The similarities were striking.

Evans drew a line connecting the names Smith and Jane Doe. Mr. Smith or his people had been behind the murder of Jane Doe. This was the part of detective work that Evans loved. It was much like science. Proposing a hypothesis and then coming up with the evidence to confirm it. He surmised that Jane Doe had been silenced because of what she knew. Her physique and appearance had suggested military training. Could she have been one of the infiltrators? The military services had been alerted and provided with her fingerprints. He would know by late morning whether she had military training.

He picked up the lapel pin and examined it more closely. It was made of gold. It was definitely a masculine piece of jewelry. It could not have belonged to Jane Doe. There was no inscription of any kind, but there was an insignia on the front. Evans laid the lapel pin down on his desk and swung a magnifying lamp into place. Examining the enlarged insignia provided no additional information. It seemed vaguely familiar, but he couldn't place it.

Evans reached into his desk drawer where he kept his FBI directory. He knew there was a guy down in the encryption division who specialized in insignias, symbols and the like. What was that guy's name? Jensen? Jasper? Jankowski! Stan Jankowski. He thumbed to the Js, found Jankowski's extension and dialed it. After a few rings, Jankowski came on the line.

"Stan Jankowski."

"Hey, Stan, it's Don Evans. Remember me?" Jankowski had helped him out on a case a few years back. He wasn't sure he would remember him.

"Sure, Don. Long time no hear. How's the family?"

"Doing great. My oldest is expecting her first come spring."

"That's great. What can I do you for?" Evans was glad to end the small talk and get down to business.

"I've got what looks like a lapel pin that was found at the murder scene. It's got some kind of insignia on it and I remembered you were the expert in that kind of thing." Flattery got you everywhere in the FBI. All the agents were supposed to be a team working together to fight crime. More often than not it was a turf battle, with everyone protecting their turf and trying to justify their existence. Jankowski was thrilled to hear the compliment and responded eagerly.

"Why don't you send it down? I'll give it the once over and get back to you ASAP."

"That would be great, and I'll be sure you get the assist on this one." Another form of flattery. A commendation in the personnel file was greatly appreciated come annual review time, especially for a desk jockey like Jankowski.

"No sweat. My pleasure."

"Great talking to you, Stan. I'll check back with you a little later."

"You too, Don. Best to the wife and kids."

Evans hung up the phone. "Marsha!" he yelled out to his secretary. She appeared at the door. "Please bring this down right away to Stan Jankowski in encryption. He's expecting it."

"Yes, sir." She took the evidence bag with the lapel pin and hustled out. The urgency in her boss's voice was clear and unusual. He never asked her to do something right away.

Evans looked down at his pad. He had four circles and three lines. The picture was woefully incomplete. He had an unsettling feeling that there were other people out there looking for Jack whose motives were less benign then his. He drew two more circles, one for Jack and one for Alison. If he didn't connect the dots soon, he was afraid that they would meet the same fate as Mr. Spivey and Jane Doe.

CHAPTER 44

Thanks to Alison's aggressive driving they reached their destination quickly. Jack filled in Alison along the way, and by the time they arrived she was champing at the bit. They pulled into the parking lot of the TV station. The TV antennae stretched high into the sky. It was a nondescript building, circa 1970, focused on energy efficiency and not architecture. Glass doors led into the lobby. Jack and Alison walked briskly from the car to the front doors of the building. Beyond the entrance door was a lobby and reception area. Inside Stan Abrams was pacing back and forth impatiently. He rushed up to meet Jack and Alison as they entered the lobby.

"It is you!" His face showed relief and exhilaration. This was the story of a lifetime and it had fallen in his lap. After the call, Abrams had notified his top reporters to be ready for a late-breaking story.

"Pleasure to meet you. May I call you Stan?" Jack asked.

"You can call me whatever you want. And I assume this must be Ms. Stevens?" He extended his hand to Alison. She shook it warmly and smiled.

"A pleasure to meet you, Stan."

"We should probably get right down to business," Jack insisted. "Alison and I are a little pressed for time."

"Of course, of course. Right this way. I thought the fewer people who know you are here the better. There's a back stairway that leads up to my office. I pulled the footage for you, and I have it set up in one our production booths, which is down the hall from my office. It's pretty quiet in the morning, but we are gearing up for the noon news, so you're going to be a little hard to hide, but we'll do the best we can." He gestured to the hallway behind him. "Follow me."

Jack and Alison fell in step behind Abrams. They walked down the hallway, through a fire door leading to the stairway, and ascended to the second floor. Jack and Alison were anxious and were right on Abrams's heels, as he climbed the steps ahead of them. If Jack was right, they were one step closer to solving the mystery. At the top of the stairway, they passed through another fire door, turned left and walked down a short corridor. Abrams's office was at the end of the hallway. A short distance away they could hear the activity of the newsroom. He ushered them into his office.

"If you can wait here for a minute, I'm going to clear out the production room. Then we can take a look at the footage in some privacy."

He left Alison and Jack in his office. Jack sat down on the sofa. Alison remained standing and began to pace.

"What does it mean if you're right, Jack?"

"Well, first of all, it means that Martinez is innocent. I suppose that's really the only important thing as far as we're concerned."

"That's a bit shortsighted, don't you think? We need to consider the impact on the country, on its social fabric."

"Alison, that's incredibly noble of you, and I mean that with all my heart, but one thing I've learned is you can only be concerned with those things that affect you personally. We're lawyers. We have a client. Our job is to defend him. The rest of it is beyond our control. What I want to do is get this thing over with as fast as possible and move on with the rest of my life. Of our lives."

"Look out for number one, is that it?"

"Yes, I'm afraid it is. But in this case, looking out for two number ones."

She was quiet for a moment, glad to hear him reaffirm his feelings for her, but it wasn't that simple. The strong conviction she felt when she left the restaurant the last night was weakening. She was still struggling with her inner demons. Her life had always been dedicated to a cause, a reason for living, beyond the ordinary day-to-day struggle under which most people lived. Until recently she had never questioned that. Now she was in an unfamiliar situation. The cause had abandoned her, it seemed. She was thus far not successful in unmasking the conspiracy, but they had made it clear that she and Jack were expendable for the greater good. Jack, on the other hand, had not abandoned her, even after she had revealed some of her darkest secrets to him. Could he be right that, in the end, you had to look out only for yourself and those you loved?

Abrams opened the door and poked his head into the office. "It's all ready for you now."

Jack and Alison followed him out of the office and down the hallway to the production studio. They entered and closed the door behind them. Inside was an array of audio-visual equipment typically found in a modern TV studio. Directly to their left was a control panel underneath a window, looking out into the studio. Abrams took a seat in front of a keyboard with a large monitor and motioned for Jack and Alison to take the chairs to either side of him.

"I've queued up the footage you wanted. This system works like a fancy DVD player. The software can play the video at whatever speed, much like a DVD, but with greater range and more control, both fast and slow. If you want it can freeze and focus on individual frames or even parts of frames like a DVD. The whiz-bang is that you can enlarge them, reduce them, enhance them in almost any way you can think. You name it, we can do it."

"Let's just start with regular speed."

Abrams hit play and the images appeared on the monitor. It was the scene outside the Kennedy Center the night of the assassination, the same feed Jack had viewed in his apartment, what seemed a lifetime ago. The clip started from the point where the president and president-elect and their wives were exchanging pleasantries. Then a man came up behind the president and whispered in his ear. The president nodded.

"Wait, that's him!" Jack yelled. "Stop!" Abrams clicked the pause icon.

Jack pointed to the man whispering in the president's ear. "Can you enlarge that image?"

"Sure can." Abrams manipulated the controls. After a moment, the frozen frame was enlarged so that the face of the man filled the screen.

"That's the guy I saw at the courthouse. Remember him, Alison?"

Alison leaned in to get a closer look. "Now that you mention it, I do. I think."

Jack looked at Abrams. "You have any idea who he is?"

"No. But based on his proximity to the president, he can only be one of two things: an adviser to the president or a Secret Service agent. Let's keep rolling the video, but first I'll print a copy of that frame." Abrams clicked the print icon and then play. The video continued. The president and the first lady walked toward their limousine. The unidentified man followed closely behind them. As they watched, it became clear that Abrams was right. The man was clearly a Secret Service agent. He walked slightly behind the president. Men dressed similarly to him walked in front of and to the side of the president. They scanned the crowd constantly. Their sole purpose was to provide protection to the president.

As the obvious sunk in, the tension in the room escalated. The president entered the limousine. Abrams clicked the stop icon. "I don't really want to see the rest of it."

"I agree," said Alison.

The color printer began to whir and produced a picture of the man on the screen. Abrams removed it from the printer and handed it to Jack.

Jack nodded his head. "That's him alright."

He looked at Alison and then at Abrams. "Stan, could you give us a minute here?"

"Sure, sure. I suspect I don't want to hear what you know anyway. Despite the journalist in me being curious, I'd prefer to live to at least fifty. If what you're saying and I'm thinking is right, you're hazardous to my health." He said it with a smile, and Jack and Alison couldn't help but chuckle.

"Just holler if you need me." He left and closed the door behind him.

"The president is in danger," Jack said gravely.

"Don't you think you're overreacting? First of all, assuming he is on the presidential detail, it could just be coincidence that he was at the courthouse. He could have been an interested spectator. Or maybe he's not even the guy you saw at the courthouse.

"No, I'm sure it's him. And if you saw the way he looked at me in the courtroom and just before they tried to kill you, you'd know it was no coincidence. He was there to make sure the job got done—and got done right. We need to warn the president."

"And how do you intend to do that? Call him up and tell him?"

"I was hoping that your friends could help me with that."

"I wouldn't count on that, Jack. They are a very secretive bunch. Going to the president would be a little more publicity than they would like."

Jack swiveled back and forth in his chair. "Well, it can't hurt to ask when I meet them. The worst they can say is no, right?"

Alison sighed with exasperation. "You know, sometimes you can be a real pain in the ass."

"It's nice to know you're beginning to appreciate my finer qualities. Now let's go tell Abrams our life story."

CHAPTER 45

The excitement in the room was almost palpable. It was late afternoon and the winter sun was dwindling. Berlin was sitting in his office with Pasqua and Broberg. They had been counting votes and canvassing electors on a nonstop basis, and were extremely close. After his discussion with the president, he had been able to use the president's name in the calls. Given the count he had from Pasqua and Broberg, he could now go back to the president and present him with the number. He also had a series of public opinion polls conducted, which showed the public favored Hampton over Simmons by almost 10 percentage points. Berlin would then be in a position to ask the president to make a few calls himself. This would probably put them over the top.

Berlin looked down at the list in front of him. There was one name left to call today, Henry Ruffolo. Berlin had talked to him twice already. Each time it gave him an uneasy feeling. Berlin had not told Broberg and Pasqua that some of the electors had needed a little persuasion. The persuasion had taken many forms: promises of favors in a second term; promises of access to the president in the second term; promises to convince the president not to veto favored legislation.

Ruffolo had wanted none of that. He wanted only one thing. Actually, a large volume of one thing 50,000 of them to be precise. This had caused a dilemma for Berlin. Promises of favors and access were perfectly legal as a form of persuasion. Offering cash payments was not. The dilemma was not whether or not to make the payment. That was easy. The problem was coming up with the cash and not getting caught doing it. Berlin had been a public servant for many years and he did not have that kind of money. He would have to find it somewhere in the White House budget. This meant that Ruffolo would now cause him to commit not one but two felonies: bribery and theft. Since he had first talked to Ruffolo, Berlin had been scouring the White House budget to see where he could come up with the funds. Fortunately the budget was a large one, and soon Berlin came across a contingency fund. It had been put in place during one of the budget deadlocks. The White House wanted to make sure that Congress would not be able to shut it down to force a compromise on the budget or any other issue. It had ten million dollars in it, which seemed like a lot at first. But when Berlin considered what it took to keep the place going, it seemed actually to be too little. After some further questions and discreet inquiries, he discovered that as the president's chief of staff he had access to the fund, provided he could get the signature of a member of the cabinet or the president. Getting the president's signature had been relatively simple. Berlin had just included the authorization in with a large stack of documents to be signed by the president. The president always signed them without question. It would be another matter Berlin would have to explain at some point, but he was thinking only about short-term goals.

Now that he had the money, he had to arrange the payment to Ruffolo. That was the purpose of his call today. He dialed the number on a secure phone in his office. The call was untraceable. The phone rang seven or eight times. Berlin was ready to hang up when he heard an answer.

"Hello?"

Berlin recognized Ruffolo's voice. "Mr. Ruffolo. Good evening. This is Mr. Parks," he said, using an assumed name. "We spoke earlier in the week."

"Yeah, it's about time you called. I was ready to call the whole thing off." This was, in fact, not true. Ruffolo already had the money spent. More accurately, some of it was owed to a local bookie who worked out of Rudy's joint. Payday was next week and Ruffolo needed the money to pay off. He was too old to get his legs broken. On the other hand, there was nothing wrong with trying to pry a few more dollars out of the situation.

Berlin did not flinch. He had brokered enough backroom deals to know a bluff when he saw it.

"I'm sorry you feel that way, but if you're not interested, I understand perfectly. I'm sorry to have troubled you." Berlin pulled the phone away from his mouth, simulating the silence that would precede hanging up.

Ruffolo was not about to let that happen. "Wait, wait. Hey, are you there?"

"Excuse me, I'm sorry. Did you say something? I was hanging up the phone."

"Yeah. I said I'm ready to do what we talked about."

"Good. Excellent. Here is how it will work. I've established a bank account in the name of Escambia Plumbing at the Citibank office in downtown Chicago. It has you listed as president of the company. Tomorrow I will deposit $10,000 in the account. Once the vote is finished you get the rest."

"Wait a minute. How do I know that you will live up to your end of the bargain?"

"Actually, you don't. It's all a matter of trust, my friend. I need you and you need me. Therefore, we can trust one another."

Ruffolo didn't like the sound of things, but he had very little choice. It so happened that $10,000 was the amount he owed the bookie. It made him a little nervous that Mr. Parks was giving him the exact amount he owed. *He couldn't have known about his bets, could he?*

"I suppose you're right. But let me tell you something. You double-cross me and I'll be sure to see that our little secret doesn't stay secret very long."

"You have nothing to worry about, Mr. Ruffolo. You can trust me and I'm sure I can count on you. Remember, Escambia Plumbing." Berlin hung up the phone. As he did, he gave the thumbs up to Pasqua across the room. "Add one more to the Hampton column."

He picked up the phone again. He needed something to relieve all his tension and excitement. "Sheila. It's Howard. You free tonight? Great. The usual place. Room 270. It's my new lucky number."

CHAPTER 46

Pettit and Hernandez had caught a lucky break. Detective work was 50 percent hard work and 50 percent luck. In this case, luck had made hard work unnecessary. They had put out the APB on Jane Doe and run her through all military services with no success. Fortunately for them, Jane Doe had a mother and the mother became very worried when she could not reach her daughter. She had called her daughter's employer and, when that had not panned out, she had called every police department in Washington and Virginia. It had taken her the better part of two days. Finally she had reached Hernandez. As soon as she began her description, Hernandez knew Jane Doe was the missing daughter. It was the part of his job he never got used to. He would be up for the next two or three nights, reliving the moment when he had told this devoted mother that he thought her daughter was dead.

After the phone call, the mother had raced down to the precinct. Her name was Joanne Bourne. Her daughter had been Melissa Bourne. Mrs. Bourne was an attractive woman, in her late fifties, impeccably dressed, and wearing expensive jewelry. Her Mclean, Virginia, address did not come as a surprise. She obviously came from wealth. She was in a state of shock but holding up remarkably well, even after she had identified the body from photographs. What did come as a surprise, and the topic of discussion as they sat in interview room "A," was her daughter's occupation. She was a member of the Secret Service.

"How long was your daughter with the Secret Service?" Pettit asked.

"About three years. She seemed to enjoy it. I tried to convince her to go to law school or business school, but she wasn't interested. I suppose it was her form of rebellion. She was the perfect child in every respect." She started to cry softly, but maintained her composure. Pettit offered her a box of tissues and she grabbed several and dabbed her eyes.

"Do you know anyone who would want to harm your daughter?" asked Hernandez.

"No. I can't begin to fathom how anyone could even consider doing such a thing to her. Everyone liked and respected Melissa." She began to sob quietly. Hernandez reached out to comfort her, but she waved off his effort. "I'm OK. I'm OK."

"When was the last time you saw or spoke to your daughter?" asked Pettit.

"I spoke to her about three days ago and I saw her about three weeks ago. She came up to the house for dinner. I didn't get to see her as much as I liked. Being on the presidential detail, she traveled quite a bit."

Pettit and Hernandez sat up in their chairs. "Excuse me, m'am. Did you say your daughter was on the presidential detail?"

"Oh, yes. She was quite proud of it actually. It's very unusual for someone so junior to get that assignment."

Hernandez rose from his seat. "Would you excuse me for a minute, Ms. Bourne? There's a call I have to make. Officer Pettit will need to ask you a few more questions. Can I get you anything to drink while I'm up?"

"No thank you, detective, but I would appreciate if you could check if my husband's arrived."

"I'll do that and make sure the duty sergeant knows to send him right in." Hernandez left the room and went to his desk in the squad room. He flipped open his case notebook to where he had written the number of Agent Evans. He dialed the number.

"Evans."

"Evans, it's Hernandez with the metro police. Listen, I have a lady down here I think you need to talk to. She's the mother of the Jane Doe we fished out of the C & O Canal last night."

"Have you determined that the murders are connected?"

"Well not exactly, but it turns out her daughter worked for the Secret Service."

"Did I hear you right, detective?"

"Yes, sir, and it gets even better."

"Go ahead."

"She worked the presidential detail."

"Have you pulled her records?"

"I wish I had that kind of clout. I just started interviewing the mother fifteen minutes ago. I figured you can get the information a lot faster than I can. Her name was Melissa Bourne."

"I'm on it. Can you keep her there a while?"

"She's waiting for her husband right now and she's pretty shook up. If you can't get here in time, we can pay her a visit at home. She'll be happy to cooperate and I'll put a couple of uniforms on her door."

"I'll do better than that. Give me her name and address and I'll put our top anti-terrorist detail on her house. She may be the break we've been looking for. We can't take any chances on this one."

Hernandez gave him the address. "Let's plan to meet at the house in an hour."

"Sounds good to me. Hopefully by then I can have the information we need."

"See you then."

"Good work, detective. I'll put a good word in for you with your lieutenant."

"Don't forget to mention my partner, Pettit."

"Will do. See you in an hour."

Hernandez headed back to the interview room. Pettit was a good detective but his people skills sometimes left a little to be desired. As he approached the interview room he could see Mrs. Bourne resting her head on Pettit's shoulder, sobbing gently. Hernandez stopped and walked back to his desk. His presence would only serve to embarrass them both. He took a deep breath and sat down at his desk. He picked up the phone.

"Hi, honey, it's me. No nothing's wrong. Can't an old man just call his daughter to say hi?"

CHAPTER 47

Martinez awoke suddenly and sat up in bed. He was disoriented. The last thing he remembered was being in the courthouse. He looked around and saw his surroundings and quickly looked down to check that all his body parts were intact. He breathed a sigh of relief. He reached for the call button to the right side of his bed. When he did, he realized his hands and legs were bound to the bed, but he had been given enough slack to reach the call button. Within seconds a nurse arrived. Two FBI agents accompanied her. Two police officers stood right outside the door to his room.

"Mr. Martinez, I am glad to see you awake. How are you feeling?" the nurse asked.

"OK, I suppose, but my head's killing me."

"That's quite common with your type of head injury. Do you know where you are?"

"A hospital, I guess."

"Do you remember what happened to you?"

"I remember being in the courthouse and then an explosion."

The nurse's questions were interrupted by the arrival of a doctor. He walked up next to the nurse and peered down at Martinez.

"Hello, Mr. Martinez. I'm Dr. Clark. How are we feeling?"

The nursed interjected, "He's complaining of a severe headache, but he seems very responsive and aware of his surroundings."

"Good. Very good. We need to keep an eye on the headache. It appears you will have a complete recovery. Nurse, get some pain killers for Mr. Martinez. See if that takes the edge off the pain and monitor him every four hours. If there is no improvement, call me stat."

"Yes, doctor."

"What happened to my lawyers? They were sitting right next to me."

The FBI agent interceded, "That's something we thought you could help us with. Doctor, If you're done here, we need a few minutes with Mr. Martinez."

"Certainly." The doctor and the nurse departed.

"Mr. Martinez, I'm Agent Duncan. I'm with the FBI. Mr. Banner and Ms. Stevens have disappeared. If you could help us find them, it would be a great help. Of course, any cooperation you give will certainly be passed along to the appropriate authorities."

"I'd love to help you, but I have no idea where they are." What Martinez was really thinking was, maybe they didn't want to be found.

"We have reason to believe they may be in grave danger. The people who tried to kill you at the courthouse are still out there, and I suspect that they are looking for them as hard as we are."

"Like I said, I can't help you. I'm not feeling that well. If you have any more questions, ask my lawyers when you find them." Martinez closed his eyes to emphasize the point. Duncan and his colleague left in disgust.

The nurse entered as they left. "Mr. Martinez, here is your medicine." She handed him a pill and a glass of water. Martinez swallowed the medication.

"I'll check back on you in a little while. If you need anything ring the buzzer. Now get some rest."

"Thanks."

The nurse left the room, passing by the two FBI agents and police officers. A dozen more were placed all over the ward, some undercover. She went out to the nurse's station and noted the medication on his chart. "Hey, Sally," she called out to a colleague. "I need a cigarette break. Can you cover for me for a few minutes?"

"Sure, Donna, no problem."

Donna headed down the hall. She pulled out her cellphone.

"He's conscious."

"And how is his condition?"

"Looks like a full recovery."

"Is the prognosis likely to change?"

"Not likely. The feds are all over the place. I don't know if he told them anything. They weren't in there very long and they came out in a huff."

"Keep me posted."

"Yes, sir."

Mr. Smith slammed the phone down. At least things couldn't get worse. The incident outside the courthouse had been a serious setback to the entire operation. Not only had they missed Martinez and the lawyers, but Ahern had gotten himself killed. The situation was getting out of control. He had to regain control. He took a deep breath and rubbed his temples. He had eliminated his first problems—the leak and the reporter. He now had three major problems left. The damn lawyers were out there somewhere and no one could find them. He found that hard to believe. They were either lucky or someone was helping them. He knew from his inside sources that the FBI didn't know where they were either. Mr. Smith didn't know what Martinez had told them, and that was dangerous.

His second problem was Martinez. He had always been the wildcard in the plan. Upon the infiltration of the Front, the first step had been to create small cells, of one or two members, who had any contact with Smith or any of his men. Only a handful of Front members had met them. None of them were alive now except for Martinez. He had seen them all together that night they had tested his resolve. Smith had hoped that after the operation he could eliminate Martinez, as he had the others. Now he was stuck in a hospital ward surrounded by FBI agents.

His third, and largest, problem was protecting his superiors from being implicated. It was not only a question of loyalty but survival. He was expendable. They knew it and Smith knew it. Just as Martinez was dangerous to Smith, so was he to those who had hired him. If they feared that his survival jeopardized theirs, his existence would be terminated. Fortunately, he had planned for this eventuality. Every operation needed a contingency plan. It was time to put his into effect.

CHAPTER 48

It was close to six by the time Jack and Alison had finished their interview with Abrams. They had found the experience enlightening. Telling the story helped them to focus on the events in an objective way. Abrams had sat in as his top two investigative reporters had questioned them. Abrams had agreed to their sole condition, that the report not be broadcast until Jack and Alison had given the go ahead. Alison and Jack had not placed any restrictions on the questions but demurred on many, on the basis of either attorney-client privilege or where the questions would have revealed more than they cared to.

Now they were both hungry and tired. It had occurred to both of them that anyone in the newsroom, including the reporters, could report their whereabouts to the police; and so they were glad when they drove out of the station parking lot unmolested. At Alison's direction, Jack had made a series of random lefts and rights for fifteen to twenty minutes, to be sure no one was following them. With that resolved, they had stopped for a quick bite at a local diner. By second nature, they chose a table in the back and kept small talk to a minimum with the waiter. Alison and Jack found they had one more thing in common: breakfast for dinner. They each ordered eggs, bacon and hash browns and coffee.

Alison looked up from her plate and caught Jack staring at her.

"You really are beautiful, you know that?" he said.

Alison blushed. "Thank you. But I'm afraid compliments won't help us with our problem."

"Problem? What problem?" Jack smiled.

"Jack, I appreciate your trying to help me, really I do. But I'd understand if you wanted to bow out now. The people I work for, and the people they know, can handle this from here." She reached out and placed her hand on top of his. "If anything happened to you it would be my fault, and I couldn't live with that."

He placed his other hand on top of hers. "Alison, I told you before, I'm in this thing to the finish. You were right back at the station. It has to be about something more than just you. If I don't stick it out, it means that I sacrifice principle for my own personal safety. Someone is trying to subvert everything we believe in. I can't walk away from that, and I sure can't walk away from you. I can't live with that. Now finish eating. We have a long night ahead of us, I suspect."

Alison pushed her plate away and gave him a mischievous look. "You know, I'm not really that hungry. I was thinking of a better way to kill a few hours."

"Check, please," Jack shouted to the waitress.

CHAPTER 49

Jack and Alison drove in silence. It was close to midnight. They had found a hotel and their lovemaking had been as passionate as the previous night. Now the tension of the meeting ahead was building. Alison had stuck by her word and refused to tell him about the people he was meeting. She had also insisted on driving. They made their way around the Beltway and then exited on Connecticut Avenue, headed south. When they passed into the District of Columbia, Alison pulled off onto a side street.

"I'm afraid I'm going to have to blindfold you."

"You're kidding, right?"

"No, I'm not." She pulled a piece of black cloth from her purse. Jack turned away from her without further protest. She placed the cloth over his eyes and tied it securely in the back. She put the car in gear.

Jack tried to navigate by memory and sense of direction, but he was soon disoriented and gave up trying. After what seemed ten to fifteen minutes, he heard the sound of a parking garage gate open and then he felt the car descending at an angle.

"We're almost there," Alison said.

"Good, because I'm getting car sick."

The car came to a halt. Jack reached for the blindfold. Alison grabbed his hands gently. "Sorry, not yet. I'll help you out of the car."

She opened the car door and went around to Jack's side. She grabbed his arm to guide him out. "Don't be alarmed, someone is here to meet us." Jack felt another pair of hands grab his other arm. He became somewhat alarmed, but his faith in Alison calmed his anxiety. They walked together for twenty steps or so and then stopped. He heard the chime signaling the arrival of an elevator. The hands guiding him prompted him to move forward. Alison did not speak with the person helping her, though Jack sensed they knew each other. The elevator ascended and then another chime sounded when it reached the intended floor. Instinctively, he stepped forward, and they helped guide him.

"Just a bit more," Alison said.

They walked down a hall and turned once or twice, then stopped. A door was opened and they passed through it and then through a second door. There were people talking in the room when they entered. The chatter stopped as they entered.

"There's a chair in front of you." It was the male companion.

Jack reached out and felt the outlines of the chair and managed to seat himself with help from Alison.

"Mr. Banner, you can remove the blindfold now."

His eyes took a moment to adjust to the light. He was in a conference room, seated at a large round conference table. The room had windows, but blinds covered them all. The blinds were closed tight. People were seated all around the table. As his eyes focused, he thought his heart might stop. Seated to his left was the chief justice of the Supreme Court, Kincaid. To his right, could it be? Yes, it was Stanley Rankine, president of Harvard University. Seated next to him was Roger Atkins, CEO and chairman of the board of RAM Industries, the number one computer company in the United States. He wanted to say something, but his shock was amplified by the person seated at the end of the table opposite him. It was Director Stevenson.

"We meet again, Jack, as I suspected we would."

Jack didn't like the tone of his voice. "Alison what the hell is this all about?"

She walked up quickly behind him and placed her hands on his shoulders reassuringly. "It's all right, Jack. I would trust these people with my life."

Jack turned around in his chair to face her. "You work for the FBI?"

"It's not that simple, Jack." It was Justice Kincaid. "None of us works for anyone or even for each other. We work only for the good of the country, for democracy."

"What the hell does that mean?"

The director got up from his chair and walked halfway down the conference table. He spread out his hands. "I assume you know many of the people here?"

Jack nodded.

"Let me introduce the less well known, but equally important, members. Then I will try to explain. Seated next to the chief justice is Elaine Symanski. Elaine is chief of investment banking at Merrill Lynch. Next to her is General Butler. He commands the 82nd Airborne Division. To my right is Manny Guiterrez, editor-in-chief of *The Miami Herald*. Me you know, of course. And I assume you know the esteemed President of Harvard University seated directly to your right? And to my left is Roger Atkins, CEO and chairman of the board of RAM Industries."

Jack could only nod in acknowledgment.

"The people you see here are merely the tip of the iceberg, Jack. There are many others, in all walks of life, dedicated to only one cause—the preservation of democracy in the face of tyranny."

"I thought that's what the people did when they vote in elections?" Jack had gotten over his initial awe.

"Yes, Jack, they do, they do," interjected Rankine. "Unfortunately, there are always forces at work trying to subvert that process. The rich, the arrogant, the power hungry. What you and Ms. Stevens have experienced is testament to that."

The director continued, "When this country was founded, it was founded on the principle that the government was of the people, by the people, for the people. It quickly became clear that it was a principle not easily preserved. If you recall, some people wanted to have George Washington become king. A group dedicated to preserving democracy was formed. We are the descendants of that secret society that has existed since shortly after the signing of the Constitution in 1789. We call ourselves the Framers, in honor of those who crafted our Constitution, vesting in the people the power to rule themselves. Dedicated people like Alison and those around this table have devoted their lives—and, sadly, sacrificed them—to preserve our democracy. I'm sorry that I had to put you through all this, but I couldn't reveal the truth until we were sure that you were not part of the broader conspiracy. Alison has vouched for you, and that's enough as far as I'm concerned."

"That's real nice of you. But how can I be sure that I can trust you?"

The General spoke up. "The way I see it, son, you have no choice. The government sure as hell can't protect you and someone obviously wants you dead. You know something and knowledge is power. That has been the key to our success; and sadly, where we have failed over the years, it has been because we didn't have people in place who had access to information. Now if you tell us what you know, we may be able to help you."

Jack stood up from his chair. "Can you give us a minute?"

"Of course. Take as much time as you need," replied the director.

Jack grabbed Alison by the arm. They moved off to one corner of the room. He turned his back to the people assembled at the table.

"It's your call," he said to her.

"Jack, these people are not perfect, you should know that. To them the ends justify the means. They wouldn't hesitate to sacrifice you or me to the cause. We are only useful to them if we can help them, and if we help them they will be true to their word and we can be free of this and maybe make a life for us."

"OK, then we do it for us."

"And for our country."

"Agreed."

They turned and walked back toward the conference table.

"OK," Jack said. "Here's the deal. We tell you what we know. In return, you agree that our involvement stays in this room. No one knows where the information came from. Second, when this thing is done, Alison is free of you and your whole secret society. You guarantee that we have safe passage, so to speak. No harm comes to me or Alison."

"Anything else?" Stevenson asked.

"Yes. I want five million dollars deposited in an account to be designated by me. That should be enough for Alison and me to disappear. Notwithstanding your honorable intentions, I'd feel much more comfortable if no one knew where we were, or at least would have to try hard to find us."

"Anything else?" the director asked, with a trace of sarcasm in his voice.

"Not that I can think of."

Stevenson looked around the table. The silence signified agreement.

"Agreed."

Alison nodded at Jack. She reached in her purse and pulled out the photograph from the TV station and the video. She handed them to Jack and he placed them on the table. "We believe that this man was involved as part of a conspiracy involving some person or persons within the government to kill the president-elect." He handed the picture to the chief justice, who gazed at it, shook his head and passed it on. As it made its way around the table, Jack continued.

"Mr. Martinez has given us some information to lend credence to this theory. Specifically, that the Front was taken over by outsiders connected in some way to the government. I can't give you any details. That would violate my ethical duty to him. However, that man was at the courthouse when the bomb went off. He was there to see if the job got done. As you can see, the man has access to the president and I suspect the president may be in great danger."

"What you have said so far confirms what we have learned," the director interjected. "We also know that they had a mole inside the FBI feeding them information about the Front that allowed them to avoid our counter-terrorism efforts."

As he spoke the picture reached the director. He picked it up and his eyes widened.

"You're sure this man is the one?"

"Without a doubt," Jack answered. Alison nodded her head in agreement.

"Well, at least one mystery is solved," the director responded.

"What's that?" asked Symanski.

"I know who this is." He placed the picture down on the table. "It also explains a few things. This is Special Agent Harkin Dow. He is one of the most senior agents in the Secret Service and head of the presidential protection detail."

"You don't seem surprised," commented Guiterrez.

"No. I suspected from the beginning that someone high up with access was involved. The forensics on the bomb showed it was an inside job, so that confirmed my suspicions. It also explains the sophisticated nature of the Front's actions. Someone in the Secret Service would have the expertise we saw in explosives and command and control. The question is who else was involved? Just this afternoon, we learned that a young female agent on the presidential detail was murdered. I suspect, perhaps, she knew too much."

"You'll have to warn the president," the general said.

"I have a meeting with him first thing in the morning."

He reached inside his suit pocket and pulled out a small cell phone and dialed. "Jenkins, I want you to get a search-and-arrest warrant for Harkin Dow. Yes, that Harkin Dow. You need to get a judge out of bed on this one. I want you to take only the best men you trust. This can't leak out. Get with the guys in legal and make sure the file is sealed. National security. Next pull the files on all the Secret Service agents on White

House duty. The details for the president, first lady, vice president, everybody. Call me back as soon as you get the warrants."

He hung up. "Well, Mr. Banner, you should be proud of yourself. You did your country a great service tonight." The assembled group murmured their approval.

"Now what?" Jack asked.

"We bring Mr. Dow in for questioning. We search his apartment, his office, all of his bank records. We turn his whole life inside out. We find out what he knows."

"And then?" Alison asked

"We prepare the country for the news. Manny, I want you to run a story tomorrow that a high FBI source has revealed that the activities of the Front were not aided by any foreign government and that, in fact, the possibility of rogue elements in the government is being investigated."

"Done," said Guiterrez.

"General, I need you to put the elements of the 82nd within your control on alert. We may need them on short notice."

"Yes, sir."

"Elaine, what do see as the impact on the financial markets when this leaks out?"

Symanski pondered the question for a moment. "Not good, but they are so far down right now, it can't get much worse. People are uncertain and uncertainty is bad for the markets."

Jack was taking it all in, trying to digest what was happening. These people saw themselves as a shadow government. The keepers of the flame. It didn't sit right with him. What gave them the right to make these decisions?

"Excuse me, but I have just one question?"

"Yes, Jack?" asked the director.

"What gives you the right to make all these decisions? These plans? Maybe the people don't want your help. Maybe the country will do just fine without you. The FBI, the police, the courts, they aren't all corrupt. Take your Agent Evans, for example. He would put his life on the line for me or for you. The things you do, the decisions you make, could just make things worse." It was said with more passion and fury than Jack had intended. The room was silent. But he was fed up with all the puppeteers trying to maneuver him and decide his fate. Despite all he had seen and been through, he remained resolute in his conviction that the system worked. Most of the people wanted it to work, because most of the people were at their core decent and good. Sure some of them were bad or corrupt, but time revealed them as such, and then the wrongs were made right. Life was inexorable. These people believed they could alter history, fix the past and change the future.

"No one gives us the right, Jack. We take it. Not because we want to, but because we have to." Justice Kincaid rose from his chair. He walked over to one of the windows, its blind drawn shut, and stretched out his arm. "I wish I could be like all those people out there—asleep and sound in their belief that the sun will come up tomorrow. I, we, don't have that luxury. I've been a judge most of my life. I've seen a lot of good and a lot of evil. For the most part the system does work, but sometimes it needs fixing. Look at slavery. McCarthyism. Vietnam. Watergate. Eventually the people do get it right, once they figure out what went wrong. That's all we are trying to do, Jack. Give them a chance to make it right. They can't do that if the truth is hidden from them. And believe me it gets hidden more than you think."

"With all due respect, Your Honor, you're missing the point," Jack replied. "If this is, as you say, a government of the people, by the people, for the people, you are acting without a mandate. If you believe in democracy and the right of people to choose, then you need to take your case to the people and say this is what we are all about. Otherwise, you are no better then the people who set off those bombs."

Alison interceded, "Jack, I don't think that's fair. These people risk their lives, dedicate their lives, to a cause. They, I, have seen many of our friends and loved ones die for that cause."

"I'm not denying the sacrifice, Alison, or your intentions. All I'm trying to say is that it's a fine line. What I'm hearing is that the ends justify the means. That's a frightening thought. If there are no checks and balances on what you do, except your own notion of what's right and wrong, that can be a very tricky balancing act."

The general was growing tired of the philosophical discourse. "Look, we don't have time for this right now. For all we know the president could be next. We need to act and we need to act fast."

The director nodded in agreement. "I'm afraid the general is right. Perhaps another time, Mr. Banner. For now there is work to be done."

The people seated around the table stirred, gathering up their belongings. Jack was still not satisfied with the answers or the situation, but he realized he had little choice. He also rose from the table.

"We have a safe house where we can take you and Alison. You will be well protected."

"Frankly, if you all don't mind, I would like to get back to my own house and my own life. I think my work here is done. And Alison and I have a client to represent."

Atkins spoke up for the first time. "I'm not sure that's a wise idea, Mr. Banner."

"Please, call me Jack. I imagine our friend the director can simply double my guard, can't you?" Jack grinned at the director.

"Jack," Atkins continued, "we don't know who might be involved in the conspiracy. No one can guarantee your safety."

"I understand. I'm willing to take that chance. I figure with my high profile the stakes are a little high for would-be assassins. Gentlemen, I thank you for your hospitality. Alison shall we?"

"Jack, I'm not going with you."

"What do you mean?" Alison looked over her shoulder, somewhat embarrassed. The others present quietly and quickly exited the room. In a few moments they were alone. Jack turned toward her; anger spread across his face.

"I'm not going to let you do this, Alison."

"Do what?" She folded her arms across her chest and turned slightly away from him, trying to increase the physical distance between them.

"Run away. You can't run forever. I love you."

Now it was her turn to be angry. "It's so simple for you. You just say the words and hope nothing else matters. You just want to feel and act and not think about the consequences. But there are other things we have to be true to besides ourselves, our feeling, our needs. I have to honor the promises I made, Jack, to those people waiting outside, to the cause. I have to see this thing through to the end; to do that I have to have a clear mind. You make me confused. I lose focus. The stakes are too high. I can't let that happen. I have to put aside my personal feelings."

Jack reached out and placed one hand on each of her arms. She tried to avoid his gaze. "I'm sorry Alison, but you're wrong. It is all about feelings. Otherwise, why bother to save the world? Why bother to risk your life and the lives of your friends? It's so two young people can fall in love and have children and raise those children in a better world. It's so we can have freedom to make choices, even they are the wrong choices. It's so we can be free to think and feel and cry and laugh. That's what freedom is. It's not an abstract principle. If you walk away from me now, your struggle is pointless and empty. When it's over, you'll be all alone. You would have fought for nothing that mattered to you, and that's what matters most."

She looked up at him and smiled slightly. "Alright. For now. But I can't make any promises, Jack. I can't see that far ahead, like you can."

Jack nodded with understanding. "Now let's get out of here."

They opened the door and the director was standing there waiting for them. "I'm afraid we have to insist on the blindfold."

Jack did not resist. He turned around and the director placed the blindfold over his eyes. As this was done, a figure stepped out of the darkness beside Alison. She was startled for a moment, until she recognized the face. "Don't forget where your loyalty lies." It was said in a low, menacing whisper.

"Don't forget my insurance policy and your promise." Alison whispered back. The director was talking to Jack as he tied the blindfold, masking Alison's conversation.

"The promise will be kept if it can be kept. If not, everyone is expendable, especially your precious Mr. Banner. Are you prepared to sacrifice your life for his?" Alison turned to answer but the figure was gone.

"You ready, Alison?" asked the director.

"Yes, I'm ready. Come on Jack." She grabbed his hand and led him down the hall. "I'll show you the way."

CHAPTER 50

Mrs. Bourne practically fainted when she opened the letter. After returning from the police station she had spent the day attending to funeral arrangements, while the detectives and the FBI had searched her house from top to bottom, finding nothing. She had made supper and then friends had come by to pay condolences. She had tried to sleep, but to no avail. Around 12:30 in the morning she had been pacing the house and then thought to check her mail. The letter had no return address. Inside was a plain white piece of paper and another envelope. On the front of the second envelope was a single word: "Mom." It was written in Melissa's handwriting. The note simply said, "You're daughter asked me to mail this to you if anything should happen to her. I am sorry for your loss."

She had wanted to tear open the letter and read it, but then she remembered that the detectives and FBI had told her to report anything suspicious right away. More than anything, she wanted to catch those responsible for her daughter's death. She had immediately gone outside and hailed down the FBI agent sitting in front of her house. Within minutes, a police car was there to drive her down to the station. Now she was sitting with detectives Pettit and Hernandez and Agent Evans. Her husband had been too distraught to accompany her.

"I know this must be difficult for you. You did the right thing coming here," Hernandez assured her.

A forensic team had taken possession of the envelope and its contents. One of the team entered the squad room, walked up to Hernandez and handed him a photocopy of the letter. The original was still undergoing some rigorous testing.

"Take your time, m'am," Evans said.

"Dear Mom . . ." but she could go no further. She started to sob. "I can't. I can't."

Evans reached out and gently removed the letter from her hands. He handed her some tissues. She dabbed her eyes and tried to regain her composure. She stopped crying. "I'm sorry."

"There's nothing to be sorry about. If you want to do this another time, we would understand," Evans said.

"No. No. Please read the letter. I need to know what it says."

Evans read the letter aloud.

Dear Mom and Dad:

If you have received this letter, obviously something bad has happened to me. I wanted you to hear the whole story directly from me and not from someone else. I'm sorry. I made some really bad choices. When I joined the Secret Service, I took an oath to protect the president with my own life if I had to. Unfortunately, I became involved with some people who I thought were trying to do good things, when in the end they were evil and misguided. I agreed with them that the country was in danger of coming under treacherous leadership and they convinced me, brainwashed me, that the only way to stop it was to kill the president-elect. The only way to protect the president was to kill his opponent. Afterwards, I realized what I had done was wrong and I prayed a lot and finally I found solace in the word of God. I realized that only the truth could set me free. I hope that reporter told the world what I told him and he published the plan I gave him. If not, I want you to go to the police or the FBI and tell them that I was involved in a conspiracy to assassinate the next president. It was all arranged and paid for by Howard Berlin. His loyalty to the president knows no bounds.

Tell them that I'm sorry. I love you Mom and Dad.
Melissa

She was weeping openly by the end of the letter.

"You can keep that copy if you like," said Hernandez. Evans rose from his seat. Actually he wanted to leap out of his seat and run to the phone, but he couldn't do that. He was able to leave the room as Hernandez and Pettit comforted her. He pulled out his cellphone once he was outside the interview room and dialed the director's number. "The cellular customer you have called is unavailable or has left the calling area."

Evans hung up and dialed Jenkins's number. "Jenkins, it's me, Evans. I'm over at the station. We just got a break. I tried to reach the director. I can't talk on this line. It's not secure. Can you reach the director and set up a meeting? It's 'your eyes only' kind of stuff."

Ordinarily he could have, but Jenkins had been unable to raise the director for the last hour. He didn't let Evans know that. "I'll find him and call you back. Return to headquarters. I should probably have located him by then."

He hoped that was true. He was getting a little nervous and maybe a little paranoid. It seemed to him that the director often disappeared at the strangest times. When questioned, his explanations were a little odd. Jenkins's immediate thought was that he was having an affair. At least that's what he hoped.

"I'll see you in twenty."

Jenkins hung up and dialed the director's phone. "The cellular . . ."

"Damn," Jenkins exclaimed as he slammed down the phone. He leaned back in his chair, hit the speakerphone and then re-dialed. Things were moving fast now, but where the hell was the director of the FBI?

CHAPTER 51

Harkin Dow was also on the phone, but he knew exactly where the person he needed to talk to was. Switzerland was seven hours ahead, which made it early morning. Mr. Lefteski would be in bed, probably alone. Although Dow had told the truth about the one million dollars in the Swiss bank account, he had left out one small detail. It required his cosignature to activate the account, after which the money would all be Lefteski's. Dow had suspected that he might need Lefteski's services and, as always, he had been right. Lefteski had been somewhat upset by this fact upon arriving at the *Suisse Bank De Credit*. The bank officer had calmly explained that a small sum of $25,000 was available, as well as a letter containing further instructions. The instructions had told him to stay put and wait. This he had done, too fearful and too poor to do otherwise.

The call did, in fact, catch him sound asleep. "Hello," he mumbled.

"Hello, Larry. Sorry to wake you."

Lefteski sat straight up in bed, now quite awake. "What . . . What do you want?"

"Your help Larry. In fact I think you might quite enjoy it. It involves computers and it involves hacking."

Lefteski was scared but also intrigued. Hacking was his one true passion. It was almost better in his mind then sex. He treaded cautiously.

"I thought I was through with you." There was a hesitation in his voice. Harkin picked up on it immediately.

"Now, now, Larry. I have been fair with you, haven't I? I've put you up in an expensive hotel, all expenses paid. I've given you freedom and a new life. And, of course, I wouldn't expect a man of your talents to work for free. There's another hundred thousand in it for you, on top of the one million."

Hacking and getting paid for it. Now that was better than sex.

"I know you have doubts Larry. Let's make a deal. I'll explain the hack. If you don't want to do it then we call it even. Sound fair?" Dow knew the answer before he even said it. His business was to know people. He looked at faces and listened to voices each day of his life, trying to divine an intention, a thought, a motive. Always looking for an edge in the continuing battle to protect Eagle One from the citizens and outside enemies who might do him harm. It did not strike him as odd that now he was trying to cover his tracks, and to put blame on others for his actions that had resulted in the death of the future president. It had been necessary to protect the country.

"I'm listening."

It took about a minute to explain, a second for Lefteski to accept and another five minutes to flesh out the details. Phase one of his contingency plan was in place. The rest was now up to him.

CHAPTER 52

Hector Rodriguiz was hatching a plot of his own. Since the Front had struck its decisive blow, Hector had been on the run. The FBI was looking for him, but they did not look too hard in the barrios of East Los Angeles. The FBI had arrested many of his compatriots, but even now they were planning how to rebuild the movement. A meeting had been called. Fortunately, there were still many of the faithful willing to give him assistance. It had been relatively easy for him to travel across the country to the nation's capital. His thoughts now were on his fellow soldier, Martinez. He had been willing to sacrifice his life for the cause and now he was a prisoner of the capitalist pigs. Hector could not stand for that.

With two others from the local Front cell, he had been staking out the hospital. It had been easy enough to befriend one of the women in the laundry room. She had willingly shared with them the details of the floor and room where Martinez was staying, as well as details on the number and placement of the agents—at least the ones she knew about. Hector had no doubt that others were carefully hidden.

There had to be a way to set Martinez free. They could not allow him to be the victim of a show trial to validate the repressive system that denied the people freedom and justice at every turn. He imagined that any escape would be bloody. That was a chance they would have to take. Historic change required no less.

CHAPTER 53

It had taken two hours but Jenkins had finally been able to locate the director. He and Evans had spent the two hours pacing and fretting. Time was against them. They did not know if the conspirators had an inkling of the information that they possessed. Each hour that passed was one more hour for them to cover their tracks. Jenkins had immediately put a team on Berlin. He practically lived in the White House and was, in fact, hard at work in the wee hours of the morning. They would have to be careful that he did not discover the surveillance. Evans had shown Jenkins the letter and described what he knew. They sat in the director's office awaiting his arrival.

"Good morning, gentlemen. What do you have for me?"

Jenkins handed him a copy of the letter. The director sat down in his desk chair and reviewed it. He looked up when he finished.

"Can we be sure it's genuine?"

"The mother swears it's her daughter's handwriting without a doubt," Evans answered.

"Well, there is one small problem."

"What's that, sir?"

"I have information pointing in another direction. It seems your friend Mr. Banner has surfaced. That's where I was, debriefing him." He explained what he had learned from Jack and Alison. "Given that information, I can't exactly burst into the White House and arrest the president's chief of staff unless I'm damn sure. Do we have any independent corroboration?"

"No, sir, but based on what we do know, what if they were in it together?" offered Jenkins.

"Explain," replied the director.

"The infiltrators described by the Front members fit to a tee special agents of the Secret Service. White, clean-cut, military types. Our bomb expert believes it was an inside job. Also, we have motive for Berlin. He's a power hungry son-of-a-bitch. He would do something like this just to have four more years with all that power."

"One other piece of information I learned," added the director. "That guy killed outside the courthouse, he was ex-CIA. Name of Nicholas Ahern. Guess who he trained at Langley?"

"Harkin Dow," Evans answered.

"Bingo. Dow was with the company, but decided it wasn't for him. Wanted to chase bad guys, not ferret out spooks."

Jenkins interjected, "So it fits. Berlin recruits Dow and he recruits the other agents. They come up with a plan to use the Front. Figure they never get caught. But why would they go along with Berlin's plan and what's the payoff?"

"There is no need for a payoff and that's the beauty of the plan," the director said. "It's all in the oath." His mind wandered back to the oath he had taken many years ago: *I will protect and defend the principles of democracy at all cost and with all means within my power. I will never forsake the principle that the government is of the people, by the people, for the people.*

"I'm afraid I don't follow you, boss," Jenkins said.

"Secret Service agents swear an oath just like you and I did. In their mind, the oath means they must protect the president at all cost. They train to sacrifice their own bodies and lives to protect the president. They live in a closed society. They view everything as a threat to the president. Throw in a power-hungry Washington political operative like Berlin and you have the perfect setting. Without a second term, Berlin has to lead a life like any other citizen, without the trappings of the presidency. He can't imagine that. So he starts thinking and soon those thoughts lead to a way to keep Hampton in office. He recruits Dow, maybe he brainwashes him, or maybe he buys him off. With the other agents it's just a matter of brainwashing. The country is in danger. The president must be protected at all cost, etc. Remember, Secret Service agents are like Marines, or even worse, the S.S. Highly trained and disciplined to carry out their duty without question or hesitation."

"So Berlin is the mastermind behind the whole thing?"

"It would appear that way."

"So do we arrest him or not?" Evans asked.

"I have to leave that up to the attorney general and the president. What we know may be enough for a search warrant. The legal guys will have to guide us on that. For now, keep the tail on Berlin. And pull out all the stops to find Dow. Determine the whereabouts of every member of the president's Secret Service detail. If anyone is missing or not where he or she is supposed to be I want to know about it. At least now we don't have to worry about the president."

"How's that?"

"The whole purpose was to keep him in office. He's the last person they would kill."

CHAPTER 54

Justice Kincaid's worst fear had come true. One of his clerks had brought him the complaint just as he had settled in behind his desk. Vice president-elect Simmons had filed it in the Federal Circuit Court for the District of Columbia. He was asking the court to declare the procedure for determining who would be the next president. The complaint would most certainly be denied by the district court as not being ripe for consideration, since it had not yet been ascertained who the electors would elect. But once denied, it would most certainly be appealed to the United States Supreme court.

He was now seated with all of the justices, who were going through the daily procedure of reviewing cases on which they had heard oral argument in the prior term. They would cast a preliminary vote and then the most senior justice in the majority would be assigned the task of writing the opinion. Kincaid interrupted the discussion of *Montego Bay Industrial and Chemical v. United States,* a particularly dull and uninteresting case regarding an arcane admiralty issue.

"Excuse me, but I believe a more important topic requires our attention."

"What's that, Donald?" asked Justice Mandel. She was the elder of the two female justices, outranking Justice Carolyn Daniels by ten years. She considered Kincaid her mentor and good friend. They had privately discussed the issue and so she was prepared to follow his lead.

"The situation with the presidential election."

"Donald, you know better than all of us that there is nothing we can do about that but wait, like everyone else," replied Justice Hawkins. He was the sole African American on the bench. He was considered a moderate. A brilliant constitutional scholar, he had already researched the issue of the election process and reached the same conclusion as David Rothstein.

"But can we afford to wait?" argued Justice Mandel. "While we fiddle, Rome may burn."

At the end of the table Justice Sullivan jumped in. "I would have to agree with Justice Mandel." His comment came as a surprise. He occupied the extreme right wing of the court. It was the first thing that he and

Mandel had agreed upon in the ten years they had been on the court together. The looks must have been too obvious.

"Well, don't look so surprised." Laughter filled the room and eased the tension. "I'm not suggesting anything drastic, like sending the Army into the street. I'm just saying that we not avoid the issue and, if possible, find a way to address it."

Kincaid was pleased with the direction of the conversation. After serious consideration and counsel with Justice Mandel, as well as the words that Jack Banner had spoken, he realized that contrary to his earlier fears about having the court decide the issue, it might be the only way to avoid a constitutional crisis and chaos. If his colleagues in the lower courts could not bring the matter to a resolution quickly, the court would have to bring its authority to bear. In thinking it through, it was clear that the only correct answer was, absent some fraudulent act, the decision of the electors in the Electoral College would have to stand. A reading of the Constitution and the law required no less. It was a lousy system, but like it or not, one with which they were stuck. It was important for the court to give it the imprint of legitimacy so that the people, including those who stood to personally gain from it, like Simmons, would accept the result.

"I had one of my clerks prepare this memo of law on the subject." He passed copies around to the justices as he spoke. "The conclusion, and one I agree with, is that the electors are free agents, for lack of a better term. They are not bound by the results of the popular vote, notwithstanding any state statute to the contrary."

"I reached the same conclusion myself," offered Justice Hawkins.

Justice Cohen shook his head in disbelief. "My clerks and I discussed the issue this morning and we were all amazed. How is it possible that a country that lauds itself on being the world's greatest democracy allows 538 people to choose its most important elected official? The man who has the power to launch nuclear weapons, to send our sons and daughters into war?"

"It's all in the memo, Alan. I won't bore you with the details."

"If we applied the principle that the case was capable of repetition, yet evading review, we could address the issue even without an actual case or controversy," Justice Hawkins volunteered. Because of the length of time involved in the appellate process, the reality of the situation could stymie the ability of the court to review the case. In abortion cases, for example, by the time the case came for review, the woman would have already given birth, and thus the court would be thwarted in its ability to review the case, because an actual case and controversy no longer existed.

"That would be consistent with prior precedent," replied Justice Mandel.

The others nodded.

"Then it is agreed. If the case is presented on a writ, we will accept jurisdiction?" asked Justice Kincaid. He scanned the table. All the heads nodded in agreement. That settled, they embarked once again upon a discussion of maritime law, but each of them was already busily scanning the memorandum of law lying before them.

CHAPTER 55

Stevenson and the president were seated in the Oval Office. They were alone but, in fact, just outside the door the Secret Service kept watch. Even with his conclusion that the likelihood of an attack on the president was small, he was still greatly concerned. Any of the Secret Service agents in the White House could potentially be part of the conspiracy.

"Mr. President, I could use a little fresh air. How about you?"

The president gave him a quizzical look. He had just made himself comfortable. "It's a bit chilly, don't you think, Gary?" It was probably no more than thirty degrees outside, gray and overcast.

"Sir, I'm afraid I have to insist."

"Very well, but you only have fifteen minutes. I have a full schedule."

They left the Oval Office. Magically the Secret Service detail appeared, with one agent holding a coat for the president. He declined it. Stevenson checked out each of the agents carefully and wished he had his service revolver. Even he had to check his weapon at the door. Stevenson and the president walked to the Rose Garden. Once there, Stevenson guided the president as far away as possible from the security detail.

"Only three people know what I am about to tell you." That was a lie but a necessary one. "We were right about the fact that the Front was assisted by members of the United States Government, and it goes very high up, sir. Very high." Stevenson looked back over his shoulder. There were three agents in the Rose Garden with them. He leaned close to the president and whispered in his ear, "Your chief of staff appears to be involved as well as some members of your Secret Service detail."

The president's head snapped back and away from Stevenson. He turned with a look of shock and surprise in his eyes. "Howard? No. Not Howard. He may have done some crazy things over the years, but murder? It's just not in his character. And Secret Service agents? Do you have proof? These are very serious allegations."

Stevenson shook his head. "Nothing solid, but it all points in that direction. I thought you should know what we know. I'm going to meet with the attorney general later today and lay out what we know, and see if he agrees that it's enough for some search warrants."

"Berlin? What could he have been thinking?" The president hung his head wistfully and slumped his shoulders. Then, just as suddenly, he straightened up. "No time for personal feelings. You have my full support, Gary, as always. If you can prove what you say, then you take it as far as you need to."

"Yes, Mr. President."

"If you don't mind, I'd like a few minutes alone."

"One more thing, Mr. President."

"Yes?"

"I'd like to put a few of my men in your Secret Service detail. I think I can sell it as a joint exercise. I'd trust them with my life."

"As you see fit, Gary. I suppose a note to Hopkins over at Treasury would smooth the way."

"It would, sir."

"Very well. Thank you, Gary. Is Ann still at Harvard?"

"Graduated last year, Mr. President."

"Time sure does fly. Damn crazy world sometimes. Damn crazy."

"Yes, sir. I'll have my men here by lunchtime."

He turned and left the president alone in the Rose Garden. He hoped he was right that there was no danger to him. He quickened his step, nodding at the members of the detail as he passed. He needed to get his men over here as fast as he could, just in case.

CHAPTER 56

The hacking had been relatively easy. In fact, in the truest sense of the word, it had not been a hack. Mr. Smith had given him all the passwords. He keyed in the account number of the Geneva account. The balance came up and Lefteski blinked twice to make sure all the zeros were not the result of his bleary eyes. No, it was $100,000,000. He regretted for a moment the paltry one million sitting in "his" account, to which he now had doubts Mr. Smith would ever give him access. At this point he didn't care. If he got out with his body parts intact he would be happy.

He processed the request for a transfer. In milliseconds, ten million of the hundred million dollars was flowing—as bits and bytes across phone wires and through servers and switches and mainframes—to be deposited at a distant location, in a branch of a local bank in the District of Columbia. He made nine other transfers to nine other banks throughout the United States, all in cities where the Front had been extremely active. As he waited for the confirmation, he wondered if all those banks actually got ten million of cold hard cash delivered to their front door from the bank in Geneva. In fact, he wondered if the whole thing was just a game. What if he, and everyone else, walked in to their banks one day and said "I'd like to close my account." Was there enough paper money to go around?

The only tricky part of the job was covering his tracks. He was using a local access provider in Switzerland to gain access to the Internet. Using a stolen credit card number, Mr. Smith had established the account in the name of a Cayman Island corporation. All that would be left was a trail leading to someone else that the FBI could follow. His task accomplished, he terminated his connection. Mr. Smith would be contacting him soon. He hoped it was with the password to his million dollars.

CHAPTER 57

The director's meeting with the attorney general had gone well. The evidence they had in hand was sufficient for search warrants and arrest warrants. The time had come to bring down the hammer. It had been a delicate matter to raise with the president, but the director had received his consent to arrest Berlin in the White House. It was important to make a statement that no one was above the law. The president had scheduled a press conference to coincide with the arrests. The arrest of Dow would be more difficult. He had disappeared off the face of the earth. His intercom buzzed.

"Yes."

"It's Agent Duncan."

The director picked up the phone. "What do you have for me?"

"An early Christmas present. Harkin Dow walked into headquarters about an hour ago. He said he heard we were looking for him. I have him down here on the third floor. I assume you want to be in on the interrogation?"

"I'll be right there." The director practically leapt from his chair. He had to stop himself from running. He started for the elevators but then turned abruptly about and headed for the stairs. He was almost out of breath when he reached the third floor. Duncan was waiting for him, as well as Jenkins. The interview area was a series of rooms with one-way windows. Duncan and Jenkins stood outside the room. Inside was Dow, sitting at a nondescript table, in a nondescript room. The interrogation rooms had no windows or clocks. The walls were bare.

"How long has he been in there?" asked Stevenson.

"About half an hour."

"Have you Mirandized him?"

"Chapter and verse."

"Let's do it." They entered the room. The director went in first, followed by Jenkins and Duncan. Dow looked up, recognition showing on his face, but little else. Stevenson pulled up a chair opposite Dow. Jenkins sat to his right. Duncan remained standing, leaning casually against a wall.

"We need to talk, Mr. Dow."

"Actually, there's not much to talk about. I've come to make a full confession. But I have one condition."

"What's that?"

"I want the right to talk to the press, explain why I did what I did."

The director pondered this for a moment. "Agreed, but only one reporter of our choosing and not for more than an hour. I don't want a circus."

"Deal. I killed the president-elect. It was me and Melissa Bourne and a group of agents under my command. Of course we were only following orders."

"Following orders? Whose orders?"

"Howard Berlin's."

The director sighed with relief. They had been right.

"Berlin and I had grown close over the years. When it looked like the president might lose, we started talking. We discussed the fact that the country was in a very fragile stage. There was, and is, I suppose, a real possibility of mass civil unrest, outbreaks of violent factionalism. Hampton is a straight shooter, a true American. This new guy wanted us to try a new way. As far as I'm concerned that way had been tried and failed. They called it Communism. Well, the more we talked, the clearer it became that we had to do something. And so we came up with a plan. We needed a cover. The Front was easily taken over. Their need for cash far outweighed their paranoia about strangers and new members taking over. We had access to money. I had the people. It was really very easy."

"You have proof? These are very serious allegations."

Dow looked at them and smiled. "Yes, I do. You just have to follow the money." He reached into his suit pocket. The agents flinched for a moment but Duncan allayed their fears.

"We frisked him. All he has is his wallet, a key to a safe-deposit box and some papers he wanted to show us that I said he could keep."

Dow withdrew the papers and the key from his suit pocket and placed them on the table. "These are a list of accounts around the United States. They are all owned by offshore entities, which are in turn owned by other offshore entities. If you dig hard enough, and I know you gentlemen are very skilled in that area, you'll see that Berlin is behind all of them. The second sheet is a list of the agents involved. You can ask them. The key is to a safe deposit box. In the box you'll find our whole contingency plan: Operation Restore Democracy. A catchy name don't you think? It lays it all out. Times, dates, places."

The director picked up the list. "Did you know Melissa Bourne is dead?" asked the director.

"Yes. I'm afraid I did. Unfortunately for her, she had a change of heart. I take promises made to me very seriously."

"So you're confessing to her murder as well?"

"Yes I am."

"You realize the seriousness of these crimes, of this confession. Why are you doing this?"

"I'm proud of what I did. It was necessary to preserve the country, to protect the president, to honor my oath. The people will thank me some day."

"I doubt that very much, sir," said the director, rising from his chair. "You are a disgrace to your country and I can't stand to be in the room with you for another minute. Arrest him and get him a lawyer."

"One man's traitor is another man's patriot." *A rather nice touch, Dow thought.*

The director turned and walked out of the room. Jenkins rose as well. "Mr. Dow, you are under arrest for the murder . . ."

CHAPTER 58

Jack awoke, opened his eyes, and then, realizing that he lay in his own bed and, even better, with Alison next to him, closed them again. She was breathing gently. He could smell her scent in the air and feel the warmth of her body next to him. He savored the moment, saddened by the fact that he was not sure it was an experience that would become a regular part of his life. After a minute, he quietly extricated himself from the bed, crossed to the bathroom and quietly closed the bathroom door. He brushed his teeth, showered and shaved. Alison was still asleep when he emerged. He threw on a T-shirt and some sweatpants and went down to the kitchen. Agent Evans was seated there, with a large smile on his face.

"Good morning, counselor."

"Good morning, Agent Evans."

"I suppose I should be really pissed off at you, seeing as how you almost cost me my job; but I'm in such a good mood, I'm willing to forget all that."

Jack got a mug from the cupboard and poured himself some coffee. "I'm sorry about that. I really had no choice."

Evans nodded.

"And what put you in such a great mood? Was it seeing me again?"

"Actually, no. I just got a call from Assistant Director Jenkins. It seems our friend Mr. Dow has made a full confession as well as implicating the president's chief of staff."

Jack almost dropped his coffee cup. He stood mute for a minute as the words sunk in. "That's fantastic news! I need to tell Alison right away."

"Tell me what?" she asked, as she walked into the kitchen wiping sleep from her eyes. Jack rushed over to her and gave her a big hug and spun her around in an impromptu dance. "We were right. That guy at the courthouse, he was the one. He confessed the whole thing to the FBI."

Alison smiled and returned Jack's hug. "So what was the reason?" she asked Evans.

"Can't really say much more. I've said enough already. My fellow agents are out right now making arrests and the president will be holding a news conference in a little while. What's a guy gotta do around here to get a little breakfast!"

"I feel like cooking," volunteered Alison. "How about some pancakes?"

"Great," said Evans.

"Great," chimed in Jack.

"Pancakes it is."

CHAPTER 59

The agents arrived in force. They wanted to leave nothing to chance. Berlin had just finished a phone call when they came bursting through the door and into the office. His secretary was close behind, flustered and trying to make sense of what was unfolding before her eyes.

"Mr. Berlin, I tried to stop them . . ."

"What the hell . . ." Duncan cut him off.

"Howard Berlin, you are under arrest for murder and conspiracy to commit murder. You have the right to remain silent. Anything you say can be used against you in a court of law. You have the right to have an attorney. If you cannot afford one, one will be appointed for you. Do you understand these rights as I have explained them?"

"Yes. I mean no. I don't understand this. Murder? I didn't murder anyone. What's going on here?"

"I'm sorry, sir, only I get to ask the questions. Barnes, cuff him."

Agent Barnes moved toward Berlin. Berlin complied by turning his back and placing his arms behind him. "I want my lawyer."

"Don't worry, you'll get one, and I hope for your sake he's a good one."

"Donaldson, Meyers, you search the place, top to bottom and don't forget the computers and all the disks. Seal this place tight. No one gets in or out."

"Yes, sir!" they replied in unison.

"Come with us, Mr. Berlin."

Duncan and Barnes each grabbed one arm and steered Berlin out the door. "Ms. Swensen," he yelled to his secretary, "call the president. And then Stan Bradley at Holland and Jones."

She nodded through the tears forming in her eyes.

"Wait until the president finds out about this. You guys are finished."

Duncan didn't much like Berlin, having heard many stories about him from Jenkins and the director. He couldn't resist one jab. "Actually, he was the one who suggested we arrest you here."

Berlin slumped, as if shot. He started to speak and then changed his mind. The less he said the better. He went along without further protest.

CHAPTER 60

The White House Press Room was filled to capacity. As the president entered, the reporters rose in unison. The president strode to the rostrum.

"Good morning. Please be seated. I have a short statement to make and then I'll answer a few questions. First, I'd like to thank the American people for their response to this tragic situation. You have acted with great calm and composure, rallying together in a time of crisis. I have never been prouder to be an American.

"I'm pleased to announce this morning that several arrests have been made in connection with the assassination of president-elect Davis." The president paused to allow the import of his words to sink in. The reporters scribbled notes furiously. "I am also saddened to announce that those arrested included members of my administration, including my chief of staff, Howard Berlin." There was an audible murmur from the reporters, and the president paused momentarily until the noise subsided.

"Apparently the old adage that absolute power corrupts absolutely has proved painfully true. Needless to say, I am shocked by this turn of events. I would remind the people and the press, however, that all persons are presumed innocent until proven guilty. The investigation is continuing and I would caution against a rush to judgment. I'll answer a few questions and then turn over the details to FBI Director Stevenson."

Every hand in the room shot up and shouted, "Mr. President."

"Ann," the president said, selecting Ann Phillips of CBS News as the first questioner.

"Mr. President, can you tell us who else has been arrested and are any more arrests expected?"

"Yes and no. Mr. Harkin Dow, of the Secret Service has been arrested. Other arrests are pending, but I can't divulge names."

The hands shot up again. "Paul." The president pointed to Paul Thomas of *The New York Times*. "Mr. President, are you telling us that what we have witnessed was an attempted *coup d'etat* and, if so, how extensive was the conspiracy? Were elements of the military involved?"

The president reflected for a moment. "I'm not sure what the formal name is, Paul, but clearly it was a plot to alter the government against the will of the people. For what purpose remains somewhat unclear. We believe the conspiracy was not widespread, as far as those involved in the government. Again, for obvious reasons I can't give specific details, but the Democratic Revolutionary Front was used as a cover. As to the military, I have at all times received the complete cooperation of all elements of the military. It appears the trail begins and ends in the White House, and with members of my staff and my administration. One more question. Steve."

Steve Carver of *The Washington Post* stood to address the president. "Mr. President, where does this leave the line of succession and who will be the next president?"

"I'm glad you asked that question, Steve. As I stated in my nationwide address the other night, the electors who were selected by the voters on Election Day are scheduled to meet in the next ten days or so. Now I'm not sure that most of the American people understand it's those electors who choose the president and vice president. On Election Day, the voters chose those electors to go to their respective state capitols and cast their vote for president. As you know, these individuals can choose whomever they want for president and vice president. The other night, I asked those men and women to follow the will of the people. I'm afraid that I have to alter that opinion given recent events. I'm not sure this country can take a chance with unproven leadership. The vice president-elect may be a very capable man, but he hasn't been tested by the fire of this office as I have. I would appeal to the electors to cast their vote for me and my capable vice president, Evan Thomas." The president paused and the reporters tried to shout out questions. The president raised his hands.

"Please, let me finish. This is not a decision I have reached lightly. Frankly, I'd grown comfortable with the thought of retirement and more free time, but I'm afraid my country needs me. I've served this country my whole life and I can't walk away when it needs me most. Thank you very much." The president strode off the podium and out of the press room as the reporters hurled questions. The assembled staff and Director Stevenson stood flabbergasted in his wake.

Jenkins turned to Stevenson. "Did you know he was going to say that?"

"Not a clue," replied Stevenson.

With the president gone, the reporters turned on Stevenson.

"Director Stevenson, can you give us any more details?"

"When will the other arrests be made?"

Stevenson waived his hands and turned to Jenkins. "Let's get out of here."

CHAPTER 61

"That son of a bitch!" exclaimed Simmons. "He's going to steal the goddamn election." He was about to hurl the remote control at the television, when Amy Hall interceded.

"Look, boss, this is no time to panic. We've come a long way, and I'll be damned if I'm going to let that s.o.b. do an end around. "Berkley!" she shouted into the other office. "Get in here with the latest canvass."

Ron Berkley entered the room. He had been canvassing the electors on a nonstop basis. His face showed the stress of the long hours and the high stakes. Just a few weeks ago they had been celebrating their victory. It looked like plum political appointments for all of them. Now that was all in jeopardy.

"If my numbers are right, the latest count makes it nip and tuck. We started out at 271 to 267. A razor thin margin and now we have slippage. We need to reverse that. Twenty-five to thirty of our original electors say they are now undecided. Fifteen of those say they are leaning to the president. With the speech this morning there's no telling what might happen. I'm canvassing right now."

"Thanks, Ron. We'll let you get back to work. Let us know when you finish the latest canvass." Berkley nodded and left.

Simmons's blood was boiling again and he started to pace the room, waving his arms about. "Great! Just great! Thirty people hold the fate of our country in their hands." He turned to Amy Hall. "Amy, get me the DNC lawyers on the phone; we need to expedite the lawsuit. Next, schedule a press conference. I think the American people need to hear both sides of the story. And get me the names from Berkley of the electors that are wavering. I want to talk to every last one of them."

"Yes, sir." Hall practically ran from the room. They were used to the hectic pace of a campaign and responded naturally.

Simmons was left alone. It was a state he rarely found himself in lately. He took it in for a moment, cherishing the silence and the chance to think. If he did win, his time alone would be even less frequent. The thought struck him as odd. Winning? Was that what it was all about? He hoped not. He took a deep breath and walked over to the window. Why did he want this thing so badly? Would it be so terrible if the president was elected for another term? The country had taken a turn for the worse, but was the president to blame? Could he have done any better in similar circumstances? Was it merely his ego or was he truly interested in the greater good? His brief reverie was interrupted as Hall returned with the list of the wavering electors. Time to get back to work. His feelings and emotions would have to wait.

CHAPTER 62

Frank Ruffulo had turned a pale shade of white after listening to the president's press conference. His breathing was labored and he was perspiring profusely. *Berlin arrested. It couldn't be. Murder? What had he gotten himself into, and all for a measly fifty grand?* He picked up the phone, his hands trembling. Maybe Berlin hadn't made the deposit. In that case maybe he was in luck. Ruffulo dialed his bank's computerized inquiry line. First his PIN number, then the options, "Press 1 to review your most recent transaction." He pushed the 1.

"Your last transaction was . . . deposit . . . fifty thousand dollars."

He hung up the phone just as his wife walked in. "Oh my God!" she exclaimed. "You're having a heart attack!"

"No . . . no," he said, waving her away as she fawned over him. "Just something I ate. Get me a Bromo." His wife rushed off, giving Ruffulo time to think. Bromo. Hell, he needed a drink. And a lawyer. Jimmy had a brother who was a lawyer. Perfect. Kill two birds with one stone. His breathing had calmed some, and he felt the color returning to his face. He rose and crossed to the front hall closet. He dressed for the cold and yelled out. "Honey, forget the Bromo. I'm going to Jimmy's." Without waiting for an answer or a protest, he left the apartment, slamming the door shut behind him.

CHAPTER 63

Detective Hernandez had not had time to watch the press conference. The night shift had been busy as usual. No murders with 9mms. A stabbing and a .38 caliber would have to do. He and Pettit were filling out reports when the phone rang.

"Hernandez."

"Detective, it's Agent Evans with the FBI."

"Good morning."

"Good morning, hopefully I'm about to make it a little better. It looks like I just cleared one of your cases."

"You did?"

"It sounds like you didn't catch the press conference this morning."

"'Fraid I didn't, what with the paperwork and all."

"Don't I know it. Well, I won't keep you in suspense. We got a confession on the Bourne murder. Apparently, she was ready to rat out her colleagues so they beat her to the punch. I thought you would want to be the one to tell her mother."

"Colleagues?"

"You don't watch CNN either?"

"Not much."

"The whole conspiracy to kill our next president was an inside job masterminded by the president's chief of staff and the Secret Service detail. They're the ones that killed Bourne too."

"Secret Service." Suddenly a light went off. "Hang on a minute, Evans."

"Sure."

Hernandez placed his hand over the receiver. "Hey Pettit, what was it that was on the computer screen of that dead reporter?"

Pettit scratched his head a moment. It was from fatigue more than anything esle. Of the two, Pettit was the smarter and had a photographic memory of names and numbers.

"The secret is . . ."

"Yeah, now I get it." He removed his hand from the receiver. "My morning just got even better. You cleared two cases with one call."

"I don't follow you, detective."

"A reporter got whacked the other night at the Jefferson Memorial."

"Right, right, now I remember."

Hernandez continued, "Same MO, 9mm to the head. On his computer screen we found the words 'the secret is', but what the poor bastard was trying to type was, 'The Secret Service.' I'd ask your suspects about that murder, too."

"You bet I will. One question though."

"Shoot."

"How do you suppose he knew it was the Secret Service?"

"He was a reporter; he gets paid to know those things."

"Maybe. But best we can tell, only a few people were involved who would have that kind of knowledge. The guy we arrested, Berlin, Melissa Bourne and three other Secret Service Agents. I doubt they would share that kind of information."

Hernandez thought for a moment. "I doubt it too, but what does it matter now?"

"It matters, because things I don't know or can't explain make me nervous."

"I hear you. I hear you." He looked over at Pettit, who was now listening to the conversation. "I imagine Detective Pettit and I could devote a little more time to the Spivey case. See who he talked to, where he went."

Pettit was vigorously shaking his head, but it was too late. "I'd appreciate that, detective. If you get any heat from your superiors, tell them to give me a call."

"Will do."

"I assume you want to tell the parents we caught the guy."

"I'd like that. Unfortunately, I don't get to make that call often enough."

"Do we lead the same life?"

Hernandez chuckled. "It seems we do. I'll get back to you with what we know."

After he hung up the phone, he faced Pettit's dagger looks. "Next time you volunteer me, can you ask me first?"

"Like you have a life," he retorted with mock indignation. "Now let's go solve us a murder like real detectives."

CHAPTER 64

Jack and Alison had decided that it would be a good idea to visit Martinez in the hospital. The FBI had cleared the visit and, once again, provided the transportation. As they arrived, the hospital was abuzz with talk of the president's news conference. Doctors, nurses, orderlies and patients were all discussing the merits of the Electoral College. When they entered Martinez's room, he smiled at them feebly. Two agents were seated in the room with him. They nodded at Agent Davis, who returned the acknowledgment.

"And how is our favorite client today?" Jack asked as he walked up to the bed. Alison stood on the other side, at the head of the bed.

"I'm OK, man. At least I'm alive."

"You heard the news I suppose?"

"No one around here is talking about anything else."

Jack glanced over at Davis. "Could you give us some time alone? Attorney-client."

Davis pondered the request. "I can give you about five minutes." He motioned to the other agent. "Let's go." They were more than happy for the break. After they had left, Jack and Alison pulled up chairs on each side of Martinez's bed.

"You guys look so serious."

"Why shouldn't we?" replied Alison.

"Why shouldn't you? Because you cracked the case, that's why. I mean you guys are heroes!"

"I wouldn't go that far, Carlos," explained Jack. "You are still in a whole lot of trouble. That's why we're here." Jack reached into his briefcase and pulled out a picture of Harkin Dow. "The government may show some leniency if you cooperate. Do you recognize this man?"

Martinez studied the picture for a moment. "Sure, man, that's the crazy dude I was telling you about. The one that put the gun to my head."

"Good. Now can you tell us anything more about any meetings with this man, or anyone else, that you thought seemed a little out of place?"

He thought for a moment. "No, not really." Their conversation was interrupted by the arrival of a nurse.

"Hi, Donna."

"Hi, Carlos." Jack and Alison nodded. The nurse was carrying a tray with a hypodermic needle and some alcohol swabs. She placed the tray on the bedside table and opened one of the swabs. She wiped Martinez's upper arm and then reached for the syringe. She uncapped the needle. Her hands must have been slippery with perspiration. It had been a while since she killed a man. The syringe slipped from her hands and clattered to the floor. She quickly picked up the syringe and moved it towards Martinez's bicep.

"Wait!" shouted Alison. "Aren't you going to sterilize that?"

"Oh, yes, of course. I'm just a little nervous with all these FBI men around."

She reached for another alcohol swab, and tore open the wrapper. As she did, an alarm started to sound. "What the hell is that?!" cried Jack.

"Sounds like a fire alarm," offered Martinez.

The two agents who had left the room came hustling back in. "Hopefully it's just a false alarm, but if it's not, we may have to evacuate. We need to stay close to Martinez."

The alarm continued to clang as the nurse finished sterilizing the needle. She was about to inject Martinez when one of the agents drew his weapon and pointed it at her. "M'am, please step away from the patient."

"Are you crazy?" the nurse asked.

"Hey, Davis," interjected the other agent, "what the hell is going on?"

"Before I went to the academy, I did one year of medical school. I've been reading his chart when I get bored. So far he hasn't had any injections intramuscular. It's all oral, or in the IV. So why one now? Plus, she's always been the afternoon nurse. This isn't her shift. So like I said, step away from the patient!" The second agent drew his weapon as well.

Instead of taking a step back, Nurse Donna lunged forward. The cause was too important. Her life was not. The first shot hit her square in the chest, but the force of her momentum carried her arm down and forward, toward Martinez's exposed bicep. He could not move because his arms were restrained for security. Alison leapt forward and threw her arm up between the descending arm of the nurse and Martinez's arm. The syringe stopped less than a millimeter from Martinez's arm. The look of shock on his face turned to one of relief. The agents rushed forward pulling the syringe from the nurse's lifeless hand and laying the assassin's body on the cold tile floor.

"Quick thinking, Ms. Stevens," said the agent with admiration in his voice. "We could use a few more like you at the academy."

"Are you alright, Mr. Martinez?"

"I think so," he replied shakily. 'What the hell was in that syringe?"

"Couldn't say. The forensic guys will be able to tell us." The commotion had brought a number of other agents to the room. A nurse who had come in coolly and professionally left and returned with a sheet to cover the body. Other curious onlookers filled the hallway. One of them could not have been more pleased. Hector Rodriquez had hoped that the fire alarm he had tripped would provide the diversion that he needed. It had taken some convincing but the maid in the laundry had come around to his persuasive discussion of the oppression of the working class and the unfair show trial to which comrade Martinez would be subjected. She had agreed to provide orderly and nurse uniforms to Hector and his colleagues, the maintenance cart he was now pushing, and ID cards, which Hector had skillfully forged. He had been approaching the security checkpoint when the shots had been fired. He thought at first that Ernie and Carla had gotten trigger-happy. They were supposed to wait in the stairwell until he signaled them over the walkie-talkie. Three more Front members were outside the hospital waiting for them to liberate Martinez. On the contrary, it had left the checkpoint unattended. It was a diversion on top of his diversion. He strained his neck to see what was happening in the room.

A nurse in front of him asked, "What happened?"

"I think they shot one of the nurses."

"Oh my God! Who was it?"

"Donna, I think."

Rodriquez pushed his way forward, the cart in front of him, clicking his walkie-talkie twice to signal Carla and Ernie.

"Did someone call for an orderly?" Rodriguez asked.

The throng in front of him parted as he moved forward. When he entered the room he reached down to the second level of the maintenance cart and pulled out an Uzi submachine gun. He got the drop on all the agents who were still assembled in the room.

"Nobody move!" Behind him Ernie and Carla arrived. They herded those out in the hallway into the room. "Everybody on the floor."

"Hector!" cried out Martinez. "What the hell are you doing here?'

"I'm here to get you out of here."

"You crazy, man. This place is surrounded with cops."

Agent Davis surveyed the scene. It was not promising. The bad guys had a clear field of fire. Civilians were in his line of fire. He nodded to the other agents and they slowly lay down on the floor. Each was looking for a chance, an opening.

"Just shut up. You!" shouted Hector pointing at Jack "Untie him."

Jack got up from his chair. As he reached for Martinez's restraints, he whispered to him, "Don't do this, Carlos. We may be able to arrange a deal for you."

Jack turned to Hector to buy time. "This man is very sick. He may die if he leaves this hospital."

Hector looked concerned. "That true, Carlos?"

Martinez looked at Jack and then at Alison. Their eyes pleaded with him, but his trust of them was outweighed by his distrust of the system. "I can travel, man."

"You heard the man, untie him."

"Come on, Hector, we're running out of time," pleaded Ernie.

"I'll take care of that." He clicked his walkie-talkie three times. Within seconds there was a clatter of machine-gun fire coming from the front of the hospital and then a whoosh, followed by a loud explosion. Then, after a moment, the sound of return fire. "That should keep them busy."

Jack had finished untying Martinez. "Carla, give him the clothes." Carla pulled some clothes and shoes out of a knapsack for Martinez. He shed his hospital gown and dressed quickly.

"Carla, cuff all of them, except the lawyer, he's coming with us." Carla quickly moved forward, handcuffing the agents to each other with one pair and then cuffing each of them to the hospital bed. She pointed her gun at Jack and motioned him toward Martinez.

Martinez tried to dissuade Rodriguiz. He respected Jack for what he was trying to do for him. He didn't want to see him get hurt.

"What you want him for man? He'll just slow us down."

"This is a big mistake," Jack added.

"You shut up." He pointed the gun menacingly at Jack. "It's insurance, Carlos. You never know when you may need it. Now let's get moving."

Despite the fact that they were handcuffed, Hector kept his gun trained on the agents as he backed out of the room. He looked at all the hospital personnel on the floor.

"Any of you try to follow us and we'll blow your head off," he threatened. To emphasize the point he let loose a few rounds over their heads, eliciting a mixture of screams and gasps.

Down the hallway, Rodriquez, Martinez, Jack and the others headed for the stairwell. They forced Jack to go first. He scanned the hallway for the possibility of escape. There was none. Two police officers lay dead at the top of the stairwell. They stepped over the bodies and headed down. It was three flights. As they exited into the lobby, the sounds of gunfire were revealed. Out front, three more of Martinez's compatriots were laying down a steady stream of fire from a van parked out front. In the hospital lobby, the police and FBI agents were returning the fire. Unbeknownst to them, they were about to be caught in a crossfire. Rodriquez reached into his coat pocket and withdrew a grenade. Carla and Bernie did likewise. Jack tried to cry out but it was too late. As they threw the grenades, they opened up with their machine guns. It was a massacre, mercifully short. Jack watched in horror as a dozen men were cut down. They continued forward toward the exit at a full run beyond the bodies and blood. Their legs were churning, filling their lungs with the cold winter air. Jack too was running hard. The last thing he wanted was to be caught out in the open, with bullets flying through the air. They would have made it were Martinez at full strength. But he had been in jail and in a hospital bed for over a week. He stumbled and then fell. Jack was running next to him. Instinctively he stopped to help him. The others stopped too. At the hospital entrance one of the FBI agents struggled to his feet, aimed his weapon, and fired. The fusillade caught the group as they tried to raise Martinez. Jack dove to the ground, unharmed. The rest were not as lucky. They fell to the ground, blood oozing, wounded, Martinez mortally so. Hector stumbled to his feet. "Long live the revolution!" he shouted and then was cut down by another burst.

Carlos Martinez stared up into the cool, blue sky. In the last few moments of his life, he was first glad that he was dying in the outdoors, under the sun. Then he realized that his legacy would be a bitter one; he would be remembered for his last desperate acts. *Only the truth can set you free.* Hector had quoted that to him once. Martinez finally understood what Hector had meant. Now the truth would never be told. He had lied to Jack. He had lied to himself. He looked up and saw Jack's face hovering over him. He reached up and grabbed Jack by the lapel of his suit and tried to pull himself up. Jack cradled him in his arms.

"You have to learn the truth," he gasped. There was a long pause as he summoned the strength to go on. He was almost gone.

Jack shook him. "Carlos! Carlos! What do you mean?" Jack thought he was dead, but then he opened his eyes briefly and stared at Jack. "Ask Alison. She knows . . . everything." And then he died.

Jack gently lowered Martinez to the ground. He heard the sound of running feet and voices and sirens. They seemed miles away. He was in a daze, a fog. Someone tapped him on the shoulder. It was Alison. He slowly rose and she embraced him.

"Are you OK?"

"I'm not hurt but to say I'm OK would be an overstatement."

"Is he . . ."

"Yes, he's dead," Jack replied vehemently. The tone took Alison by surprise and she stepped back. "I'm covered with blood. I just watched this man die. No, I'm not OK."

What Jack was thinking was that he was far from OK. What Martinez had said made no sense to him: Ask Alison, she knows everything. He did not want to make sense of it. He wanted to run from this place and never come back. What did it all mean? Was it true, as he had suspected all along, that Alison was not who she seemed? Jack had kept the thought far from his conscious mind. When it entered he had pushed it away. As the walls she had erected around herself had tumbled he had been happy to rush in. A fool for love. Was it all a calculated plan to lure him in, seduce him and use him to give legitimacy to the solution of the crime? The chance meeting at the wall. The flight from the courthouse. The midnight meeting with the protectors of democracy. Was this all part of the plan? Dow, Berlin, Alison and others. He needed time to think. Time alone.

"I need to get out of here." He looked at her and summoned his most sincere expression. It was hard to lie to her, despite the thoughts in his head. "Would you mind if I said I wanted to be alone? I need to deal with all this in my own way."

"Of course, I understand. I'll see you . . ." Jack did not wait for her to finish. He walked briskly away. An FBI sedan was waiting for him at the curb. He got in without looking back, and drove off.

CHAPTER 65

Ed Simmons's press conference had gotten off to a good start. His opening statement had been forceful, but not overbearing or desperate. The people needed to see a strong and confident leader, not a man who was trying to save an election won by hard work.

"And let me just conclude by saying that the people have spoken in the election and I would prefer to place my trust in the hands of the people. The decisions of the electors may be uncertain at this time, but I urge them to follow the will of the people. I respect the president for what he has done for the country, but now it is time for him to step aside and let the process work. I considered Arthur Davis my friend. I want to honor that friendship by finishing the work that he never got a chance to start and lead this country to greatness. That would be my greatest honor. Now I'll take any questions you might have."

"Mr. Simmons. John Evans, Reuters. What do you have to say about the president's comment that you lack his experience, and now is not the time for untested leadership?"

"Well, John, an old friend of mine used to say that experience teaches you that when you run into a wall, it hurts. You need intelligence and creativity to get around, under, or over the wall. My record in the Senate shows what I can accomplish. I introduced the bill and passed the legislation that handled the Social Security problem. I cosponsored the revised environmental cleanup legislation. I've sat on the Senate Foreign Relations Committee and helped shape foreign policy. I can get the job done."

His pause signaled the need for another question. The reporters were eager to oblige. "Sandra Hughes, *Time* magazine."

"Good to see you, Sandra."

"What is the status of your declaratory action and do you think it is in the best interest of the country? Why not just let the electors decide as the Constitution provides?"

Simmons paused for a moment to ponder the question. He had expected the question. He and Sandra went back a long way. The pause had the effect of conveying serious and thoughtful deliberation.

"I don't have time to go into the details of the procedural aspects. In fact there is a hearing scheduled in just about an hour. But let me say this. This is important enough that all the constitutional aspects should be explored. It is the job of the courts to interpret the law. The specific question is a narrow one and not clearly addressed by the Constitution. I will honor whatever decision the courts make. If they hold that the electors can, in fact, elect President Hampton, I will support his presidency as all Americans should. If they find otherwise, I hope he would honor their decision and peacefully step down from office." A misstep. He knew it as soon as the words left his lips. The practice and preparation had been for naught. The reporters pounced.

"Are you suggesting, sir, that the president might refuse to step down and resort to military force if not re-elected?" It was Sandra Hughes. Maybe they weren't such great friends.

"I never said that, Sandra, and you know it. Of course that's not what I meant."

He was saved by the murmur that began at the back of the room and spread like a wildfire. The whispers became an audible hum. Finally a reporter stood up.

"Mr. Simmons, we're receiving reports that Carlos Martinez was just killed attempting to escape. Were you aware of this and what are your thoughts and feelings?"

Simmons was truly caught by surprise by the news and collected his thoughts. He didn't want to stumble on this one.

"No, I was not aware. It shocks me. I think it shows that difficult times lie ahead. It is time to put aside divisiveness and to join together. This whole ugly incident in our country's history should cause us each to examine who we are, what we stand for, and how we can make America a better place. That's what I intend to do as president. I hope I get the chance. Thank you." He quickly left the podium. No point in risking any more damage.

CHAPTER 66

The United States District Court for the District of Columbia was used to hearing cases with constitutional implications. The one before them this day far outweighed the others. Because of the importance of the case and the need for a prompt determination, the chief judge of the court had decided to hear it *en banc*. All fifteen judges on the court would participate, not just a panel of three. They sat on the bench, with the Chief Judge Owen Casgill presiding. Below them, across the courtroom, sat the proponents and opponents of the petition. The petitioner was the Democratic National Committee. The opponent was the Republican National Committee. The jurisdictional question was the first order of business.

The chief judge addressed Samuel Paulson, chief legal counsel for the Democratic National Committee. "Mr. Paulson, as you know, we have a significant procedural question before we can even address the merits of your petition."

Samuel Paulson was prepared as always. He was a brilliant constitutional scholar and a practicing lawyer as well. A rare combination. He took a deep breath and rose to his feet to address the court.

"Yes, Your Honor, I'm aware of that. I assume the court is concerned about whether a case or controversy exists." The other judges nodded, as did the chief judge, and Paulson waded in.

"It is the position of the petitioner that the case and controversy requirement is met due to the fact that the case is capable of repetition, yet evading review."

His hope of a quick summary was dashed by Judge Tomlison.

"Excuse me, Mr. Paulson, but isn't this case distinguishable from those cases in that the likelihood of repetition is remote. Those cases stem from a desire to give guidance to a future plaintiff where it might not otherwise exist. Your client is asking us for an advisory opinion on a constitutional issue that might not even come into question and hopefully not likely to occur again. Is not one of the possibilities that Mr. Simmons will be elected president thus mooting his petition?"

Paulson was ready for the question. The DNC staff had spent many hours tossing around potential questions and arguments. This had been the one that had occupied a large part of the discussion. As he prepared to respond, Paulson considered the fact that this argument was a formality. No matter what the decision, it would be appealed first as a matter of right to the United States Circuit Court for the District of Columbia and then hopefully to the Supreme Court. They could only be hopeful, because the Supreme Court's jurisdiction was discretionary. They assumed the Supreme Court would agree to hear the case given the importance of the question. Alternatively, the court of appeals could certify the question, asking the Supreme Court to resolve the important unsettled question of law. Again, the Supreme Court had discretion to accept or reject the invitation by the court of appeals to review the dispute and pass judgment.

"With all due respect to the court, that is just the point. Because it is so unlikely to happen again, the need for a determination is all the more important. The result, if there is a constitutional crisis and deadlock, is too great to allow the question not to be addressed."

The chief judge came to his rescue, albeit briefly. "I'm afraid that I agree with Mr. Paulson. Moreover, the majority of the judges find this case to be of such import that we took the unusual step of briefing it and discussing it prior to argument. We assume there will be an appeal, and time being of the essence we thought it prudent to act quickly. We've come to the conclusion by a 14-1 vote that the electors are free, as a matter of federal and constitutional law, to cast their vote for whomever they please. Therefore, your petition for declaratory relief is denied. In reaching that conclusion, we do not address the legality under state law or what recourse you might have in that regard. I assume you intend to appeal?"

"Yes we do, Your Honor."

"Very well. The final order will be signed within the hour." The chief judge turned to the attorney for the Republican National Committee. "I assume, with the decision, you don't wish to be heard."

The RNC lawyer wasn't one to look a gift horse in the mouth. He rose to address the court. "No, Your Honor. I have nothing to add."

"Very well, then, we're adjourned. The judges rose from the bench and filed out. The others in the courtroom stood as well. Paulson was disappointed by the result but pleased at its swiftness. The judges could have avoided the issue by finding a lack of jurisdiction. Now it was on to the court of appeals. The result would probably be the same, and again in the Supreme Court. Paulson had considered all the arguments on either side. The Constitution was, at best, ambiguous on the subject, if not silent, so far as a final resolution of this unprecedented situation was concerned. The Twelfth Amendment does state, however, that the electors meet and choose the president, and the Supreme Court judges had become strict constructionists of late. A literal reading of the Constitution could seemingly lead to only one result. A suit in the states where an elector was required to pledge support for a particular candidate, to enforce that pledge, would be too time consuming. Even worse, not all states even required an elector to swear an oath. He gathered up his papers and legal pads and placed them in his briefcase. He was an advocate for his position. He would continue on behalf of his client within the bounds of the law and his ethical duty until no more appeals were left. He was a lawyer. That's what he did, for better or worse, in good times and bad. This looked like one of the bad ones.

CHAPTER 67

Jack wasn't sure what to do next. He lie on his bed looking up at the ceiling, Martinez's last words racing through his mind over and over again. Each time his mind would try to focus on the problem and a solution, the words would intrude again. In the maelstrom into which he had been thrust, Alison had been the only one he thought he could trust. Now he was alone. The ringing of the phone caused him to start. He let it ring five, six times. He knew it was Alison. Despite his resolve, he could not let it go unanswered. He snatched the phone from its cradle.

"Jack." It was her. "Are you OK?"

"Yeah, I'm fine. Just trying to digest it all."

"I know, it was horrible. Guilty or innocent, Carlos seemed like an honest and decent man, a victim of circumstances."

Jack did not respond and there was an awkward silence. Alison sensed it. "You sure you're OK?"

"I said I was fine." His tone was rigid and heightened.

"Can you come over and see me later? There's a lot we have to talk about. I'll make us some dinner."

Jack caught an edge in her voice as well. "Sure. How about six? I'll bring the wine."

"See you then." Alison sat on the other end of the line, holding the receiver.

"Does he know?" asked her visitor.

"No," Alison lied. "He's just upset about what happened at the hospital."

"You're sure?"

"Yes. I know him well and he trusts me."

"That's what we're counting on."

Alison turned and fixed a gaze on the speaker. "We had a deal. Nothing happens to him. And don't forget about my insurance policy."

The visitor scooped up a winter coat from the sofa. "The deal depends on you completing the mission. Keep him off track."

"I'll get it done. I always do."

"Good, good. Why don't you walk me out?"

"You know the way," Alison said with spite.

"As you wish. Just remember my dear, that insurance is often overrated. I'd be careful if I were you." There was a momentary breeze as the front door opened and then slammed shut.

After her visitor had gone, Alison reclined on her sofa and breathed a sigh of relief. It was only temporary. Something was wrong with Jack but she didn't know what. He was suddenly cold and aloof, which he had never been before. It was more than the shock of the incident at the hospital. She didn't have the luxury of time to find out. She was caught in-between two forces. To save Jack and herself, she had to hide what she knew from him. She might lose him because of that, but she had no choice. The force pushing her from the other side would settle for nothing less than complete victory. Her whole impetus and value set was disjointed. She felt like Alice through the looking-glass. Never before had she questioned those who directed her every move. The anger welled up in her. Her whole life had been controlled and programmed for the good of the country and sacrificed on the altar of democracy, on which they prayed. That was going to stop. And to do that, she would have to tell Jack the whole truth. What his reaction might be scared her. Alison was prepared to step away from the life she had known. To do it alone was more than she could bear. The timing would have to be perfect for her to pull off her plan. She had some calls to make, some favors to call in. A lifetime of doing for others was about to pay its rewards.

CHAPTER 68

Howard Berlin was just hoping that his nightmare would end soon. Stan Bradley was with him in an interview room at FBI headquarters. The desperate call from Berlin's secretary had interrupted what had promised to be a quiet day in his otherwise hectic criminal practice.

"Howard, I have to tell you it doesn't look good for you. How could you have been so stupid?" Berlin had told Bradley about his activities in trying to sway the electoral vote, including his dealings with Ruffolo.

"Stan, I know it looks bad, but I didn't kill anyone. I swear."

"Well, then how do you explain Dow's confession and the wire transfers with your name all over them?"

"He's a liar and those records are a setup. If I could just talk to the president, he would straighten this whole thing out."

"I'm afraid he's not returning my calls, and now with Martinez dead, the only link left is Dow and the other Secret Service agents who have mysteriously disappeared. I suspect they are either dead or in a foreign country with no extradition treaty and strict bank secrecy laws."

Berlin could not believe this was happening.

Bradley stood up to go. "Howard, you better start thinking of something you know that they don't. The name of this game is Pin the Tail on the Donkey, and right now you're the donkey."

"I'll try to think of something. Really I will."

"Look, it's unlikely you're going to get bail. Is there anything I can bring you?"

"Just get me out of here."

"I'm a great lawyer, Howard, but I'm not a miracle worker. Make the best of it because you're going to be here for a while."

CHAPTER 69

From the outside the restaurant did not look unusual. It was family owned and operated and had been for three generations. It was nestled in the middle of a strip mall on Lee Highway in Arlington, Virginia. The awning was a faded green and the stenciled lettering on the windows was peeled off in places: Carlucci's *Ristorante*. If you weren't looking for it, you would go right by it. Alison was looking for it. The bells on the door rang loudly as she entered. It was dark inside and it took a moment for her eyes to adjust. Although it was lunchtime, the restaurant was almost empty. Just inside the door was a counter where the hostess sat greeting the patrons. The hostess, in this case, was hardly friendly.

"What do you want." It was a demand not a question.

"I'd like to see Salvatore Carlucci."

"He ain't here right now."

Alison glanced toward the back of the restaurant. It was not very big. At the back table sat a man, in his late 60s. On either side of him were two much younger men. The elder man was eating a bowl of pasta.

"Isn't that him in the back?" asked Alison.

"No, you're mistaken. Now unless you want to order somethin' . . ."

Alison ignored the woman and started walking to the back of the restaurant.

"Hey, you can't go back there!" she cried.

Her cry caught the attention of the men at the table. The two younger men stood up and started toward Alison. The older man looked up from his bowl of pasta and squinted at her. The first of the two men walked directly toward Alison, his hands outstretched. "You can't come back here, this is a private party." The second man's hand disappeared into the folds of his designer suit.

Alison stopped. "I'm an old friend of Salvatore's."

"Mr. Carlucci's not taking any visitors right now." The first man had reached Alison. He gently put his hand on her arm and tried to steer her back toward the door.

He was interrupted by a booming voice, "Alison is that you?"

"Yes, it's me, Salvatore."

"Boys, let her through." The boys complied and Alison walked toward the table. Salvatore Carlucci had a wide smile on his face. He pounded the chair next to him.

"Come here and sit next to me. When you left, you promised you'd come back and visit. Three years, I don' hear anything from you. Is that any way to treat an old man?"

As she sat down he gave her a warm and sturdy embrace and kissed both cheeks. "I'm sorry, Salvatore. You know if I could have come I would."

"I know, sweetie. I know. Sometimes we're a prisoner to our responsibilities. You want something to eat?"

"No thanks, Salvatore. I don't have much time."

"What you talkin' about? Margie, bring us another bowl of pasta and some Chianti," he yelled toward the front of the restaurant.

"Really, Sal. I'm here to ask a favor." Salvatore became quiet and serious. He looked at the two men who had again positioned themselves on either side of him.

"Boys, go smoke a cigarette or somethin'." Without a word the two men left. Salvatore turned to Alison.

"I knew this day would come and I owe you; but I have to ask, how come you're here and not one of the others?"

"The others don't know I'm here, Sal. This isn't a favor for them or the others; it's a favor for me."

He reached across the table and placed his hand on her arm. "You in some kind of trouble, sweetie?"

"You might say that, but nothing I can't handle. My problem is I need to find a couple of guys and I don't have much time or the resources. I know this puts you in a bind but I thought I could come to you."

"Of course. Of course. You did the right thing coming here. You saved my life when those bloodsucker politicians wanted to put me out of business if I didn't pay off. I'm a legitimate businessman. I don't pay bribes to no one."

Alison's mind wandered to that time three years earlier, when a strange alliance was struck between her organization and one that denied it existed. Salvatore Carlucci's family had come from Sicily to escape Mussolini's fascist rule. The importance of freedom and democracy made an impression on the small boy. Although Salvatore was the don for all of

Northern Virginia, he believed in democracy above all else. Sure he peddled in drugs, gambling and prostitution, but he never paid a bribe or countenanced anyone who did. The people had placed their trust in the politicians. That trust could not be violated or the end result would be fascism and tyranny. When he had been approached with a demand for payoffs for the district attorney and police to leave him alone he was livid. He was ready to go to war when a mysterious figure appeared in his restaurant, and explained that others cherished democracy and were willing to sacrifice their lives for it. He refused to pay the bribes and went public. It had been quite a scandal when it hit the papers. Lots of politicians went to jail. A few mysteriously vanished. Salvatore and his family came off as heroes.

An up-and-coming lieutenant was not enamored of Salvatore's respect for the Constitution. He had paid the bribes. When the don's disclosure turned up the heat, he turned on the don and a gang war had ensued. When it looked like the don would be ousted, Alison and some others had been sent in. Alison discovered later that the protection of democracy could be lucrative. 'Round-the-clock protection was expensive. The don's legitimate business did, in fact, turn a hefty profit, a percentage of which now went to fund the activities of the Framers. On a cold, rainy night the young lieutenant and his followers had come for the don. They expected a few muscle men. Instead they were met by withering fire and a team of well-trained assassins. The numbers favored the opponent and, despite their training, Alison and her team were pushed to the brink of defeat. In the back of the restaurant they had made their final stand. Alison had draped her body over Salvatore, who had been wounded. The last of the insurgents came within twelve feet before Alison gunned him down. Now, as was her right, she had come to call in the favor.

The wine and the bowl of steaming pasta with red sauce arrived. It did smell good and she did not want to insult Salvatore. They had grown close in their short time together. He was a killer, no doubt about it, but so was she, and that bonded them together in a way few could understand.

She took a bite. "You still make the best red sauce."

"I know. So who are these guys you need to find?"

She swallowed the bite and wiped her mouth with a napkin. "Men who tried to kill the next president."

"Those sons of bitches! When—and I say when, not if—I find these guys, what do I do with them?"

"Call me. I'll need to be there." She took a few more bites of the pasta.

"You got names for these guys?"

She nodded her head and spoke between bites. "Ted Washington and Hal Parsons. They were Secret Service agents on the president's detail. They were in on the plot and now they've disappeared. I need to find them before my friends do. I have a strange suspicion that if I don't they won't be around long to tell their story."

"I saw on TV they already arrested the guys responsible."

"Well, my information says there's more than meets the eye." She pulled a piece of paper from her purse. "Here's their last known address and social security numbers. I need this fast." She pleaded and looked him straight in the eye.

"Don't you worry, sweetie, your Uncle Sal won't let you down. Now eat your pasta. You're all skin and bones."

CHAPTER 70

Jack had decided to go into the office for awhile to take his mind off things. He presumed he still had a job, his recent absence notwithstanding, but it wouldn't hurt to make an appearance. Elaine had a stack of messages waiting, which he had ignored. After reading through his mail, with constant interruptions from his curious coworkers, he decided that he had to see Jim Kelly. Jack needed to talk to someone about his dilemma.

Ms. Hathaway was at her usual place. "Good morning," she greeted Jack as he approached.

"Good morning. Is Mr. Kelly in?"

"He is. Let me see if he can see you." She picked up the phone and pressed the intercom button. "Mr. Banner is here to see you." She paused to listen then said, "Very well."

She hung up the phone. "He said to go right on in."

Jack walked past her secretarial station and into Kelly's office just beyond. As Jack entered, Kelly stood up and crossed the room to meet him. "Jack, how are you?" Kelly extended his hand and Jack grasped it in a firm shake.

"Reasonably well, under the circumstances."

"I can imagine. Come on in and have seat." He motioned to the sitting area to the right. Jack observed that it was considerably larger and more well-appointed then his own.

"I spoke with Gary Stevenson. He filled me in on what's transpired. I'm sure you're glad this whole thing is over."

Jack paused before responding. He wasn't sure why, but he trusted Kelly and felt he could confide in him. His instincts had better be right. There was little choice, in any event. He needed people with power and influence to find out what he needed to know. Kelly had that kind of influence.

"Actually, I don't think it is over."

"What do you mean?"

"Can I trust you with my life, sir? And I don't mean that the way it sounds, impertinent; I really mean it. Because if I'm wrong about you, it could cost me my life."

Kelly looked at him for a moment. He started to speak and then held up his hand, stopped and stood up. He walked over to the door and closed it, then returned to where Jack was sitting.

"Son, I've taken on the worst sons of bitches in this town and beat everyone; and the way I've done it is by always being a straight shooter. When I say I'm going to do something, I do it, and when I say something is so, it is so." He leaned in close to Jack. "You can trust me with your life. And just to prove it to you I'm going to tell you something that will give you the power to threaten my life, so you can know that I have something to lose if I screw you. How is your memory?"

"Pretty good." Jack wasn't sure he wanted to hear what was coming next.

"It better be excellent, because I'm only going to say this once. So listen carefully." Kelly leaned back in his chair. He was enjoying the moment because it gave him a chance to unburden his soul and to gain the trust and confidence of another man. Once that happened, he could always count on that person being there for him when he needed a favor. The favor might be insignificant or it might be a question of life and death. It didn't matter, the opportunity was there; the request had to be honored.

"Do you remember the Metz Commission?"

"Sure. The congressional committee formed to investigate charges of bribes to DEA members in return for ignoring the Colombian cartel's activity in the United States. They concluded no wrongdoing took place. This firm represented some of the cartel members, didn't it?"

"Yes, we did. And we helped them get away with it."

"You what?"

"You heard me. The firm was retained to assist in their defense. I was able to . . . convince certain key members of the congressional committee of the fallacy of their supposition. That's pretty fancy talk from a coal miner's son, don't you think?" Kelly chuckled. "Anyway, money was no object to the cartel, as well as other more subtle means of persuasion. The best part was that the firm received a nice fee. I believe part of your bonus that year came from that money. Now here comes the memory part. You sure you want to trust me? Because if you do, someday I'm going to ask for your trust, and I have to know that you will be prepared to do whatever I need to trust in you. So you think on it a minute while I ask Ms. Hathaway to bring us some coffee."

Kelly got up and left the room. Jack stood up and started to pace around. He stopped and looked out the window and down at the White House. Just when he thought things couldn't get any more complicated, he proved himself wrong. Jesus, the whole damn world was corrupt and he had never noticed it before. Playing with the big boys was rough. He knew he had little choice. Alison was hiding something. He needed to find out what it was. He hoped and prayed it was something that she needed to hide, in order to protect her and him, and not part of some scheme to use him in something she had been part of all along. He had to trust Jim Kelly. Alison meant too much to him to do otherwise.

His thoughts were interrupted by Ms. Hathaway's return. She placed the cup of coffee on the table, smiled at Jack and left. Kelly came in and closed the door. He looked at Jack.

"So?"

"You can count on me when you need a favor."

"Excellent. In the Suisse Credit Bank in Geneva is an account. In that account is one hundred million dollars of the cartel's money, all from legitimate businesses, I might add. Only two people know the account number. I'm one of them. I'm about to make you the third. If anything should happen to that money, the cartel will come to me and they will kill me, as well they should, seeing as how they would be under the impression that I took the money. As additional insurance, in a separate account is a safe-deposit box that the cartel does not know exists. In it is all the documentation on the Metz Commission. I suggest that when I give you these account numbers you write them down somewhere safe, with instructions to someone you trust to withdraw the money and send the documents to *The Washington Post*. Are you still with me?"

"Yes, 100 percent."

"The first account number is 0149299. The second account number is 0387489."

Jack grabbed a pencil and wrote the numbers down.

"Now, take as long as you need to memorize them and then destroy that paper, agreed?"

"Agreed."

"Now, are you ready to tell me your big secret?"

"Well, I suppose it pales compared to yours." This time Kelly laughed out loud and Jack smiled with him.

"Like I said before, you're a real wiseass."

"I suppose I am. In all seriousness, the pieces of the assassination don't add up and I think the whole thing, Martinez included, was a setup. Someone is hiding something and I need to find out what. I need you to find out everything you can about Alison Stevens. She is the key. She is the link to something I can't tell you about yet. Once you find out about her, then we can talk again. Fair?"

"I don't know, kid. I need a little more than that."

Jack thought for a moment, then related what Martinez had told him as he had died. When he finished, Kelly said, "Maybe he was delirious."

"I don't think so. If we check out Alison and she comes up clean then maybe he was. I can't afford to be wrong. I have to know for a lot of reasons."

"You're sweet on her, is that it?"

"That's part of it. I also believe in the Constitution and our democratic system, as hokey as that may seem. Someone is trying to subvert it and that pisses me off."

"Alright, I think we can do business. I'll call the people I know. I should be able to get you an answer by the morning."

"Good, and thanks for your help."

Jack got up and walked toward the door. "You must be real sweet on her to take these kinds of risks," said Kelly. Jack stopped and turned to face him.

"I've always felt risk is relative to the reward. High reward is worth high risk. She's the highest reward I can think of."

"A romantic, as well as a wiseass. A dangerous combination."

"How about you?" Jack replied. "What's in it for you?"

"I'm an old man now. I need these kinds of thrills to keep me alive and virile. Besides, I like you. I see some of me in you."

"Is that a compliment?"

"Yeah, kid. It is. Now get out of here and bill some hours. The firm needs the revenue."

CHAPTER 71

Pettit and Hernandez were glad to make the drive. It wasn't often enough that they had the chance to tell a crime victim's family that they had caught the perpetrator. Mrs. Bourne was expecting them. Unlike their prior meetings she seemed deeply depressed. They had not told her why they were coming but she must have known. The relief, in turn, brought the final realization that her child would not be coming home.

She greeted them at the door. "You found the people who killed Melissa, haven't you?"

"Yes, m'am, we have," answered Hernandez.

"Please excuse my manners. Can I invite you gentlemen in?"

"No excuse necessary, Mrs. Bourne. We just wanted to come personally and tell you that the man they arrested for the murder of the president-elect confessed to the murder of your daughter. We hope it brings you a measure of peace."

She bowed her head slightly as if in prayer, then looked up. "Do you have any children?" Petitt shook his head.

"I do m'am. Two," said Hernandez.

"Then you must know that there will never be any peace in this house again."

"Yes, m'am, I do."

"Thank you for coming by. It was very thoughtful of you."

"It was the least we could do." They turned to leave. As they walked down the stairs she called after them, "I almost forgot. I got another letter from Melissa. Actually, a package. I couldn't bear to open it. Would you like to see it?"

"Yes, m'am, I think we should."

Mrs. Bourne went inside and then returned with a manila envelope. She handed it to Hernandez. He had donned plastic gloves and examined the envelope. It was sealed and taped. On the front was Mrs. Bourne's address and a P.O. Box with a return address. He flipped it over but nothing was written on the back. It was about an inch thick and felt as if it contained paper. He placed the envelope in an evidence bag, held open by Pettit. Then he took out his pad and pen and jotted down the P.O. Box number.

"Thank you. We will let you know what it is. If it's something personal I'll have it returned."

"You're welcome. I hope it helps. I'm not a vengeful woman, but I hope the men who did this rot in hell." Tears formed in her eyes and then gently rolled down her cheeks. She didn't try to wipe them away.

"Again, m'am, we're sorry for your loss." She could only nod. Hernandez and Pettit turned and walked down the steps toward the car.

"What do you think is in there?" asked Pettit.

"No idea. We best let the forensics guys open it, while we check out the P.O. Box."

"Seems to be warming up a little," observed Pettit.

"Yeah, right. But remember, it's seventy-five degrees in Miami."

CHAPTER 72

Henry Ruffolo had to wait for Jimmy's brother for a good part of the day. The guy had never been on time in his life. By the time he arrived, Ruffolo had thrown back more than a few too many. Ruffolo related his story as comprehensibly as possible under the circumstances. Frank scratched his head a couple of times, reached for his whiskey and took a large swig.

"You've got one big fucking problem, Hank." Ruffolo ignored Frank's use of the nickname he hated. Frank had always called him that, and Ruffolo corrected him each time. Today he was too upset and too drunk to care. Frank scratched his head again. He was in way over his head. The biggest case he had ever handled was a DUI.

"Gee, thanks, Frank. Like I didn't know that already. Can you help me?"

"No fucking way. You need someone a lot smarter than me."

"I can't afford anyone one else but you. You're my last hope, Frank." Ruffolo began to cry. He lay his head in his arms and began to sob softly.

"Jesus, Hank. Enough with the tears." He motioned to Jimmy. "We need some coffee over here." He reached over and patted Ruffolo on the arm. "OK, OK, I'll try and help the best I can, but I can't promise results. You may be goin' up the river."

Ruffolo looked up and then wiped the tears from his eyes. "That's all I'm asking, Frankie. Just give it your best shot. Besides, don't you think my story might be worth something?"

Frank was intrigued by the possibility. "I suppose it might. I could make a few calls. Some of the guys I know from law school might be able to help. Maybe it was a good thing after all that you called me. Hey, Jimmy, another round over here. We might have somethin' to celebrate after all."

CHAPTER 73

Jack was nervous as he approached the door to Alison's townhouse. He hesitated for a moment before ringing the doorbell. His heart won out over his mind and he reached for the bell and pressed it twice. When the door swung open, Jack knew he had made the right choice. Just like the first time he had seen her at the wall, she took his breath away. She was dressed in a black turtleneck sweater and black slacks. Her auburn hair practically shimmered in the light from the vestibule. She smiled and he wanted to reach out and gather her up in his arms. Instead, he smiled back and held up the bottle of wine.

"I brought the wine."

"Good. Dinner is almost ready. Come on in, it's cold out."

He walked in and slipped off his coat, which Alison placed in the hall closet. Jack admired the decor. It was warm and stunning at the same time. Alison, or someone, had a flair for decorating. Jack suspected it was not her because her skills seemed to be in less artistic areas.

"This place is beautiful," he said.

"I wish I could take the credit. I have a great decorator if you need one."

"I think I'll stick to my basic bachelor pad."

There was an awkward silence. Jack could not bear the small talk a second longer. "Listen, Alison, can we cut through all the smoke? I have something I need to say."

"I know. I do too, but can it wait for just a minute? Let's put on some music, open the wine and act like normal people for just a few minutes."

Jack laughed. "That would be nice. Like a first date."

"Exactly." She started toward the living room and pointed in the opposite direction. "The kitchen is that way. The corkscrew is in the drawer by the fridge. I'll put on the music."

Jack wandered through the dining room and into the kitchen. It was as nicely appointed as the rest of the house and, again, decidedly different from his taste. Her decorator liked French Country. He found the corkscrew in the drawer and then proceeded to search for some wineglasses. The sound of jazz music wafted in from the living room. It took him several tries before he found the right cabinet. Jack walked back toward the living room.

"I found the corkscrew and the wine glasses. Now can we talk?"

She was seated on the sofa and put one finger up to her lips and then pointed to her ears. Alison got up and walked over to the stereo and turned up the volume until the music filled the room. She motioned for him to come closer. They met in the middle of the room and she pulled him close to her.

"We can't talk here," she whispered in his ear. "Meet me tonight at midnight. You know where. Now let's give them something to really listen to." She kissed him passionately and pulled him close to her. Jack wanted to resist. He managed to push her away. She stepped back for a moment and then pulled her sweater up over her head and tossed it aside. The curve of her breasts was barely concealed beneath a black lace bra. Jack reached out and pulled her towards him. His mind told him that he could not, should not, but the rest of his body instantly overrode his mind.

CHAPTER 74

Al Bolton examined the package carefully. The District of Columbia crime lab was relatively quiet. He would miss dinner as he often did, but the detectives had insisted it was a rush. He didn't mind too much. He could use the overtime, assuming the city could find it in its budget. The explosives guys had ruled out any possibility of a bomb, allaying his biggest fear. His care was directed toward not destroying any potentially valuable evidence in the way of fingerprints, fibers, or other clues about the origin of the package. Its purported sender was known: Melissa Bourne, P.O. Box 18432, Bethesda, MD. Unfortunately, the envelope had been handled by a number of people in the course of its journey. Melissa Bourne had been one of them. Her fingerprints had been clearly identified. Eight other sets were also present. Based on the information he had received from the detectives, he assumed one set was her mother's. The rest could be any number of postal employees who had handled the package. The envelope itself was nondistinct and could be purchased at any drug store or stationary store in the D.C. metropolitan area. Bolton had examined the package under a high-powered microscope and removed a number of fibers, none of which appeared significant. But more analysis was needed.

The envelope had not been sealed but merely fastened with the two copper prongs at the top. He gently pried them up with tweezers and then gently lifted the flap up. He spread the opening and, shining a light inside, saw a sheaf of papers. Using a bigger tweezers he reached in and pulled out the papers and placed them to the side. He spread the envelope again and peered inside. Nothing else was visible. He tipped the envelope over and gently tapped on the end, collecting whatever invisible debris fell out in the clean cloth he had laid underneath for future examination.

He placed the envelope aside and turned his attention to the papers at his side, which were lying face down. He flipped them over. On the front was typed the words OPERATION RESTORE DEMOCRACY. Bolton carefully turned over the first page with his tweezers. The second page was titled Executive Summary of Action Plan. His eyes scanned the summary. He stopped and blinked twice and then adjusted his glasses. This document could not be what it said. The contents were incredible but its existence was even more incredible. He would not have believed it but for the fact that what it recommended had, in fact, occurred—the assassination of the president-elect. He had to read it again.

> *The recommended course of action is the assassination of the president-elect. The desired result, retention of President Hampton, is not guaranteed given the uncertain legal procedure in the event of the death of an elected president prior to taking the oath of office. However, under the circumstances, this is the only viable solution at the present time and therefore is recommended.*

Bolton kept reading it over and over hoping the words would change, but they did not. He flipped to the next page and the next and the next. He had to read each page twice. It took him about thirty minutes to finish the twenty-five pages of neatly typed double-spaced text. The plot to kill the president-elect laid out in black and white. The last page froze his heart. At the top of the page was typed the words ROUTING LIST AND APPROVAL. It was the list of names and apparent signatures that were the cause of his intense consternation. He slowly removed his glasses and laid them on the table. He got up from his stool and paced back and forth. He reached for the phone, started to dial Detective Hernandez, and then hung up the phone. He paced some more and then picked up the phone, was about to dial his wife and then thought the better of it. One thing he was sure of: The fewer people who knew he had read the document the more likely his chances of survival. What to do? What to do?

His urge for a cigarette, a habit he had kicked twenty years ago, came hurtling back to him. He used the mental imagery and the sensation of inhaling smoke to calm him. *Think! Think!* The detectives had told him that Bourne's mother had not opened the package. The detectives had clearly not opened it. That meant no one knew what was inside except the sender and she was dead. Bolton could replace the memo with something completely innocuous and no one would be the wiser. But what if someone did know? He could go to jail for destroying evidence. Better than being dead. The memo had made clear the objective, which had been carried out with deadly efficiency. He picked up the memo and walked over to the shredder. He turned on the power and the shredder whirred to life. All he had to do was drop it in and then put the bits and pieces in the evidence room incinerator. He looked at the document again. OPERATION RESTORE DEMOCRACY. The last word jumped out at him. Bolton had voted for Davis. Someone was trying to render his vote and all the other votes meaningless. In his hands he held the power to change that, or least to hold someone accountable. Could he ever look his children straight in the eyes if he took the cowardly approach? Could he live with himself? The answer was obvious. He reached down and shut off the shredder. He walked back to his desk and picked up the phone.

"Detective, you'd better get over here right away. There is something you have to see. I can't say what it is, but you best hurry before I change my mind and throw it in the shredder, like I almost did before I called you."

Bolton hung up the phone and laid the memo on his desk. He sat on the stool and prayed that Hernandez was a fast driver. He thought about cigarettes again and then prayed some more that his own newly found courage would not leave him.

CHAPTER 75

Jack had wanted to stay longer but Alison insisted that he leave in order to draw less attention to their planned meeting. As Jack approached his house he saw a large Mercedes parked out in front. His headlights shone on Jim Kelly leaning against the car. Jack slowed down next to Kelly and lowered his window.

"What are you doing here?"

"We need to talk. Park your car and let's go for a walk."

Jack rolled up the window and pulled into his driveway. It was one of the perks of his house. Parking was at a premium in Georgetown. He locked the car and walked back out into the street. Kelly was waiting for him, leaning on the hood of his car.

"Your girlfriend is something of a mystery."

The word girlfriend was said with sarcasm that Jack did not appreciate.

"Could you be a little more specific?"

"Well, for starters, she died about eighteen years ago."

"Look, quit fucking around."

"I'm perfectly serious. Alison Stevens died over eighteen years ago in a traffic accident. The woman you know that calls herself Alison Stevens first appeared shortly thereafter. You see, we traced her backwards. Employment, jobs, law school, college. The trail ends where the real Alison Stevens died. Scared the hell out of my guys when they found out. Don't see that kind of thing very often. Only someone with a lot of juice could do that. Someone went to great lengths to create her cover. I suspect they would be most upset if it were revealed."

"What else did they find out?"

"She has a strange habit of turning up in hot spots around the world. Someone is renting her out as a kind of mercenary. A freedom fighter if you will. When there was a military coup a few years back in Honduras she was there, helping out the democratically elected government fight off the coup. Same thing in the Ukraine after that. A few other places are suspected, but not confirmed. She is on lots of watch lists. Different names and descriptions, but it's her."

"She told me there were things about her I wouldn't want to know."

Kelly stopped and faced Jack, who stopped as well. "That's not the worst of it."

Jack took a deep breath. "Let me have it."

"Three months ago she was seen with various Front members. No one could figure out why. Her MO has always been to support democratically elected governments. The Front stands for violent overthrow. Then she disappeared until you discovered her or, rather, she discovered you."

"Nice try, Kelly. I already figured out that our meeting was a setup. I'm not an idiot. But I've met the people she works for. Their objectives seem honorable, if a bit zealous."

"What do you mean you've met them?" Jack explained his meeting with the Framers, the evidence he had shown them and the resulting arrests. It seemed perfectly plausible.

"You really are a sap. You believed that pile of bull. Committed to democracy!"

"I believe in Alison. She asked me to trust her and that's enough for me."

"Yeah, but why is she hanging out with members of the Front and telling you she is opposed to their methods?"

"I don't know, but I aim to find out."

"I hope your aim is good. No, great! You're in way over your head. These people are professional killers, including Alison. You're just a lawyer."

"I have no choice, do I? I have to see it through to the end, whatever it is."

"I guess you do."

"And I could use a little moral support, if nothing else. How about a drink?"

"Why the hell not. But you have to promise me one thing."

"Sure."

"Don't tell any of my junior partners. I wouldn't want to ruin my reputation as an s.o.b."

CHAPTER 76

Hernandez was, in fact, a very fast driver. His siren helped. Bolton's resolve and courage was greater than he expected. Unfortunately for him the old pack of cigarettes he hid in his desk drawer had been put to use. He was sure he could quit easily. Hernandez and Pettit had read the report, and now wore the same ashen expression as Bolton upon his first reading.

"This can't be for real. It's a hoax," Pettit said.

"A week ago I would have agreed with you," replied Hernandez. "But after what we've seen, I believe it. Nothing else makes sense."

Bolton spoke up, "But what the hell do we do with it? Assuming it's true, if we go to the wrong people we're all dead." They contemplated the truth of the statement, considering the next step to take. Hernandez pulled out his cellphone.

"Evans. It's Hernandez. I need to know if I can trust you with my life. I don't mean that touchy-feely cop-to-cop bullshit. I mean on your children's lives kind of trust."

"What the hell are you talking about?" asked Evans.

"Let's just say that things aren't what they seem. Can we meet in two hours?"

"Sure, you name the place."

It was a spot only a cop would go late at night, but one where Hernandez could feel comfortable. Evans understood.

"Don't tell anyone and come alone."

"I thought they only said that shit in the movies."

"That's perfect, because this is stranger than life. See you in two."

He hung up the phone and turned to Bolton. "How long can you stall your report?"

Bolton smiled. "This is the District of Columbia. The paperwork can take weeks, but you know that."

"Perfect. Come on Pettit, we have work to do."

CHAPTER 77

The drinks with Kelly had made Jack a little mellow. That was a good thing as he waited in front of the wall. To his right was the Washington Monument, named after the first President of the United States who had led his men into battle and the colonies to freedom and the birth of a new nation. To his left was the Lincoln Memorial, named after the man who had saved the Union, almost torn asunder, and ordered men into battle to die a horrible death, as old battle tactics faced new and modern weaponry. And in the middle, the Vietnam Memorial, named after the war of many presidents, none of whom wanted it, nor could figure a way to rid themselves of it. So many had died for no grand purpose, as in the wars represented by the monuments that flanked it.

He had stayed far away from the part with Tommy's name on it. That was part of his Sunday visit. He paced nervously back and forth, oblivious to the cold wind. He checked his watch for the umpteenth time—12:05—and then scanned the area around the wall. He turned 360 degrees and, at the end of the circle, he saw Alison in the distance. He smiled inside. She came walking toward him.

"Let's keep walking," she said as she approached. Jack fell in step and they started down along the path bordering the wall.

"Jack, I left out some details about my life. I need to tell you about them. I suspect you'll be angry when I tell you. I'd understand if you were."

"Alison," he replied, "I told you before that it doesn't matter what you've done in the past. I have no right to judge you."

By now they had reached the end of the wall. They kept walking in silence toward a little park beside a lake beyond the wall. Near a deserted snack bar they found a bench in front of the manmade lake and sat down. They just stared at each other for a moment, as Alison summoned the courage to go on. She had to tell him the truth now. Things had gone too far. He had a right to know his destiny so he could make a choice to try to change it or accept it.

"I assume you knew our first meeting here was a setup?"

"Of course."

"And I think you know that Dow's confession was not the whole story?"

"I suspected so." He hesitated, deciding whether or not to tell her what Martinez had said as he died or what Kelly had revealed to him. He decided against it for the moment.

"I could tell by your body language. What did Martinez tell you when he died?"

Jack looked at her with surprise.

"Jack, I know you better then you think. From the moment Martinez died, you've looked at me differently, touched me differently."

Jack took a breath. "He told me you knew everything. What did he mean by that?

It was her turn to take a deep breath. "Martinez worked for the Framers. He was in deep cover with the Front. I was a member of the Front as well for a while, too. We had intelligence that the Front had been taken over and that a violent revolution was planned. Our plan was to infiltrate the Front and stop whatever was planned. Unfortunately, Martinez and I were separated. I had the sense my cover had been blown. I had to leave the Front and leave Martinez behind. When Martinez was arrested it could have been an enormous embarrassment to the Framers. Even worse, our existence and our activities could have been revealed. I was sent to keep track of you, to throw you off track. At least that is what I was told."

"The director, the others I met, they were involved in this?"

"No, they knew nothing of my activities. I was directed by others in positions of power above those you met."

"So you lied to me from the start and you were prepared to let an innocent man go to jail, let alone exposing others to danger and possibly death?"

"Yes, I did, and I'm not proud of it. And I won't make excuses, but I've lived in a different world than you Jack, one where the rules that apply to the rest of the world don't exist. I was an orphan, Jack, raised by the Framers, indoctrinated by them . . . actually, brainwashed. But since I've met you, I realized I have to get out of that world. Jack, I love you and I want us to be together."

Jack was stunned and also uncertain. For the first time she had told him that she loved him. But could he ever truly forgive her? Could he believe her now after she admitted to lying to him? It was a true test—his greatest. Could his love be stronger than the evil she had committed?

"Jack, I would understand if you walked away and never wanted to see me again. But at least give me a chance to prove to you that I've changed. I think that I'm being misled. Things don't add up. Someone in the Framers is lying to me, hiding something. I'm going to find the real truth and expose the whole thing, even if it means I have to go to jail. Can you at least give me that chance?"

Jack did not answer. They sat quietly for a moment, staring out at the Washington Monument, bathed in light, a small red light blinking atop the pinnacle. Another couple walked by, arm in arm, huddling together to keep warm. Jack moved closer to Alison and she leaned her head on his shoulder. For a moment they were just another couple, enjoying a cold, crisp night and the beauty of the mall. It was a moment they both needed. Neither of them wanted to leave, and so they sat pretending that the normalcy would last, knowing that it wouldn't, and hoping that some day it might.

CHAPTER 78

"This better be good." The director was dressed in his bathrobe. He rubbed his eyes and yawned. Agent Evans looked at Detectives Hernandez and Pettit. He hoped they knew what they were doing. Their call had woken him and they had insisted that they had to see the director right away. Evans demanded to know why he had been deflected. The detectives had been persistent. So now they stood in the foyer of the director's McClean, Virginia, home to legitimately explain, Evans hoped, why they had awoken his boss from what appeared to have been a sound sleep.

"It is, sir," insisted Hernandez. "We have information about the president-elect's murder, information that is so sensitive we could not dare to show it to anyone but you—and only in person. In fact, sir, we're trusting you with our lives by coming here. My partner was opposed to coming here. It took a hell of a lot of convincing."

The director was coming out of his deep sleep. "Won't you gentlemen come in?" he offered. He pointed his arm in the direction of the den off the foyer. They walked in as a group. Pettit and Hernandez sat down on a large, overstuffed sofa. Evans pulled up an easy chair and the director took a seat in another overstuffed chair.

"Alright, what is it?"

Hernandez pulled out the manila envelope and handed it over to the director. "As far as we know, only three people have seen this document. You are the fourth. Agent Evans has not seen it. We believe it is proof of the assassination plot. It contains evidence contrary to what we think you believe at this time."

The director lifted the envelope, flipped it over and opened the flap. He took a deep breath and pulled out the papers. When he read the title, he breathed a sigh of relief.

"I appreciate your efforts, gentlemen, I really do, but a copy of this was in the safe-deposit box of Harkin Dow. He personally gave me the key during his confession."

"What?" Pettit said and glanced at Hernandez. "That's not possible. If it was, more arrests would have been made, the whole plot exposed."

The director looked at them quizzically. "We did make the arrests, of all those implicated in this document." He raised the papers up as if to emphasize his point.

"A loyal soldier to the end," Pettit said.

"Excuse me detective, I don't understand."

"Dow. He played you like a fiddle. He's protecting his superiors to the bitter end. I suggest you take a minute, sir, and read that report. I think you'll find it somewhat different, especially the last page."

The director leaned back in his chair and reached up to flip on a reading lamp. He put on his reading glasses that lie on the side table next to his chair. He read for some fifteen minutes, glancing up occasionally with furrowed brow. When he flipped to the last page he let out an audible gasp. He removed his glasses, slowly folded them, and placed them back on the table with great deliberation.

"You're right, it is substantially different from my version. Is this the only copy of this?"

"On that point, sir, I listened to my partner, Detective Pettit. We kept a copy for safekeeping, in case that one might be destroyed in an accident or something."

"You were right to trust no one, not even me, although I'm telling you, you can. Does Jack Banner know about this?"

"No," answered Hernandez.

"He needs to and has a right to before we do anything else. Agent Evans, get a detail out to his house and tell him I need to see him right away."

"Yes, sir." Evans got up to use the phone.

"Before you go, Agent Evans, you have a right to read this and then decide if you wish to obey my order. I give you the option of saying no." He handed Evans the papers. "Gentlemen, can I offer you some coffee? I think it's going to be a long night."

They nodded and he led them into the kitchen. They sat and waited for the coffee to brew. As they were pouring the first cup, Agent Evans came in. Hernandez and Pettit recognized the look in his eyes. It was the same look they had seen in Bolton's eyes when they arrived in his office, the same look they had seen in each other's eyes, and then in the director's eyes: a look of disbelief and of fear.

CHAPTER 79

Jack and Alison had sat for some time at the lake, until the cold and their fatigue caused them to reenter the reality they faced. No decisions had been made. What could either of them say? The silence led Alison to believe that Jack was at least considering what she had said. As they drove up to Jack's house they were surprised to find a detail of FBI agents at the doorstep.

Agent Duncan greeted them as they got out of the car. "The director and Agent Evans need to see you ASAP. I'm here to drive you to the director's house."

"What's this all about?" Jack asked.

"Couldn't say. I'm just . . ."

"I know, following orders. OK, but do you mind if we follow in our car?"

"That would be OK."

Jack and Alison climbed back in the car and waited as Duncan got into his car, started it, and executed a three-point turn on the narrow Georgetown street.

"What do you suppose is going on?" asked Alison as they waited.

"Don't know, but I'm sure it's important, and it could be information that we need."

"Hopefully . . ." The ringing of her cellphone interrupted her.

"Hello."

"Hey, sweetie. It's your Uncle Sal. We found your friends."

"Really? That's great! When can we meet?"

"It better be soon, at the spot we discussed. As soon as you can." The line went dead. Jack was putting the car in gear.

"Stop," yelled Alison. "I have to go. It's the friends I told you about. I need the car. Can you go with them?"

"No way. I'm going with you."

"No, Jack. We don't have time and we have a lot of ground to cover. You go meet with the director. Find out what he knows. We'll meet up later. Call me on my cellphone. Here's the number." She pulled a piece of paper and a pen from her purse and scribbled down the number.

Jack looked at her for a moment. "Alison . . ."

"Not now, Jack, you need time to think. I told you, I can wait for your answer."

Jack was glad she had interrupted him. He was not ready to give her his answer. Jack got out and waved down Duncan. The backup lights on the sedan went on and the car pulled back toward Jack. Alison got out and walked around to the driver's door. The FBI car pulled up next to Jack with the window rolled down. "What's going on?"

"Alison's not feeling well. I need the ride after all."

"Hop in." Jack opened the rear door and climbed in. He glanced at Alison again. She smiled and waved. He felt a gnawing fear growing deep in the pit of his stomach as she pulled away. He had felt that way before but couldn't remember when. Then suddenly, an image hurtled from the back of his mind into his consciousness: a uniform, a knock at the door. He threw the car door open and jumped out.

"Wait!" he yelled, but it was too late. Jack stood there waving his arms as the taillights disappeared into the darkness. He slumped against the car door. Duncan leaned into the back seat.

"You OK?"x

"Yeah."

"Then get in. The director is waiting for us."

Jack got into the car. As they drove, he closed his eyes and pictured Alison in his mind. He tried to burn the image into his memory, afraid that he would never see her again, and knowing that if he did not, the image would slowly fade. It was a thought that frightened him to the core, and revealed in him a love he did not know could exist. Perhaps he knew the answer after all.

CHAPTER 80

The self-storage unit was not far from Carlucci's *Ristorante*. Alison killed the lights as she pulled up. It was long structure composed of concrete block, covered with corrugated steel, with a number of storage bays. The office was in front with a driveway around the back, closed off by a fence to prevent unauthorized entry. A light was on in the office. As Alison pulled up, one of Salvatore's boys she had met the other day came out to meet her. She lowered her window.

"Drive around back. Unit 105. Sal's waitin' for ya."

Without a word she raised the window. The gate slowly opened and she drove through and followed the driveway. The bays were lit and soon she found number 105. She parked the car and got out. The bay door opened and Alison ducked under and into the storage bay. Sal's other goon was there to close the door behind her. It was fairly large, maybe twenty feet square. Salvatore greeted her with a hug and a smile. His company was less happy to see her. In the center, securely tied to two chairs, were Secret Service Agents Washington and Parsons. They were completely naked and were bound so that they could not move their arms, legs or bodies. It appeared that Sal had not been patient enough to wait for her. Their faces were bloody and bruised, but that was just for softening up. He had left the hard work for Alison.

"What have they told you?" she asked.

"Nothing. They're pretty tough bastards, but I told them I was the good cop and they should talk before you got here. They didn't take my advice."

"That was a mistake." Alison directed her comment at the prisoners. She had not wanted Jack to come for the reason she had said, but also because, on top of what she had told him, no matter how much he loved her, if he were to see what she was about to do, of what she was capable, he could never have felt the same for her again. No man could. Alison did not relish what she was about to do, but some part of her enjoyed it.

"Did you bring what I asked for?"

Salvatore nodded and snapped his finger. The second of his bodyguards wheeled a dolly out, with a tray on top, and placed it in front of the prisoners. A linen cloth covered the contents of the tray. Their eyes widened but they remained silent. Alison walked over to Washington.

"Tell me what you know about the assassination." It was said in a flat, monotone voice with no stress or urgency. If the prisoner saw your emotions he assumed he could play on them, that somewhere there was a human being with compassion and feelings. It was met by silence.

Alison turned toward the dolly and pulled it close. She whipped off the cloth and picked up one of the instruments that were arrayed on the tray. It was a scalpel. It shone in the harsh light of the storage area. "Did you know it's possible to surgically remove all of a person's skin and still have them live? The pain is intense of course and you pass out, but if you're skilled, and I am, there is very little blood. What kills you is the infection that invades the body; it kills you slowly. Amazing how important skin can be. Now, who wants to be first?"

She advanced towards Washington, the scalpel outstretched, turning it over, edge to edge and waving it in the air. "Of course, because I'm in a hurry, I'm going to get right to the point." She kneeled down in front of him and lowered the scalpel to his groin area, touching the blade firmly to his flesh.

"No, Jesus, no!" he screamed.

"Now listen, you seem like a nice guy. I'm not a very nice lady and you should know that I will do whatever it takes to get you to tell me what you know. And if you die, then I start working on your friend. One of you will talk, there is no doubt about that. Sal, you've seen me work. Tell 'em."

"I wouldn't fuck with her boys. I once saw her turn a guy twice your size into a crying baby."

Washington shut his eyes firmly and shook his head. Alison stood up quickly, grasped his left wrist with her left hand and then made a quick cutting motion with her right hand. He screamed in pain and tried to move about, as the top portion of his left index finger fell to the concrete floor. Alison waited for the screaming to subside.

"That was just your index finger. If you're lucky and you get to a hospital fast enough they might be able to reattach it. Hey, Tony, why don't you put that finger on ice, just in case." Tony was standing wide-eyed and as far away as possible. He had seen a lot of things working for Sal, but this lady was the scariest by far.

"Tony, you heard the lady. Do it," Sal said. Tony moved in cautiously, keeping a safe distance from Alison. He picked up some gauze from the dolly and then picked up the finger. There was dry ice in a cooler. She had even thought of that.

"Now here's the deal, gentlemen. The next thing I cut won't be re-attachable and you're going to miss it a lot more than a finger. Whoever talks first gets to walk out of here in one piece. The other one I'm going to carve up like a turkey and leave you so disfigured you'll wish you were dead." She pointed the scalpel at each of them, the blood and bits of flesh clearly visible. As she suspected, the words came spilling out, each in a contest to beat the other. When they were done, Alison's worst suspicions were confirmed. She had been lied to. She, as well, was just a pawn in their game.

"Sal, can you keep them on ice for awhile?"

"No problem."

"Get that one a doctor. Patch him up the best you can."

"Hey, what about my finger? You said they could reattach it," complained Washington.

"You should have talked the first time. I need you guys to tell your story, and until then no one can know where you are."

Her cellular phone rang. It was probably Jack.

"Hello."

"Alison, I'm with the director. You're not going to believe what I just found out."

"I think I am, if it's the same story I just heard." She related the confessions of Washington and Parsons, leaving out the details of what motivated them.

"That jibes with what we know." Jack related the discovery of the detectives. "The only question is, what do we do with the information?"

"I have an idea. Tell me where you are and I'll meet you."

Jack gave her directions to the director's house. "I'll be there in two hours."

Ordinarily Alison would have been more careful about what was said over an unsecured line. The excitement and adrenaline were still flowing and caused her to be careless. Her cellular phone, in fact, had a listening device implanted in the mouthpiece. In the control center, in the basement of an office tower, someone was listening. That someone made note of the contents of the conversation and the intended meeting. He picked up the phone and placed the call.

"As we expected, she found out the truth. You trained her well."

"I expected no less. But I did not expect the betrayal. Who else knows?"

"Banner and the director. They're at his house right now. I'm not sure who else is there."

"Are the teams ready?"

"Affirmative."

"Go get the memo. Put Washington and Parsons on ice. We may need them. Kill the rest of them."

"The director too?" asked the caller.

"Unfortunately, yes. He has outlived his usefulness. His cover has been compromised."

"What about Alison?"

He paused. It was a difficult decision, even for a man like him. "Eliminate her."

The phone went dead and the caller placed another call, this one internally, to the floor just above him.

"Get the teams ready. We move out in twenty minutes."

CHAPTER 81

The phone rang again, immediately after he had hung up. He thought, perhaps, it was the mission commander again.

"What do you want?" he said somewhat impatiently.

"It's Alison." His tone surprised her. In all the years she had never known him to be angry or impatient. He sounded both. The call had caught him by surprise and he quickly changed his tone, trying to recover. He sensed the uncertainty in her voice.

"Is everything alright?"

"Yes and no. I've found out the truth and tomorrow the whole world will know. You betrayed me, used me. After all that I've done for you, for the cause, this is how I am repaid?"

"Please, Alison, it was all for the greater good. You of all people should understand that."

"Yeah, right. The greater good? I've come to realize that all those years you spent talking about the greater good were just a way of stealing my life away from me. The cause was more important than anything, including my happiness. I'm through with all that. It's time for me to live my life and to stop being used by you and the almighty cause." The anger in her voice left the caller speechless. It validated his decision to eliminate Banner and her. His silence allowed her to continue.

"Alison, please, let's talk about this."

The answer was a dial tone. He slammed down the phone and called the team leader. "Get the team moving fast, were running out of time!"

CHAPTER 82

After the phone call to Alison, they had gone over all the options and decided on a course of action. It was a decision reached by unanimous consent. They all knew that their lives hung in the balance, and all pretenses of rank and privilege were abandoned. Evans gave no quarter to the director, and the two D.C. cops showed no respect for the high-priced lawyer. In the give and take, a plan was formulated. Now all that was required was for it to be executed. The director had decided that it would be best for them all to get some rest before Alison's arrival. He retired upstairs, but not before arranging for his wife to be taken to a FBI safe house. She had protested mightily, but agreed in the end.

Pettit and Hernandez began dozing on the overstuffed couches. Jack was too anxious to even try to rest. Evans was awake as well. He had brewed some coffee for the two of them. After flipping through the stations on the TV over and over again in the kitchen with Evans, he had taken to wandering through the director's house, examining his bookshelves and pictures in order to gain an understanding of the man. His movements were being tracked through night-vision goggles. The two FBI agents parked in front of the house had been eliminated. The team now faced several problems. The first one was time. The security unit was required to check in every thirty minutes with a designated password. If the check-in was not made, additional units would be dispatched in force. The second problem was a lack of intelligence on the layout of the house. The urgency had not allowed that. Finally, the team had no idea how many people were in the house or if they were armed. They assumed the director was inside and they could see Jack Banner wandering throughout the house where the sight lines permitted. Drawn shades or large tree limbs blocked many of the windows. The team leader was not at all comfortable with the situation, but he had no choice other than to proceed.

"Alpha One, this is team leader. On my lead."

The house was set high on a hill along a curving road. To reach the house they had to climb a long set of stairs set in the steep hill. A total of six men had been dispatched. It was fewer than he had wanted, but the rest of his men were on their way to collect Washington and Parsons. He crossed the road from his hiding place in the woods across the way. Two other members of the team joined him from the flanks of the house. At least one thing was in their favor. The house was in a remote area and it was a moonless night. The rest of his team was covering the back entrance. They climbed the stairs, smoothly and silently. Someone looking right at them would not have seen them. At the door, one member of the team withdrew his instruments to pick the lock while another shone a small light on the lock.

Inside, Jack's wanderings had him crossing the vestibule at the moment that the lock was being picked. The lock picker was an expert and made almost no noise as he worked. In his former life, Jack would never have noticed a thing, but his recent experiences had given him a newly found sixth sense. He saw the door move a fraction and the handle jiggle ever so slightly. He quickened his pace across the vestibule and into the den.

He shook Pettit and Hernandez awake. "We have company," he whispered loudly.

They awoke instantly and instinctively reached for their weapons, rolling off the couches and onto the floor. They were moving toward the kitchen when the lock was picked and the door flung open. In an instant, the first man was through the door. Pettit and Hernandez opened fire and the man fell mortally wounded. The team leader's worst fears were being realized. He had lost the element of surprise. The second man on the team tossed in a stun grenade. It exploded with a bright flash but was useless. Jack and the others had already retreated to the kitchen. The director was less fortunate. The firing had awoken him. He had grabbed his weapon from his bedside drawer and made his way down the hall to the stairs. The team leader saw him out of the corner of his eye, turned and let loose a burst of fire from his machine pistol, catching the director full across the chest. His body slumped against the wall and then gently crumbled and rolled down the stairs.

The team leader motioned up the stairs and his colleague went upstairs to check. He headed for the kitchen. A swinging door separated the rooms. He fired a burst through the door and then kicked it open. The room was empty. He looked to his right and saw the back stairs leading to the cellar. He smiled. The rats were scurrying into the trap. The rest of his team at the back door would take care of them.

"Alpha Two, anyone upstairs?"

"Negative."

"Meet me downstairs in the kitchen. Alpha Three, they're in the basement. Find the exit and wait for my orders." A double click of the mike signaled acknowledgment. The team leader started down the stairs and stopped halfway. It led to a large basement where Jack and the others huddled together in the dark to quickly plot strategy.

"There's probably a team at the back door waiting for us," Evans whispered. The others nodded.

"And the other one, or more, are coming up behind us."

"Agreed."

Their deliberations were interrupted by a voice from the stairwell.

"You're trapped down there. You might as well give up." The team leader hoped they believed him. Time was running out. Assaulting a dark basement with no knowledge of the number of defenders or their weapons was not something he wanted to do, but if they refused to surrender he would have no choice. His three remaining men were poised at the back door to the basement waiting for his orders.

"If you're so sure why don't you come down and get us," Jack called out.

His suggestion was greeted by silence.

"Jack, we have to get you out of here with that memo," said Evans. "The rest of us can hold off the troops. If we can draw them in, you may be able to sneak around them and out."

"No way," Jack replied. "That's suicide. You're shooting pop guns compared to their firepower."

"It's the only way," Hernandez insisted. "We need you alive to tell the story. The rest of us are expendable."

"That's very noble but let's try and think with our heads. We have an advantage in that they have to come in and find us. They can't wait forever. So let's just wait them out." It was a lawyer's answer to a nonlegal predicament. He was out of his league and Evans tried to set him straight.

"Look, Banner, you may be a good lawyer, but you don't know shit about combat. Those guys have night-vision gear. They have machine pistols and grenades. The one thing they don't have is you and that memo. I suspect they could care less about you, but the memo they want." Jack reflexively gripped the sheaf of papers under his arm. He had grabbed it as they had fled toward the kitchen. Jack was about to mention a thought but was interrupted by the voice from their pursuer.

"You have sixty seconds to decide and then you will die."

Their eyes had become accustomed to the dark and they stared at each other hoping for a solution. The sound of broken glass was followed by the clatter of a canister on the concrete floor.

"Tear gas!" yelled Pettit. They moved further back into the basement as the gas hissed out of the canister. The ceiling became lower toward the back. Jack tripped over some debris and then righted himself, scrambling on all fours toward the back of the basement. He started to stand up and bumped his head on a pipe. He lowered his head and reached up to rub the spot. It was at that moment that he felt a slight breeze on his left cheek. He looked to his left and glimpsed a small window, slightly ajar, the cold winter breeze blowing in. "Over here!" he hissed in a low voice. He heard scuffling noises as the others came crawling toward him, coughing as the teargas filled the basement.

"We might be able to squeeze through that window." Jack pointed up. They scrambled over to the window, the teargas stinging at their eyes and lungs.

"Banner, you first," commanded Evans. Pettit and Evans grabbed Jack's legs and hoisted him up to the window. Jack pried the window all the way open and then wiggled his head and shoulders out. The window opened out to the ground. He hesitated and then tossed the memo out the window and onto the ground, hoping he would soon be following behind. He reached his arms out and grabbed the ground and the dirt and anything he could grab hold of and tried to haul himself out of the window. Pettit and Evans pushed from below and suddenly he was free. He looked around for any sign of danger and, seeing none, stuck his head down into the window.

"All clear, come on!" he implored the others. Jack reached down and grabbed a hand. He pulled and in a moment the face of Agent Evans appeared. Jack hauled him out and then reached back down for another hand, but no one was there to grab it. He heard a loud crash as the basement door was forced open and then gunfire, followed by return fire from below.

"Banner, you get out of here, we'll catch up to you," Hernandez shouted.

"I'll try to work my way around back," explained Evans. "Banner, get moving."

Jack wanted to stay and help the others but he knew he could not. The papers in his hand were more important than the lives of the three men trapped below. Suddenly, he realized how Alison must have felt all those years, sacrificing her own needs and the lives of others for a greater good. He did not like the feeling and his compassion for her grew, knowing the bitterness those acts must have caused in her. The self-hate, the doubting. She must have been, must be, incredibly strong to have survived it. He hesitated a moment more, gave Evans a pat on the shoulder, and then straightened himself, turned and ran. At least he would do what he could to help them. He ran as fast as he could towards the lights of the nearest neighbor. It seemed miles away and Jack dug down deep to run at full speed. He banged on the door like a madman, ringing the doorbell as well. Lights came on in the house and then a voice was at the door.

"Who's there?" asked a nervous voice.

"I need you to call 911. Tell them that the director of the FBI has been attacked and to send help. Please, right away!"

The door started to open but Jack yelled out, "No! Don't open the door. You want to be able to say you never saw me. It's safer that way. Just call 911 like I asked."

"I will. I promise."

Then Jack turned and ran. He wasn't sure where he was going but knew he needed to be as far away as possible. As he ran, he remembered what he wanted to say to the others. Besides those in the house, only two other people knew about the memo: the forensic guy at the D.C. lab and Alison. One of them had told someone else.

CHAPTER 83

Alison knew something was wrong the minute she drove up to the house. The security car in front of the house showed no sign of activity as she approached. In the distance she heard sirens. She scanned the terrain around the house but could see nothing. Alison grabbed her weapon from her purse, got out of the car and carefully approached the security vehicle. As she reached the passenger door she saw the two agents, heads back, the vacant look of death in their eyes. Jack was in trouble. She walked briskly but carefully up the walkway leading up the hill to the house. The sound of the sirens was getting closer. Her caution saved her life. The explosion lit up the sky and threw her to the ground, showering debris from the house all around her. She could feel the heat of the flames. She got up and tried to move toward the house but the heat and flames were too intense.

Instead she ran back down the hill and grabbed her cellphone from her car.

"911."

"There's been an explosion at 4582 Tidewater Drive, Mclean. We need paramedics and the fire department."

"Can we have your name, m'am?"

Alison hung up and turned to see several police cars and two FBI sedans screaming up the street. The FBI sedans pulled up to the curb and the agents jumped out. One ran for the security car, the other stared up at what was left of the director's house. "Oh my God!" he shouted and reached for his radio to call for help.

A third agent ran up to Alison. "What the hell happened here?"

"I have no idea. I just got here. Who called you?"

"The security car didn't check in and we couldn't raise them. I wonder what the local cops are doing here."

The street was filling with curious neighbors in their night clothes. The cops were moving them out of the street and away from the house. A patrolman raced up to them.

"What happened?"

"Maybe it was a gas leak," offered one of the agents.

"This was no gas leak," Alison stated flatly. "Who called you?" she asked the policeman.

"A neighbor called 911. Said a man knocked on her door and told her to call the police because the director's house had been attacked."

Alison's heart leapt. "What did he look like?"

"She never saw him. She wanted to open the door but he insisted that she shouldn't."

The fire engines came racing up the street, their hoses unfurling as they approached the house. The fire had died down somewhat and the fireman attacked the fire with precision and determination. The captain came over to the assembled group.

"Anyone know how many people were in there?"

"Four that I know of," Alison offered. "Any hope of survivors?"

"Not likely, m'am. The explosion was pretty large and those flames look to be mighty hot. It would take a miracle, based on what I see."

"Thanks." The captain nodded and went to check on the progress of his crew.

Another FBI car drove up and Jenkins leapt from the vehicle and ran over to Alison. "Oh my God! The director? Was he in there?"

"I think so."

"Anyone else in there?"

"Don't know." She pulled him aside, away from the others. "I was supposed to meet Jack and the director here. I got here and the agents in front are dead and then boom the whole place goes up in smoke."

"Who the hell would do this?"

"Someone who is afraid of the truth."

"What truth?"

"Sorry, Jenkins. I can't say anymore. Will you call my house and let me know what you find. I assume you know the number."

"Aren't you going to stay and find out if they're alive?"

"Why? If they are, I can't help them. If they're not, I'm wasting time here when I could be trying to find their killers."

She walked away and Jenkins shook his head.

CHAPTER 84

The team assigned to eliminate Salvatore was not under the same constraints as the one assigned to Jack and the others. They had the luxury of patience. They had staked out the warehouse and reconnoitered the area. The front office was deserted, which meant that they must be in one of the storage lockers. The homing device in Alison's phone gave them a general location, but not with the precision necessary. No one had come in or out of the warehouse. They did not know for sure if anyone was inside and, if so, how many. The team was composed of eight men, smaller than one would have liked. There were over two hundred storage lockers. It would be impossible to search each and every one. So they waited. Their patience was rewarded. A large, black limousine pulled up to the storage area. The security gate opened slowly and the car entered and turned right, down the road dissecting the lockers. The team leader clicked his mike once and his men began following the limousine, moving in the shadows. The limousine stopped at unit 105 and honked twice. The gate of the storage unit was rolled up and the doors of the limousine opened. Two men got out and moved towards the storage area. Salvatore and two men inside the storage area came toward the car, with Washington and Parsons in tow.

The team leader clicked his microphone two times and the team swung into action. They knew what to do without communication. It was important to move in as close as possible. Indiscriminate fire might kill the agents, and their orders were to be sure that didn't happen. The sharpshooter trained his scope on one of Salvatore's men. When the first shot was fired, he would also fire. The team leader heard two clicks in his headset. The team was in position. There was no time to waste. They were almost to the limousine. He gave the signal. One click. The sharpshooter squeezed the trigger and one of the men holding Washington went down. This caused the others to whirl around in his direction. In the confusion the rest of the team leapt from the shadows, took aim and fired, taking out the other man holding Washington. The rest of Salvatore's men reached for their weapons. They got off a shot or two before being gunned down. The team leader watched in horror as one of the bullets hit Washington squarely in the chest. He crumpled to the ground, a red stain spreading across his shirt. Salvatore, despite his age, was quick as a cat. He had survived more than one hit in his lifetime. He quickly reached over and grabbed Parsons, throwing him in the car and then diving on top of him.

"Go! Go!" he shouted. The driver was expertly trained and immediately stepped on the gas. The limousine was constructed for just such a situation. It was armor-plated and could be driven even if the tires were blown out. The team reacted quickly, directing fire at the limousine. The bullets ricocheted off the armor plating as the car wove in and out, and then turned sharply around the corner of the warehouse out of the line of fire and toward the front gate.

"He's headed toward the front gate," screamed one of the team into his headset.

The team leader responded quickly. "Unit C, cut them off. You can't let them get away!"

The limousine screeched around the second corner in front of the storage facility, fishtailed and then regained its balance, as it accelerated toward the front gate. The men in unit C were waiting. One of them shouldered an RPG and aimed it at the oncoming car.

"Shit!" yelled the driver.

"Floor it!" commanded Salvatore.

The driver did as commanded and the car lurched forward. The team did not yield. The one holding the RPG aimed and fired. A tongue of flame jetted out of the back of the launcher and the projectile was on its way. It was not a smart bomb and its success would depend on the skill of the marksman. The team leader held his breath, viewing the unfolding scene through his night-vision glasses. The future of the nation depended on the arc of an explosive projectile.

CHAPTER 85

Jack was exhausted. He had run until he was out of breath, and then walked until he had found a strip mall. He had fifty dollars in his pocket, enough for a cab but not a hotel. Alison's lesson in the train station made him know not to use his credit cards. The cab dropped him at his office. No one would expect him to go there. The building was eerily silent. He climbed the stairs the ten floors and then made his way to Jim Kelly's office. He flipped on the light switch and headed for his phone. His intuition was right. Kelly's home number was on speed dial. He pushed the button. The numbers flashed on the LCD panel and Jack jotted it down, tore off the paper and thrust it into his pocket. The phone rang five, six times.

"Answer it," muttered Jack.

"Hello." The voice was Kelly's.

"It's Banner. I'm in trouble."

Kelly was alert now as he sat up in bed. "Where are you?"

"I can't say. Now is your chance to prove what kind of pull you have in this town. I need a name and address." Jack told him who the person was. "Can you do it?"

"No problem, but it may take an hour or two. People will be hard to reach at this time of the night."

"I'll call you back in a bit."

Jack hung up, turned off the light, and then went down to his office and lay on his couch. He needed some sleep. He set the alarm on his watch for an hour and closed his eyes. The memo was tucked securely under him. Surprisingly, sleep came quickly.

CHAPTER 86

Alison wished she could be sleeping but she did not have the luxury of time. Besides, she was too angry to have slept anyway. She had been betrayed. They never intended to let Jack live. She had been lied to from the start. It should not have surprised her, given her own experiences over the years; everyone was expendable. She assumed Jack was alive and still thought of him in the present tense. Now she was on the most-wanted list. She had no doubt that they would kill her if they found her. She was waiting outside Salvatore's restaurant. It was deserted. She had tried to reach him on her new cellphone without success. As soon as she arrived at the director's house, she knew her cellphone was bugged. It was sitting by the side of the beltway where she had stopped and left it. The director was most likely dead. Not knowing how many of her colleagues were part of the betrayal, none could be trusted. She was on her own.

Several cars pulled up to the restaurant and screeched to a halt. A bunch of men quickly got out and entered the restaurant on the run. When the light went on inside, Alison got out of the car and crossed the street. On the same side as the restaurant, she slowly worked her way down toward it. She approached one of the cars from behind and slipped up to the driver's side. The car was empty. They were in a real hurry. Something must have happened to Salvatore. Her heart sank. He was her last hope. She turned and walked toward the restaurant door. It was open and she entered noisily to attract attention.

The men, eight to ten, were all seated in the back, guns in various stages of display, and talking animatedly. "It had to be that bastard Cardoni. He always wanted to be the don."

"Hello," Alison yelled.

"Who the hell are you and what are you doing here?" demanded one of the men. Several others leveled their weapons at her.

"I'm a friend of Salvatore. Has something happened to him?"

"Like I said, who the hell are you?"

"She's OK," said a lady from the back. Out of the shadows stepped the hostess from the other day. "Salvatore told me about her. You can trust her. I know he did."

She came forward and gestured for Alison to take a seat. Alison demurred and moved closer but remained standing.

"Sal was supposed to make a pickup and delivery last night. When he didn't show I sent some of the boys to look for him. They found his limo blown up, but no sign of him or the others."

"And my package he was going to deliver?"

"It's gone too."

"I tell you it was that damn Cardoni family."

Alison turned to the man. "By the time this is over you're going to wish this was a family matter. I'm afraid it's a lot bigger than that." She turned to the lady. "Is this the best you have?"

"No, lady, they're the ones that got here first. The real troops should be here within an hour."

"Great. We're going to need all the help we can get. I'm Alison." She extended her hand.

"I'm Judy."

"Judy, nice to meet you. Is there any coffee around?"

"I'm brewing it right now."

"Great. When the others come, I'll lay it all out for you."

Judy turned and then looked at Alison with concern in her eyes. "Do you think Sal is alive?"

"You known Sal for awhile?"

"Long enough."

"Then what do you think?"

"The devil himself couldn't take old Sal if he wasn't ready."

Alison nodded. She hoped the same was true about Jack.

CHAPTER 87

Kelly had come through with the phone number and address for Jack. The street was not too far from Jack's house. The black sedan parked in front with two FBI agents and a uniformed patrolman walking the beat marked that it was the right house. Jack stood down the corner from the house, glanced at his watch and waited. The man he needed to see had agreed to meet him. As unusual as it may have seemed, he emerged from the house at close to four a.m. The FBI agent and the police officer quickly walked up to him.

"Is everything alright, sir?" asked the agent anxiously.

The old man dismissed him with a wave. "Yes. Yes. Just a little trouble sleeping. Just wait until you get to be my age. You'll know what I mean. Thought the fresh air might do me good."

"Would you like us to go with you?"

"That's not necessary. I'm just going to go up to the corner and back. Smoke one of these." He brought a cigar up to the light of the agent's flashlight. "The wife will kill me if I smoke this inside."

"I hear that, Mr. Chief Justice," said the FBI agent. "We can keep an eye on you from here."

The chief justice nodded and started his walk down to the corner. Jack backed around the corner and waited. In a moment, Chief Justice Kincaid was standing at the corner lighting a cigar. Jack stood at the corner, the building blocking him from the agents' view.

"I hope this is good. You took a big chance coming here."

"I had nowhere else to go," Jack explained. "The director is dead and it's only dumb luck that I'm not."

The chief justice wanted to whip his head around, but resisted the urge. "Dead. How?"

"By machine gun fire; and if that didn't kill him, the explosion that obliterated his house finished the job. I have some information that will end this thing, but I need to get in and see the president. I'd call him for an appointment, but I suspect he won't see me. But he will see you."

"The president? Why him?"

"I don't have time to explain now. Can you get me in to see him?"

"Yes. Meet me at the White House. Pennsylvania entrance at six a.m. I suspect they will let me in."

The chief justice took a long draw from his cigar and the glow illuminated his face.

"I hope that's not a Cuban."

The chief justice chuckled and the smoke entering his lungs caused him to cough. He turned and glanced down at the agents. They were watching him, but not intently. He turned to face Jack.

"You're a brave man, Mr. Banner. Alison was right to care about you."

"Thank you, sir. Coming from you, that's a great compliment. But let's not congratulate ourselves quite yet. The final chapter has yet to be written on our little tale."

"I'll see you in a few hours. I should be going. My watchdogs are probably a little nervous."

"Understood. Save one of those for me. Hopefully we can smoke one together when this thing is over."

"For that I will break out the Cubans."

CHAPTER 88

Alison knew the safe house as if it were her own. It had to be the place where they would bring Sal and the others, assuming they were alive. It also brought back distant memories and the pain they caused. She could feel the caress of his hands, the curve of his body against her. She pushed the thoughts aside. There was no time for them now. There never was.

Through her night-vision glasses she could see the sentries on patrol. This started her adrenaline pumping. Sentries meant live people. She had Sal's finest men with her. At the restaurant, she had outlined the details of the house. This information was to her advantage. It was an old farmhouse and her men were scattered about the perimeter on the neighboring acreage, at the outside range of the detection equipment. This was another piece of information to their advantage. Even with the information she was worried. Although her troops were trained killers, the defenders of the safe house were also trained killers, and had the additional advantage of being the defender in a highly secure facility. The sky would soon be lit by the first rays of the dawn and so they had to move fast. Alison laid down her weapon and then patted her leg to make sure her second weapon was in place. Then she boldly strode straight toward the house across the open field. There was no fence, as this would stand out. Sensors would announce the arrival of any unwanted visitors. When she came within five hundred feet of the house the sensors detected her, and automatically a searchlight shone on her; a second after that two sentries rushed towards her, guns pointed at her head.

"Stop! Move no closer! This is a secure government facility!"

Alison slowly raised her hands in clear sight. "I'm Alison Stevens. Code name Panther Express. I need to see the director of operations."

The sentries were momentarily confused. An agent in the middle of the field? This was not within their instruction set. As any good drone, they needed instruction from the queen bee.

"Control. This is position X-5. We have a lady out here. Says she is Panther Express. Do you copy?"

"That's a roger, X-5. Bring her in."

The two sentries motioned with their guns toward the farmhouse. Alison started toward it, searching her memories for details of the inside of the house. It had a stairway immediately in front of the door leading up to the second floor and then a second stairway toward the back near the kitchen. That stairway led to the operations center two stories below, where it had been carved out of the rock. She had to take control of that room. As she hoped, they did not search her. Her legitimacy had no reason to be questioned. Unfortunately for them, they had not bothered to check at the highest level. The man in charge of the control room had no reason to question her loyalty. She noticed also that the guards let down their vigilance the moment her identity had been confirmed.

One sentry remained outside and the second escorted her inside, where they were joined by a new sentry. Together they led Alison toward the back stairway as she had hoped. She could see no sign of Sal or the others, but she knew someone was being held here. She saw two more men and a woman in the kitchen, as they passed by. They were armed but not on duty. Alison and the sentry walked down the stairway. At the bottom there was a solid steel door and a sensor. Alison placed her eye on the sensor. It read her retinal pattern, and then the locks on the door released and the door slowly opened. She walked in while the sentry stayed outside.

Inside, a man sat at a control panel in front of a large screen. On the screen were scenes of the perimeter from the surveillance cameras. The man looked away from the screen and smiled at Alison, his face brimming with happiness.

"It's been a long time, Alison."

"Yes it has, Frank. It is good to see you. I didn't know you'd be on duty tonight." In fact it upset her greatly. It saddened Alison to think she would have to kill him. He had been, and still was, a friend. Maybe it wouldn't come to that.

"The high council will be eager to speak with you. I understand they've been looking for you."

"Have you spoken with them?" she asked anxiously. She hoped the tone of her last conversation with her superiors had not reached Frank. Paranoia and suspicion ran deep here.

"No. I was just getting ready to call and let them know you had appeared."

Alison nodded in agreement and scanned the room. There were two others in the control room. They were deeply engrossed in their activities. There was no need to pay attention to her. Frank turned to pick up the phone. Alison walked up to a chair next to him. She reached for it with her left hand and, in the same motion, reached down to her ankle with the other. She whipped the gun from its holster and, with a single motion, shot the two attendants dead. Then she trained her gun on Frank. He remained motionless, with no sign of emotion. Though surprised by her actions, he knew that he could not let his emotions betray him.

"I don't know what this is about, Alison, but you know to get out of here you're going to have to kill me."

"I know that, Frank. All I ask, in the name of friendship and what we've been through together, is that you give me five minutes to explain. If not for me, then for Ben. You owe him that."

She knew the appeal would work. When a man saved your life you had no choice but to listen to the woman he had loved with all his heart. Many a night Ben had expounded on his love for Alison to Frank. As best friends often do, they had both been in love with the same girl, but Frank had never stood a chance and he knew it. He had become the dutiful friend and third wheel in their escapades.

"Five minutes, Alison, and then I reach for the phone and you have to kill me. So this better be good."

"It will be, Frank. It will be. It's all about power and greed and how it corrupts everything good. Once you hear it, you'll want to help me. I know you will."

CHAPTER 89

Howard Berlin was having a dream. He was sitting in the Oval Office with the president. No. He *was* the president. He was sitting behind the president's desk and in front of him was the president. They were going over the day's schedule. Suddenly, his lawyer, Stan Bradley, walked in.

"Stan. What are you doing here?"

"You called me, Howard. You said you had thought of something to help you out of this jam."

"Jam? Peanut butter and jelly? What do you mean?"

"To get you out of here, Howard."

"Out of here? This is the Oval Office. I'm the president. Why would I want to leave?"

"Howard. You're in deep shit. Remember? You have to think of something to get you out of here. Anything."

"I'll think of something. Something to get you out of here." Berlin pushed a buzzer on his desk and in came several Secret Service agents.

"You rang, Mr. President?"

"Please shoot this man," he said, pointing at Bradley.

The agents took out their guns and pulled the triggers. The bits of brain and flesh and blood splattered all over Berlin, and he gasped. Then he was conscious, frantically wiping the imaginary blood from his face, slowly awakening to his surroundings, seeing the steel bars and feeling the coarse sheets beneath him. The realization of where he was, compared to where he had been, came upon him like a storm front. Berlin swung his feet off the bed and walked toward the steel bars, gripping them in his hands and leaning his head against them. He slowly tapped his head on the bars.

"Think, think," he muttered to himself. Somewhere in the back of his mind he knew something was there, something he had forgotten but had to remember. He let go of the bars, turned around and then slid to the floor, pulling up his knees to his chest. It comforted him, as it had as a small boy. He took a deep breath to clear his mind. He needed to focus. He needed to remember all the events of the past ten days. Berlin started with the most recent events and worked backwards. Then he went forward again: the assassinations; the meetings at the White House; his efforts to sway the Electoral College vote; his arrest. Nothing stuck out. No clues or smoking guns. Then, suddenly, he remembered something. It was seemingly inconsequential, but then he put it together with a few other small, seemingly inconsequential things. And then he knew.

He stood up and turned to face the bars. "Guard! Guard!" he yelled.

The other prisoners in the cellblock started to stir. "Shut the fuck up," one yelled. The others started to chime in, "Guard! The pansy ass wants his mommy!"

Berlin ignored them. "Guard!" he yelled again.

The light came on in the cellblock, followed by the sound of running feet. Strict orders had been given to make sure nothing happened to Berlin.

"What the hell is going on here?" demand the guard as he rushed up to the cell.

"I need to see my lawyer right away."

The guard was relieved that the important prisoner was OK. But then he became annoyed. His nap had been interrupted for nothing.

"Listen. You may be some hotshot on the outside, but in here you're just another number. In the morning you can call your lawyer, but for now shut the fuck up and go back to bed."

"But you don't understand . . ." The guard interrupted.

"Yes, I do. Now quit hollering. You can't talk to your lawyer until morning—and that's final!"

Berlin saw the futility in arguing and retreated to his cot. Sleep would not come but the anticipation of his release and vindication was enough. Morning would come soon. Hopefully it would be his last night in prison.

CHAPTER 90

Alison's men were becoming concerned. The signal was to have been the shutdown of the searchlights, signifying her takeover of the control room. It had been over fifteen minutes and the searchlights still shone brightly, sweeping the perimeter. She had told them that once twenty minutes had passed they were to abandon the perimeter. They had no means to communicate with one another. Only the synchronization of their watches let them know that only five minutes remained. The leader of Sal's men was Bobby Scanlon, Sal's top lieutenant. He was prepared to sacrifice his life for Sal, as were the others. Sal had made them all rich beyond their wildest dreams and, more important, had bestowed honor on their families. He glanced at his watch again. Only three minutes left. He made a decision. No matter what, when twenty minutes passed he would rush the safe house and, hopefully, the others would follow. No one was going to stand in their way. What the hell was taking so long? He moved forward in the underbrush and motioned to the two others beside him to follow. They did so without question or protest. They advanced to within ten feet of the outer perimeter. He motioned for them to ready themselves and checked his watch again. Three minutes left. The lights still burned brightly. Thirty seconds. Ten seconds. He raised himself to a crouch and moved forward to the very edge of the security fence. The searchlight began its arc toward him, its light threatening to reveal him to the enemy. He raised his M-16 rifle to his shoulder and aimed at the guards closest to the house. Just as the light reached him, it disappeared, as did all the other lights around the house. Scanlon and the others rushed forward, guns blazing. They had the advantage and pressed forward.

The return fire came quickly but the defenders were relying on their defense system, which was now inoperative. They could not communicate to coordinate a defense. Their central command post issued no orders. The attackers had to move quickly. The police would be called and the defenders would most likely kill the hostages. Scanlon was thirty feet from the door when fire came from his left flank. One of his men went down but he kept moving forward, turning to the left and firing as he moved toward the front door. To his right, one of his men hurled a concussion grenade that detonated on the front stoop, clearing the front porch. Alison had warned them that the front door was fortified steel. One of Scanlon's men ran up to the door and placed a charge of C-4. It was the same type of explosive that had killed the next President of the United States. He lit the charge and they ducked down on either side of the door. The charge blew the door open and they sprinted through, spraying fire left and right. The guards in the kitchen reacted quickly to the gunfire. They returned fire on Scanlon and his men as they tried to enter, forcing them back out on to the porch. Another concussion grenade was thrown in. Gunfire erupted from the back of the house. The second wave of his men was assaulting from the rear. The guards inside were caught in a crossfire. Scanlon nodded and a third grenade went in. They followed in behind it, firing toward the kitchen. To the left was a dining room, and they dove in ahead of the fire, which peppered the wall above their heads.

The numbers favored the attackers and they soon had the defenders subject to a withering crossfire. Scanlon saw three more of his men come to the front door.

"We have the perimeter secured," one yelled, and then ducked out as bullets thudded around the doorframe. Scanlon looked around. Where the hell was Alison? He suspected she had been killed disabling the security system. Too bad. She had guts. He turned his attention back to the kitchen, assessing the situation. It was a standoff. Eventually, his numbers would sway the battle in his favor. He couldn't wait that long. He looked across the front hallway and to the flight of steps leading upstairs. That would be where Sal and the others would be according to Alison. He turned to the man beside him. "Cover me."

The man peaked around the corner and fired a stream of bullets toward the kitchen. Scanlon ducked his head and dashed across the open space, then flung himself onto the stairs as the bullets whizzed by in the air. Once on the stairwell he was shielded from the kitchen. He slowly climbed the stairs. There was a landing halfway up and then the stairs turned to the left, up three steps, and then another ninety-degree turn to the left. Slowly he went around the corners expecting to confront the enemy but found no one. Secure in their defense, they had posted no guards on the second floor. He moved down the hallway. There were two doors on his right and one door straight ahead. He tried the handles on each of the doors as he went. They were all locked.

"Sal!" he yelled. "Are you up here?"

He heard a muffled voice from the door at the end of the hallway. He trained his assault rifle on the door handle.

"Stand back," he shouted. A single burst shattered the lock and the doorknob. He kicked the door open. Sal was lying on a bed, tied up and bruised, but alive. Scanlon unsheathed the knife from its ankle holster and cut the ropes, then lifted Sal gently to a sitting position.

"Ain't you a sight for sore eyes," he mumbled. He tried to lift his body up and then slumped back in Scanlon's arms.

"Come on, Sal, we have to get out of here. Can you walk?"

Sal nodded his head and Scanlon lifted him from the bed and placed his arm around his neck, supporting Sal's weight as they moved towards the door.

"Do you know where the others are?"

"Washington is dead. I think Parsons is in one of these rooms up here," gasped Sal. "They grabbed him when they grabbed me." The firing from downstairs was continuing unabated. Scanlon wasn't sure how he was going to get Sal out through the crossfire. He was obviously in great distress. Alison had stressed the importance of finding Washington or Parsons. Without one of them, the rest of the information she had was not worth a damn. He couldn't leave Sal behind but Parsons was just as important. He stopped halfway down the hall and eased Sal against the wall.

"Wait here. I'll be back for you."

"I know you will, kid. Now go do what you have to do."

Scanlon nodded and walked down the hallway to the first door. A quick burst shattered the lock. He kicked open the door. The room was empty. He darted back in to the hall and down to the next door, shattering the lock and entering the room. Parsons was there, tied to a bed, but unharmed. Obviously they had more use for him than they did for Sal.

"You have two choices, pal. Die right now or come with me and do as I say. What's it gonna be?" Scanlon pointed his assault rifle to make his point clear. Parsons considered the situation and the odds. He nodded his head in assent.

"Sal, can you make it in here?" Scanlon yelled out into the hall.

"On my way," Sal rasped from the hall. He came into the room with a slow but steady gait. Scanlon handed him his knife.

"Cut him loose, but keep his hands tied." Sal did as he was instructed and Scanlon motioned for Parsons to get up and move toward the door.

Scanlon made a wide berth and motioned Parsons through the door. "You first."

Parsons went through the door followed by Scanlon and Sal bringing up the rear. They descended the stairs. Scanlon motioned for them to stop at the landing halfway down. He pulled a pistol from his waistband and handed it to Sal.

"Stay here. If he moves, shoot him."

Scanlon inched down the stairs, his back flush to the wall until he could see down into the front hallway. The gunfire was still intense. He could see that one of his men lie wounded in the middle of the front hallway. Across the hall his men still had the guards pinned down in the kitchen. Scanlon yelled across the hallway to get their attention but it was no use. He was trying to think of another way to get their attention when, suddenly, the firing from the kitchen lessened and then stopped all together. His men, in turn, also stopped. The house was eerily quiet. Acrid smoke and the cries of wounded men filled the air.

From the kitchen a voice yelled, "We've been instructed to call a ceasefire for ten minutes, for you to withdraw your men. Our reinforcements are on the way. You can take the old man but Parsons stays here."

Scanlon was pondering a response when a second voice called out from down below, "You can cancel that order. New orders just arrived."

Scanlon peeked over the railing and saw Alison standing at the head of the stairs that led up from the basement. She had a tight grip on the man in front of her, a pistol trained at his head. His body stood between her and the defenders in the kitchen.

"You let us out of here or I blow his head off," she threatened.

"No way, lady. Now let him go."

"No," Frank commanded. "Do as she says."

"You're a coward."

"No, Richards. I'm thinking only of the movement. The police will be here any minute. We can't allow ourselves to be exposed. That's more important than the old man and Parsons. We can survive the loss, but not the loss of secrecy. That's our most valuable asset."

There was silence for a moment and then the sound of weapons being lowered and placed on the floor. "We're coming out."

They came out with their arms held high. Alison backed away as they emerged, keeping Frank in-between her and the others. Scanlon motioned for Sal to come down, and he slowly descended the stairs behind Scanlon, keeping his gun trained on Parsons. The two groups met in the vestibule, with Scanlon's men keeping a close eye on the disarmed defenders.

Scanlon looked at Alison. "You get the others out of here. Me and my men will cover the retreat."

Alison wanted to protest but realized that Scanlon was right. Sadly, he and his men were expendable. She and the others were not.

"You're a brave man. I hope we can work together again."

"I know we will. What about him?" he asked, pointing to Frank.

"He saved our butts by disarming the defense system. That whole scene back there was just for show."

Scanlon smiled. "You best get moving. I imagine the cavalry is on the way."

Alison smiled back and reached out to touch him on the arm, then jerked her head toward the door. "Let's get moving."

One of Sal's men led the way, followed by Sal and Parsons. Alison and Frank brought up the rear. She kept her gun trained on him to maintain the charade. They headed down the path leading to the front gate a good two hundred feet away. Just outside the gate a van was idling, waiting to pick them up at the prearranged time. Alison looked to her left, down the long drive that led up to the country estate. In the distance, headlights wove along the road leading to the house.

"We have to hurry," she urged, prodding the others to move by pushing Frank in front of her at a faster pace. The others complied, increasing their pace to match hers. Alison trailed the group in front by about twenty feet. She breathed a sigh of relief as they neared the waiting van. About ten feet from the car Alison saw a blur of movement to her left. She turned instinctively and saw a figure emerging from the bushes. One of the defenders had avoided the ambush and laid in wait. His gun was trained on her.

"No!" yelled Frank as he threw his body in front of hers. She swung her pistol around in the same moment and fired, her bullet finding her mark. The shot was a moment too late. Frank lay at her feet. She bent down and gently rolled him over. His breathing was labored. A red stain spread across his chest. He opened his eyes and looked up at her.

"Ben would have never forgiven me if I had let anything happen to you. He made me promise."

"I know, Frank." She held his hand gently in hers and then leaned down to kiss him on the forehead. "I love you, Frank. I always did," she lied.

"Ben would be proud of you if he could see what you've done," he whispered, his voice fading.

"You can tell him yourself when you see him."

He nodded and closed his eyes. She released his hand and folded it gently on his chest. Scanlon came racing down the path.

"Come on, we have to go. Now!" he yelled. Alison took one last look at Frank. Another good person that the Framers had taken from her. Alison hoped it would be the last. She got in the car behind Scanlon. The driver started backing up.

"No!" shouted Alison. "We can't get out that way. Go straight ahead and then make a left at the first dirt road." The driver put the van in gear. The wheels spun for a moment on the dirt road and then the van lurched forward. Alison turned and looked behind her. The approaching headlights were getting nearer.

"Kill the lights," she commanded.

"What?" asked the driver.

"Just do it. The fork on your left is just around the next bend. Slow down just a bit and you can't miss it."

The driver looked at Scanlon. He nodded. The driver killed the lights and slowed the van. They were all relieved when Alison proved to be right. The driver swung the van left onto a second dirt road.

"This road goes straight to the highway. Just keep it steady and straight."

Alison turned around and watched anxiously. The headlights of the other vehicles were stopped. They had reached the house. It would take them a few minutes to sort out the mess back at the safe house. After that it would take another few minutes before they started searching for them. That was enough time, she hoped. The main road was only half a mile away. Once on the main road they would be home free. Her hopes were realized when the sound of the tires on the ground changed: asphalt.

"About another 100 feet ahead is the main road. Go slow. There could be traffic out there."

The driver slowed down and they all strained to see when their road would meet the main road. They were surrounded by trees and shrubs, which occasionally brushed up against the van. Then, ahead, they saw a flash of light, and then another.

"Roll down the window," Scanlon said.

The driver rolled down the window and they all listened. The sound of passing cars was clearly audible.

"OK. Hit the lights and go for it." The driver flipped on the headlights, illuminating the road ahead, and pressed the accelerator firmly. The car lurched forward. He paused when the road met the highway, looked left for any sign of traffic, then pulled on to the highway, wheels spinning on the dirt between the two roads. The passengers all breathed a sigh of relief. The driver brought the van up to fifty-five miles per hour and then pulled to the right lane of the two-lane highway.

"Where do we go from here?" Scanlon asked.

Alison knew that there was only one place to go, and she instructed the driver. He looked at her, and then to Scanlon for approval. He nodded.

"I sure hope you know what you're doing," said Scanlon.

"So do I," said Alison.

As they drove, her thoughts turned to Jack. Deep in her heart she knew he was alive, even though she had no objective facts to support her feeling. She also knew that if he were alive, he would be going to the same place she was. She prayed silently that he would be there when she arrived.

CHAPTER 91

The guard at the gate to the White House was extremely nervous. The man in front of him did appear to be the Chief Justice of the United States Supreme Court. He even had the credentials to back it up. Of course documents could be forged. If it was the chief justice, then that was a problem he could deal with. Of greater concern was the chief justice's request to wake the president immediately. It was almost laughable.

"I'm sorry, sir, but I can't just wake up the president. I need to get clearance to even let you in."

"Well, call whomever you need to. This is a matter of national security."

"I'll do what I can, sir," the guard responded wearily. *Only twelve more months until retirement with a full pension and now this potential bump in the road.* He took the chief justice's credentials and the driver's license of his companion, Jack Banner. The guard had to read it twice to be sure. Now he was really nervous. The guy's name and picture had been in all the newspapers and on television. He retreated to the back of the guard shack while his partner kept an eye on the chief justice and Jack and picked up the phone.

"Lieutenant. This is Donaldson down at the Pennsylvania entrance. You're not going to believe this, sir, but I have the chief justice down here with that lawyer guy, Jack Banner, and they're insisting on seeing the president right away."

"Donaldson, would you quit the bullshit. Chief justice of what?"

"I'm 100 percent serious, sir. Of the Supreme Court. I think you should come see for yourself."

"I'll alert the boys upstairs and then be right down."

Donaldson hung up the phone and then walked back to the front of the guard gate. A thick bulletproof glass separated him from the outside. He motioned toward the White House. "I've called for instructions. I'm afraid I'm going to have to ask you to wait here, Mr. Chief Justice."

"That's not a problem. We understand you're only doing your job."

Donaldson nodded and then lapsed into an awkward silence. Jack and the chief justice moved away a few steps.

"I sure hope this works," whispered Jack.

"It has to. I'm sorry to say that we don't have the time or the luxury to allow the legal process to run its course. Do you have the memo to show the president?" Jack patted his coat pocket. They stared out onto what had once been the continuation of Pennsylvania Avenue. It was now closed off to vehicular traffic due to threat of a terrorist attack. It was a pedestrian thoroughfare now. From the White House driveway three figures came down to the guard gate. It was Donaldson's supervisor, Lieutenant Antill, and two other guards. The lieutenant wore an expression of disgust. A good nap interrupted. Even worse, a light snow mixed with rain had begun to fall. They walked gingerly down the sloped driveway, testing the footing.

The guardhouse was half inside and half outside the White House grounds. A metal fence surrounding the White House split the guardhouse in two. The lieutenant approached the gate and Donaldson exited the rear of the guardhouse and joined him as he approached the gate. He handed him the identification, which he examined under the security lights. It was bright enough to read a book in small print. He looked at the IDs and then at the chief justice and Jack. He then leaned over and whispered to Donaldson, who just shrugged his shoulders. The decision would not be his. The lieutenant motioned for the others to wait and walked toward the gate.

"Sir, do you really want me to do this?" he asked the chief justice.

"Son, I know this may seem out of the ordinary, but believe me, it's necessary. I alone will take the blame and make clear to the president that I insisted on seeing him."

That seemed to cinch it. "Very well, sir. Donaldson let them in and let the Secret Service boys up at the big house know that the president has some visitors."

"Yes, sir."

Donaldson approached the gate and opened it. "I'm afraid I'll have to search you." Jack and the chief justice raised their arms and Donaldson patted them down. He felt a bulge in Jack's overcoat. Jack removed the papers and handed them to the officer. He flipped through them and, finding nothing dangerous or lethal, returned them to Jack. A second officer stepped forward and passed a magnetic wand over them, searching for weapons. It made no noise and the officer stepped away. Donaldson stepped aside as well.

"Follow me," said Lieutenant Antill.

CHAPTER 92

They were shown into the Oval Office. Jack had to admit that he was intimidated. The chief justice seemed less impressed. He must have been here before, thought Jack. It was what he had expected visually but not emotionally. The room vibrated with the energy of history and power. It overwhelmed him. He reached out to steady himself, then realized he was leaning on the president's desk. He quickly removed his hand and stepped away from the desk. He tried to take in his surroundings. The door suddenly opened and the president entered with his Secret Service detail. He was dressed in sweatpants and a sweatshirt. *Hardly an impressive first meeting with the president, thought Jack.* He looked tired and angry.

"This had better be good, Donald," he said to the chief justice. "Generally, only acts of war get me up at this hour."

"I apologize, Mr. President. As you can imagine, this is of the utmost importance."

The president seemed to notice Jack for the first time. The chief justice observed the reaction and interceded.

"This is Jack Banner. I assume you've seen his picture in the papers and are aware of his involvement." The president nodded.

"He has important information, Mr. President, and I'm afraid it is for your eyes only."

The president waved his hands at the Secret Service agents and they departed. He crossed over to his desk and sat down in the chair. Jack and the chief justice stood in front of the desk. The president leaned back in his chair.

"Let's have it," he demanded.

The chief justice nodded at Jack. He crossed to the front of the desk. "It's all in this memo, Mr. President." Jack pulled the memo from his coat pocket and laid it on the president's desk. The president leaned forward in his chair.

"Operation Restore Democracy? What is this?" he asked.

"It's the plan to overthrow the government of the United States. As you will see, certain members of your administration felt that the new president would destabilize the country. His populist positions gave them great concern. They believed his administration would lead to armed insurrection. They plotted to kill him and to have you elected, using the peculiarities of the Electoral College, to nullify the popular vote. They used the Secret Service to gain access to the president-elect. Then they tried to frame the Front. My client, Mr. Martinez, was a patsy."

"Then the director was right, and he paid for it with his life."

"Yes, Mr. President. That is correct, in part." Jack continued, "In fact, it was that memo they were after when they attacked his house. I managed to escape with a copy and make contact with the chief justice."

"So far you've danced around the most important question. Who was behind this?"

"It's right there in the memo, Mr. President, on the last page. It lists the people who reviewed and approved the plan." The president reached out and pulled the memo toward him. He leafed through it, turning to the last page. His eyes scanned the list. He looked up at Jack and the chief justice and then read the list again.

"Howard Berlin. Harkin Dow. Agents Washington, Parsons, Bourne. That fits with what the director said. I'll need to get the attorney general on the phone. You gentlemen should be commended. You have done a great service for your country. Now if you'll excuse me, I have some urgent matters to attend to."

"Actually, Mr. President, there is one more thing," said the chief justice.

"What's that, Donald?"

"There's one name missing from that list," Jack interjected.

"A name missing? Whose?"

"Yours, Mr. President," Jack stated, his tone flat but firm, trying to conceal the fear and trepidation in his voice.

The president looked at the chief justice. "Donald, what has gotten into this young man?"

The chief justice did not reply. Jack continued, "That memo in front of you was the copy found in Harkin Dow's safe-deposit box. The safe-deposit box to which he directed the FBI. The director gave me a copy at his house earlier tonight. This copy came from Melissa Bourne." Jack reached into his other pocket and flung the memo on the desk. It landed with a loud thud. The president made no attempt to reach for it.

"Your assassins thought they had killed her in time and recovered it when they killed Glen Spivey. But Ms. Bourne was well trained. She mailed another copy to her mother and, I suspect, some other places as well. In that copy, your name is in the place of Howard Berlin's. There is one other name on the list I didn't recognize, but the chief justice did. The Founding Father. I had no idea what it meant. But you do. It was brilliant really. Use the head of the Framers to help you retain power. Corrupt the very organization that stood for everything that led to your first election, a free democracy. I hoped it wasn't true. We had to be sure. Your reaction to the first memo was the final piece of the puzzle."

The president stood up and leaned forward with his hands on his desk. "This is ludicrous. You come into the Oval Office and accuse the President of the United States of murder. If it wasn't for my longstanding relationship with Donald, I'd have you arrested."

Jack was too far along to turn back. He was too angry and fighting for something too important. He placed his hands on the desk and leaned toward the president. They were face to face across the desk.

"Is it that ludicrous?" Jack said. "A friend once told me to follow the money. In this case it's follow the power. It's obvious, actually. Who had the most to gain from the death of the president-elect? You did. Why would Harkin Dow risk everything to save you? He wouldn't—unless you, as his commander-in-chief, ordered him to do so. It's the only explanation. The use of the Front and the Framers, that was brilliant. Playing Berlin for the fool, even better. He was so obsessed with power that the smallest suggestion of your reelection would motivate him to act toward that goal. As to the others, what did you promise them? Power, I bet. Access to power and all its trappings. The world's most powerful aphrodisiac."

The president slumped back in his chair and was silent for a moment. And then he began to smile. "You'll never be able to prove a thing," he whispered, almost to himself. "No one will believe you."

"They will now." The voice made them all jump and Jack's heart soar. Her clothes were torn and soiled. Her hair was disheveled. Her face was worn with fatigue, but Jack had never seen a more beautiful sight. He wanted to rush over and gather her in his arms and pull her close enough to smell her sweet aroma. Sal stood beside her.

"Alison." He could only say her name and nothing else.

She smiled at him, then turned to the president. "I've got your man Parsons on ice; he'll verify the story. I can also testify that the Founding Father used me, among others. I was sent in to try to cover up the embarrassment of the Framers' failure to infiltrate the Front and stop the assassination. He didn't tell me the real truth—that he and you were behind the conspiracy; that he and you had corrupted all the values for which the Framers stand. If it hadn't been for Jack, who knows what would have happened?"

"How did you get in here?" demanded the president.

"I let them in," said the director, entering the room. He walked gingerly, his wounds tightly bandaged.

"Jesus, I thought you were dead!" exclaimed Jack.

"I would be if it weren't for Agent Evans and those two police officers. They managed to neutralize the team sent to kill me and get me out before my house was reduced to matchsticks. I see you've read the memo, Mr. President. The only question now is how this is all going to end."

"What do you mean?" asked Jack. "Arrest him," he said, pointing to the president.

"It's not that easy, Jack. We have to think of the good of the country. The specter of a president committing these acts would be devastating. The country might not survive it."

"He's right, Jack," agreed the chief justice. "A resignation for medical reasons would be best, with the vice president to succeed the president."

"What the hell are you talking about?" Jack was about to lose his temper. "There you go again, making decisions for the benefit of the people and the country. How many times do I have to tell you, that's what democracy is for. We elect politicians who pass laws that are enforced by the courts. This man should be treated no differently."

"That's very noble of you, Mr. Banner, really it is." It was the president. In the heat of the moment they had all seemed to forget him. He stood up and walked out from behind his desk and crossed over to the sitting area. "But you have forgotten one small matter of constitutional law. It really is rather fundamental. My escape plan as it were. He reached into a drawer in a side table by one of the couches and pulled out some sheets of paper. He crossed over to where the others were standing, aligned in a semicircle around his desk. He handed the papers to the chief justice.

"What are those?" asked Jack.

The chief justice scanned them for a few moments. "They appear to be presidential pardons for all those involved, including the president."

"Can he do that?" asked Alison, as she reached for the papers. "Can he pardon himself?"

"I suppose he can. I've never fully addressed the issue," answered the chief justice. "Of course it only extends to crimes against the United States. He would still be subject to prosecution by the individual states for any state crimes."

The president laughed derisively. "Do you think that Alabama or Arkansas or any other state is going to try and prosecute the President of the United States? A resignation followed by a quiet retirement. I'll even agree to support whomever you desire before the Electoral College vote. Mr. Banner, this way we all win. You make the world safe for democracy. I keep my reputation and honor."

The room fell quiet. Jack scanned the room, looking for an ally. If just one person joined him, he could sway the others. His eyes bored deeply into the others, pleading with them. There were no takers.

"Well, I don't want any part of this," Jack stated and headed for the door.

Alison chased after him and reached out and grabbed his arm. "Jack, please don't go."

Jack turned and faced her, absorbing her beauty, storing the image in his mind. "I'm sorry, Alison, but I can't stay. Please come with me. Together we can reveal the truth."

"It's not that easy for me, Jack. I've been part of this for so long. It's not easy to break free. You could help me. Just do this one last thing and I can be out of this forever, and we can be together."

"No we can't, Allison. Not like this. I would resent you for making me do it and that would doom us."

"I understand, Jack, but I have to do what I think is right too. I've done so many things for the wrong reason. Now I have to do what is truly best for the country, instead of what some other person tells me is the right thing to do."

Jack summoned up all the courage, all the resolve he could muster. Behind her, the others waited expectantly, trying to ignore the exchange between them, but tuned in just the same. Here was his whole life laid in front of him. A pivotal moment. There were so few where you could say that the moment truly defined you. Often, after the fact it seemed clear, but at the exact moment, seldom was it so. It was true, he knew. If he went against the truth, the right thing, he would end up resenting her for compromising his principles. Eventually that resentment would harden his heart. But what would life be without her? The essence of being that she thrust into his life, into his heart, into his soul, would be gone and an empty void would return. A heart filled with so many disappointments and compromises to fill up the empty spaces would once again toll its weary beat. His voice caught in his throat. He tried to say something but failed and fled. Alison stood alone, stunned. She turned back to the others.

"So what's it going to be?" asked the president.

Alison tried to compose herself. So much had happened and her mind was numb. All her training and life experience up to that moment steered her toward the rational decision. The system had to be preserved. The nation could not be torn asunder by the controversy and conflict that would follow. But now another force pulled at her. The emotional forces that Jack had stirred in her could not be easily suppressed. Slowly over time she had been corrupted by those who professed to do righteous work. To their own end the system had been manipulated. All along, Jack had impressed upon her that the ends did not justify the means. To find true happiness Alison would have to follow her heart and her conscience, not the rules and ideas of others foisted upon her as the one truth.

"I'm sorry, but Jack is right, we can't be a part of this. I can't be a part of this."

The chief justice nodded and then smiled. "And neither can I."

The president stood his ground. "Well, there's not much you can do about it, given those pardons I showed you. You must respect the Constitution."

"I suppose you're right," said the chief justice. "The courts will have to sort it out but, in the meantime, the American people deserve the truth and I intend to give it to them. Mr. Banner was right. It's time we let them decide. Jefferson, Madison and the rest would have wanted it that way. If you want to stop us just go ahead and try."

He turned to leave. The others followed. The president did not move from his chair and in a few moments he was left alone. He thought about calling out the army, declaring martial law, and arresting the whole lot of them. But after a moment of reflection he swiveled around and looked out the window, and then swiveled his chair again to take one last look around the Oval Office. Then he picked up the phone.

"Marcia."

"Yes, Mr. President."

"Tell them to get Air Force One ready within an hour."

"And where should I tell them you're going?"

"Remember that vacation I told you I needed?"

"To a deserted island?" she joked.

"That's the one."

"Right away, Mr. President. It's going to require quite a bit of rescheduling. You have the British ambassador scheduled tomorrow."

"I know. Call the vice president's office and ask them to arrange for him to cover my schedule for the foreseeable future."

"Is anything wrong, Mr. President?" she asked with concern in her voice.

"No, Marcia. I just figure he could use some practice being president."

"Very well, Mr. President."

He hung up the phone and then stared at the presidential seal embroidered into the carpet of the Oval Office. He would miss the trappings of the place. The power, the prestige, the respect. But it had been worth the chance. Banner and the others had been wrong. It was not about power. It was about responsibility and the courage to do what was needed for the good of the country. The country could not afford to take a chance with someone like Davis, calling for radical change. He had worked too hard and too long to allow that to happen. He would live out his life in dishonor, condemned and misunderstood, but knowing in his own mind that he did what was asked of him when called upon by his nation.

CHAPTER 93

The chamber of the House of Representatives was usually empty on this day that came every four years. It was in past years a formality, prescribed by the Constitution, and always a foregone conclusion. The vote of the Electoral College had been taken in each of the states and then sealed and sent on to the House of Representatives, as required by law. The revelation of the circumstances behind the assassination and the flight of the president to a remote South Pacific island had essentially ended the suspense over who would be elected, but history was about to be made and everyone wanted to say that they had been there. So today the chamber was full and C-Span had its largest network share ever. Vice president-elect Simmons was there. No sense in taking any chances. So was Howard Berlin. His nightmarish experiences with the law gave him a new view on life. He was considering a life dedicated to real public service, after finishing his memoirs, of course. Harkin Dow was not so lucky. As all good soldiers, he had fallen on his sword. In time he would escape from prison, never to be heard from again. Eventually, rumor had it that he and the president played golf every Wednesday on their island retreat. Larry Lefteski watched the whole thing on TV in Brazil. Otherwise he was on the beach with the beautiful people. In fact, he was now one of them. Dow had been true to his word, and the million dollars would last Larry long enough to invent some very sophisticated and sought-after encryption software, giving him millions more the old fashioned way. The president had followed through on his promise, issuing pardons to all those involved, including himself. That issue would be litigated in the courts for years to come, with the outcome uncertain. Any trial would require the president to return voluntarily or be wrested from the island, which was, in fact, a separate sovereign nation. Any removal by force would be a violation of international law. The Speaker of the House was there to read the votes and the envelopes were stacked in front of him. He opened the first envelope with slow deliberation. "From the state of Alabama . . ."

And so it went, until 270 electoral votes were cast for vice president-elect Simmons. A loud cheer went up in the chamber.

Alison was there, alone. Jack had not been heard from in months. He had simply disappeared without a trace. No forwarding address. No phone calls returning her calls to his office and voice mail. Jim Kelly knew where he was but was sworn to secrecy. A vow he took seriously. Messages were relayed to him about the position that Alison and the others had taken in the end, to no avail. The director stood next to her as the cheer went up. Simmons gleefully strode through the chamber, shaking hands, accepting congratulations.

The director turned to Alison. "You've done a great service to your country, one it can never repay." He embraced her in a strong and firm hug.

"I wish I could feel that way, but I have the blood of many good men on my hands. I should be in jail or worse."

"Alison, that would accomplish nothing. It's over and done with. It's time to get on with your life."

"I'll try, I promise I will."

He gave her another warm embrace.

"I have to go. I have a meeting to attend," she said.

"You don't have to be there. The others would understand."

"I want to be there. I need to be there to put all this insanity behind me and to move on. If that's possible."

"Where will you go?"

"I'm not sure."

"Keep in touch," he said.

"I'll try, but right now I'm living one day to the next."

The director nodded with a knowing smile. She had been through a lot and the strain showed on her face. She turned and walked away, the weariness apparent in her gait and posture. He committed himself to double his efforts to find Jack.

The meeting of the Framers was filled with gloom and foreboding. In its two hundred years of existence, the serving Founding Father had never before gone over to the dark side, subverting their most fundamental tenets. Now he was underground with his coconspirator, former President Hampton, on his private island, attempting to rally other members to their cause. If it was to be civil war then the Framers were prepared to do battle.

"We have no choice but to destroy them and their followers," intoned General Butler.

The others nodded in agreement. There was no dissent. Alison looked on forlorn. Her mind was on other things.

"Then war it shall be," declared the general.

In Miami Beach, a young pickpocket was not watching the proceedings in the House of Representatives. He had more important matters to attend to. He had easy marks in the elderly German tourists. Their bags and purses were wide open, wallets ripe for the picking. Absorbed in a tourist map, they never saw him coming. He realized his error as his hands plucked the wallet and he continued on down the sidewalk. A figure came at him from his left and grabbed him roughly by the shoulders. Another appeared in front of him, blocking his escape.

"Miami Vice, Sammy. I think you have something that doesn't belong to you."

The pickpocket's shoulders slumped. It had been too easy. Now he would have to pay the price. The two detectives pushed him up against a wall.

"Sammy. I think this is three strikes, isn't it?" one of the detectives asked him.

Sammy muttered an obscenity under his breath.

"I think he's saying something about your mother," said Hernandez.

"That's the thing I love about Miami," replied Pettit. "It's so beautiful here, there's just no reason to get mad about the little things."

"Ain't that right," said Hernandez, with a big smile.

Frank Ruffulo could not believe his good fortune. Not a single word from anyone regarding his dealings with Washington. In Rudy's, the television was tuned to the proceedings in Washington. Ruffulo had gone to Springfield and cast his vote, with his conscience. The Sunday before he had even gone to church. It made him feel good about himself and the future. Things were going to have to change. No more taking the shortcuts for him.

Rudy intruded in his thoughts. "Hey, Ruff, who do you like in Sunday's game?"

"Not sure, Rudy, but I've got some extra cash lying around. I suppose I should put it to good use."

Tomorrow was as good as the next day to start a new life.

The sun was rising on a new day, its first rays peeking over the horizon. The cold winter still filled the air. Alison approached the wall as she had each Sunday for the last three months. Each time it was with anticipation, followed by disappointment. She came over the rise, past the statue of the soldiers and looked down on the wall. She had to look twice. She caught her breath; her heart quickened. She walked down to the wall. He was standing where he always stood. She came up alongside him.

"I knew that sooner or later I'd find you here. I've been coming every week," she whispered. He did not turn to face her, but kept looking straight ahead. Alison did the same.

"I'm sorry I left. I needed some time to think."

"I understand." The wind gusted, blowing her hair across her face. She brushed it aside, pulling her overcoat closer, against the wind. They stood silently, swaying slightly as the wind gusts would come up and then subside.

"I shouldn't have come. It's too soon. You need some more time." She said it all quickly, hoping he would interrupt her and tell her she was wrong. But he didn't. She started to walk away but he reached out and grabbed her hand.

"I'm glad you came," he said, never taking his eyes off the wall.

They stood there, holding hands, as the rising sun warmed them, their images reflected in the smooth, polished, black granite of the wall. For the first time in all the years that Jack had stood before the wall he smiled and, in the reflection of the wall, he could see Alison smiling too.